About the author

Rob Watkins studied art at college then went into industry, working his way up a large food processing company before becoming a house-husband when his wife Juli's career took off. She, like his heroine in *How to Kill a Minority Shareholder*, was the main breadwinner, and Rob – like his hero, Bob – spent his time looking after their son by day and working shifts by night.

However, art was always Rob's first love, so when their son left school he went into business as a painter and decorator, specialising in murals. When demand for the artistic side of his work fell off, Rob decided to indulge his creative talents by writing his first novel, a revenge thriller based on the underhand tactics he witnessed in big business. Rob lives in Tamworth, Staffs.

How to Kill a Minority Shareholder (and Get Away With It!)

Rob Watkins

Book Guild Publishing
Sussex, England

First published in Great Britain in 2015 by
The Book Guild Ltd
The Werks
45 Church Road
Hove, BN3 2BE

Typesetting in Sabon by
Nat-Type, Cheshire

Printed in Great Britain by
CPI Group (UK) Ltd, Croydon, CR0 4YY

A catalogue record for this book is available from
The British Library.

ISBN 978 1 910298 55 8

Contents

CONTENTS

1

Humble Beginnings

Well, where to start?

Here he was, sitting in a small, inconspicuous, borrowed white van of indeterminable age in the middle of the Staffordshire countryside. It was the early hours of what would be just another normal working day for almost anyone else and he was waiting for the lights to go on in the large but lonely, modernised farmhouse (with lots of potential, as they say) out there in the darkness.

He was watching from a discreet distance, even though he was on a lonely, poorly-travelled country lane in the back of beyond. There was no one else around, not even any irritating neighbours to disturb the peace and tranquillity of those who owned the farmhouse. The radio in the van was on but the volume was down and AC/DC had just finished blasting out 'Highway to Hell'. Well, a muted, not-to-be-overheard version, anyway. Bob didn't want to draw attention to his presence, even in this expanse of country nothingness. But boredom is a killer whenever you are waiting to do something and you have little or no control over all the variables. And he had been waiting for his chance and his number to come up in the Argos queue of life for a very long time ... and the chance to end the homeowner's life. The owner of the house that was sitting there in the still dark, the bitch who had destroyed all that he had believed in and who had taken away everything of value from his life.

He wasn't here because he had been hired to do it, or blackmailed into it to pay off some outstanding gambling debt owed to the wrong people. And no, for once this was not an ex-wife getting her just rewards. But this was very personal and all his other options had been explored and found wanting.

How did he get to this point? He is overweight, fifty-plus and invisible. Nice to most people and with no real issues. He has a few friends here and there to talk to once in a while (if he really has to). The answer is sadly very simple: greed. GREED, in big, fat, ugly letters. All-consuming, addictive and out of control, with a little jealousy thrown in for good measure … and not even his own greed and jealousy, but someone else's.

His name is Bob. It is cold and it is dark and he is a little early, so he listens as the radio continues with the AC/DC tribute – and as it rolls out 'Dirty Deeds Done Dirt Cheap', I will take a moment to tell you his story. Well, we really haven't got anything better to do, and to be honest, neither has Bob until the lights go on a few hundred yards away. I will give the edited highs and bad, bad lows that have brought our hero – or maybe villain (if that is your viewpoint after you have read and judged his story) – to this moment in time. Don't go wandering off, now. It's a story that builds and builds … 'from humble beginnings', as they say.

OK, it's not a particularly good or bad life in the beginning but later there are guns, murder, mayhem and – if you stick with it – even a visit to Thailand that includes a very sexy ladyboy. Maybe it even needed these things to happen to our hero to give his nice, quiet, comfortable life a good old touch with the business end of a Taser and put a little focus back into his life. A life story where Mr Nice and Cuddly gets pushed just a 'Touch Too Much', to milk the AC/DC theme. The radio tribute is at an end and something new and unknown is playing, so I will begin …

Life started in the early sixties with a working-class mum and dad trying to make the best of a poor lot (which over the years, despite their best efforts never really got any better). The family lived and grew up in a two-up, two-down terraced house. Two up and two down was being generous and a better description than it deserved with the loo at the top of the garden. That's not a bucket and spade job, it wasn't that bad and it was only the Midlands after all, not the Third World. It was just the way it was back in the sixties; old people will confirm that not all homes boasted an indoor loo back then, or central heating for that matter, or even SKY plus.

With all these hardships to endure, surprisingly Bob wasn't traumatised for life and his parents managed to bring him up with a strong moral and ethical code. Honesty and integrity compulsory as only the not-so-rich can buy into. All that 'work hard and keep your nose clean and you will get on' crap we all get told as a kid.

Bob worked hard through school and got good, if not spectacular, grades. He found a girlfriend in high school who turned out to be 'the one' and the love of his life – thirty-odd years and counting. Their life was one kid and a lot of sex and laughs on the journey, which is better than most these days. He tried college, but this was back in the day when paying your way meant actually paying your way, not some deferred loan scheme that you never have to pay back, unless of course you earn that much you're not going to notice the odd £5 a month wrenched from your account. The only concession back then from the education system was reduced fares on the local train to take him the fifty or so miles to college, where Bob had to compete with the talentless but seriously well-off at the nearest art and design college.

Just to give a little insight into our hero's situation, 'There once was a girl called Sue'. Well, in Bob's case, a beautiful, spaced-out junkie called Sue. Just after starting college, Bob witnessed Junkie Sue reach her twenty-first birthday (she was much older) and receive a brand new Mercedes convertible from her parents. A gift presented, Bob supposed and reflected on, for the young lady in question because she presumably had made it to twenty-one without dying in the process from an overdose and upsetting the family. Still, she was gorgeous (the girl not the car) and Bob can always re-live the memories of her paddling bare foot in the snow one winter with nothing on but a silk mini kimono tight against her cold chest. Was college worthwhile? Well, for that week at least the answer was probably yes. Thank you, Sue, for the memories and a temptation to the dark side only just resisted.

When it got to the stage that the little money Bob earned doing part-time work over a year plus the small amounts his loving but poor parents could afford to contribute only bought enough second-hand books and basic art materials to last a couple of weeks, a promising career in the art world bit the dust.

To be fair, the college was glad to see our hero go after a year-and-a-half. Enhancing fellow students' work to help fund his studies was frowned upon. Grades shot through the roof until end-of-term exams arrived and work had to be done for real on the day by the actual student presenting it. Perhaps forgery should have been our hero's next career move – who knows?

Even back then the qualifications were more important than the talent. Bob tried but could not get work in advertising, marketing or design and the 'Damn, you're good and much better than what we have, but you really need the qualifications' responses took their toll. The last straw was reached when our hero was interviewed by a national car manufacturer. Same old story: enthusiasm, grand tour and 'You're better free-hand than the interns using state-of-the-art equipment' and Bob still got the 'Come back when you're qualified' speech (Yeah, no problem if I don't bloody starve to death first). Enough was enough and rightly or wrongly the art career was binned.

Bob's girlfriend Deb – later his wife – had had the same sort of family upbringing ... just throw in a repressed Catholic mother, a couple of younger siblings and a house with one more bedroom. Also, they had been privileged enough to have an inside loo, flash bastards, but it was one of the newer council estates, after all.

Bob and Deb wanted to better themselves and felt together they could achieve something more substantial and maybe even great. They aspired never to rely on anyone else, moved in together, got jobs and looked after themselves without the help of government hand-outs or feeling the need to become religious zealots.

Bob's working life after college was OK. He had a few small jobs through the early years, got experience and then joined a bigger company, working quickly up the ranks. Later he used what he had learned to run the factory for seven years and taking it to top spot within the national group but with a baby on the way, his career took second place to income. The food industry didn't pay that well at the time despite Bob being in a senior position, so Land Rover called. He doubled his earnings overnight and did a boring job for a while for the good of the family.

Dear reader, stop fidgeting and let it build. Stick with it or we shall run out of things to talk about and Bob could be here waiting for a long time yet. Our hero wasn't made overnight after all.

Bob's wife Deb was the real star. It was the seventies and she chose to take on the Midlands car industry and joined on an engineering apprenticeship. Can you remember the seventies? It was the age of 'Red Robbo' and lightning strikes. The attitude back then towards women was that all of them should be at home with the kids. Except for nurses, secretaries and shop assistants of course. Deb was strong and motivated and flourished in the hostile environment, even though she had to be twice as good as any of her male counterparts and had to continually stomach all the prejudices and resentments that women today cannot even imagine. Her first major job after qualifying had been to run a large section of production area and the all-male work force had shown their displeasure by throwing bottles of urine in her direction whenever they thought they could get away with it. 'Hostile and prejudiced' described her charges but she soon won them over.

Despite all the trials and tribulations, Deb qualified and advanced, one of a small elite group of professional women, and took the first small step towards her future. With her skills and abilities she was soon running miles of production line, helping to get new manufacturing systems up and running, also changing the attitudes of all around her to female employees.

You have to remember the women of the day hadn't then whipped their men into shape in the bedroom, let alone the workplace, and were still waiting for *Emmanuelle* and the Second Wave to show the way. No man felt comfortable with a woman in charge and 'Maggie's' influence hadn't really got going enough to save the world as yet.

What Deb had achieved so far wasn't a surprise to anyone who knew her. Even in their domestic life she had the ability to overcome and take it all in her stride. Way back in the mists of time we all struggled to find our first mortgage, and our hero and heroine were no different. Bob had worked on the shop floor in the food plant and Deb was in an apprenticeship and their combined wages barely covered the rent and living expenses, so saving for a deposit was almost impossible. Added to that, most weekends were spent in local scrapyards finding bits to keep their old Ford on the road so they could get to work the following week. But they still found time to look at the housing market and dream.

Finally they found their first home and, as all young couples did (no Internet back then), they spent days going from building society to building society and then to the banks, trying to get a mortgage. But with no deposit and no credit rating, they were turned down again and again. They were both employed so what was the damn problem? Drastic action was needed.

* * *

'Another refusal. I am getting really pissed off with this. We can't keep going around and around in circles. If they're not going to give us credit to get a credit rating, what's the point?' Bob looked in Deb's direction and continued. 'Some twat agreeing that we are already paying more on rent than we need to pay a mortgage and then refusing to give us one really isn't that helpful.'

Deb was deep in thought. 'We can't get a mortgage until we have a deposit. We can't save a deposit until we have a mortgage. The answer is obvious.' She gave young Bob a sweet smile.

'What the hell are you on about? You going to go on the game or something? Or maybe ask Mum-sie and Dad-sie for a loan?' Bob's sarcasm came more from bottled-up frustration than anything else. 'In case you've forgotten, we don't come from a background where Mum-sie and Dad-sie can give us a deposit. Please, enlighten me if you have any ideas, because being dragged from twat to twat for days is really beginning to play havoc with my outwardly happy persona.'

'I'm only doing it because I love you, dear,' said Deb, pecking him quickly on the cheek before heading for the nearest bank with Bob in tow. Fifteen minutes later, they were the proud owners of their first credit card. A quick cash withdrawal and twenty minutes later the building society was doing the 'sign here and press hard' speech and Bob and Deb were well on the way to being home owners. It is surprising how easy and how willing banks are to give you something that tempts you to run up bills but have very little interest in you if you are one of the sensible and grown-up types. Of course our lovebirds had not been totally up-front about what they were going to use the card for. Good old Access weren't going to be interested in what the cash was for anyway. With interest rates already in double figures and set to rise even higher (boy, you don't know how lucky you are today and how easy you have it) they set off up the property ladder.

Don't get our heroes wrong – buying your first house on a credit card isn't for everyone. OK, it was only the deposit but needs must and all that. The card was paid off as soon as possible using the money saved from buying rather than renting and then it was ripped up, job done. They bought their first home on Access and never looked back.

Right! Back to our history lesson before it gets light and Bob trundles off to get violent. Deb – having worked in engineering and production and achieving great things in both – went on to have equal success in purchasing. Negotiating contracts worth hundreds of thousands of pounds and even millions on a regular basis. Then after a few years she went on to recruitment and training, where she transformed the way recruitment was being done and used it to get the right people into the right job and to move away from a system where people were just fed into jobs they were not suitable for or not even trained to do just because they were next on the list. It was all part of Deb's master plan. She learned as much as she could from each discipline and area and then applied her knowledge, leaving these areas much improved as she moved forward.

Bob and Deb were a team and complemented each other, as all good couples do. Bob was now working nights at Land Rover so he could look after their son in the day and work on the house they were living in, preparing it ready for the next move. Growing up is a scary thing but these are not the times that turned our hero from 'mild-mannered spouse' to 'killer in waiting', so onwards and upwards.

2

At the Bottom of the Garden

Deb eventually left the car industry and joined a large civil engineering company. In her eyes this was needed to round off her vast array of experience and qualifications so she could then achieve her ultimate goal: to be a director of a company she had helped to create and build. After a couple of years the chance came along. From the network of friends and colleagues she had built over the years an opportunity presented itself: the chance to join a small, struggling family-run company that had potential, if she could only guide it onto the right path and in the right direction.

Our hero was against it from the start. He was earning good money, even if the job itself was tedious. Their son was getting older and they had continued moving up the property ladder, all Deb's new 'opportunity' offered was a wage decrease, an uncertain future and a big, big risk. The company had a few good ideas and some potential but like nearly all family-run businesses there was so much internal bickering, back-stabbing and clique mentality that the business was grinding to a halt and on the brink of destruction.

People were in jobs that they had been given or promoted to because of who they were in the family, who they were related to or who they were married to. Some were just there because of who they were friends with. The company was already running on re-mortgaged funds and the owner seemed the only one willing to employ the rest of his extended family. Yet Deb believed she had the knowledge and the know-how to take the few good ideas and misdirected enthusiasm and turn it into a multi-million pound profit-making company.

Bob and Deb were summoned to a little mansion in the Midlands to be scrutinised by the family … 'I don't know why I am here, am I just eye candy? Ha bloody ha!' Bob said, as they pulled onto the drive.

'No, dear, we are here to meet the main players before I get all professional on their arses and rock their badly run little world.' This barbecue-cum-pool party had the potential to be a dire little get-together. Bob contemplated later that the main man at least knew enough to realise things needed sorting out in the company and that his company's future lay pretty much in Deb's knowledge and abilities. He was all sales and no sense of humour as they were introduced briefly. He did joke (or Bob assumed he was joking) that he didn't want to restrain and restrict Deb in her efforts but he still wanted his expensive and revolutionary digital cameras, his sit-on lawnmowers and his gardeners to be the priority and to put them through the company books – 'There's a good girl.'

OK, OK, I'm sure we'd all do the same if we were in his position. But to Bob it seemed if you were already up to your ears in shit you should be looking for ways to get out of it – ways to get up and running again and forget the un-needed little luxuries that only helped to keep you down and struggling.

Deb talked later about her new boss and his attitude, and the problems it caused. The guy was a salesman first and struggled with the big picture. He was unable to understand that promising the stuff they produced to the customer, taking their money and then not being able to meet his commitments wasn't the most profitable and sustainable way to run a business long term. If you go to all the trouble and hard sell to get the customer interested and are then given your chance and your sales bullshit hits the fan, you shouldn't be surprised when the customers are not that interested the next time you come calling. Like all crap generals he was getting his army into position, then asking if anyone had brought their guns; and was there any ammunition or did anyone know who they were fighting and where were the food and tents? Still, he was the one with the mansion, even if it was re-mortgaged.

The party, as feared, was not up to much. It was the late eighties now. They were at a mansion with a swimming pool and for once the British summer was actually playing fair and was sunny and hot. Old and young alike were running around with their bits barely covered by their bathing cozzies. It was fair to say that some looked better than others. Bob suspected the better-looking ones were guests, because the family colouring was ginger, anaemic white and of course, freckles! The food and drink was free and plentiful, with the caterers doing a great job in the kitchen, but this party was still like pulling teeth. He had known or at least suspected it was a party that would never grace the pages of the *News of The World* to the shame of all concerned, but still.

Bob didn't want to ruin it for his better half and he couldn't say he saw what she saw in these people but he did his duty and mingled and ended up talking to the guy who was in charge of production at the factory and praying for the god of boredom and blank smiley faces to send someone in his direction with a tray of drinks. He guessed that the guy was one of the relatives and there had been a lot of who you knew, not what you knew, involved with his appointment.

This guy was actually bragging that in three years he had only needed to visit the shop floor twice. Bob was stunned, amazed and left trying to figure out how the man could even open the door himself, let alone actually do what he was paid to do for the company. Sadly, that was pretty much the standard throughout the whole show.

As the conversation went on, Bob found out that the shop floor staff were left alone to get on with it the best they could.

They did the job at their own pace and made the best of it in their own way, just about keeping the company going. The owner seemed a nice enough guy and was prepared to give family and friends the pick of the jobs. But even he was now realising that if he wanted to keep the lifestyle he had, wanted things to get better and for there to be a long-term future for his company, things would have to change. Freeloaders and the brain-dead needed to go before the Bentley in the fifth garage became a thing of memory. Deb was going to get a real ear-bending when Bob could find her, getting involved with idiots like this.

Bob couldn't know what the owner's motivations were and what had inspired the change in his attitude. Maybe he just wanted to surround himself with attractive women at his beck and call rather than ginger, overweight, freckled relatives. Frank must have thought all his Christmases had come at once when Deb showed up. Vital statistics of 38-26-34 were not to everyone's taste but in a nice tight business suit it worked for Bob and with the brains to actually do what she was employed to do, what a bonus!

Personally, Bob thought, he'd like to drop something electrical and switched on into the swimming pool and empty the gene pool. It would have solved at least half the company's problems in one minor little accident.

Well, there is doing your duty and then doing your duty. Bob decided to slink away and be nosey. As the 'Stray Cat Strut' blasted out from the record deck by the pool, he strutted away from the main party, dodging about like he was in Vietnam watching for snipers. He passed Deb at a distance across the other side of the pool and tried to convey his deepest sympathies as he went. She too was trapped talking to two of the dead wood and trying hard to play nice because of the situation she was in. She was obviously big and brave enough to lay down the law and tell her new boss what was required to save his sorry arse but there is a time and a place. She was professional and kind enough not to make what she had to do as unpleasant as possible for all concerned and at least she would wait for the right time and place. From her gesture to Bob across the pool, her husband believed she wanted two drinks. Maybe he would do the right thing and save her … later?

She could look after herself. Frank, her new boss, had said when they had arrived to feel free to look around the grounds, so Bob was going to escape the party from hell for a while and do exactly that. The party itself seemed contained to the pool area and the kitchen, so once he had slipped between the pool hut and the first set of out-buildings, he was on his own and free to explore. He set off past some flowerbeds and skirted a small attempt at a vegetable patch, a little surprised by the small token effort to be self-sufficient. He had expected something a lot more spectacular, especially considering the four full-time gardeners Frank had bragged about earlier. Bob and Deb had passed the factory as they drove to the party and that fully tarmacked car park could not be what was keeping these mysterious gardeners fully employed. More hangers-on, no doubt. Maybe they should be disposed of by burying them in the gardens somewhere; poetic justice, you could say. It wasn't Bob's problem so he wasn't going to dwell on it.

Once past the vegetable patch and self-setting herb garden it was onwards to some more old and decaying out-buildings. The money was obviously spent only on the places people might see. The hope now for Bob was to find hidden or forgotten treasure, such as an old BSA or Triumph motorcycle maybe. He would even settle for a fully kitted-out swingers' dungeon. That would amuse the hell out of him and brighten up the conversation on the way back home. 'Oh, by the way dear, did you know what your new boss has at the bottom of his garden?' Sadly there was only rotting compost, discarded furniture and a pile of rust that might once have had a use in its past life. Nothing of interest here so the quest continued.

From the very brief first meeting, Frank had not seemed too

bad. A bit disorganised, scatter-brained and with the attention span of a gnat but all-in-all, OK. He was a small, rotund man (his own words, everyone else would go with short and fat) with a ginger, Bobby Charlton comb-over and a ginger moustache, oh yeah, baby!

So as Bob wandered around the corner of yet more derelict outbuildings it was a surprise to see that Frank seemed to have had the same view of his own little get-together as our hero. Unlike Bob, though, Frank had brought along a little friend to help relieve the boredom, amongst other things.

Bob casually backtracked a little so as not to disturb his host, even though it looked like his attention was elsewhere. The young lady had been kneeling in front of Frank and was sucking away like she was earning a big bonus. With her back to Bob she was probably not in the best position to see that she and Frank had been discovered.

Bob knew this wasn't Frank's wife, as he had been introduced to them as a couple together briefly earlier when Deb and he had first arrived. The wife had been an old, dyed-blonde stick insect who had held that title for years. She was painfully thin, suggesting she only nibbled on greens, and Bob had deduced from the slight sway as she tried to stand still when she was talking that her only calorie intake of note was probably gin-based. True, he could see she had been good looking when she had been younger but she wasn't ageing so well, despite being preserved in alcohol. Maybe you need to be immersed in it to do any real good rather than drinking it?

The kneeling woman was buxom, if not a few stones overweight, and even at this distance you could see freckles all across her shoulders and a large mass of ginger hair bobbing in and out of Frank's groin. The lime green and orange bikini was trying to keep everything in but the fight was nearly up.

One more quick glance out of morbid fascination and Bob decided he would retreat and leave them to it. It must have been the schoolboy in him – the time when you caught the gym mistress at the back of the science lab with the French supply teacher and you had to take just one more look. To be honest, Bob was a little bit jealous. It seemed a much better way to be filling your time rather than spending your afternoon being at some party that had died on its feet a long time ago. They say money talks, no shit.

Just like at school, when taking that one last peek when you could have got clean away and ended up getting you a detention, Frank chose that split second to look blearily straight at our hero. The mystery lady guest was still totally focused on the job in hand and her arse was wriggling in the air. Fair play to Frank, being spied on didn't put him off his game. Just a thumbs-up, a stupid grin and absolutely no intention of stopping.

What was the protocol for this type of situation? A small, embarrassed wave or a silent applaud? Bob took option three and backtracked a little quicker than he arrived, heading back towards the party praying that he would not meet any other guests en-route coming in the opposite direction. He didn't feel he should be the one to act as a diversion and distract strolling guests from the little tableau being acted out behind him. It wasn't his job to save Frank's dignity after all. Anyway he wanted to get the gossip back to his 'better half' and it was really worth saving her from the mob for this. He hastened down the not-so-well trodden path, hoping he was out of earshot of the impending climax. Thankfully the music was belting away and he arrived back at the pool without incident.

He soon found Deb and joined her conversation, hoping to prise her away from her duties and dish the gossip on Frank. Well, who wouldn't? But after what seemed like only a few moments Frank and the buxom bird with the memorable bikini came back to the party and headed straight for Deb and her little crowd, which also now included Bob. Frank dismissed his clan, which left just the four of them. They were then formally introduced to Ms Summer Ponsenbury, Frank's chief executive. He joked how these two lovely ladies in front of him were going to make him a fortune with an accompanying theatrical wink and ‘nudge, nudge, say no more’ comedy-style routine the Pythons made famous.

Summer had parents who owned a casino and hotel group in Hawaii, a marketing degree and this was her first real job in the big wide world after working for a family friend for a few years to find her feet. It was clear Frank could not have found two more different work backgrounds for his ladies if he had tried. Or maybe he had, and Summer was going to be more ‘special projects’ while Deb took care of the ‘business end’, for want of a better phrase. It was clear Summer was already established within the company but it was unclear what she had actually improved or introduced to help the company in her time there. There was small talk between them all with Bob becoming increasingly sure Frank didn’t recognise him from earlier, thanks to the blurry vision of a man distracted. Bob recalled later that all he remembered of the stilted chat was Credence Clearwater Revival playing ’Bad Moon Rising‘ in the background – an ominous sign of things to come, if only he had realised it at the time.

Frank never mentioned the outbuilding blow job and what he had been seen doing, so Bob assumed that his own identity and voyeuristic indiscretion was safe, and he was sure Summer never knew what had been witnessed. On reflection, it explained a lot about what went on over the years and how Summer got the company.

Both ladies were ambitious. Deb was the ultimate professional, very experienced and with an unshakable ethical and moral code. Whatever happened, Deb had made her decision and she was not going to let anyone down and she would do her part. In her words, ‘It was Frank’s company and he could meddle as much as he wanted but ultimately she would be there to repair and contain the damage as she went along and put things right.’

Summer, Bob was certain, was going to take a very different approach. Well, it became increasingly obvious that Frank had his opinion of how he was going to play the game and it was clear he had every intention of getting the best of both worlds.

Bob knew that his wife would achieve all she had promised for the company and more but didn't want to add to the stress levels unnecessarily, so he made the choice not to tell her what he had seen. So the earlier incident went unreported. He warned her in general to watch her back and said that he didn't expect her peers to match her high standards.

The way Deb saw it was that she had her job, and that was first to save the company, then to make it profitable. That was what she was going to do and the rest would be dragged along in her wake.

3

Hidden Agenda

The 'new' girl had been a surprise to Summer and that little shit Frank had some explaining to do when she could corner him. She had tried after the party but there had been too many of his bloody relatives milling about and all of them worse for wear after all the free booze (and that included herself) and she didn't want to blow her chances for the sake of one drunken rant. She had tried to get Frank alone on several occasions when they had passed or met but the party had dragged on and on and then finally petered out. He hadn't even fallen for the promise of a second blow job or a 'quickie'. He knew she was pissed off and he wasn't stupid enough to risk his genitalia anywhere near her teeth just yet.

When his priorities earlier had been to find time and a quiet place for her first performance of the day, things had been different. Perhaps she would have to withhold company perks to get his attention. Now she wanted to talk, she had found him suddenly being the perfect host with all his guests, and diving for cover every time she spied him free and started heading in his direction. Tonight she would give up and drive home to bed. There was always tomorrow.

* * *

It was morning now and they should both be at work. Summer had been cornered and had to listen to one of Frank's whingeing relatives going on about something already forgotten, and now it was time to hunt Frank down – and she knew the most likely hiding place. The drive into work had been dangerous for her and the other road users. She was a bad driver at the best of times but in this foul mood, god help the slow and careful. Frank had given her a high-powered BMW in an attempt to impress her. It had been his but he had scared himself silly with it. Well, boys will be boys and she was now picking up speeding tickets on an almost daily basis, except when the damned thing was in the garage having the latest dent taken care of and knocked out of the over-powered erection substitute. Still his royal sweetness was paying for it all, and paying for the fuel as well. She didn't know why she disliked it so much. It was certainly more status symbol than practicality and it screamed 'excess' and 'superior' in the car park. Perhaps it just wasn't a NEW one?

She knocked on his office door, not stopping to wait for the expected invitation to 'come in' before she opened it. Good job no-one else was so brazen or Frank and she might literally have been caught with their pants down on more than one occasion. Good, the little ginger weasel (she had never noticed the colour match before, how appropriate) was hiding out here all alone. The office was large and opulent, all high-quality furniture and expensive executive ornaments collecting dust. She had had him improve the sound-proofing under the guise of redecorating. All for when she took over one day in the future.

'WHAT THE FUCK ARE YOU PLAYING AT?' she ranted. Then a little calmer: 'Why did you keep avoiding me last night, you little shit? We have to talk now.' She crossed the office and finished by aggressively leaning forward over the desk with her ample chest heaving and staring at him sat on the other side.

Frank sat behind the overly large antique desk she had picked for him and for once he was glad of its size. He knew she would not be happy about his decision and knew the next few minutes were going to be uncomfortable.

'I am very, very unhappy. You promised me the company when

you retired and you are already sneaking in another woman to replace me.' Frank raised his hands in what he hoped was a calming, non-aggressive posture. 'Don't I fuck you when you want, suck you when you want, and look after your little company for you? I placate that old, dry wife of yours and say what a wonderful couple you make so she doesn't divorce you and take all your FUCKING MONEY.'

A pause and deep breath. 'I do more than my fair share and you bring in some feral factory whore to run everything – or is she your new shag?' It was a tirade of accusations, questions and hidden threats brought on by the surprise new rival for – as she saw it – Frank's affections, and, more importantly, his money. Summer was going to make sure that this new bitch never got her working-class hands on either.

'Summer, please calm down.' The party had dragged on and on until finally the drunken rabble and a few designated drivers had staggered to their cars and gone home. He had seen she had not been happy about the new appointment but it was still his company. The sex was fun but Summer was not what the company needed. He had realised soon after her appointment that he needed someone more talented and experienced than the both of them to turn the company around and turn his dreams into tangible profits. Yes, the blow jobs were nice and the sweaty couple of minutes across the desk or in a hotel were equally pleasant but that was not going to rekindle his quickly dwindling fortune.

His wife spent like it was the end of the world, thinking nothing of forking out the amount of a small family car on curtains for one room. He had found jobs for all the family and his close friends and had let them into his company and they all just saw it as an excuse to sit back on their overpaid laurels, do nothing and still be able to pick up their pay cheques at the end of the month. He had thought he could and would be able to inspire them with his dreams and they would help him to forge ahead. Fuck, he paid them enough. He had thought Summer, a friend's daughter who had marketing and business degrees, was his saviour. But the bits of paper had not been a real and cheaper substitute for actual experience he had hoped for. Once she had her claws into him, he had realised she didn't have the talent to improve things, but by then they were having sex and it was too late.

He knew he was short, fat, ginger and unattractive and she really wanted the job and the company, almost a year of clandestine bonking had improved his mood but not his bank balance. He had in hindsight been a little hasty making all those promises about her getting the company when he retired. The negotiations he remembered had taken place after a few drinks, with him sat in a big comfortable chair with only his vest and socks on while she sucked hard and negotiated between mouthfuls. It had been a long time since that night when Summer had insisted on stopping at an expensive hotel after the trade fair, even though it was only a few hours' drive home. The separate rooms had seemed innocent enough. She had spent the evening meal topping up his wine glass and massaging his ego and later, hinting about what she wanted to get out of the company. He should have seen the warning signs then. Once it had got to the naked, sweaty stage he was lost and the blow job had finished any resistance from him. It had been so long since anybody had done that for him. Some long ago Christmas or birthday, he couldn't remember.

All those promises he had made just to help resurrect a flagging libido. Well, he wasn't the first and he wouldn't be the last and it was his company until he retired, so she would just have to wait and bend over the desk once in a while.

'Summer, please, it is OK. This woman will make us both very rich. Your marketing skill, my love, is only worth anything if the company is still running and we have something to sell. Deb is an engineer, she has worked in a high pressure job for years. Look at her resumé; production, negotiations, recruitment, training, even bloody civil engineering, human resources and corporate admin and all for international companies. I have spoken to her past employers and she is the perfect employee.'

Summer glanced at the papers he passed across his desk and still found time to glare daggers in his direction. All she could see and hear were warning bells proclaiming 'rival' and 'replacement'.

'Summer, listen to me. With her background and talents she will make us both very, very rich. I have promised you the company when I leave.' He stepped around the desk and held her by the shoulders at arm's length, trying to massage the tops of her arms. In his mind's eye it was a reassuring and calming gesture. It did flash across his mind for a split second that he was now standing face to face in front of a very large, bad-tempered and aggressive woman with his defenceless genitalia protected by only a couple of layers of cotton and nylon. Well, if she doesn't knee him in the groin he must have made his argument. She gets it or she will at least listen whilst he makes his point.

He lessened his grip with that slightly embarrassed but friendly little pat to the upper arms only older men seem to think is appropriate when they have no idea what to do next.

'You better be right. If you are thinking of replacing me now after what I have done for you, just be absolutely sure that I will have no qualms about telling your wife and everyone else what you made me do to keep my job.'

'Don't be like that … It's not like that. I don't want to stop our relationship or even change it.' He stepped forward again and just about stopped himself making the old man gesture again, managing to turn it into the outspread arms of the universal accepted pose of the 'Trust me, I am innocent and have nothing to hide' pose that we have all seen from every piece of crap salesman who has ever tried to sell us something we don't need.

'Sit back and let this woman work. Take her advice and learn from her and play the game. We are both – how can I put it? – dedicated to our improved finances and this golden goose has just fallen into our laps. She is talented, motivated and is as honest as the day is long. She will work tirelessly if we allow her to think that in the future she will be generously rewarded. She will work like a fanatic because she has always had to, to survive. That is all she knows, working in and coming from a hostile, male-dominated environment. She will have a giant chip on her shoulder to try and show that she is at least as good as us rich people because she came from a council estate background and wants to be accepted and prove that she can deliver everything she has promised she can. All you have to do is find a way to exploit her talents and make sure we keep all of the winnings.' A slight pause. 'With her running the show we might even be able to spend some time abroad looking for new markets?' He emphasised the innuendo with a wink, a raised eyebrow and a stupid grin.

'You think she is that good?'

'Yes! I would bet [if I had any money, he thinks] that she has always had to be at least three times as good as her male counterparts and her conduct will have been exemplary because the establishment would have been looking for any excuse to knock her down and get rid of her.'

'So we take a back seat and enjoy the gains. I can live with that.' Now Summer also had a stupid grin. Frank opened a drawer and pulled out a very expensive bottle of Scotch and a couple of crystal tumblers. The cogs were turning and the wheels moving. 'So I watch her, make out I am a friend and encourage her to keep her sweet.'

Frank didn't hear the irony.

'Babe, you will get the company. I am sure as hell not selling it or giving it to any of the scrounging relatives out there,' he said, with a general wave in the direction of the factory with the hand holding the bottle.

'OK, this might work and be a good thing after all. I have plenty of time to work away in the background and prepare. I can discuss what is legal and what is just ethical with the company lawyers and see if they have any suggestions to make this work. I am sure there will be a way to keep her motivated and making us money until I don't need her any more.'

'WE don't need her,' Frank half-heartedly corrected.

'Yes, whatever.' Summer downed the alcohol she had been passed in one gulp even though it was barely 9.30 in the morning. Frank now had the appearance of the grinning Cheshire cat from *Alice in Wonderland.* She walked past him, took the IN A MEETING sign from the back of the door and hung it outside the office, closing the door and dropping the latch before turning on her prey and advancing. She grabbed his tie as she passed him and dragged him in her wake to the desk. She deftly removed her underwear, hitched up her skirt and leant across the desk.

She looked back over her shoulder at him. 'It has turned out to be a very promising morning and you have been a good boy after all.' Frank took the hint and waddled up behind her, erection in hand and trousers around his ankles.

4

Growth and Success

Deb rolled up her sleeves and got stuck into the job. A few weeks in and she had to confess that the company was in much worse shape than the figures Frank had spun in front of her to get her to join up had showed. Bob manned up and confessed to what he had seen on the day of the party, hoping that would be the final straw and Deb would leave and get her old job back, and this disaster could be nipped in the bud.

Unfortunately, his confession had the opposite effect. Deb was now determined to turn the fortunes of the company around. She viewed his version of what had gone on at the party as a made-up story, a ploy to get her to leave. She accused him of being jealous of her success and of not wanting to move home again and rebuild yet another house. She pointed out that if she succeeded and the company kept its promises they could look forward to a secure and happy retirement. The arguments petered out. It was obvious which way Deb had decided to go and all Bob could do was give her his total support – as he had always done.

The company was just about managing to pay the workers and keep its debts under control. It would take only one small push in the wrong direction to bring everyone's dreams crashing down. Maybe Frank and Summer didn't realise how close they had taken the company to going under? All the management had come from marketing and sales backgrounds if they had any background at all, and they had a simple mantra: 'Promise what you have to, to get the sale.' Those few words were as far as their commitment went.

The general idea of the company was good (it made sauces, flavourings and ready meals for the catering trade) but those in charge did not have the technical background or depth of knowledge and experience needed to make it a true success. They could not understand what it took to get what they were trying to sell produced in big enough quantities and of good enough quality to make it profitable and earn repeat sales. They could not see what it took to turn dreams into profitable reality.

The factory conditions were poor: machinery practically useless, too old and run down or the wrong equipment for the job. Evil salesmen ripping off the company because of their lack of knowledge, just as the company sales team treated their own customers. Most of the pre-Deb equipment was of no real use and unable to be used for the jobs it had been bought to do. All that could be said for it was that it was nice and shiny and looked very expensive! It had taken a large chunk of money out of the company that could have been put to much better use if there had only been someone there that had known what they were doing.

Because of lack of leadership and knowledge from above, the workforce were untrained and dysfunctional. Their products were inconsistent in quality, and their success depended on who was making them on that particular day. Everyone had their own rule of thumb. There were no fixed company procedures, processes or policies, and the small sales successes were due to the rip-off and move-on tactics of the sales staff.

It was a question of what to put right first for Deb. She wrote and implemented training programmes for all the staff so they knew how to do their jobs and what was expected from them. She found, bargained and modified equipment herself so it was capable of doing what it was required to do, carrying out repair and instillation work herself to keep costs down. She wrote company manuals and procedures so that the products were actually produced the same every time, and were of consistent quality. No longer did the salesmen in the field have to make excuses when products they were selling were different quality from week to week as was the case before.

She slashed stock levels and negotiated better deals with suppliers, and improved production times, which rolled on to improved delivery times. She also found time to install and implement a new computer system for the customer service department and invoicing. It was a hard fight and it was not instant but soon the company was on the up. This was the first time she saved the company but would not be the last.

Summer was seen very little through the hard times. There were lots of offsite meetings, sales conferences and seminars, nearly always with Frank in tow, none of which ever really seemed to contribute anything of any value, although it did give Deb space to do real work. Summer always appeared to take the praise and do the window dressing at meetings with the bankers but again it was Deb who presented the bones of these meetings, the forecasts, the figures, strategies and investments to improve things. That part of history I am sure has been rewritten more to Summer's tastes by now, maybe even casting herself as the saviour of the company as fewer and fewer people remember the truth. Despite all Deb's hard work it was obvious to all that Summer was still Frank's choice of successor. She had earned the nickname 'Frank's little ego boost' around the company, but it was never said out loud so she could hear.

Even though the company was getting it together, there was a small, hard core of the old guard who nearly destroyed everything. Deb had brought in codes of conduct, sales targets and ethics but in return she had given everyone security, reliability and the chance to achieve their goals and make big profits if they followed her lead and guidance. Most could see the company had turned around and was on the up. Working conditions were greatly improved and some products now being made in hours and not days, unlike under the old systems, which meant the cost of manufacturing came down. This in turn made the company more profitable and competitive, with more money to develop new and better products – a luxury few competitors had at the time. Most seemed happy to live hand-to-mouth and copy other people's ideas, just like Frank had done in the past.

This old guard had been taken on in the period before Deb and were determined to continue to work under the style of the bad old days, fleecing customers for as much as they could and then moving on and hoping they could keep recycling new 'suckers and victims'. It only takes a few to spoil the party, and soon the company was being torn apart, the old guard convincing the short-sighted that a return to the old ways would be best now that there was an upturn in the market place. But the upturn was imaginary; it was Deb's hard work that was making the company successful but these people were in for the quick profit and easy escape and didn't concern themselves with the future. No company overlords, no targets and no checks were the types of sales pitch many fell for, the grass always looking greener on the other side.

Luckily for the company Frank and Summer miraculously followed Deb's lead. The company split came and went. Good and bad were lost to both sides but despite all the hardships and uncertainty Deb steered the company through the storm and out the other side, leaner, more professional and with a hunger to be the best. She made them the real deal and the full package that the competition couldn't compete with. She hadn't started the company but it was a success because of her.

Some competitors tried to copy what she had achieved but all they saw were the finished products in the marketplace and thought all they needed were newer vans and flashier labels on their products. They thought the last couple of per cent of the job was all that was important and failed to see the bedrock Deb had built to support her company. It was that that made all the difference. It isn't the new sales technique that is instantly copied that makes the difference in the long term. Like always, the new trend, new product or technique will only give you a small advantage until the competition copies it. As with most successful companies, it was the work behind the scenes that made the difference and created a successful company – but the people with the ability to achieve that are always the ones least appreciated.

Twenty years on and Summer still boasts how it was the sales technique she and Frank copied and adopted that saved the company even though many competitors followed suit, copied the same thing and failed. The success of course was more likely down to Deb's hard work. As the company grew, the competition was swallowed up. There were highs and lows through company splits, bad economic times and even recessions but the company marched forward. Deb used her time to fine tune and even redesign recruitment procedures to find the right people and put them in the right job with the minimum amount of fuss. Deb even designed the recruitment criteria to help Summer take on the right type of people for the sales network. The main criteria was no longer only that the person wanting to join could pay the franchise fee and was able to open the door by themselves. The company now saw the benefits of offering those willing to invest and take the risks a long and successful career, being rewarded for their efforts and making good profits for the company.

Everyone knew it had been Deb's endless hours and total commitment that had saved the company. Bob and Deb had even been visited one evening when everything still hung in the balance by Frank's wife. She was in tears, because even she realised the company was on the brink of going under. After a couple of hours sharing her woes and fears for the business and even for her marriage, she left telling Deb to do what was necessary to save the company because she knew Summer was not up to the task. Frank's wife's description of Summer running around with her hands in the air telling everyone it was all right the sky wasn't falling in and jumping on and off the company vans in a mini skirt, flashing her crotch, wasn't really that helpful, even if it was not an entirely inaccurate description of how far Summer's efforts went. But the crisis was averted.

After the bad times came the good. Deb continually upgraded and improved everything she could. Manufacturing, training, you name it, she found a way and improved it. She designed and built the company's own in-house canning plant that saved hundreds of thousands of pounds and improved quality, and modernised and changed the labelling processes. With her innovation making the department much more flexible and creative and saving the company half a million pounds in the first year alone in better stock levels, storage and not being at the mercy of outside printers. What savings all this made over the years as the company grew and grew and in the future went past four times its size compared even to then. All this improvement soon achieving Deb's aim of making the company totally self-sufficient as far as production went, other than buying in the raw materials.

She had time for everyone and if she couldn't help she found someone who could. No one was scared to ask her advice and they all valued her input, even when it came to their personal lives. She had proved to be the company's guardian angel.

She even managed to save Frank a fortune when his financial advisers tried to pull the wool over his eyes and Summer – now the marketing and financial director – had not picked it up and was letting him continue to take bad advice. After Deb's efforts, Frank would soon be able to sell up, ship out and enjoy retirement.

A few years before, Deb had become a director as thanks and reward for her efforts. Frank, under the guidance and influence of Summer, had taken on two other directors and in Deb's eyes these new people did not measure up, but it was his company. Deb felt it was now her baby, she had mothered and trained it and cleaned up its messes but she agreed it was now far too big for her to control alone.

5

Sidekicks and Conspirators

Deb headed towards Harry's office – one of Summer's 'must have' appointments who she had brought into the company a year earlier to be Sales Director. With the impending retirement of Frank, Deb had known things would change, but this guy didn't seem to be the calibre of person she would have hoped they were now aiming for. It also irritated her quite a bit that he had walked straight into a directorship and looked an odds-on bet to be a shareholder soon, yet he had contributed very little, other than making sure his expenses were done on time. Still, she was not the sort to bitch, and as always she would find a way to keep the company moving forward.

One of Harry's jobs should have been to update and implement all the new training programmes for the company sales team. Deb had, of course, been the first one to do this years before when she first arrived but now there were many more products and she had improved sales methods. Everything needed amalgamating to finish the job and give the company a training programme for the next twenty years with new and old members of the sales team all working and selling the same way, ensuring there were no inconsistencies.

Her own job swallowed her time. With more money in the kitty it was time to overhaul and renew. But she always found time to help in other areas when her experience and knowledge were needed. Hell, that was what she had joined a small company for, to show them how it should be done. A bold statement but accurate if the success she had brought to the company was anything to go by.

But Harry just bumbled along and over the year he had been there he had neither improved nor helped to move the company forward. In Deb's arms were weeks of work he should have done which she had ended up doing herself. All because Summer now thought or had decided that it would be better if someone with Deb's experience did it whilst Harry focused on special projects and found his feet. 'Special projects, my arse' was Deb's view. She had known everyone in the company for years. She had recruited and trained most of them and all she heard from the sales team was how wonderful Harry was, always ready to take them golfing or for a meal out to relax them and listen to them talk and bitch about how hard-done-by they were. She had trained them, and she had built the infrastructure to support them in the field. Some of them now earned well over £100,000 a year just as salesmen because of her, yet all it took was a free meal to make them forget all that she had done for them. She was not impressed.

And she had still had all her own work to do, the biggest part being the design and installation of the new labelling system. It had taken lots of late nights and stupidly long working days but the result was that she had again saved the company hundreds of thousands of pounds. Even conservative estimates predicted that well over half a million pounds would be saved in the first year. All that and she was still doing the work of other directors. On reflection, that at least meant she knew it had been done right in the first place and wouldn't have to be redone and would serve the company for years with just an occasional tweak.

She struggled through the office doorway with her arms full of hard copy Harry would have to sign off before it officially became company policy.

'Here, let me help.' Ha bloody ha, all he had done was move an old coffee cup so she could put the ring binders on his desk.

'Well, hi, Deb, you should have got one of the plebs to help you. You can't give the workers the wrong impression. I always call someone to do my filing and photocopying and all that sort of thing, even though the photocopier is only next door.' He points in its general direction and there is a stifled snigger from Andy Sapp, the Head Chef and development director, sitting across from Harry. It turns into a choke as Deb's glare falls upon him. He wishes he had stayed inconspicuous.

'And what impression would that be? That us directors sit on our arses all day and do nothing?'

'Hey, if we're the bosses there have to be some perks.' Same smug grin as always from the tall Del Boy clone sat behind the desk in front of her. Did they really need this wide-boy running such an important part of the company?

Harry – full name Harry Grant – was liking his first year or so in the company and he was quite happy with the decision to change jobs, moving up from London to the Midlands. He wasn't sure whether it was the accents up here or whether the scum that were employed here were taking the mickey but they seemed to get Harry Grant to sound more like 'ArryGrunt', all one word. Twats. He was the one with the cushy job and big pay cheque.

Harry had been a salesman of sorts all his life, selling insurance for most of it because the work was done over the phone and he never had to leave the office. He had taken a punt when he had been scrolling through the jobs section of whichever recruitment agency he had Googled by accident to fill the boring hours before he went home from work. Once he had an interview lined up, he had used the Internet to brush up on the 'in' words and phrases to use, exaggerated everything on his C.V. and had then done the same in the interview.

He had a moment of panic when they had confirmed his appointment pending confirmation from his previous employer of all he had said but that had been easy to manipulate. His boss rarely came in, so when the letter arrived with his potential new company's logo on he had taken it upon himself to open and answer the letter on his boss's behalf. He had learnt, since he had been there, that the 'fanatic' Deb had always done all the recruiting until the CEO had interviewed him, and he had been glad Deb had not been involved with his appointment. He didn't know whether he had successfully duped Frank and Summer or whether he had just fitted their requirements. Frank was the owner but Ms Ponsenbury had taken the lead and it was her agenda he had seemed to meet. She had recognised the snivelling 'yes' man he was willing to be for the excessive amounts of cash she was offering for the job. And that part of the job he had done superbly well since he had joined the company.

He had learnt about the company history and made a point of telling all who would listen (which included the new, the innocent and the plain stupid) how he had helped the company through its troubles, always failing to point out to his audience that he wasn't actually at the company then, and always missing out a few similar minor details about most things that concerned him. When he writes his memoirs he will fall into the category of those who 'never inhaled' and 'yes I did actually save the world', honest.

Grunt was tall and lanky, with the appearance of Lurch from The Addams Family but without the nice personality. He had a legendary, jet-black, flat top hair-do whatever the decade, which he will probably still have when he dies. He was a man capable of bringing the whole factory to a standstill in his quest to get someone else to do his photocopying, or any other work for that matter. If only someone had found the time to record the amount of time this guy would spend over the years trawling from office to office, trying to hunt down the naive and then convince them to do something he classes as menial and beneath himself, whilst still claiming to be overworked and rushed off his feet.

He had no kids, claiming he and his wife couldn't stand the thought of it. No-one was sure whether he meant the expense, the mess, the pain or just physically having to touch each other to produce one? He was a man prepared to bring the poor ethics and non-existent moral code of the insurance world to his workplace whenever he could. The type of man who could stand and proclaim to all: 'I know you did not follow procedure or follow the instructions or use any common sense but I am sure we can screw your boss over, you are the victim. Just learn your lines and I will help you sue, sue, sue.' After years of Deb getting the company in general, and the sales force in particular, to raise their game and develop a few ethics and a moral code, Harry arrived quoting: 'It is not a case of no ethics, it is just a short-term commercial decision'.

'Here, if you are sat down, um…' Deb struggled to find the words she wanted, and settled for sarcasm 'working, start reading all these training courses. Once you have signed them off I will start getting everything in place and up to speed and we can start training your staff to do their jobs properly. Won't that be nice?' She had not meant to be that cutting. Maybe the long hours were catching up with her, or was it that all she saw in Harry was the potential for the company to jump straight back into the past and lose everything she had worked for and achieved? She had trained the sales force to be much, much better than the competition but it just wasn't as good as she knew she could get them. These latest revised courses would put that right.

'Don't be like that,' replied Harry. 'I really appreciate all you've done for me since I joined the company. A woman can always type faster than a man. It would have taken months for me to do this. You know with all these special projects my time is precious.'

Andy Sapp was still sitting there in the office, hoping no one expected him to join in. He made a mental note that he would have to find another place to skive off. It was getting too unsettling in Harry's office. He and Harry spent hours talking man stuff as the world passed by and things still got done. As Harry said: 'That's the wonder of delegation, and when things go tits up there is always someone else to take the blame.'

Now Deb was talking again. 'Just read. Input what you want and sign them. I will put any changes into the master copies and we can get it up and running.'

'Hell, I know how good your work is and I doubt I could even come close,' responded Harry. 'Why waste my time? How many signatures do you want?'

'First, this is important for the future of the company – it's your department and it should have been your job. And second, I want to know you have had to look at least at the first and last page of each section so that's two signatures a course, if it's not too much trouble. Initial amendments and sections at their ends so when you try and come back whingeing about something in there you don't like, I can point out you have read and approved it. There are twenty-five product ranges with five to eight sections to each product course. Do it over the weekend and let me have them back Monday morning.'

'Hold on, you want them back Monday? It's already fucking Wednesday.'

'For once, just do it. If you want motivation, the training and improvements in your staff will make your bonuses even better and you haven't even raised a finger to help.' She turned and walked to the door, with one last glare in his direction. 'Monday, remember.'

Harry casually flicked open the first binder and started signing.

'Hold on,' Sapp piped up. 'Aren't you going to read any of that? It is for your department after all.'

'Yes, it is my department – and no, I'm not going to waste my time reading any of it. It is going to be much better than I could have possibly done and when it comes down to it, it will be my signature on it and everyone will assume I was the one who did the work. I will get all the credit and no one will know I didn't write it.' He looked up at Sapp. 'How have you survived this long without me?' he asked. 'Life is too short to waste working, especially if you can get some idiot to do it for you.'

'Still, surely you should know what's in it? What if you disagree with any of it?'

'Andy, I sold insurance before I came here to be Summer's right-hand man. All I have to do is agree with all that woman says and sack the people she wants me to sack and my life becomes very sweet. If that stupid cow (waving an arm in Deb's general direction) wants to help and do everything for the "good" of the company I will let her get on with it and I am sure as hell not going to stop her. Anyway, it's a bit "pot calling the kettle black". She takes those few crappy buckets of product that you actually don't have to empty down the drain because they don't work, and finds a way to produce them in bulk and on a large scale, and at a profit and that keeps us all in a job.'

'Well, er ... that's different.'

'Grow up. She makes us all look good and she is then stupid enough to let us take the credit for what she does. When it comes down to it we will all be here long after she is gone.'

Sapp didn't miss the implication. 'What do you mean? She has been the one that's made it all work for years. She lives for the company. She won't ever leave. Her damn funeral will probably take place here in the car park.'

Harry leant forward. 'Nudge, nudge, wink, wink, as they say.' He tapped his nose at the same time. 'Just be ready to step up and do what's right for us when the time comes – and choose the right side. If you need a clue to what side that is, think about who pays your wages, my pudgy little friend, for all of life's luxuries you can now afford.' Again the stupid Del Boy grin, and Harry returned to blindly signing the documents in front of him. Andy was a little uncomfortable with the way this discussion had ended. Maybe it was time to go and do a little work somewhere else.

Surely Summer wasn't thinking about getting rid of Deb when the buy-out came? No date was fixed yet but Frank wouldn't be here much longer. Was she really that greedy or jealous?

* * *

Sapp was back behind his own desk and thinking hard about Harry's comments. He knew Summer was the only daughter of painfully rich parents and didn't need the money. He must have misunderstood.

To look at, Sapp was Frank's 'Mini Me'. A lot younger and with more hair on his head and no big ginger moustache – but there was a striking resemblance. He was always quick to point out that he was no relation (there really must be a website where you can find a 'ginger' to fill your every need). Originally a chef, he had been nicknamed the 'chemist' because of all the additives, 'E' numbers and preservatives he added to the products to make people like them. Sapp managed to land the development director's job when the original candidate snapped and ran off to live in a commune. He was the only one left and got the job by default. He had been here even before Deb had arrived and he'd seen all that she had achieved.

Andrew S Sapp ... parents can be so cruel. Even though most people in his life had known that the 'S' actually stood for Samuel, they all liked to think it really stood for 'Sad' because it was more appropriate and he, sadly, could see their inspiration. He had many of Frank's traits – short, ginger and rotund – and he made everything even more cringingly bad, just like many forty-somethings, by squeezing into tight designer or fake designer clothes he hoped would magically change and transform how people viewed him. In his mind he was young, trendy and hip, which again sadly was not a view shared by many.

Admittedly he must have had some talent, considering he hadn't bothered with exams, at the time trying to appear young, wild and reckless to the 'in' crowd at school. They had let him call them his mates so he would share his pocket money with them and buy the fags. Well, if his family had been poor, Sad's story would probably have died there and then and he would have ended up on some council estate looking like a Noddy Holder wannabe. Of course, his parents had paid for college and re-sits once Sapp had found out his fair-weather friends were friends only because he had money. Once they had jobs and cash of their own he was no longer required.

He married a nice Indian college girl after a drunken party they both attended. Reasons for their haste becoming more apparent over the months ahead until they became proud parents of a little boy, her parents disowning her and Sapp benefitting and gaining a much better spouse than he rightly deserved. The child seemed to get hidden away a lot. Having no control over his genetic make-up, the poor kid followed in his dad's footsteps. Maybe fat, ginger and now with dark skin was not the best possible combination from the union …

'Sad' himself had a nice, clean, up-to-date laboratory and development kitchen to play in and it was packed with groovy toys, thanks to Deb's efforts at making the company profitable. He had come up with some good products, thanks to the cash now in the system for research and development – but maybe Harry was right in his implications? It was Deb who made it all work and made it all profitable. He hadn't really thought about what happened after he had finished mixing up a gallon or two of new goo in the lab and how many failures he had to empty down the drain before he found something slightly better than what it was replacing. He would then make up a few scientific-sounding sound bites to enhance the pitch for the sales team, using made-up terminology so they could make it sound better as they went into the world trying to sell it.

He felt a little deflated now he realised he wasn't the saviour of the universe as he liked to brag to anyone he could find who would listen. Just sitting alone in his office he could see he was just the start of the process – or could he even claim to be that? He didn't have the know-how or inclination to make millions of portions of something. All he did was to get a little of it to work in the lab.

Once the goo left the lab it was down to everyone else to make it a commercial success. Deb would refine and fine-tune the production process to suit the product, finding or inventing new equipment or processes as required, replacing ingredients when those he had used were too expensive or too obscure to be commercially viable. He could hide his mistakes and failures down the drain and he did so almost daily, but the company would notice if she ever got it wrong and an industrial-scaled mix of 20,000 or 30,000 gallons of product had to be disposed of. In all the years he had been here working with her she had never failed to get it right and it was something everyone now just took for granted. The correct cooling and heating methods and the mixing processes were all hers. He knew from experience that adding the base ingredients in the wrong order could sometimes turn product into something unsellable.

Shit, why was he getting down on himself? Production wasn't his job and it had nothing to do with him once it left the lab. Why should she get all the credit? He would make sure he was on the right side when the time came, if Harry wasn't just mouthing off again? Sad was getting very comfortable in his lifestyle, thank you very much, and he would do what he had to to keep it.

6

Cracks and Doubts

Bob pulled up in the company car park, as he had many times before. His wife had, without question, been the mainstay of the company and the inspiration for its success ever since she had joined all those years ago. He hadn't believed in her choice at the time but she had proved him wrong. The ride had been bumpy. All the old guard were well gone now and the company was achieving new highs almost every day. He was proud of her success. They were proud of her success. She had shown all the employees that a company totally reliant on customer sales and satisfaction could lead the way in their market place if they were the ones that set the standards of honesty and integrity, backed up with a little help from the best manufacturing system in the sector, thanks to her.

Still, he could remember when you could enter the car park and it would be less than ten per cent full. Now he had prowled around and eventually given up and triple-parked, like all the other late-comers. The lack of space was testament to the company's growing success. Today he would not be long, dropping off a few quotes for a little work needed by the maintenance department. They had tried to get him to join the company several times over the years and he had even tried a few of the job offers. But every time he did, someone tried to play politics and he felt it wasn't for him. This was Deb's baby and he was quite happy being self-employed, enjoying the freedoms that came with it now their son had grown up.

Deb and Bob met up sometimes for lunch when he was working in the area, or at the company. Today was just a flying visit, though. A quick once around reception, drop off some paperwork and then back to the real world. Even that plan could take half an hour if everyone was feeling chatty and needed to tell him every gruesome detail of gossip he had missed because he hadn't been there for a couple of weeks.

He left his car more abandoned than parked. It was mid-morning on a work day, so no one should be leaving, and he could see the car from reception if anyone did want to flee the scene. Why did he need to struggle when it wasn't necessary? It never helped that there were always several new company trucks parked at the back of the car park waiting to be handed over to their new owners. Today was no exception and there were four of them taking up eight or so car-sized spaces that could have been filled by employee cars.

Quote in hand, he headed for reception, magnolia in colour like almost every other one he had ever visited, with a few solid-looking low chairs that would turn to mush as you sat on them and probably put your back out as you struggled to get out of their grip when the time came to move. There were also a couple of glass and steel coffee tables to gouge the shins of the clumsy. And in the corner was the non-specific plastic foliage next to the water butt. There was a locked door into the factory and offices with a sliding, frosted-glass window in one wall, which the receptionist hid behind until you summoned her forth by pressing the buzzer.

The window seemed more appropriate to a sex clinic or drug abuse centre as shown on a TV documentary. Clients shuffling along to ring the bell and then have it opened by someone clearly addicted to something and with all the sexually transmitted diseases you could ever possibly want, and willing to share if that was what you had called in for. In this case though, the receptionist, Penny, was a well-mannered and well-informed, middle-aged woman. She always knew what, when or who the answer was to the subject of any request you put to her.

Reception was completely empty for once. Good timing on his part. One tap on the glass (the bell was for newbies) and Penny opened the window.

'Hi. Anything for genital warts?'

'Hi Bob. Complete decapitation normally works, I hear,' Penny replied, without batting an eyelid. Having known each other for years now the customary formal hellos had disappeared and been replaced by supposedly witty repartee.

'Well, pleasantries over with, and by the way that does seem a little drastic. Was there some bitter break-up in the past we should all know about?' he pried.

'Ha-ha very witty. I should tell Deb I am being sexually harassed by her husband.'

'She wouldn't believe you ... Anyway, I've seen and heard you flirting with the sales team in the past so don't act the innocent with me, young lady.'

'Just doing my job and keeping them friendly. You know I wouldn't risk it if I didn't have this big strong wall to protect me,' she said with a grin.

'OK, if it is company policy I will let it slip.' He passed the quote over to Penny. 'Here, if you could just pass that on to maintenance. It's not urgent, just throw it in their daily post. See you around. I better get back and do some real work.'

As he turned to go, Penny asked, 'What you think of the new logo designs on the trucks at the end of the yard? Should be on everything in the next couple of weeks.'

'Didn't notice but I will have a quick look as I go. You have had years of complete rubbish so far from Summer and her motley crew and their wonderful marketing background. You have had stupid colours, shapes and childish designs. What has she come up with this time? She doesn't seem to have a clue what market you're in. You should all be grateful she hasn't got all of you giving out a plastic flower with every purchase to bring a ray of sunlight into everyone's life.'

'OK, I know they have been a bit naff in the past but this one is better. She had some big design company come in and help. Take a look, everyone is really impressed,' she said, with a conspiratorial smile and a wave goodbye. With that the sex clinic window closed.

Can he be bothered to go and look? The trucks are all head-on, so he will have to walk all the way down the car park to see the sides. Is it too far? He had tried several times to help but every time he had been snubbed by Summer. It was a good job the company relied on the salesmen actually demonstrating what they sold. Bob thinks about it and decides, 'Why not? This could be fun going on past efforts.' Another little catastrophe waiting to happen and he didn't have any excuse not to at least have a quick look because it wasn't even raining. It would more than likely be as inappropriate as all her other efforts but you can live in hope. You couldn't do a lot with Frank's Fine Fare.

No-one else is in the car park as he walks towards the trucks. The more he could see, the more familiar the designs seem. At first he could not place it. Had Deb had these designs mixed in with the work she always brings home every night and he had glimpsed it then, mixed in with everything else?

When he can fully see the side of the truck his memory clicks into gear and he knows why what is in front of him is so familiar. Well, well, it had taken them more than two years – almost three, in fact, but they had finally used one of his designs. There it is in all its glory. He could say with pride that it was sixty minutes of his time well spent. There were a few minor add-ons but there was no doubt that was his design. When he had sent the original artwork to Summer via his wife it had received a very cold reception. Summer must have finally exhausted all her feeble attempts.

He was in two minds to go in and take the glory but he had

work to do. He did wonder why Deb hadn't mentioned it. Maybe there would be a little cash in it for him? Well, back to work and he would see tonight.

* * *

Later that evening he was in the kitchen when he saw the car pull up at the side of the house. He was making himself a coffee so it took little effort to make a second cup for Deb. As usual the dog, all enthusiastic to get its first fuss of the night, had met her at the back door as she came in through the garage. With the dog calmed and Deb's coat and bag abandoned at the bottom of the stairs she came into the kitchen.

'Good day? There's a hot coffee here,' he added, pointing to the cup next to the kettle.

Thanks were followed by a quick hug and a peck on the cheek. As always the dog received the most fuss.

'Saw the new trucks today when I dropped by.' It was his opening gambit. He had been happy all afternoon. Circumstances had meant that he hadn't followed his heart and had given up on a possibly promising design career when Deb's career had taken off. And circumstances being what they were he had never had the opportunity to return to what he enjoyed. But having your designs on the trucks of an international company, even if he had done it for free, was a boost and worth a few Brownie points.

'Yes, it is a really good design,' was her only comment. There was no reference to his part in it and no comment on how long it had actually taken the company to use it.

'Well, am I getting anything for it? You know, a car, some cash or just a nice thank you for your help?'

She seemed confused. 'What are you on about?'

'The design … it's mine, from a couple of years ago.' Now he was the one getting confused by her lack of reaction.

'It could have been similar but Summer has paid over fifty

grand to have it done professionally. At least it is better than her other attempts.'

'Wait! Hold on a minute, you are telling me you all think someone else did that? You took the designs in to Summer for me. I still have them in the attic with all my old art crap from years ago. I am sure I have.'

'Dear, if your design was similar what can I say? Great minds think alike. She got professionals in. Spent shitloads of money and had lots of lunches out paid for on our company expenses to get that design.'

'NO, no she can't do that. Surely I have copyright? Wait here, I will prove it to you.' Bob disappeared upstairs.

After rummaging around in the attic for several minutes and searching through years of accumulated clutter he emerged with the offending designs that confirmed what he already knew.

Deb had retired to the lounge and was watching some mindless game show on TV. It was her way of slowing down and re-setting at the end of the day before she put in another couple of hours before bedtime. Bob presented the papers in his hand. 'Look at these. There is almost no difference.'

She took the designs. She could see why he was upset. It was a long time ago when she took these in for Summer to look at, and if she was honest she hadn't taken much notice once they had been rejected and returned. 'You are right, they are very similar.'

'SIMILAR! They are identical. All that is different is that they've underlined the icons I used. Look, they are even in the same damn order.'

'Dear, the company has spent a lot of money on these designs. It was Summer's project. What can I say?' Bob got the sympathy look and not a lot else.

'Look at the comments on the back. Here, I will read them out to you. "Thank you for your interest. It is so nice when a spouse wishes to contribute. Unfortunately I will have to reject these designs. I have been brought into the company to remove the colonial image and attitude it has now and give it a more international feel. With that in mind I would be happy to receive any further designs using those guidelines. This design screams British patriotism and is totally unsuitable for our future marketing plans." There, you see? Signed and dated, Summer Ponsenbury etc etc.'

'What do you want me to say? Yes, you were right and attitudes have moved on and people are willing to accept that the workforce is patriotic and we are all proud to be a British company doing well? Now it is acceptable to say such things – you know how things can be now we have to be politically correct about everything. Maybe it wasn't right for the company two years ago. I cannot comment on her decision. It is the only department she is interested in and having her leaving the rest of the company alone makes my life much easier. Go see her if you want to talk to her about it but I know all she will say is that was then and this is now. As far as she is concerned, the design company wins. Look, be proud it took you a few minutes to design something it took a professional design firm six months to do. Go chat with her if you want but honestly you will be wasting your time. She isn't going to give you any credit for these.' Deb raises the sheets of paper in her hand.

The night had been spoilt. It was naive to think life was fair but surely he deserved a little recognition. He knew it wasn't Deb's decision so he dropped the subject – but tomorrow he would call on Ms Ponsenbury and see what she had to say.

* * *

It was late in the afternoon when he finally found time to call into the company. He parked in the crowded car park and he could see the large, flashy, over-the-top, executive, four-wheeled waste of money that signalled Summer was still in the building. She might be in a meeting but if she was he would wait.

He went into the reception and headed straight for the key-coded door to take him into the main building. There were a few people milling about but he would not disturb them. Everyone knew who he was at the company, so even when the codes were changed there was no problem getting someone to update him.

He inputted the latest four-digit number he knew and it was still current. They changed on a monthly basis, but they only repeated the same four sets of numbers based on the birthdays of the directors and shareholders-in-waiting, so if the first had been wrong it would have only taken another three attempts at worst to get in. He suspected Summer had suggested it because it meant all those craving favour knew exactly when to arrive bearing gifts in hand for her latest and current special day (and being only four digits, it didn't give away date of manufacture, so to speak, just day and month).

He closed the door behind him and the real world was left behind. Then he headed for the grandeur of Summer's office. She wasn't the owner yet but everyone knew she was Frank's replacement and taking over Frank's office was just another step closer to the inevitable. Only a few knew exactly how she had made it; a few more suspected but the majority just saw the plaque on the door and thought she must be really good at her job.

Tap, tap on the door. Confident but not angry and intimidating, he had promised himself he wouldn't lose it straightaway. He would listen to her side and judge the lay of the land before acting.

'Come in!' How could a woman so big have such a high-pitched squeal of a voice, even if it was all airs and graces when she needed it.

Bob entered into the opulent and expensively decorated office that had now been vacated by Frank. He didn't really need it now anyway. Thanks to Deb he could sit at home and count his wad and just call in now and again to 'touch base' with Summer.

'Hi Summer, have you got a minute? I have a little matter I want to throw your way. It won't take long.'

'Yes, no problem if you're quick. I have a few minutes spare.' A few minutes spare! He knew all his wife did for the company and who benefitted the most. Summer must come in and put the 'In A Meeting' sign up outside on the office door and sleep most the day, or at least get the play-station out to kill her time. He repeated to himself, 'Keep your cool, keep your cool'.

'I have just seen the new designs for the trucks.'

'Yes, I'm glad the professionals and myself managed to come up with something so eye-catching and in tune with how the company wants to project itself in the market place.'

'Yeah! About that…' Bob unrolled the three sheets of paper he had been carrying that had the original designs on. 'You see, I believe these are my designs that you rejected over two years ago. Now I am not going to fall out over it, but as you can see there is no question it is my design. So what is going on?'

'They are very similar but I have no recollection of you ever showing me these. All our artwork was professionally done and original and has taken many weeks to finalise.' She browses the sheets in front of her as though they are someone's attempt to copy what she now claims are the originals.

'Summer, I gave you these over two years ago.' Bob completed the gesture with hands open and an eyebrow raised in what he hoped was a 'Come on, what's the game?' sort of look.

Summer played her part. 'I have never seen these before. Why should I try and take credit for something you have done if these were genuine, and that was the case? I assume no one ever saw these and I am sure no one here was influenced at all by them.'

'Is that a fact?' Bob feigned surprise and sat down in the comfortable leather armchair across from Ms P. 'If that is the case, can you please explain your comments and your signature on the back and, of course, the date? Because I feel I should get some, if not all, the credit for the future corporate identity of this company.'

Bob felt he had played his hand well and kept his cool as he presented his evidence. 'As far as I can see, MY designs pre-date anything from anyone else by two years at the very least and you seem to have just copied them like for like.'

Ms P watched as Bob turned the sheets of paper over to prove his point and then sat back waiting for her reply. After a quick inspection to confirm what he suspected she already remembered, Summer picked up the sheets and tidied them into one pile. 'Well, I don't know what to say. You obviously feel I may have hijacked your work or feel you are owed something.'

Bob nodded his agreement. 'Summer, you can see clearly that this is my work which I gave the company for free. Just give me the credit I deserve. I tried to help and you told me I was wasting my time but it seems despite all the negative comments you wrote about my efforts, I was right all along. At worst if you had listened to me straight away it would not have cost the company tens of thousands of pounds.'

There was a pause as Ms P contemplated her next move. 'Robert, why should I give you credit for this? To all concerned my department came up with the original idea and the professionals fine-tuned it. The people I feel deserve credit will get it.' Summer was menacing but still civil.

Bob was sure the last comment meant she was claiming the credit herself. 'Hold on. If you've already started repainting the trucks you will have started relabelling the product, and there will be new stationery to tie it all in, new uniforms and sales material ready for the big launch. These are clearly my designs and I haven't yet said you can use them.' The argument was gaining momentum. In Bob's eyes the company could stand to lose hundreds of thousands of pounds if they had to rework all they'd already done because he wouldn't give permission for his designs to be used. How could she question any of it with the proof right there in her hands?

'Wouldn't there be some question of copyright if I presented those to a lawyer?' Bob said, pointing to the three sheets of paper.

'Presented what to a lawyer?' Summer swivelled in her chair, grabbed the papers and put all his evidence through the shredder at the side of the desk. It was such a fluid movement that he realised too late what she was going to do. Even as he reached across the desk, the papers were being quickly consumed, pulled down into the body of the shredding machine. With the monstrously big desk between them, she and the evidence had been well out of his reach.

'WHAT THE FUCK? You bitch.'

'Business, Robert, business. If it helps, they were good designs. I don't know why you gave it up. Face it, I'm not letting anyone else steal my thunder. This meeting is over and your evidence is gone. I remember Deborah brought them in for you. I looked at them and sent them back and that means only three people know about them or will ever know about them and your efforts. Good day.'

'You can't do that.'

'I just did. No evidence, no proof, no claim. Go!' She got up, crossed to the door and opened it for him.

'You are fucking sick.' Bob was stunned.

'Yes, but I am also very, very rich so goodbye.' The door closed behind him and he was back in the corridor leading back to reception.

* * *

Later that evening at home, Bob and Deb went over and over the same ground many times. Bob had had hours to let what had happened earlier evolve into something bitter and twisted and the argument had ebbed and flowed since his wife had returned from work. In twenty years of marriage, only a handful of major arguments had taken place, so they were probably luckier than most. When it happened it was always about work and Deb taking the high ground for the greater good (too many episodes of *Star Trek* and Mr Spock sacrificing the one for the good of the many crap when she was a kid).

'You cannot be serious about staying in business with this woman and the rest of these morons. How can you trust any of them?'

'I am a director of the company and when Frank leaves I will become a shareholder and we will be very rich. I know she has turned you over but in the grand scheme of things, what's painted on the side of the wagons isn't what makes the company money. I've spent years and years building this company up and making it better than any of the competitors. I am the one who has made it profitable beyond everyone's hopes and wildest dreams. The money we will make in the end far outweighs making a stand about this here and now.'

He knew she should be right about the future, but where she saw positives, he saw potential for deception and people taking advantage. Deb played by the rules and was good enough to still make things work better than anyone else but she always gave the benefit of the doubt and saw the best in people – too often, for his liking.

'Deb, I gave up my career so that you could have yours and I do everything I can to help. I am telling you now as an outsider looking in, this woman has no intention of letting you have anything out of this company – money or credit for what you have achieved on their behalf. She will find a way to fuck you over like she's just done to me – and you have a lot more at stake.'

Deb went over to him and took both of his hands in hers. 'Bob, please. It is only weeks until I sign the share agreement. If it will stop you worrying I will ask the questions again with you there and get the answers and make sure we are safe. We have always known Summer is going to be the next owner and CEO. I can do nothing about that. But if things get screwed up between me and the company now, I will have worked eighty hours a week for the last ten years for nothing. You have to be positive and think that in fifteen years' time we retire rich.'

'Deb, I know the promises she is making to keep you there and I don't believe them. Please just go somewhere else before it is too late. I don't know how I am so certain but I know that she is going to find a way to screw you over – and she will. The paperwork you sign will be worth nothing in the end, she will make sure of that.'

'I will go over it with the company lawyers and we will make sure that does not happen. I know she wants guarantees from me about staying for the full fifteen years ... I have made the company so strong, so powerful and so profitable, our future is with them. Trust me.'

Deb was smiling and trying to calm him down. She had a few minor doubts now herself but she had to stand firm; all the guarantees and benefits the company had talked about would not be on offer if they were planning on getting rid of her. 'I know what she did to you but there will be lots more witnesses for me. There will be the other shareholders there and they will be in the same boat as me. Also the company lawyers. Even Frank and his wife. If I cannot trust these people how can I work for the company?'

'That's my point! You cannot trust these people. You know how she can manipulate those around her. You have seen it over the years. The office she wants, the car she wants, her friends getting promoted over better candidates. If you had not been there the company would have jumped straight back to how it was when you arrived. Don't put your faith in Grant and Sapp, they're morons. You keep helping them out for the "good of the damned company" and letting them take credit for work you've done but they will jump as high as Summer orders them to. She pays their wages, just like she pays the wages of the company lawyers. They'll say one thing to your face and something very different behind your back.'

'The company is bigger and better than that. We set the standards now. That was how it almost failed before and these games won't come back now.' She sounded fully committed, as always. 'Please, if I have to start all over again our future will not be assured. All of the company knows what I have done and achieved for it. I do not have to stand there blowing my own trumpet for doing the job I am supposed to do or signing things I haven't written or contributed to ... or buy my friends, for that matter. Just fifteen years and we get all we ever wanted. Let's face it, the hardest part is done and the foundations are fully built. All I have to do is keep the company out in front. Come on, let it drop. It's the only real contribution Summer has made to the company since I joined and she will take the credit for it whatever you say.' The accompanying smile Deb gave went a long way towards winning the argument, which she knew was nearly over.

'Deb, that's what worries me the most. You let all of them take the credit for your work and the extra stuff you do for them. People believe what they see and if it is not your signature but someone else's it is the other person who is going to get all the credit. Please be careful; you see the good in people too much. You do not have to give them the chance to shit on you before you learn not to trust them.'

Deb was struggling to keep the happy front going and let go of his hands. 'Enough! Please, to go through life not trusting anyone is not healthy.'

'Better to trust no-one and be pleasantly surprised than the other way around.' He reached for the wine and glasses. 'It's your choice. You've earned the right to make that decision, and I don't work with these people day in and day out. Again, as an outsider looking in, these people are not to be trusted.' He'd poured the wine as he talked and now handed his wife a glass, signalling the end of the topic – at least for the night.

7

The Signing

A few months after the argument over Deb's future at the company it had all died down. Even Bob seemed more on-board, or at least he was keeping his doubts to himself. And today was the biggest day of her career so far, a culmination of all she had achieved and a reward for the total commitment and total dedication of all her efforts in her working life. She had slept well but was now wide awake as she lay next to her sleeping husband. It was still only 5.30 a.m. The alarm would go off at 6 a.m. as normal but she did not want to deprive him of that last half an hour, so she just lay there. She was sure that deep down he was as pleased as she was with what was going to happen today. The company had decided only the shareholders and the lawyers would be involved and present, so for Bob it was going to be a normal day at work. Deb thought it would have been much better if spouses had been there to witness it all and share the moment with their partners but that was not going to happen.

By the end of the day, Deb would be an officially recognised shareholder in the company she had spent most of her working life building into a major success story. She had contributed the most by far. She had made the journey from council estate teenager being told by the school careers adviser that women should consider being a housewife first, and if that was not good enough there was secretary or sales assistant, and if she was really dedicated she could even become a nurse. She had been told the jobs she had been aiming for after school were unsuitable for women and she should be prepared for something less ambitious. There was nothing wrong with housewife, secretary or nurse but they had not been her first choice options. Back then it was men who were the breadwinners. It was a different time now and she considered that she had been one of those who had helped to enlighten people's attitudes to women workers. How would modern women have coped in the seventies when the things they now take for granted did not really exist?

She had ignored the school's advice and taken on an engineering apprenticeship, one girl in a college of hundreds of men and boys. She had passed that with flying colours, then worked up through senior production and management jobs. Then negotiations, sales and recruitment with a little bit of civil engineering just to keep things interesting, all completed with complete success, all her achievements making it a little more acceptable and easier for the girls and women who followed her now to go into more interesting and significant careers.

She wasn't a feminist but she had proved that a woman could be as good as or better than her male rivals. She hoped that she had showed it should be on merit and not just what sex you happened to be, or what post code you came from.

The new suit, her one small indulgence for the day, hung in the wardrobe waiting for the alarm to go off. Summer would get the lion's share of the shares and become the new CEO when everything was finalised today and they officially bought out the old owner. She had always known the job of CEO wasn't going to be hers and, if she was honest, she had never wanted it. She enjoyed having full run of the company and being where the action was and where she was needed. She believed you could never run a company without knowing how it worked and what part the people working for you played. She could name everyone in the factory, reel out their histories and training and could still sit down and laugh and joke and talk about their families with them. She had helped many with their personal problems in her own time. She was in touch with all parts of the company and she knew how to do all jobs within the company. The only departments that she felt she should know more about were the development and research labs. But even there, she was the one who took Andy's experiments and what his department produced and turned them into commercial-sized production runs whatever it took.

Yes, Summer could keep the CEO's job but Deb felt her own rewards would and should be bigger. It did sting a bit that she had worked tirelessly for the company and everyone concerned knew that the company was only there, growing and profitable due to her efforts. The list of what she had done for the company was practically endless and no one had been able to contribute a tenth of what she had to the company's success. What had really grated had been Summer awarding the sales director, Grant, and the research director, Sapp, more of the remaining pot than she was going to get. Neither had contributed as much as she had. Grant had only been with the company a couple of years and she had had to do most of his work for him.

Maybe Bob was right? Allowing someone to take credit for your work wasn't the right thing to do, even if it was for the greater good of the company in the long run. She had written all the courses that were used to train the sales team. She had taught Grant most of what he was using to do his job now, even though she didn't class sales as her specialist subject. The guy just seemed a liability. He was vindictive, a throwback to the unethical and dishonest sales teams of the past that had nearly destroyed the company before, the type who had been dumped to help the company and its reputation grow. She was intelligent enough to realise now he had only been taken on to make Summer's position more secure. Again, not Deb's choice but she would have to live with it.

Sapp had at least been in the company longer than she had, but his work ethic was questionable. She supposed that was because she was marking him against her own efforts. He had produced over the years the product range the company now sold but his interest stopped though once his goo left the lab. She'd tried to show him how much of the process remained after it left his lab and how hard it was to get things to work and then be profitable for the company to make. He had shrugged and said he'd done his bit. No more interest or input, he was much happier making up scientific but non-existent spiel to help the sales team sell to their customers. The same customers who also would not know these words and phrases didn't mean anything and if they could be bothered and looked them up in any dictionary they couldn't be found.

In her mind she was beginning to take the shine off the day already, lying there as she was, contemplating her career. To herself she said, 'Nothing is going to spoil today. I know I deserve more but I am not greedy. Even the two-and-a-half per cent of the company will be worth millions when I retire, and I'm doing a job I love, which is way more than most people can say about their jobs.'

The clock ticked over to 6 a.m. The alarm rang and the day began.

* * *

Out in the country, Summer also woke at exactly 6 a.m. She had planned and schemed to get to today and she hoped all was in place. She had to watch that council tart build up the company for her ever since Frank had taken Deb on without her permission. She had been resentful and bitter about Deb from the start. Now it was total hatred and jealousy and the stupid bitch thought they were best buddies. Ha!

It should have been she who'd saved the company, not that pleb Deb. Her parents in Hawaii owned a casino and bar chain. She had had a private education and all the social contacts you could want and when Mummy and Daddy were gone, being the only child, she would get everything. This was a well-paid make-do job until then. Well, it would have been without Deb. Now there was too much money to be made out of the company. The 'soon-to-be' her company.

Summer had been given her chance by Frank, who had fallen for the uplift bra and a few dodgy resumés. There had been much she didn't know or understand about the business but she'd bluffed her way along quite nicely and by the time Frank saw through her it was way too late for Frank and he was hooked. Little Miss Council Estate had been brought in to do the actual work. Well, well done her, and today with the advice and help of the company lawyers she was going to make Deb a shareholder and she would go away and work even harder, thinking she was going to get big rewards in the end for all her efforts and hard work ... Like that was ever going to happen?

If what the legal eagles (more like vultures) had said was true, she was setting that bitch up so that when the time came and she had had enough of that grating, working class accent, she could take away everything that slut had hoped for, and there would be nothing she could do about it. What had Mr Fox said? 'Not illegal, just immoral and unethical,' and they had all laughed. Summer had thought that the lawyers might have baulked a little at her request. They had worked a lot with Deb over the years and they liked her. In the end Fox and Smite had simply turned around and said, 'No problem'. Money talked, as ever. Their company catchphrase should be 'Fox you over and Smite you down'.

The stupid bitch had even settled for two-and-a-half per cent after a little wheeling and dealing and the occasional veiled threat about finding someone new. Summer had made the offer so low because she hoped Deb would throw her dummy out of the pram and piss off. With hindsight, there was still work the bitch could do, so there was a little relief when Deb had accepted the insulting offer. Summer had had to make sure Grant and Sapp knew a little of her plan and that they would be suitably well looked after if they played their part.

By the end of the day Deb would have signed her retirement away and all hope of getting anything at all, and the best part was she wouldn't even know she had done it. The company was now international but Summer estimated there was about another seven to ten years left for Deb to beaver away until she could just sit back and watch the company run itself and let it just keep pumping the profit into her bank account, and then it was bye-bye Deb. Thanks for everything and all that, now just bugger off. Damn, this was going to be such a good day.

Summer stretched and disturbed her better half, Anthony. 'Sod off, will ya! Let me sleep.' She didn't know what the attraction was – a bit of rough, she supposed – but she kept him around and bought him lots of expensive toys to play with to keep him loyal. She'd fucked Frank for her career. She now fucked Harry Grant for the amusement and power thrill. When she was away from home she'd occasionally get smashed and take a total stranger to bed, just because she could splash the cash. It helped to know she could still pull fit young men even if it took more money these days, but she always came home to Anthony in the end.

She slipped out of bed, which wasn't easy for someone her size, and left him to sleep on. He would probably rouse himself about ten-ish but she would be long gone by then.

* * *

Summer had arrived and toured the factory, something she very rarely did. She didn't want to mix with the riff-raff but she felt the need to walk around all she would soon own and gloat inwardly about the millions these idiots on minimum wage were making for her and would put into her bank account over their working lives. It also gave her the chance to remind her co-conspirators of their obligations.

As she walked around she had taken congratulations from the plebs who were interested enough to know what was happening later that day. She had not kept it secret but she had not made it a big thing either. It didn't affect most of the staff and she didn't want them using it as an excuse to slack off. There had been quite a few remarks like, 'Don't you think Deb deserves more?' and a few 'You're lucky to have Deb'. There had even been a small number of 'You're lucky to keep Deb for that', which had started and rekindled that little annoying itch of jealousy and resentment. She had simply smiled serenely and said, 'I know, I know!'

When these morons had their jobs on the line and they had to choose sides in a few years, she knew they would all keep their mouths shut, their heads down and get on with their work as she dumped the trailer trash and moved on. It would be her factory, her company and her money that paid the wages and she would be the one who allowed them their jobs. None would dare point out it was Deb who had created the jobs in the first place and had masterminded the company's success. God, she hated the workforce. If they were not making her money she could not bear to be near them.

It had been bad enough in Daddy's casinos and nightclubs back in Hawaii but at least the staff there knew their place and knew that their jobs depended on sucking up and giving some respect. She should have gone to America, Harvard maybe, rather than being sent back to the UK by her mother to a stupid old finishing school to get a 'nice accent', as mother put it. She had not been born here or had any ties here. Surely as an only child her parents should have loved her enough to let her choose?

* * *

The conference room had been chosen for the signings. Charity's office would have been large enough but she could not be bothered to supply extra seating and neutral territory seemed to be sending the right signals. We are all in this together, we are all one team. Someone had arranged for a few bunches of flowers and a couple of bottles of champagne and glasses. What a pathetic waste of money. There were even a few congratulation cards. It all smelt of Deb yet again, how could anyone this naff possibly have succeeded where she had not? She could not bring herself to even think the word 'failed'. Let the silly bitch have her warm fuzzy moments. She, Summer Ponsenbury, was getting all the profits and that was how you won the game.

The room was empty except for herself but in a few minutes people would start arriving. There would be the three new shareholders joining her. Frank, the old boss, had already sold his home and with his old wrinkled wife had retired to a tropical beach somewhere. He was going to join them for 'old times' sake' whatever that meant. If he was hoping for one last shag or blow job he was very much mistaken. Once he had signed where he was asked and pressed hard and it was all completed she probably would not even be polite or civil and he could take his stubby ginger cock and shove it up his own arse for all she would care. Lastly, the lawyers, loyal to her because she paid them the most.

At least Deb's efforts had made this day possible a lot quicker than anyone could have hoped or imagined. Summer should be grateful for that. Frank was almost gone, off counting his money in the sun. It hadn't taken much to convince him to sell up and move on after a few years' profit had arrived in his bank account to bolster the balance. Nice black figures rather than the horrible red, as in the past.

There was a knock on the door and the lawyers arrived to put all the paperwork in the correct places before the others arrived. She could hear the faint droning of some pop song that she would not normally have even registered existed – 'Another One Bites the Dust' by some group called Queenie or something, how appropriate. The image of Frank's dick was forgotten. There was lots more scheming and manipulating to be done even now for the sake of her own bulging bank balance. Thank god for men with dicks and poor people wanting to be accepted as part of the team. It really was too easy.

Soon all who needed to be there were there and the pleasantries had passed around, great day and great future etc. The lawyers had given their little spiel about what a great and generous contract it was and how considerate Summer was being, sharing her good fortune with them all and guaranteeing all their futures.

In the days running up to today she had revealed what she was putting into their contracts and all the nice things they could expect. Deb had queried the fact that none of the generous promises were going to appear in the Articles of Association they were all going to sign. Summer had expected and planned for this. That had been the time the lawyers had needed to step up and earn their expensive pay-outs.

At the private meeting a few days earlier 'Ms Smith, Deborah' the man from Fox & Smite had started with. 'Ms Ponsenbury is being very fair. More than fair in fact and all she is asking for is that you guarantee you will stay until you have completed the time agreed. It is to protect her from you taking the money and running. Not that we are implying that you would do such a thing. It is all standard procedure in this sort of transaction and designed to protect everyone involved, even yourself. In effect Ms Ponsenbury is guaranteeing you employment for the next fifteen years with a big pay-out once you have completed the time agreed. Ms Ponsenbury has even indicated that she sees no reason for any of you to part company after this time has been completed, and sees a very long and profitable future for you all with ever increasing benefits.'

'I have no doubt she feels she is being generous,' said Deb. 'I am just asking why none of all the generous things she is claiming we will all be given and entitled to will appear in the Articles. I have no reason to think I will want to leave the company, it's the whole of my life, but what happens if Summer decides she wants any of us gone and it is not our fault we cannot complete this fifteen year agreement? The contract itself seems far too vague and meaningless.'

Mr Fox paused and steepled his fingers on the desk as though he was deep in thought, even though his answer had already been agreed and approved. 'Ms Smith, it is a basic Articles of Association contract my company deals with all the time and everyone is always happy with the deal. Your doubts are not uncommon, that is why I have suggested that Ms Ponsenbury does what many of our clients do. As the company grows, and I am sure it will under your guidance looking back on your past achievements, we suggest that Ms Ponsenbury annually or more often if she prefers, issues a company headed note or document listing what incentives and guarantees you have accumulated. As the company grows I am sure this list will get bigger and bigger. Having this separate document simply means that there is no need to pay an amendment charge every time something is added to yours or anyone else's package in the Articles of Association. She has already indicated to us that if any of you lose your jobs because of, shall we say, movement within the company, that she is prepared to pay seventy five per cent of market value of the shares as a thank you for past services.'

'But shouldn't that be in the Articles, not on a separate document?'

'Deborah, as directors and soon to be shareholders, you already have insurance cover if you are too ill to work or if you die and the company has to buy the shares back at market value, so that you and your families will not be left out of pocket. You all accept that as a separate document. This new document just keeps track of the detail for you and keeps the cost down for the company because it will not need a legal team involved every time anything is added.'

'As long as you are sure it is legally binding. We're all friends now but who knows what problems might occur in ten years' time?'

'Very astute – but I am sure you and the company will not have any problems at all. As for the documents we have just talked about, if they are issued and signed by Ms Ponsenbury on headed paper I assure and guarantee you as the company's lawyer and as someone you have worked with for years that they will stand up in court (liar, liar pants on fire, but how was Deb to know?). Please have no concerns or worries.'

Deb was sifting through the paperwork in front of her as Mr Fox was talking. Summer was sitting to one side and had not said anything so far. For this to sound convincing it was better for Mr Fox to do all the talking and Deb to do all the assuming. As Mr Fox concluded and Deb read through the contract again she did not see the little nod of gratitude from Summer in the direction of the lawyer as he acted out his final scene of the day.

'I'm not trying to delay or stop anything moving forward,' said Deb, looking up from what she has been reading and glancing around the room almost apologetically. 'If you're absolutely sure that all of what you are saying is true and legally binding I have no problems – but I have always been the one who has sorted out all legal problems and contract disputes for all the company. I'm sure if the contracts had been this vague, both for the people who worked for the company and the franchisees, there would have been problems.'

'For Christ's sake, Deb!' It was an irritated expression of exasperation rather than an angry outburst, but only just. There was too much at stake for Summer to lose complete control. 'We've been working together for years and I class you as one of my closest friends. We're the leaders of the company. What has to be in the contracts to stop the scheming salesmen or the snivelling ungrateful workforce taking us to the cleaners is one thing. We're not going to be trying to rip each other off. If you cannot trust what your best friend and company CEO or the company lawyers are saying to you, what other guarantees can we give? You want my first born, if ever I have any, to keep as security?'

Summer regained control. 'We make the contracts inflexible for the plebs because they cannot be trusted. You have helped us all and I am the first to admit the company would not be here if it wasn't for you.' She concedes to herself that this was almost as bad as sucking dick and she bites her tongue. Summer realised that if her prey was spooked, Deb could get the hump and leave. She'd soon get a job with a competitor and it wouldn't take her long to do for them what she had already done for this company. Summer decided she'd eat a very small piece of humble pie this time, just to seal the deal.

'I've agreed to let you all use your bonuses to pay for the shares so they cost you nothing in real terms and I've agreed to you having them at market value now, so your investment won't increase as the company gets bigger and their worth goes up. It's like you've actually bought them now.' That had been a brilliant move; the cash never left the company. Deb was the only one organised enough and sensible enough to be able to pay for the shares straight away. Summer had pointed out this fact as praise but had then influenced Deb into going along with the rest and not buying now because no one else could. Suggesting that Deb would feel guilty if she was seen to make loads of money when the other two were struggling and it would be better for the company if she was seen as part of the team, sharing a little hardship at the start of their 'time as company leaders', but of course getting all the rewards in the future, and that had led to Deb agreeing the same terms as the other two. The soft idiot had fallen for the sob story sales pitch. Deb wouldn't even see the benefits of the dividend pay-outs before she was dumped, the stupid bitch.

* * *

A week or so after that meeting between Deb, Summer and the lawyers and they were all there for the contract signing. Harry and Andy had joined the group, pens in hand, ready to sign on the dotted line. Deb felt as though she had been pushed into a corner. She still felt uneasy about the contracts. She could not put her finger on what it was that worried her the most or even if there was anything to worry about. Maybe it was just Bob and his doubts, because nobody else seemed worried. When she had tried to talk to the lads they'd just kept telling her to sign and make big plans for how she was going to spend her cut. Deb didn't want to lose all she had worked for, and as Summer had pointed out on more than one occasion, if she couldn't trust her and the lawyers after all these years, who could she trust? They all seemed more interested in getting the deal done and opening the champagne in celebration.

Summer moved closer. Deb seemed a little jittery and waited for a final round of reassurances but then decided to open the chat first. 'OK, you are right. I will be here until I retire and by then who knows how much we'll be worth? It's a better investment than the lottery,' she joked.

'I'll drink to that,' Harry and Andy said in unison, giggling like school kids.

Summer stepped back, looking smug. She went to sit at the head of the table presiding over the meeting. There had been a few minor heart flutters on the way but she only needed the signatures now. Then she'd have everything she wanted – and she'd have nailed the bitch Deb, too. Those pathetic, ethical, honest people always assume everyone else deep down inside are just like themselves, ha bloody ha.

* * *

'You cannot be happy with this? Are you happy about this?' Bob questioned Deb. 'From what you've said it is very much weighted in the company's favour. I know you see yourselves as one big happy family and all that crap but, to me, it is the same old story. She is out to turn you over.' He had just heard the details. He had known what was happening that day and had left it in Deb's normally reliable hands.

'I know you don't trust her,' said Deb. 'You have made that blindingly obvious. You think she is out to stitch everyone up but you see the worst in everybody.'

'Deb, trouble is people very rarely prove me wrong. You don't have to be an all-seeing Greek oracle. This is not set up to help anyone but her. You are brilliant at the work you do. You can see every other con-artist and skiver there is but you have got one massive blind spot when it comes to Summer and her cronies.'

Deb was a little mellow from the champagne she had brought home and drunk on an empty stomach. It had all been an anti-climax. She had wanted to be out celebrating, rejoicing over the culmination of years of work and dedication and reaching a major stepping stone to health, wealth and happiness in old age. As soon as the documents had been signed, there had been a couple of publicity photos for the company website and then they'd gone back to work. Surely this was a special day for everyone? Summer and the lads didn't want to celebrate at all and if she hadn't bought two bottles of champagne out of her own pocket to mark the occasion she was sure the photos would have had them all clutching empty glasses.

The others had gulped down one glass and left. She had salvaged the second unopened bottle for herself. There had been no celebratory lunch on the company or announcement of a small get-together of those present and their families to share an evening in celebration. Surely there should have been more to mark this special occasion? Deb wasn't extravagant but buying the company had obviously meant more to her than anyone else. Pinnacle of your achievements so far and all that claptrap.

Over the years she had seen the receipts and bills put forward by the others on their numerous days out wining and dining on the company expense account. She wasn't jealous of their high-rolling on the company credit cards but she was always the one left at the factory keeping everything running smoothly and making the profits that turned into these golf days and race days and drive-a- Ferrari days. This day of all days should have had more oomph!

The lawyers had packed up and gone while the ink was still drying. The others had just left to get back to their own little worlds, which was totally the reverse of any other time there was free booze on offer. Maybe she felt it more because she had come the furthest and worked the hardest. All the others had come from rich families and could have enjoyed a comfortable life, even if they had not joined the working masses. Summer, even in that category, had more than most. Her family was worth millions already and now with Deb's efforts her new CEO's wage packet, with all the bonuses and dividends, would be over a million pounds a year and would only get bigger and bigger, thanks to the work she, Deb, had done.

She took another long gulp straight from the bottle. Maybe it was the alcohol awakening all the little demons but she couldn't see why Summer was even bothering. She did very little and Mummy and Daddy's millions would arrive in her lap at some point and the family business would be passed over to her as well. Summer should be back in Hawaii learning the ins and outs of that business, not here giving everyone the royal wave as she kept them as far away as possible. Deb could see no inspiration or motivation that Summer could possibly have. She hated the workforce and was not interested in the slightest in their welfare and futures. She already had access to more money than she could ever spend and she did very little to help the company even when she was there. Perhaps Bob was right and Summer's ego was so big that she needed to parade it up and down and rub it in everyone's faces. Deb just knew deep down inside that if she had had that amount of money, the contacts and the head start Summer had had just by birth right, she was sure she could and would have achieved much more with it.

How would that woman have coped with bottles of urine being thrown at her or the threats for taking a man's job after she was given her first substantial promotion? With three miles of production line full of militant, racist and prejudiced workers all out to stop her achieving anything just because they didn't want a woman in charge? You sink or swim in those conditions and you can't swim with a cocktail in each hand.

Deb drained the bottle. Damn, she was sounding like her husband. It was the only thing they ever disagreed on and the only matter on which they were polarised. They could not both be right – she just hoped it wasn't her who was wrong. All that honesty, integrity, hard work and ethics must count for something.

Let down by the day itself, she now just wanted Bob to help revive the day and to share the moment with her. Again the small doubts and fears she saw as only minor possibilities way off in the future Bob saw as inevitable catastrophes just around the corner. He had been watching her and not saying a word. She felt very fuzzy around the edges. She never drank that much at any other time, so it showed how pissed off she was. They were in the kitchen, so she got up and poured herself a glass of water from the tap.

'Deb, I know they have wrapped this contract up and sold it you as being totally in your favour and claiming all this protection for you in the future. But the way it is written means both sides can interpret exactly what they want from it. You only write something this vague when you are going to use it in your favour at some point in the future going, "Sorry you must have misunderstood".'

These same arguments that turned into shouting matches kept flaring up over and over and they covered the same ground again and again. He had given her total support throughout her career, even working permanent nights so she could continue and they would not have to pay stupid amounts for childcare. Even now when it was pure business he was there for her – but it had gotten to the stage where she only had to mention one of three or four people at the top of the company and his anger was instant.

She turned to face him, the cold water reviving her a little. 'Why can't this be good?' she asked.

There was a pause. He was obviously thinking about not commenting and just letting it drop, but then said: 'I know these people and they are not like you. I have seen you build and carry this company and the people connected to it for years. You hire them, you train them and you build the equipment and teach them how to use it. You find the ingredients to make the products and you do it all more profitably and more smoothly than any other person could have. These people around you at best use the crib sheets you write for them to do their jobs and you still have to spend half your time watching their every move, putting their mistakes right and stopping them continually fucking up.'

He'd walked over to her and put his arms around her protectively as he was speaking. She was now holding him back and she looked up. 'So what can I do? It's not my company. I know what you're saying but if I walk away now after spending years making everyone else rich, I walk away with nothing. Or I stay and get a small share which will still give us millions to retire with.'

'Go to a rival company; they all know you. They've all tried to recruit you in the past. They all know what you are worth to them and their offers have always been way better than what you're getting. Stop thinking loyalty and go for it. Say to them, "This is what I've done and this is what I can do for you," and get a bloody good deal from the start. Then drive these scum you are being conned by off the face of the planet.'

'You think I could give them a fifteen-year head start? Give them market share and a totally self-sufficient company and be able to make a dent in their sales? I built a company to be better than the rest and good enough not to have to worry about looking over their shoulders, because we lead from the front.' She felt totally sober again now.

'You deserve more than this after all you have done for these people.'

'Please, none of the bad things will happen, I promise. When I joined this company I gave my word to all the employees that I'd bring them wealth and job security, and I have. Yes, I am pissed off that Summer got so much for just cuddling up to Frank but she is the boss now and that is all there is to it.'

'Deb, she is jealous, vindictive and resentful of you and what you have achieved. She WILL stab you in the back.'

'How can she be jealous of me? I've had to work up to eighty hours a week ever since I joined the company, finding ways to do absolutely everything that needs doing, trying to keep it moving forward and stopping it destroying itself. I know they sit back and watch me work and make fun of my commitment. If I'm making money for them I'm making money for us at the same time. I can watch them and keep their screw-ups to a minimum. If Summer is out test-driving her latest company sports car or getting her personal shopper to spend three hours picking a suit for work with her or any of the other non-work crap she fills her time with, that's great, because I can get on with the job and the real work. If she's spending all that money I'm making for her, you'd hope she wouldn't kill the goose laying the golden eggs.'

He took a big breath and sighed. 'Stop thinking of everyone else in the company and protect yourself. As soon as you've written enough 'how to do this' books and put in the best equipment for the job, they will get rid of you.'

'I know that is what you think, but the company will keep evolving and getting bigger. Summer and the lawyers are guaranteeing the promises she is making in a different document that is all. It keeps the Articles simple. No one else is even slightly concerned. All they talk about is the money they are going to make, the benefits they will get and the lack of risk. I have to trust the system.'

'OK, let it go.' Bob had had enough arguing. 'It's done now but personally I would expect the worst and watch your back. And if it all actually comes good, that will be a nice surprise for us all, won't it?' He couldn't hide the sarcasm and didn't even bother to try.

Deb perked up, grabbing her husband's arse with both hands. 'Look, no-one else wants to celebrate. It's a big day for me and I'm sure they'll prove you wrong in the end. Come on, you cynical old Hector, go and get spruced up and let's salvage the night.'

He walked to the kitchen door and turned back to face her. Half-jokingly he added: 'You know where it says the meek shall inherit the earth? They found the second page that had been lost and the real end finishes "... when they have enough money to hire the big boys to get it for them".'

She smiled, stuck out her chest and grabbed a carving knife off the kitchen counter, pointing it in his direction. 'Meek, am I?'

8

Dirty Harry

It was a few years on from the buyout. Things had not really changed as far as personnel went. Deb was still the mainstay of the company and keeping things moving in the right direction, mopping up the messes along the way as they happened. The company had got bigger and was expanding internationally. This in the main was down to the company salesmen making so much money out of their sixty per cent profit margins that they were now selling up in the UK and following Frank's example in finding warmer climes to ply their wares. Thanks to these hardy few leading the way, and the locals around where they had settled who had joined the company, export sales were growing with very little help at all. Because of the honesty and ethics Deb had painstakingly instilled into the sales team, the company's reputation had soared to great heights. Now they had lists of potential people to fill every vacancy and could cherry-pick the best of the lot.

A long time ago, Deb had written questionnaires and crib sheets to help Summer and Harry find the right people because as the company grew she knew it was now physically impossible for her to do everything. It had meant that the others did actually have to do a little to warrant their fabulous pay cheques her hard work was giving them. Unlike before, when Summer and Frank recruited the salesmen, the criteria was no longer 'if the candidate has the cash to buy a franchise, can sign his name and open the door himself he was taken on'. The cash had always been really the only important thing. Someone could usually be found to help them spell their names and open the door for them, if needed.

Deb had hated this attitude but it was Summer and Frank, and then Summer and Harry, who now recruited the sales team and had the final say on who joined. Many were taken on and their money absorbed into the company funds but they were the wrong people for the job and ultimately failed, losing their money, and then they were replaced with the next victim and history was repeated. Again it was Deb who had fought for better people to represent the company and changed the company attitude.

After the buy-out, Harry had gone to Germany to try and get the company up and running there. It seemed a good potential market but Harry seemed unable to deliver on the hyped-up and projected sales figures he had put forward. Deb suspected that it was down to Harry and his wife having a really good time at the company's expense and work not being at the top of their to-do list. They had no kids and were living an idyllic lifestyle in the German countryside in a big country farmhouse paid for by the company. The couple had made sure it was not too close to anywhere too large where Harry could actually do some work, and Deb was sure Harry and his wife had been having a damn good time over the last couple of years with no real return on the company investment. She had talked about it to Summer who had simply put it down to a lot of ground work that needed doing before things took a big step forward. Deb suspected it was more marketing and sales hype. Who needs facts when you can get away with fantasy?

Harry had been a pain in the backside ever since he had joined the company and it wasn't just his work ethic, or lack of it. At every staff conference or party Harry was there, sowing his wild oats and womanising. It had been toned down a little in recent times because most of the staff now knew he was married, but there were a few ladies within the company who still just wanted to party with one of the bosses in the hope it would improve their own status within the company, and Harry had proved himself the most likely candidate to take full advantage of the situation. Even Summer had been shocked though, when Harry's sex-ploits had spilled over into the workplace – or so Deb had thought. If she had known about what Summer and Harry were doing on company time she might have recognised a little jealousy or anger, because the implications from Harry's actions were that Summer was just another notch on the bedpost. Summer obviously thought a little time to reflect on his loyalty away from the luxuries at work was in order, and the German invasion had begun.

What had caused this disturbance in the camp had been an incident a few weeks prior to the German announcement which had resulted in Harry's move to Germany. Deb had been walking through the factory as she tried to do at least once every day, workload permitting. She had been in a reflective mood. All the great work she had done since she had joined surrounded her and it was her pride and joy. Staff were happy and well-trained and all the factory's component parts worked in harmony. None of the competitors could match this. The company was self-sufficient with everything made in-house, as profitably as it could possibly be. The rest of them could whine on about the unique sales format that every competitor had copied within a few weeks or months of them taking it to the marketplace some twenty years earlier, but what surrounded her now was what had actually been the cause of all the company's success. Anyone with half a brain could surely see that this copied idea wasn't what had made the company as successful as it was. When they had started selling that way it was unique to the sector but the advantage was lost as competitors followed their lead and did the same. Deb knew the company line was that their unique sales pitch gave them the edge but even salesmen should be able to see through that. Especially with every customer won having had the same sales pitch and equipment from the guy before.

She knew it was her continued improvements and inspirations that kept the company up at the front. How many competitors had sunk without trace over the years because they thought all they had to do was copy how her company sold its products? Nobody ever saw the processes, the training, the logistics and everything else that went into making this unique sales technique work. It was just like the brand new, shiny sports car of your dreams sitting in the showroom and all you had to do was walk in and buy it. You never considered what it took to get it there. Still, she appreciated what she had achieved and the staff were happy.

As she did her rounds she noticed the factory was a little quieter than normal. Maybe there was a staff briefing or something. It was close to break time and the production manager did tend to aim for that sort of time to cut down on interruptions and questions, even if the input could be useful. The workers were more worried about getting to the canteen a few seconds late rather than hearing about or contributing something that could make their working life easier. She smiled to herself; she had never understood that attitude.

She entered the main warehouse and spied a gathering in the far corner which seemed to comprise of most of the missing staff. A strange place to have a meeting, she mused, heading towards the group. A few of the workers at the back started to break away and head towards her on their way to the canteen. There was a mixture of giggling and embarrassed looks as they passed. Deb suspected it was something set up for a worker about to get married or a birthday she hadn't heard about. Normally the staff were good when it came to this sort of thing and it was set up for the end of shift but this was the middle of the morning, so she made a mental note to have a quiet word with the shift manager. She didn't want to stop this tradition (one that is honoured by every work force in every factory in the country) but just keep it to a less disruptive time. As one of the older members of staff passed her, she commented: 'Deb, I wouldn't go over there, you will get embarrassed.'

People misjudged Deb's professionalism as being prim and proper and perhaps a little frumpy. After being the only female worker in a male-dominated workforce for years there was probably nothing that could shock her. The worker's comments only seemed to confirm her suspicions that maybe someone was having the mickey being good-naturedly taken out of them? She was usually informed of these occasional happenings so that they were not discovered by accident by important visitors or if there were people who didn't want to be involved and wanted to be somewhere else, they could arrange to be elsewhere.

She remembered passing the production manager going in the other direction at the start of her tour – there was no way he could have got past her and back here to supervise and make sure that things didn't get out of hand. If this was the staff taking matters into their own hands, maybe a few good-natured words might be in order, just to re-enforce a few small ground rules. The staff were usually excellent and it wasn't like them to swing the lead and be slacking off during work hours just because their manager was away doing something else.

She closed in on the crowd, which was getting noisy and boisterous. Cheers and slow hand clapping were coming from most of the participants. Deb was guessing it could be a strip-a-gram so that could be male or female in this day and age. Everyone had their backs to her, so she placed her hand on the shoulder of the person in front, one of the tall lads from the warehouse. He turned to let her past but was trying hard to continue watching what was going on at the front of the crowd. He glanced down and realised who he was letting past, and like the ripples of a stone thrown into deep water the rest of the crowd started to realise they had been caught, dispersing as quickly as they possibly could. Like a biblical parting of the waves the human sea parted to reveal ... Harry!

The sales director and shareholder was sitting with his trousers around his ankles on a small stack of pallets with one of the pretty Polish female temps giving him a blow job, all done for the amusement of the now quickly dispersing crowd.

'What the fuck are you doing, you moronic pervert?' yelled Deb. The blonde Polish girl realised she and Harry were the only ones left. She quickly stopped what she was doing, got up, snatched up her top and bra, then disappeared as fast as the rest of the crowd, clutching her jiggling breasts with her hands as she ran for cover. 'Of all the stupid damn things you have ever done since you joined this company ...' Deb could not find the words to complete what she was going to say.

Harry was nonchalant and stood up casually, pulling up his trousers and tucking his wilting erection back inside its more customary hiding place.

'What the hell are you doing? What the hell were you thinking?' Deb asked.

'Relax, just trying to get to know the workforce. It was only a bit of light-hearted fun.' Harry seemed quite proud of himself.

'Are you insane?' Deb was enraged, and Harry's lack of guilt wasn't helping the situation. 'How can you get someone to do that here?' She made a grand gesture to show she meant the warehouse. There were only the two of them left now.

'Big tip, dear,' he brayed, and grabbed his crotch. After what she had just seen she was positive he was talking monetary value rather than anything else, despite his gesture.

'We need to talk. My office, now.'

'Don't talk to me like that. I am the same grade as you.'

'And that makes all this OK does it?'

'No harm done, and now you've spoilt my tea break I'm going back to work.'

Deb was stunned by his attitude. 'This isn't the dark ages. You are not lord of the fucking manor. You cannot just come down here and roger a peasant to fill your tea break. What if she sues the company? What if any of them sue the company? Haven't you heard of sexual harassment?'

'Sorry Deb, we own the company and there have to be a few perks in that. Lighten up a little.' Harry turned away and headed off in the general direction of his office. Deb wanted to scream and shout but she was too professional to lose her temper here and followed after him.

Harry entered his office and tried to close the door on her. Deb was going to have her say and barged past. One of Harry's lackeys was already there and waiting to see his boss. 'Mick, can you give us five minutes?' Deb asked.

'Hey this is my office. I say who goes and who stays. Mick's here for a meeting and me and you are finished.'

'You want Mick to stay whilst we "chat", do you?' Mick picked up on the anger in the room and got up out of his chair to leave.

'Sit down,' Harry commanded. 'This will not take long. She just caught me getting a blow job off that little blonde Polish tart in production and spoilt my big finish.' All this was said with a stupid grin on his face. Mick was hovering, not knowing whether to sit back down or stand up and leave but his boss was waving at him to sit, so that is what he did. 'It was a bit of fun, that's all. No production was lost in the process of making me happy, OK,' Harry announced, followed by a conspiratorial snigger between the two lads.

'You disgusting, arrogant bastard. You don't have the power of a Roman Emperor, whatever you think. You cannot just go up to the female staff and get them to give you sexual favours.'

'Well, I did. Or would have if you had given me a couple more minutes.' Renewed sniggering.

'Seriously, what if she sues for sexual harassment? Apart from all the other employment laws and codes of conduct you have chosen to ignore. Yes, we own the company so we have to set the standards, not abuse our position. You are a director and shareholder of an international company. What if this crap made the local papers? I employed that girl on a youth scheme; she is only just out of school. Three weeks ago you could have been done for under-age sex, you creep.'

'Nothing will happen, we were all just larking about. Now, bye-bye, mother, I have work to do.'

'You are sick. If she comes to me with a claim against you I will be on her side and I will wipe that stupid grin off your face.'

'I know you think it is your company, luv.' Harry had come to stand in front of her. 'But I am one of the new guard and we don't give a fuck about what you did for the company in the past or what you do for it now.'

Deb stormed out, slamming the door behind her. She had discussed with Summer the type and standard of the people she was now bringing into the company, over-ruling Deb's choices and recommendations in favour of people whose only real talent seemed to be the ability to run roughshod over everything Deb had built, and having undying and unquestioning loyalty to their CEO and no-one else. It was becoming harder to stop these people eroding all the good work she and the company had done over the years. It had taken complete dedication and all her experience to repair the damage this type of person had done to the company the first time around. The only saving grace was that she had now made the company bomb-proof, ensuring there were enough systems in place to limit the damage any one person could do.

Later she spoke to Summer about the incident and was again surprised by the way it had been dismissed like some harmless prank. But it had not been long until Harry had been sent to Germany, something only talked about and considered after Harry's Polish incident, despite the company stating it had been in the pipeline for a long time.

Two years or so later and the word was that Harry was on the way back to the UK. Deb was holding out for a German national to be found to take Harry's place. In the few places where they had tried 'the foreign national' approach it had worked a lot better than UK lads arriving and trying to start new markets.

The main candidate to replace Harry was one of the few employees there before Deb's arrival, and was not the foreign national she had hoped for. The candidate was OK at best but at least he had some experience of this type of work at a junior level within the company. Summer was trying to influence the selection with her own choice and her candidate was a skinny, poisonous, black lesbian woman called Yvette, who was her close friend. The candidates' nickname around the company was the 'Black Queen'. This had stemmed from an incident at one of the company get-togethers. One of the many salesmen had got into a heated argument with Yvette. He had been drinking all night and was very drunk and he had tried to negotiate an opportunity to show Yvette what she was missing in the bedroom department. As the argument escalated he had got his gender insults politically incorrect and mixed up, and called her a Black Queen in front of everyone – and the tag had instantly stuck. Newer people who heard the tag assumed it was based on the colour of her skin. Those who had been with the company longer suspected that it had more to do with how treacherous and spiteful she was. She was, or seemed to be, the font of all malicious gossip around the company. She would sit in state in her office next to Summer's with all her snipes and snitches in attendance, whispering and scheming against any poor unfortunate who had gained their displeasure.

No one was quite sure of Yvette's origins, although they could guess from her nondescript English accent that she was most likely an American. Since Summer had taken her on, Yvette had played the minority card again and again to get out of trouble. Somehow she always managed to get someone else blamed for what she had done or not done when it all went wrong, but she had a talent for being associated with and taking the credit even when she had nothing to do with things that went right. When the situation was really bad she always had the 'I am lesbian and black' get-out-of jail-free card and was not afraid to use it.

Most of the longer-serving members of staff had attended several of Yvette's coming-out parties over the years and these parties had usually heralded an announcement that all was not going to plan on something she was working on, despite all her best efforts. Still, most people saw it as a good excuse to go out and have a party, all the while secretly wishing that this was going to be the time Yvette would get what she deserved – but she never did and she never would. Yvette was Summer's best friend and had her full protection, and Deb knew it.

Yvette had arrived not long after Summer had joined the company. What their relationship had been before that was open to debate. The rumours ranged from the outrageous (that she was Summer's father's illegitimate love child and she was given her job as a favour and for the purpose of keeping her away and out of sight of Summer's mother) to the more salacious (that she was really Summer's lesbian lover), to the mundane (she and Summer had worked together and Summer liked her). Harry had been useless in Germany and Yvette had the potential to be no better in Deb's eyes. She could only hope that they would both stay as far away from the company and for as long as possible. You could always hope.

* * *

Harry was glad to be back in the fold, realising he might have gone a little too far with his Polish prank a couple of years earlier. Summer had not blown a gasket or anything like that but he had got the message loud and clear that she wasn't happy when she had declared what a great opportunity it would be for him to prove himself in Germany and sent him off, even though all their research had shown that it might be more trouble than it was worth. There had been many easier targets to go for and most had at least a few ex-UK salesmen living in the country to give him a hand. He didn't even speak German, for fuck sake.

He had been very lucky to land this job with Summer. There

was the fabricated CV and the opportunity to make sure the company had believed it. Then that idiot Deb did most of his work for him and for no better reason than to keep the company moving forward whilst he got up to speed. He suspected she had figured out he wasn't all he claimed to be. But it was too late now as long as he didn't blow it with Summer. His feet were well and truly under the table. All that great work Deb had done had his signature on it and everyone thought he had done it all and that was all that really mattered. He made sure he bought enough drinks and sandwiches when he was out on the road for the sales team to think he was a wonderful boss, not that he ever taught them anything useful or helpful that was originally contributed by himself. He was no more than the messenger, if the truth be known. But as far as his team were concerned he was God because they believed the words he spoke were all his own. When it came down to it, he was going to be here long after Deb was a fading memory. Or that was the implication from Summer, anyway. He just had to keep himself under control and on the right side of his CEO.

He had been like a kid in a sweet shop. It had been a whole new world. He knew before he joined the company physically he had very little pulling power. Poor physique and an insurance salesman doesn't come high on attractive girls' wish lists for potential partners. He had had to settle for a partner who he had once overheard being described as a man in drag. It was true she was nearly as tall and lanky as him and as ungraceful as himself. She had a very small chest but she had the right equipment 'downstairs'. He had won her over easily enough, the salesman in him taking over and giving him the words to say what was needed to get the deal done.

One of his so-called friends and colleagues had said to all that would listen in the local pub one dinner time 'that once a woman was on her back and the lights were off they were all the same height, same shape and whatever colour you wanted them to be'. Harry suspected there was some truth in what the man had said but on the other hand he wouldn't be at all surprised if the guy had been getting even less than he was.

Jackie was his wife's name. They copulated maybe twice a month and that was his love life until he joined the company. Jackie's family were fairly well off, so he wouldn't jeopardise that and break up their happy home but the flash executive car that was now his, thanks to the company and the flash suits he had invested in had certainly been babe magnets. On the road he had found wherever he stayed there was always one of these bitches on heat and ready to flex the company credit card with him. He would confess to himself that not all the conquests had been that attractive but the observations of his friend had been accurate. When he first joined the company he had made it home no matter what, arriving late and out early in the morning. Now Jackie was happy that it was the workload keeping him out and not anything more sinister, he took full advantage of his new-found extra wealth and freedom.

Even within the company he found to his amazement that his pulling power was greatly enhanced because of his position. Jackie was always kept at home for the company get-togethers. They weren't her thing, anyway. With a little more salesmanship about how he would be working all night and had to mingle and be seen as part of the team and she would be left all alone, it wasn't hard to show up at these little get-togethers partner-less and on the prowl.

The tarts in the offices or on the shop floor were ready to give in and give out by the end of the evening. Their husbands at home with the kids and themselves bitter because they deserved more and better. Of course he spent the evening getting as much alcohol into his chosen victim of the night as possible, the amount of drinks administered through the evening guaranteeing a pliant, willing and disorientated partner. Some had even passed out as they were on-the-job. He had finished and woken them enough to help them out of his room. One had even thrown up half way through their little illicit activities. She had twisted over on to her front to retch over the side of the bed. Once she was finished he had hung her over the other side of the bed so he wouldn't have to stare down on a pile of puke and shafted her doggie style. Each conquest ending in the stagger of shame as he insisted they leave his room once he was satisfied.

To his knowledge, Summer had never been upset by any of these indiscretions. Hell, she was never at these company do's anyway. However, the Polish thing had not been one of his best decisions. Not everyone gets to do their boss doggie style over her desk and pulls in a shed load of cash as well. He knew he was lucky and for this type of bonus he now realised he was expected to be completely loyal and obedient. He had innocently thought the loyalty stuff was just work-related.

Still, he was on the way back now and had quite enjoyed getting paid to do practically nothing for two years. His in-depth reports were more the product of time spent on the Internet with just the occasional visit to some German town or city to get a few compliments slips and introduction cards to enhance and sell the report as genuine. You couldn't call yourself a salesman if you couldn't come up with a few rigged figures to keep your boss off your back, now, could you?

He had been back and forth to the UK a few times in the last month and he was now sitting in Summer's office, waiting for their meeting to start. She had called him in when he had knocked on her door but had been on the phone so he was sat waiting for the call to end. He hadn't heard the whole conversation and what he had didn't really make sense so he had given up concentrating.

She put the phone down. There was some small talk. She was glad he was nearly back and she wished that Germany had progressed quicker. He countered with a line or two about it being a harder market to crack than first thought, a speech he had prepared for the occasion. Adding that it would all be worth it in the end.

'Well, I feel it is time for you to return here full-time. Things have moved on since you have been gone and I need my loyalist workers here with me. I want Yvette to take over from you in Germany. She deserves her chance and I want to give her free rein to show us what she can do. I don't know why people dislike her so much here. You should hear the gossip she has to endure and put up with.'

Harry thinks it's 'gossip' she starts and spreads herself most likely but keeps it to himself. Germany isn't the worst place he could have been sent and Yvette is one of Summer's blind spots – even he knows that.

'I had Barry in mind. He is good, hardworking, can work on his own and he has done this sort of thing for us a couple of times already in the past. His sales results are double his closest rival and to be honest, that isn't even Yvette.' There is a slight pause and he says the next sentence in a slightly embarrassed voice. 'And I don't think Germany is the right place for a black lesbian to be representing us.'

'When I want your opinion I will tell you what I want you to say.' The calm presentation and the accompanying sickly sweet smile didn't hide the fact that this was a decree and not a discussion.

'It is just that everyone will expect Barry to be the one; he is by far the best candidate. He might get the hump and see it as a slight and a put-down to lose out to Yvette.' Why did he say that? Why didn't he just keep quiet and do as Summer ordered.

'What?'

'I am just saying it could get messy. If Barry thinks you don't rate him or that he is going to be replaced, he has been here long enough to stir up the muck. We can't just give Yvette the job if there is someone more deserving.' He knows he is treading on very thin ice. The company has been carrying Yvette and overlooking her failures and shortcomings since before Harry himself joined. Now Harry is a shareholder it is his profit as well and he wants the best candidate to make his own profits that much better. Barry would do a better job and make them all more money. 'I am just thinking of your profits; Barry would do better.' He hopes the last comment will show his loyalty is still in the right place and with the right person.

'I appreciate your input and your concerns. I have already told Yvette she has the job, so make it happen. I suggest you fall out with Barry over something and play the spiteful boss card. I don't care how you justify it, get Yvette to Germany.'

There is a small pause. Harry has a small dilemma and crisis to solve and because it is one of his own loyal crew that is about to be shat on he doesn't want it to snowball and lose the rest and their loyalty. Normally when Summer wants something like this set up it is from someone else's department. The pause seems to have been a signal to Summer that he is unsure what to do next and that she needs to take control and explain what is expected from him.

Summer starts again and it is obvious she already has the outlines of a plan he could use. 'You both like skiing, don't you? I know since you've been here you have been out with the boys a couple of times for weeks away, splashing a little cash at the start and then letting those snivelling salesmen fight to buy your drinks for the rest of the holiday if you have any sense and self-respect.' She leaned forward and he glanced at her boobs. 'I suggest you get a trip organised quickly. Get a few loyal members of your team going, including Barry, and orchestrate a very messy and public falling out. Surely you can manage to arrange that.'

Another pause and a blank look from Harry. 'Get Barry drunk.' Summer is now spelling out her plan to get Harry going in the right direction and on the right track. Who would have thought it would take so much effort? 'Everyone knows that once he is drunk, Barry's stock-in-trade comments are always the same. He gets morbid and the stupid little twerp starts telling all the wives and girlfriends that they are all way too good for their partners and that their partners don't deserve them.'

Harry cringed a little internally; the scenario is not totally unique to Barry, only Barry doesn't take advantage of the situation.

Summer continued. 'You take the hump and get angry. Accuse him of trying to fuck your wife and chat her up in front of all your friends and staff. Accuse him of doing it to humiliate you and disrespect you. How hard can that be?'

'Barry is not like that. He wouldn't do it for that reason. He is just a prat and can't see that it could be taken the wrong way. All he is trying to do in his own crazy way is to be nice.'

'Am I having a problem with you again?' Summer asked, looking up from the paperwork on the desk in front of her. She folded her arms and leans slightly forward. 'Harry, you need to have this very public falling out. When you come back, make him very uncomfortable. Make sure he knows you have fallen out with him and when he comes crying to me because I am your boss and asking can I make things right, I will calm him down and take the opportunity to encourage him to see this as a golden opportunity to reach for his own dreams and ambitions and treat it as a sign it is time to leave and fly higher and prove you wrong.' She had that same smug smile again. Where does she come up with these plans?

If Harry only knew ... Summer had become friends with a local therapist-cum-councillor she had started seeing. She had read an article in a magazine that had declared they were the latest 'must have' accessory for the modern business person and of course she had then had to get one. The article had been young and trendy; unfortunately – or fortunately – the therapist had been better than she had been ready for. He had latched on to her 'daddy' issues and he had denounced the hard businesswoman thing just as an act, trying to impress her father and win his support and approval, something she had already convinced herself would have come naturally if she had just been a boy. All the money, cars and flashy everything were just prizes she was displaying to convince him of her abilities. She would get the family business one day, but she was bitter. If she had been a boy it would have been Harvard, not some shitty finishing school in the UK. She knew if 'she' had been 'he' she would be standing side by side with her father learning the business and being part of it now and not in some awful business in the dullest part of the damned world. She was just waiting for father to call her back proclaiming the time was now right. Maybe father knew more than she gave him credit for and knew she was just taking the credit for someone else's work.

Summer had been making millions out of Deb's work for years, so damned right she was a real businesswoman. It was her name on the top of the list and that should be all her father saw and all that mattered.

The therapist had also picked up on the jealousy and hatred thing she felt for Deb and had pointed out it wasn't a weakness. This need to show power and crush the opposition was a strength. It wasn't insecurity knowing that this person was much better than you, when you were the one making the money and enjoying all the perks as they toiled away for you day in, day out.

Summer had suspected the therapist was going to help her influence and manipulate the people around her even more. She had talked increasingly about how to get people to do what you wanted in their later sessions, rather than talking about herself. It had taken extra cash to talk specific cases but she was ready to put her new source of information to the test. Deb's little charts and tests had Barry down as hard working, committed and loyal. It also said he had underlying tendencies to believe he was far better than he was and that he would flee from confrontation from someone superior if he felt he had upset them. The therapist had confirmed the evaluation and together they had discussed a scenario involving poor Barry that would result in the outcome Summer wanted.

The plan was to panic Barry into thinking he had lost favour with his boss and that it would stop him advancing in the company. Next she would convince him he was wasted in the company although he was much better than people gave him credit for, but unfortunately it wasn't her decision. Harry was his boss and it was his choice and she would have to abide by the decision. Then it was all about leaving the company and showing Harry how wrong he was about holding Barry back, positioning this as a chance to go it alone. Barry would be inspired by her little speech and motivated to hand in his notice to go and achieve his dreams – whatever they might be – and she wouldn't even have to pay the poor sap redundancy. Deb's profile had, of course, revealed poor Barry was likely to succeed in a more controlled and risk-free environment as part of a team but no one wants to hear you're only good enough to be a team member. If the therapist was right, and the plan they had constructed worked, Barry would be leaving of his own free will with no come-back on her. Disgrace the guy, build him up and then lead him on until he left of his own free will on his new grand adventure ... but first she needed Harry to get off his fat arse and do his part.

She had found over the years with very few exceptions that the way to get a man to do what you wanted was sex. She hadn't given poor Harry any for two years so it was about time he had a little incentive. She had had her diversions over the same time period. Of course, money will get you whatever you want. When you are out of sight and away from anyone who might know you there are certain encounters that are very acceptable. On the other hand when you are using it as a bit of leverage and manipulation, the whole thing always seems to be accompanied by men with their trousers around their ankles and their socks pulled up to just under their knees with their shoes still on.

Money could always get you the bodies you really wanted to play with and they stripped exactly the way you told them to. Oh, power and money were great. And if she was really desperate there was always her own husband.

'Harry, lock the door. I think it is time for a little bonus to get you motivated again.' By the time he was shuffling back she had removed her underwear, hitched up her skirt and had assumed the position on his side of the desk. Harry was in straight from behind. She was a little dry and it was a little uncomfortable. Old age must be creeping up on her. There was a time she could be wet and ready as soon as she needed to be. A little discreet lubrication might be needed these days. Still, it was quite amusing and pleasant hearing the little moans and whimpers behind her.

Harry obviously wasn't getting it as regularly as he used to, not that he ever lasted that long. Not a good performance … the occasion was obviously getting to him. In a couple of minutes it was all over and he was gone. A new man on a new mission. She had a handful of tissues stuffed in the crotch of her panties so she didn't have to sit in a damp patch and was ready to carry on looking busy.

9

Back to Normal?

It had been several years now since the buy-out and the company had grown and grown. The excitement Deb now felt about her job was about being there and watching something she'd built and nurtured succeed above all expectations. She had the joy of knowing that all the years painstakingly ensuring that the foundations were in place and then building on them meant that the company was damn near indestructible. All it now needed to do was to expand to meet growing demand or fine tune to meet changes in legislation. Before the buy-out the company profits were already lottery-win size. Now they were in the realms of a multi-rollover Euro-millions jackpots.

There had been problems at first when they had all been made shareholders. Deb had been worried when the lads had acted like kids in a sweet shop with no restrictions. New cars, new houses and flashier lifestyles, spending money the company had not even yet made. Concerned, she had questioned their restraint at the end of a meeting one day, only to find out Summer was handing out interest-free loans to the directors of the company, which Deb knew to be illegal. Summer had also been wheeling and dealing with the company finances on schemes she and her company accountant had cooked up. Large profits had suddenly disappeared and big plans were put on hold. It took Deb weeks to sort the mess out and get the company legal again.

Most people didn't find out what had happened and the only

casualty was the company accountant, who was allowed to leave after taking the blame. Deb was sure it was all done on Summer's instructions and that Summer had full knowledge of what was going on. Summer's department, Summer's instructions and Summer's watch but never ever Summer's fault. The company was well past that particular problem now but again it had been Deb's vigilance that had diverted the accident waiting to happen.

* * *

Deb should have been happy! She should have been ecstatic! She was in South Africa following the British Lions rugby on tour and she was with her husband celebrating twenty-five years of marriage but it had been a really shitty eighteen months at work and she could not put her finger on what was causing her all the grief. The company was still expanding, still making unbelievable profits and in the main she was still loving her job.

There was only another eighteen months or so until she could leave the company if she wanted to, as the agreement that she'd had to sign before Summer would allow her to become a shareholder was coming to an end. The way she felt now she was tempted to take advantage of the guaranteed pay-out of the get-out clause Summer had insisted on including in the articles they had all signed. If she did, though, it would mean losing out on much greater rewards in the future, rewards she deserved and had earned. But she had never been greedy.

Deb shook her head to clear her thoughts. Of course she would never leave the company, she'd be letting everyone down. What would they think? As soon as she got back off holiday she'd get all the minor troubles sorted. It had just been a hard time to get through. It wasn't the hours or the work, it just felt as if there was more than usual going wrong, and it was taking longer to put things right when people messed up because they were not doing what she was asking them to do to solve the problems. It had been easier in the past when the company was smaller. Things were now spending longer under the radar before they were found out, giving them time to fester before they could be put right. People could hide in the shadows and not pull their weight, or not work in the company way. Working in much larger companies before she had seen the problems created from what seemed minor issues and problems or people with the wrong attitudes. But maybe the reason she was down was because she seemed to be the only one who could see these minor cracks and no-one else was worried.

Well, she was going to make the best of her break. Summer had insisted that Deb had celebrated her twenty-five years of marriage bliss in style, despite the problems at work. Summer's suggestions had ranged from buying a grand new home to buying expensive new cars for her and Bob. They had finally agreed on something a little less extravagant and had settled on a three-week holiday on tour with the Lions. Bob was wary of spending large amounts of money they couldn't guarantee replacing but they had still spent a large enough amount to clear a good chunk of savings.

Summer had continually pointed out that everything was safe because of the bonuses Deb was going to receive from this point on. All the work was now done and the company shareholders could sit back and take their profits. Deb had managed to keep the profits so high that the shares had all been paid for in the last couple of months, and for the first time the bonuses would be theirs to spend and not paid straight back to the company. Again, she had completed the task way in front of estimated completion dates.

After years of work it had been great to sit back and take a three-week holiday. However, it had been a surprise when Andy Sapp had announced only a couple of weeks before they were due to fly out that he was coming on tour too. Luckily, so far he had been located in different hotels for most of the time. Deb and Bob had booked reasonably early and were placed in hotels for families, couples and older people, which seemed to mean quieter and better run places. Sapp had been put into one of the young, free and on-tour groups, which meant their paths only seemed to cross on match days.

When they did meet up, Sapp spent all his time trying to get them to join expensive trips or enticing them to spend stupid amounts on fashion or jewellery. Deb and Bob had got to the point where they were prepared to avoid Sapp at all costs. If they wanted to spend their money they would; it wasn't going to be spent for them by some tag-along work friend.

They had both been surprised when Andy had announced his plans to come on tour. It had always been company policy to allow only one executive off at a time and in all the years Deb could remember that rule had never been broken. When he had unveiled his plans, she had made sure she already had 'dibs' on this holiday. Summer had been very dismissive about the whole thing, claiming the company was now in a position to bend a few rules and seeing no problems with them both being away from the company for so long.

Maybe the biggest surprise of all was the fact that Deb had worked with Sapp for twenty-odd years and he had never shown any interest in rugby – or any other sport for that matter. Deb and Bob had always loved their sports and rugby was their common ground. Even at work the company had the usual split and good-natured discussions between footie and rugger fans that took place most working days, in or out of season. Both parties disowned cricket fans, if ever they confessed in public.

Andy Sapp had never shown any interest in any of it until a few weeks ago. They had also been a little surprised when he had announced he wasn't bringing his wife and family. On the few occasions they had all met at company functions, sport had never appeared on the list of topics talked about so Deb was sure Andy's wife was no sports fan. But this was three weeks away from the family and there would only be four actual days when there would be matches played and that would only really account for four, maybe five, hours on those days. The rest was all holiday time. Wives were not expected to sit through the matches and could just sit by the pool and relax as their husbands rode the rollercoaster of emotions at the match on their behalf.

It would have probably been nice to get to know Sapp's family a little away from a works setting but Bob and Deb presumed he must be meeting up with a gang of old friends for a boy's reunion, some heavy drinking and reliving of the past. But Sapp didn't seem the type and Deb suspected there were no great gangs of friends waiting to all meet up. In fact there was very little reason or evidence that would explain why Sapp was going on tour on his own, to a place he didn't like, to support a sport he didn't seem interested in, surrounded at all times by people talking mostly about rugby.

As the holiday went on and they met up for the matches, they noted that at least Sapp now knew a few names of players and their positions and joined in a little with the conversation. There had been no appearance of any gang of buddies and it still seemed a little strange to Deb and Bob, but it was his money to spend. They had blanched a little at the cost but at least it was on their sports bucket list and they could use the big anniversary to justify some of the expense. Sapp seemed to be signing up for three weeks in his own private purgatory.

* * *

Two weeks into the break, Deb was finally beginning to wind down and switch off from work. It had been her year from hell, starting innocently enough when Summer asked her to review the work Yvette was doing in Germany and see if she could make some helpful suggestions. Yvette had been there ever since Harry had returned and had had about as much success. In other words, she had been as useless as Harry, and once Deb had arrived and started investigating it hadn't taken long to find out how little work was actually being done on the company's behalf and to uncover the creative accounting Yvette was using to 'prove' all was going well and keep herself in a nice cushy little number.

Deb had taken with her a candidate she had found to be Yvette's assistant. He was tall, good looking and an ex-professional footballer. He was also a German national who she'd found when he had applied for one of her English jobs. When he had proved himself worthy after all the tests and interviews she had known he had the potential to help them break into his home country, Germany. She had been honest and told him about the politics between Summer, Yvette and the rest of the company, and that he would have to bide his time and play at being Yvette's assistant until Yvette got bored and moved on around the company. He would then be in a position to do the job properly and become a country manager. The German was happy with the plan. He had come to find work and it was a bonus that he was actually able to go back home to do just that. The only problem again was that Deb had done something for the good of the company but it would earn someone else the brownie points. She couldn't force Yvette to take the guy on, so she would have to make it seem that Yvette was doing it of her own free will. She was sure it wouldn't be too hard to convince Yvette that an assistant was needed to do most of the German stuff, and the bonus would be to free up some of Yvette's own time. It should be an easy sell.

There had been many criticisms and obvious faults in the way Yvette was running the show in Germany but when you were only answerable to Summer, that was to be expected. The biggest problem was Yvette claiming she had new starters and the company was setting everything up, and then the new starters never appeared, wasting everyone's time but still being classed as Yvette completing her part of the process. In the UK, deposits, franchise fees and orders were paid up front, so the new starter was committed. Yvette claimed it wasn't the German way, along with doing interviews in coffee shops and restaurants that projected a far-from-professional image of the company. Deb suspected that quite a few of the new starters never really existed at all. Yvette wasn't even using all the tried and trusted interview systems and forms, so Deb could not review the candidates herself and find out what the problems were, even if they had been real. Either Yvette was being continually duped or the candidates were imaginary so she could pad her stats.

Yvette had got the hump when Deb had gone through everything and pointed out what was needed to make things work. By the time she left though, Deb had made sure the company had an office, the German had been taken on and a proper advert had been placed in real German, not schoolboy German, as the new assistant had pointed out quietly under his breath, for her ears only.

She reported all her actions back to Summer, except for her German employee coup preferring to get the right person in place and let someone else have the credit rather than have Yvette dismiss him only because he was Deb's choice, and not hers.

When she returned home from Germany, Deb was confused by the lack of support or commitment from Summer, and came out of a meeting feeling that her CEO thought she was being harsh on poor Yvette. Salesmen who hadn't been lucky enough to have the CEO as a best buddy had been dismissed for far less than fiddling important figures. As always, Deb had done her work, but no-one took any notice.

* * *

One of the unfortunate outcomes of the German's placement and success was that Yvette had lots more spare time and when a major Finnish customer called Hawkken had his yearly sales conference, Yvette was sent as the company's representative. Over the years it had always been a director and it had normally been Deb who'd gone because she had worked closely with the guy since he had started and she and Bob had become good friends with him and his wife. Also, Deb could answer all the technical and annoying questions everyone wanted to ask at this sort of thing. Bob and Deb had even tried to help when the Hawkken and his wife had been divorced but after years of marriage the Finnish couple had said that they had drifted apart. Work, the unsociable hours and the Finnish taste for drinking to excess had finally taken its toll on the couple's marriage and with no kids to worry about they split and went their separate ways.

Hawkken had joined the company years ago, around the time it was splitting and reforming. The big, blond guy had shown up with his long hair pulled back into a ponytail, a long Viking beard and a large bundle of cash he was ready to invest. Frank and Summer had instantly been ready to sell him the rights to Finland. Their plan was to take his money to keep the UK company going, using him as a cash cow and nothing else. The hope was that once his money had dwindled and he had not received the support promised, he would bugger off, putting it down to a poor choice on his part with his cash being well looked after by Frank and Summer. If by chance the guy did manage to hold on and succeed on his own that would be a bonus.

Deb had seen the potential in the business proposition and in the ability of Hawkken, and she had fought to get him treated fairly and ethically from the start. Her knowledge and experience turned the situation from a short-term and short-sighted snatch-and-grab on the poor guy and his money into the most successful foreign franchise the company had ever had. Having fought for this franchisee every step of the way and putting great pressure on her working relationships with Frank and Summer, Deb had been proven right. Hawkken was now a customer spending millions of pounds with the company every year.

But this year, Summer had decided to send Yvette to represent the company. Germany was just down the road, so to speak, from Finland, and a country manager was good enough to show they hadn't forgotten the Finnish connection. There were to be no real big announcements or changes this time, so Summer felt she wouldn't waste anyone who was of any importance on the jolly. Yvette could go and let her hair down and get smashed on the company. The German national had taken to the job like a duck to water, so Yvette's presence wasn't essential and this two-day jolly would remind Yvette who still pulled the strings and where her loyalties should lie in the grand scheme of things.

* * *

The first day back to work after the conference, Deb had received a phone call from a livid Hawkken threatening to quit and never deal with the company again. His mood wasn't helped by the time difference between the two countries, which meant he'd had to wait before starting his rant. He had used the time to wind himself up to explosion point. Deb finally got him to calm down enough to talk to her properly and explain why he was in such a foul mood after what was usually the highlight of his year. The problem was Yvette!

Hawkken went into vivid detail about the trail of hostility and humiliation left in Yvette's wake and how she had totally embarrassed everyone and had shown up the company. He described how Yvette had spent her time drinking all day. A little bit of 'pot calling the kettle black', thought Deb, the Finn's not being known as teetotallers. It hadn't been uncommon to see some of the Finnish staff ending the conference and party being so drunk that they had to crawl on hands and knees back to their cars to drive home. Many of them had owned their own breathalysers and one of their favourite party games was to see how far away you could get and blow at (yes, at – not into) the machine and set it off. But as the events of the weekend were recounted, it was obvious that it had not been the amount of alcohol consumed that was the whole issue with Yvette.

A drunk Yvette was acceptable, even expected, but a drunken Yvette accosting Finnish wives and girlfriends in public toilets had crossed the line. Hawkken explained that he had been called to explain several times to an increasingly belligerent Yvette that his staff were not interested in gay sex and to try and get her to tone down her act. There had been a few small scuffles when the Finns had started ignoring their English co-worker and Yvette had started doing the 'Don't you know who I am?' and 'I can get you all sacked' act. The evening had taken an even more unwanted twist when Yvette had cornered one of the salesmen's wives alone in one of the ladies toilets of the night club they were using for the party.

Yvette had tried to take advantage of the wife, pressuring the poor woman and telling her how she couldn't say 'no' to her advances because she had the power to ruin the woman's husband, Hawkken's career and the Finnish company. She had tried to kiss the salesman's wife, who had been shocked, which had quickly escalated to fear when Yvette had dropped her trousers and then put her hand up the woman's dress. She claimed she was going to 'pleasure' the now- terrified wife better than her husband ever could. The Finnish woman had pushed Yvette away and fled. Yvette had been totally smashed and with her trousers around her ankles she had lost her balance, falling and ripping the nearest cubicle door off its hinges in a futile attempt to regain her balance and not end up in an undignified heap on the floor.

Of course Hawkken was livid about the company sending someone like that to a family conference. Some 'little black pervert', as he put it, attacking a member of his staff, and with some of Hawkken's biggest customers present to hear about, if not actually see the incident.

Yvette had left the scene claiming she had done nothing wrong and saying it was the Finnish woman who had pestered her, claiming the salesman's wife was after a 'bit of black'. When she had said no, the Finnish woman had got into a shoving match that had caused the damage and then the wife had run off leaving poor Yvette to take the blame.

Deb was sure the salesman's wife's version was more likely to be the most accurate and she had followed company procedure and taken as many details as possible over the phone. Unfortunately there was no unbiased witness to the main part of the complaint. Deb assured Hawkken she would see to it that Summer was given all the facts, given Yvette was from Summer's department, and that the matter would be resolved appropriately.

Hawkken had started off threatening to quit and throw all the company's property into the sea. He was still mad but had calmed down enough to say he would carry on as long as Yvette was dealt with severely.

The outcome of it all was a surreal meeting with Summer, who dismissed the grievance out of hand, calmly stating that it sounded like any other conference or staff party she had ever been to or heard about, and that any of the foreign salesmen or their wives should have been glad that someone like Yvette had found any of them remotely worth her time. If it had been a salesman or franchisee with a female member of staff, no-one would even have mentioned it or cared. Deb was stunned with what Summer was implying. Summer stated that the Finnish woman should take it as a compliment Yvette was attracted to her and that she should be reprimanded for spreading malicious gossip. Deb resisted making the comparison of how it was Yvette that was normally the one doing the spreading gossip, but received a glare as she pointed out both statements couldn't be valid. They couldn't expect the wife to be happy with someone forcefully sexually harassing her and there was no evidence that the woman was spreading gossip – she had just reported the incident to her husband's boss.

Deb was between a rock and a hard place. She had witnessed the type of person Yvette was and her questionable attitudes and actions at their own company functions. She needed to keep Hawkken happy and show that the company was acting responsibly but she also need to keep Summer happy because she obviously felt her little Yvette was the one being wronged.

The three way shit-storm stopped as quickly as it had all blown up. To Deb's amazement, *she* somehow came away as the bad guy in all of it. Years of good working relationships and friendship with Hawkken seemed in jeopardy because Summer would not allow the incident to be investigated and no guilt ascertained, which meant no suitable punishment could be handed out. Hawkken raged that the company had no respect for him or his staff and Summer was angry that the matter – a minor problem, not worth wasting time on – had not been instantly quashed. Deb knew if an assault on a female employee had taken place in the UK all hell would have broken out, the culprit more than likely sacked and maybe even facing criminal charges.

Then there was Yvette. Deb had never liked, trusted or rated the Black Queen and she was now twisting and manipulating this and making it look like a personal vendetta that was aimed against her because of the colour of her skin, with Deb out to get her. These false accusations about Deb started to stick. She had never spoken to anyone but those involved, and she would never make any of the details public knowledge, just like the debacle in Germany but somehow all the details were again becoming public knowledge.

Yvette took every opportunity to accuse Deb of bullying her because of who and what she was. The reverse was actually true. Deb knew more than most about bullying and victimisation of minority groups, having been on the receiving end for years because she was a woman in a perceived man's industry. Because of that she had always been acutely aware of any minorities and always made sure that they were not victimised.

People were actually siding with Yvette and even asking why Deb had not fought Yvette's corner against the accusations. It had become 'them against us' and the 'them' in this case was those bloody foreigners. Deb suspected all the rumours and details were being leaked by Yvette and her inner circle. But everyone believed it was Deb. Deb hadn't been the one sexually assaulting a guy's wife in a public toilet after twenty-four hours of binge drinking or the one fiddling figures to preserve her job.

Even when members of Deb's own department stood up for her and had confirmed that it wasn't Deb leaking all this stuff, and pointing out Deb's past record and that she had dealt with the whole mess as discreetly and professionally as ever, people's views didn't change. Her staff were accused of sticking up for their boss and their statements and claims dismissed. Deb meanwhile, was traumatised that people she had known and worked closely with for years would even consider her a bully, a racist and a homophobe.

Deb had always been the strongest member of the company but all the false accusations took their toll. Soon she was taking anti-depressants and having sleepless, nightmare-filled nights. Matters were not helped when Summer started calling her in to private meetings or bringing up the subject out of the blue. Summer of course sided with Yvette and even forced Deb to apologise for her actions although she must have known they were imaginary accusations and had nothing to do with Deb. Yvette always played the hurt-but-willing-to-forgive, brave little soldier and Summer swung from 'it is all behind us now' to 'the company is getting the police involved'. Whenever the matter was dying down, somehow it seemed to raise its ugly head to continue tormenting Deb.

Deb had wanted to talk to Bob or someone about this but had convinced herself they would judge her the same way and not believe her side of the story, which she couldn't face. Added to that were the long hours she was doing because her own department was woefully undermanned. Summer always finding something else to allocate the money to rather than putting it where it was truly needed and just relied on Deb to put the hours in to make it all work.

Then there were problems with the recruitment side. Deb had

always done most of this and she was immensely proud of her success rate. Now the company was bigger, the department directors recruited for their own areas. Her crib sheets, tests and files along with all the training she had given out should have meant a seamless change in the way things were done, but either people were not using the tried and trusted methods or were not taking any notice of the results and recommendations produced. People were being recruited who were wrong for the jobs on offer and many were failing, or at best struggling, in their new positions. When questioned, the recruiters blamed poor candidates, an urgent position to be filled and no time to find the best people, or people just not living up to their test scores and profiles. Deb had done the job for years and knew it wasn't her system that was failing but again, she was taking the blame or the blame was being pointed in her direction.

A proven system did not fail overnight and you didn't go from near perfection for years before to struggling now for no reason. Again it was something else that had eroded her confidence and standing within the company. Summer, Grant and Sapp were either ignoring her work or over-ruling the results. She and the system were both working fine and were as good as ever but they were both being ignored. People were not questioning the failures or trying to find out why, just blaming her because they knew that it had been her job and her job alone in the past, even though that wasn't the case now.

Even when she tried to help, things were ending up all cock-eyed and messed up. She had always discussed work and bounced ideas off Bob to get a different perspective and it had always worked well. She couldn't remember what the original conversation was about but Bob had come up with a good idea after seeing a rival company's attempt at a cost control system when he was out on the road working for her company, but even that had gone wrong.

The conversation had got around to a mixer-cum-cost control system Bob had used in the factory he had run years ago. It was a simple, water-run system that would drag the ingredients and chemicals through a tube using water pressure and mix it all up to the required percentages and dilutions. If it worked elsewhere surely it could work for her company. Deb was ecstatic! It was a simple solution to a problem the company had had for years. If she could find the right equipment, health and safety would be improved, dilutions and mixes could be guaranteed and customers would get a cost control system that would eliminate wastage. She had searched the Internet for a few minutes and found loads of variations of the suggested system. All she needed was to sell it to the rest of the board.

Sales was Harry's domain and he and the new production manager were given the project. Deb had lit the blue touch paper but it wasn't her department so she did all she could, then handed the project over. Soon the company was selling and installing these new systems all over its market place with more success than even Deb had hoped for. The customers loved the safety, continuity and security of the new system. But Harry even found a way to compromise this and risk the company name.

The customers had all loved Deb and bought into her professionalism. It had been easy for Harry to squeeze extra out of her systems; everyone was just too trusting. He just had to show the salesmen how to 'enhance their sales potential'. Deb's approach got them the business but he made sure they squeezed the suckers for as much as they could. He also made sure the salesmen all knew the excuses to use if they were caught – and he did it all with Summer's blessing.

Deb had spent years salvaging the company's reputation, proving honesty was the best policy. This wasn't the way to do business – they were better than that, and she was annoyed that Harry had compromised something she had come up with to help the customer. He'd found a way to use it to abuse the customers and she had innocently supplied the ammunition. She was feeling isolated and alone and that wasn't helping her health with everything else that was going on, just adding fuel and stoking the fire.

Summer had caused much of Deb's grief before the holiday. She had over the last year to eighteen months seemed to change her views, her requirements, her loyalties and her goals for the company at the drop of a hat. Projects started and things promised were shelved or scrapped without notice and it all seemed to be Deb's stuff. Every meeting became a battlefield with accusations and recriminations, all without facts or anything substantial. Summer seemed to be getting Deb working on one thing and going in one direction and then the next minute she'd change what she wanted to the exact opposite of the meeting before. It was scatty, even for Summer. Deb resolved to sort it all out, but after her holiday. She was below par and not at her best, on prescription meds and not getting enough sleep, but she was still better than the rest. And that had been how she felt before her holiday.

* * *

She and Bob were sitting in the hotel restaurant with new friends they had made on the rugby tour, having a late breakfast, or early lunch – it was one of those sorts of days. There was no Lions match today and no organised trip, so it was a day to relax and chill out. Deb and Bob had got up late, gone for a swim, then finally made their way to the restaurant.

The hotels so far had been great but this one couldn't live up to their high standards. It was functional at best, more prisoner-of-war camp than anything else. It had quickly become the running joke with the 'inmates' to stand and shake the imaginary dirt out of their trouser legs so the guards wouldn't find the tunnels, even when standing at the bars ordering drinks. There was also an unofficial competition going on to come up with the most dumb-arse escape plan. Whether anyone would attempt the winning plan was unsure but when you had all started drinking way too early it gave you something to talk about other than rugby, because that wasn't going too well.

The hotel could have been an ex-army base. There were high, solid gates at the front, regimented rows of guest bungalows with a tall, white-painted wall topped with obligatory razor wire surrounding the lot. It was also big enough to hold many of the army of British rugby fans in one place. Deb and Bob had managed to continue to avoid Sapp because of the sheer size of the place.

As they came into the restaurant, they had been waved over by a couple of slightly older, single ladies they had met and been travelling with since the first hotel. Taking a short detour to claim a plateful of food each, they headed for the ladies' table and the awaiting customary and now traditional gossip over their meal. The Africans were good at making a passable full English breakfast with lots of fruit and muesli for those who felt the need. Cheese and ham were also on offer for the lightweights and there was some pretty horrible local fare tucked away around the edges that seemed to get few takers but no one ever returning for a second helping.

'Morning, ladies, how was your part of the "stalag" last night?' was Bob's happy greeting. They had all arrived two days before by coach, load after load arriving and spilling out passengers over the car park in front of reception. The red army of Lions fans were now all sweaty because they had dressed for the weather they had encountered so far and not the searing heat they had arrived in or were basked in now. The driving rain, storms and howling winds were now forgotten, thanks to the alcohol and blazing sun. They had all registered at reception and then everyone had been shipped off to their allotted rooms or cell blocks. To be fair to the place, once you did venture out into the heat it wasn't too bad. There were pools, bars, and a nightclub. The rooms were well-equipped, clean and tidy but no one could say it was modern.

'Very loud. They have given us a room near the nightclub.

Why they couldn't keep us all together I will never know.' This was a reference to the family and old peoples' group that had travelled together since the start of the tour. 'I mean, us poor old ladies being put by the damn nightclub? What do they think we are going to do, break-dance and jive all night for everyone's amusement? We arrived as a group and if they had kept us as a group surely it would have made more sense.'

'Maybe they just wanted us to all mingle and find new friends. We can't all have the best rooms near the bars and clubs, can we?' Bob teased, as he tucked in to his breakfast.

'Robert, there is already enough "mingling" going on over by us without anyone trying to help make it happen. The bars and the nightclub are open to all hours and we can hear them going all night.' Barbara leant forward conspiratorially. 'We're sure the security men are bringing in black lady prostitutes. There are loads of black girls milling around at all times of the night.'

Barbara was a small, feisty woman with big-rimmed glasses and she was the font of all things rugby. She knew everyone, spoke to everyone ... and listened to no-one. Her friend Sue was a little taller with no glasses and a little less knowledge of rugby, but listened a little better. Both ladies had been recently widowed and had been friends for years. They had travelled to chosen matches in the past as a foursome for years but now travelled as a two. Both were very fit for their age but going on the evidence of the tour so far, quite happy with a nightcap and bed as soon as it got to 9.30ish.

'Didn't have you down as a party pooper,' Bob commented, knowing Barbara would bite and rant a little longer and he could concentrate on the food in front of him. The ladies were already on their second coffee of the day and at the reading the papers stage with the breakfast things cleared away long ago.

'I don't mind a little partying. If the young people are getting on I'm not going to stop them or start complaining. But you should see them, the girls are arriving with almost nothing on. You know, skirts so tight and so short.' Bob thought about the clubs and bars in Birmingham and concluded to himself, 'Broad Street' on any given night. 'The men, well … not all of them will be single, will they? Half these idiots will go back to their families with AIDS or something equally nasty.'

There was a short pause for breath and then: 'The young people with the young people isn't so bad, but for god's sake, you should see the old men making fools of themselves with these young black girls. Who is going to look after all these half-caste babies? No-one cares about a half-caste baby here, you know.'

'I'm sure either the men or the girls for that matter will be careful. No girl is going to want a baby from a one-night stand, especially here,' commented Deb, as she thought to herself how happy she was that they were at the quiet end of the hotel. 'I'm sure they'll move you if you ask at reception.'

'I'm sure some of the other lads would pay for the privilege to move if you put it on the notice board.' Bob threw this into the conversation and got an icy glare from Barbara.

'We've asked for a move, but they won't or can't,' Sue put in. 'We are only here two more days after all. We can survive.'

'I'm glad we're in the family group if this is what it's been like at the other hotels.' Barbara had started again. 'If all the unaccompanied men are doing is getting drunk, rowdy and trying to fornicate with anything that moves, I'm glad we're not part of it.'

'What happens on tour stays on tour,' Bob said, innocently enough. The painful bruise that appeared instantly on his shin was testament to the fact that Deb thought otherwise.

'We're rugby fans, not football hooligans. There is rarely trouble on the pitch, let alone off the pitch.' The statement was punctuated with another icy glare from Barbara. 'I conclude that most of these men are not rugby fans and don't follow rugby at all. They're simply just using it as an excuse for a holiday.'

Bob found it hard to eat, not cry out with pain and not to snigger all at once.

'They just keep bringing in the girls and the booze. I mean, these old men are just using them. What are the girls getting out of it?'

Bob was about to comment but Deb gripped his thigh tightly and squeezed with nails digging into flesh.

'We have one of these dirty old men next to us. He is a little monster. Overweight, sweaty and ginger, he really is an ugly little man.' Barbara continued. 'He has had three different girls visit him in his room since we arrived.' Bob thought about questioning how they knew these things, then thought better of it, but was soon enlightened anyway. 'If this horrible little man is still with his wife she is bound to catch something off him when he gets back. He is staggering around half-cut whenever we see him. Then when he is in his room all you can hear is the bed squealing and him grunting. Thank god it doesn't last long. You can't tell me someone that drunk and depraved would bother with a condom or worry about the consequences?'

'Barbara, we cannot do anything about it,' piped up Sue.

'But it is disgusting!'

Bob and Deb had their backs to the entrance, the 'ladies that lunch' having claimed the better seats long before they arrived.

'Oh my god, that's him. That horrible little man has just come in. At least he isn't swaying and he is alone. Stop! Don't look around.' Bob and Deb stopped mid-turn and waited. 'He is going over to the buffet. Watch what he has – I don't want anything he has touched. Quick, he isn't looking in this direction. Just see the type of man we have to put up with. What sort of man must he be? Just look at those sweat stains. Hasn't he heard of deodorant? Please let's hope he doesn't sit down-wind of us or it will be hell.'

Firstly, it had been the only place so far on tour that had been hot enough to make anyone sweat. Howling winds, driving rain and freezing conditions had been the constant, with tour organisers making a killing selling winter gear to unsuspecting tour followers expecting South Africa to be somewhat warmer.

Secondly, and more importantly, if Deb and Bob hadn't turned around at that point to see the evil little fiend, Andy Sapp might have sat away from their little group and not realised they were there. Once he had seen them, however, it was too late and there was no stopping him from coming over and joining their clique. The ladies were horrified as Sapp dragged the nearest table over one-handed, so he could sit closer, his other hand balancing his plate and mountain of food and trying desperately not to spill anything. The screech of the table being dragged was soon followed by the cutlery that had been laid out upon it beginning to bounce and clatter on the floor. He had managed to disturb everyone in the room and it was left for Deb to try her best to introduce Sapp and explain how she knew him to the ladies.

Andy, of course, registered none of the hostility sent his way by everyone around him, especially the two old ladies sitting with Deb and her husband. After the brief introductions, Sapp launched into yet another attempt to get Deb and Bob out and about and spending their hard-earned cash, as he put it. Deb was trying to explain they were fully committed to just relaxing after the hectic schedule they had been on. She was having a little pang of sympathy for Andy and felt he might just be feeling lonely. Bob felt more inclined to point out how Andy was having no problems finding 'friends' in the evening and it wasn't up to them to keep him amused. It was their anniversary and together-time and babysitting Sapp was not on Bob's agenda and things-to-do on holiday list.

They managed to keep all parties involved civil but everyone was glad when they all moved on with the tour to the next set of hotels. Andy was again sent back to his single traveller group. Life became much simpler and Andy only had to be watched out for at the matches.

Deb and Bob did do most of the tours laid on by the Lions but South Africa didn't win many Brownie points. There were areas of outstanding beauty, and the safaris and visits to tribal villages were fantastic, but they were overshadowed by oppression.

Razor wire and large, vicious dogs accompanied almost every white residential area and the white South Africans in and around the tour all wished the land would be cleansed of the blacks by a stronger, more virulent strain of AIDS. The black Africans did nothing either to help their cause when you heard or saw their take on life and their complete apathy even when people were interested in them or trying to help.

The three weeks passed quickly, although sadly the rugby never lived up to the hype. The country itself was a place deeply divided and damaged but at least Deb was ready to embrace work head-on again.

10

The Grand Scam

A few busy months had passed since they had returned from their anniversary holiday in Africa and Deb was beginning to feel that things were getting back to normal and she, too, could claim to be almost back to her best. She was still fighting depression and her demons, thanks to all the false accusations that had preceded the holiday and the full time rumour-mill that had seemed to spring from nowhere and then been dedicated to her, or at the least trash talking about her. She had been warned that it would take a while to fully recover, so she kept taking the pills even though it was totally against all she stood for and believed in health-wise. The threat of returning to where she had been was too great; she never wanted to revisit the dark places other people's lies had taken her ever again. Since her return she had felt people were keeping their distance but that could easily be a small amount of paranoia creeping in. Surely that was understandable after all she had been put through behind the scenes, including her efforts not to involve others in her problems and drag them into her own private hell.

Well, that part of her recent history was now tucked away and hidden and the memories were slowly fading. Back from Africa she had been on top of her game, sorting the things that had needed sorting and immersing herself totally back into her work with all the commitment she had always shown. Even things between the Black Queen and herself were better, if not totally repaired, and the situation was working to some degree. Deb was moving on for the good of the company but felt now that trust was always going to be an issue.

There had been one incident since she had been back – a misunderstanding or something? She was reading more into the incident than was actually there, according to Summer and her peers, although Deb wasn't entirely convinced of the incident's innocence.

Only a couple of months after her return, there had been the regular company summer shut-down. Up until that point Deb had always visited the deserted site several times during the holiday period to check that everything was all right. Living so close to the factory, it meant only a relatively small amount of time taken out of her break. Everyone else at a senior level lived miles away and mostly used the shut-down for family holidays. Deb had always seen it as a nice gesture on her part to take responsibility. It also gave her time to think and plan towards the next wave of improvements in relative peace, and a chance to work on the fine detail. As a trained engineer, she could also do the essential maintenance needed so no-one else's holiday need be disturbed. Security was always there but in essence she had the factory to herself and that time alone always yielded improvements and savings for the company.

This year Summer insisted that the new production director, Gavin, be the one to do the checks. Deb was not put out and could see the argument that now she was more senior and her perceived standing in the company much higher, this sort of job should be handed over to the next generation. But she felt like a parent of a teenage son who was going out to work or stopping away for the weekend for the first time. You feel you should worry a little but in reality you know they are grown up and can look after themselves. Things have just moved on and the relationship has just changed a little, that's all.

This summer's holiday had been very relaxing. Of course there had been work she had taken home but she had found time to lounge in the summer sun in the back garden and found time to walk the dog in the countryside. She had finally given in, however, the day before everyone was due to return to work and had visited the factory. There were many things that needed doing to get the factory ready so they could hit the floor running. She planned on just making sure the new guy had followed the instructions and not missed anything important. Ten, maybe fifteen minutes, tops. A quick coffee if he wanted one and then a 'see you tomorrow'.

As she pulled into the car park she felt something was wrong. There were only two cars in the car park, the new director's and the security guard's, and that should have been a good sign – but one look at the row of office windows and she knew there was trouble. Every window she could see was closed but steamed up and condensation was running down the glass.

She did not park but pulled up next to the main door, abandoning the car and searching in her bag to find her keys for the main entrance. She knew the security codes so without too much fuss she got into the main part of the building. Reception had been ok but the admin, training and main computer offices were a giant steam room and the hot humid air took her breath away and dampened her clothes immediately. All the carpet tiles had been removed but there were several millimetres of dirty water on the floor in places. She quickly inspected each office. All were in the same sorry state and all had the addition to their usual equipment of an industrial gas heater blasting away into the mist at full power, raising the heat and moisture levels to unbearable in every room.

The suspended ceilings sagged dramatically from the moisture. All the paperwork and posters wilted on the walls and water glistened on every plastic or metal surface. Every electrical item in the offices was wet to the touch. She resisted the temptation to switch on the lights, fearing she would be instantly electrocuted. She re-ran her route, opening as many windows as she could to let the Turkish bath-like conditions vent outside into the mid-morning sun.

The offices were deserted. The only rooms surviving intact were the sales, marketing and development offices, which were further down the hall. Her search became almost frantic trying to find someone who could tell her what had happened. Finally she discovered two of the maintenance crew (they must have parked at the back of the factory) in the warehouse with loads of floor tiles draped across stacks of wooden pallets, trying to dry them using the same style of industrial heater as were in the offices, but with a little more success because of the wide open space they were working in. A quick question and answer session and she had the low-down.

The new guy had called them in the day before. He had come in to do his final checks and found the place flooded. A radiator pipe had pulled out of one of the radiators in the main administration office and had been losing water for days. Luckily, the doors to marketing and beyond had been tightly shut. Unfortunately training, admin, records and the main computer offices had not been so lucky. The new guy had commented that the employees in these offices had contributed to the damage by carelessly leaving doors open in their rush to get away on holiday. Deb would dispute that statement later. This was all her area and her staff were well trained and always locked all doors to their offices whenever they were not there. She herself knew she had locked her own office but she had found it open today and when they had all left for the holiday she was sure none of the doors had been open. As one of the last to leave, as always, she would have noticed she was certain of that.

The lads confirmed they had fixed the mysterious leak and followed the director's instructions. He had sent them all over to find heaters for hire. They had stripped the floor tiles and fired up the heaters keeping the windows shut, under his instructions to get the temperature up and dry everything out. From the amount of water and damage, Deb felt the leak must have started almost immediately they had left, so she was concerned as to why it had not been found more quickly. The new guy would have had to have passed these offices several times in the last two weeks and security should have passed them several times a day. The call to keep the windows shut seemed a stupid one; without the windows open to vent, the hot moisture had nowhere to go, she thought.

She questioned the two lads a little longer. It seemed the security guy had been told that there was no need for the internal checks and not to enter the factory as no-one was left in the building over the holiday period. He and his team had been told just to do more perimeter checks. This worried Deb; part of having security do these internal checks over the holiday or at night was to pick up this sort of problem, even if it was a very rare occurrence. The new guy obviously needed talking to about the importance of the systems already in place. Hopefully he would learn quickly from his mistake this time.

The lads also confirmed that the new guy had been certain that there was no evidence of the leak a couple of days earlier when he had been here. This Deb found hard to believe, taking in the area that had been damaged.

It had been the new guy who had over-ruled the drying-out procedure as well. The two lads had opened all the windows originally but he had made them close them straight away, saying they were stupid to let the heat out and leaving the windows open would compromise the security of the factory. The lads had simply followed orders. There was still the question of how the pipe had come loose after working perfectly well for years. Deb had never heard of something like this happening at home, at friends or at any of the factories she had worked at before but accidents did happen, she supposed.

The lads said the director had wandered off and gone for breakfast hours ago but they didn't expect him back soon, so – yet again – it was up to Deb to sort things out.

Deb called in the IT guy and his assistants and as soon as they had arrived they set about moving the equipment and setting it up in conference rooms, unoccupied offices and any suitable rooms she could find, so the company could at least return to work the following day. After two weeks' holiday, all hell broke loose on the company's return to work in a normal year, so a contingency plan for the essential offices had to be implemented. With the windows open, the equipment dried enough to move it to safety, and as the rooms were cleared, Deb got the two lads to use the industrial floor scrubbers from the factory to suck up the excess water, a few scrapes to the décor small price to pay to get the water up quickly. It would be days, if not weeks, before these rooms could be used again. The ruined paperwork could be dealt with and cleaned up tomorrow.

Deb rang her staff, preparing them for the chaos they would face the following day. Those she couldn't speak to she left messages for, saying jeans and T-shirts would be the practical advice rather than their more formal normal attire.

Gavin finally arrived back. He was angry he had been overruled, believing he'd had the situation under control. But Deb knew if she had not acted, the likely outcome would have been thousands and thousands of pounds worth of equipment written off and a company unprepared and in chaos starting back after the holiday at the start of the busiest period of the year. She hoped this was not the best performance and attitude the new recruit was capable of. As always recently, Summer had chosen him and had not called on Deb's experience, and again, sworn loyalty to the CEO seemed more important than actual skill and commitment to the job.

Deb spent most of the day at the company and got it to a point where they could start work on Monday morning and most things were usable, saving equipment and clearing away most of the water. The few people there had done an outstanding job for the company but there would be lots to do before it was all back to normal.

* * *

Deb was a little upset when Gavin was given the credit for the clean-up job, although she was well used to other people getting credit for her work. It had stung when Summer had so openly praised the guy for his command of the situation and his quick thinking. As far as Deb could see, the only thing the new guy had proved was how incompetent he was. Only the few people she had called in knew the truth of who had done all the organising but in the grand scheme of things it was only a small insult. Summer seemed very impressed with Gavin, so Deb wasn't going to risk the new, shaky status quo for a few glorifications.

If the guy was incompetent he was incompetent; any other explanation for the list of events became quite sinister and had implications of some sort of insurance scam but Deb put that sort of thinking down as another minor case of paranoia. She couldn't put her finger on it but yet again it felt as though people were blaming her for what had happened. If she had done what she had always done this would not have happened, or would have been contained quickly. The general consensus seemed to be that she had not done her job and people blamed her, even though it was no longer her job to do. And worse that Gavin had stepped in to save the day, but nothing could have been further from the truth.

* * *

Deb had always done the company's forward-planning and forecasts. It was one of her favourite jobs to present to the shareholders the success story so far (and a subtle way of blowing her own trumpet for once) and then present the way forward for even more company success. The presentations covered everything from new equipment available to new possible markets, personnel requirements and improving the loyalty of the workforce, keeping everyone happy and working in the same direction. Some of her work was over-ruled or dismissed by Summer, who lacked Deb's overview and insight. Small things done that yielded great rewards later was not Summer's style; to her, the details were not that important. Summer was more 'wait until it broke completely and then make a giant performance about getting it fixed' rather than get it done with minimum fuss before it became a major problem. The trouble was, most people were impressed with that attitude. Not many could see that over-reacting wasn't as good as not creating the problem in the first place.

Deb's presentations were always laid out the same; lots of detail for the year ahead and then more vague predictions and recommendations for the following three years, plus a wish list for five years down the road. This year was going to be different. Soon after Deb had returned from holiday, Summer had called her in to discuss the following year's forecasts.

Deb went with trepidation. She knew her work had not slackened and was as accurate as ever but with the Black Queen incident not too far in the past she was worried Summer might not give her the free rein she had done previously. But when the meeting was over Deb had been amazed: Summer's commitment and faith in her had been even greater, requesting even more detailed reports than usual. This time Summer had insisted there had to be a full plan and strategy not only for the next few years but for the next decade. She had also insisted that the company was now at a point where they could look way into the future, and this information was vital to their continued success. Deb agreed wholeheartedly, as it had always been her own view, too, although in the past no-one had shared that same interest. Normally Deb had trouble keeping their attention past the immediate next few days or weeks. Maybe it was a sign that Summer was growing into her role as CEO and finally taking her responsibilities seriously.

Whatever the reason, Deb felt she was now back in the heart

of the team and had dedicated long hours to the documents that held the secrets to the next decade of company growth. Of course, things could change and outside influences were unpredictable but the core would be right and the foundations laid out. Summer had commented and enthused how brilliant her work had been when Deb had presented it to the shareholders.

* * *

Deb sat in her office, the usual array of work-related paperwork spread across her desk, good and bad, you had to make time for it all. The phone rang and the receptionist announced it was an outside call from the company's insurance brokers. Deb had always dealt with this type of work for the company, so she knew everything was legal. If it was delegated to someone else she felt they might not give it the attention needed because it was such a mundane but important job.

The short conversation was fairly chatty. She had been dealing with this company for a long time and had known the person on the other end of the line for at least four years. He had always been spot-on with his advice and work done on the company's behalf but today's was a strange conversation. He was informing her of a minor oversight after Ms Ponsenbury had reviewed the shareholders' and directors' policies earlier that week.

Deb had done the work on this, forwarding it to Summer to look at and confirm it was the cover she wanted for everyone, but Deb wasn't intending to act on it until the end of the month, after their meeting. Part of the policy's cover was for the shareholders, if they became too ill to work and the company had to buy them out or if they died in service. It was a prudent precaution so that the company had the funds to buy back the shares immediately and it guaranteed market value for the shareholder or their family if the worst happened. It also meant that it wasn't the company's money being paid out.

Deb knew her small amount of shares would not be a problem for the company's coffers but the others would be for much bigger amounts. This phone call had been a courtesy to say that for some reason her own details had not been forwarded with the others, and that the oversight was no big problem. Summer needed to confirm everything, so they could dot the i's and cross the t's on the minor admin mistake. Deb confirmed she would sort it out later that day if Summer was in and thanked the guy for his vigilance. Usually Deb would get Summer's required signatures and then check it all through herself before she sent it off to stop this kind of thing happening. Why was it when someone took it upon themselves to help it always seemed to create more work for her?

* * *

It was much later in the afternoon than she had planned before she visited Summer's palatial office. Deb knocked, and a muffled 'enter' came from inside. 'Yes? What can I do for you, Deborah?' was the greeting as she entered the office.

'A minor admin problem with the insurance … I need you to have a quick look at so I can clear it up. Nothing too bad.'

'OK, be quick. I was about to leave for a keep-fit class.'

What dedication to the company, Deb thought, a little sarcastically to herself. She should be used to this by now. Keep fit wouldn't have been Deb's first guess off 'the non-work stuff Summer does on company time' list? It was 2 p.m., for appearance's sake, couldn't she say she had an offsite meeting? No, stop being bitchy, she told herself. You are better than this.

'I just have to get you to sign this insurance for me and I will get it sent off. They have everyone else's. I brought a copy just in case you had misplaced the original.' She leant across the immense desk. 'You need to sign there and there.'

Summer did not reach for a pen. Instead she sat back. 'Oh! That was vigilant of them. Never mind. Please, sit.' Deb sat out of politeness. How long could it take to sign your name twice on the same piece of paper?

'Well, you might as well know. It's like this. I really don't need you any more.'

'Pardon? What ... what are you saying?'

'Come on, you're a bright girl. Can't you work it out? I don't need you any more, the company doesn't need you any more. I am telling you you're fired. Now don't make a scene – just go.' Summer waved dismissively in the general direction of the office door.

'Is this some kind of joke? I have done absolutely everything for this company. I am a shareholder. I have rights.'

'Dear, what you think you have is meaningless and your rights are worthless. I have made sure of that.'

Deb sat stock-still, trying to take in what had just been said. Her knuckles were white as she gripped the arms of the leather chair to keep control, her heart now pounding fit to burst in her chest.

'How dare you!' she said, angrily. 'I've built this company up from next to nothing. I've worked with total commitment for the good of the company so it will benefit us all. I've always been your friend – I class you as one of my oldest friends ... I've worked to make the company and you richer and I've made you and the company millions and millions of pounds. You put millions into your personal account every year because of what I've accomplished here.'

'Yes, yes, and we all thank you from the bottom of our hearts for what you have done,' Summer condescendingly replied. She stood up, so she could tower over her victim. 'Now just go. I've spent a lot of time and money making sure you will take absolutely nothing from me and my company.'

Deb's world was spinning. Is this a bluff? 'I have rights,' she replied, the conviction in her voice not as strong as it was. Deb picked up pen and paper, scribbling down figures while Summer looked on, amused.

She turned the piece of paper so Summer could see what had been written.

'My first job when I arrived here was to sort out production. This was my first step towards doing that. I reduced this first process in this one small vat and one product from three batches a week to three a day. That meant thirteen extra mixes a week. We work fifty weeks a year. Thirteen mixes x 2,000 litres (vat size) divide by five (the size the product is sold in) x £15 (the rough price per tin) x 50 (production weeks a year) and that works out to £3.9 million pounds a year for that one vat alone. That one small job has funded everything this company has ever done. Even today that one small vat produces more turnover and profit for this company than marketing and national accounts combined. The profit alone is more than the whole turnover of Harry's national accounts.'

Deb continued. 'THAT is the smallest vat we have. We now have them up to 14,000 litres. Plus what about everything else that I have done for the company – and for you?'

'I am sales and marketing, dear, I could produce a hundred documents if I wanted to and dispute your figures ... that's if I wanted to or needed to. As for the rest, it's all in place and running smoothly. I now even have a detailed ten-year plan I can follow. Thanks for that, by the way.'

Words like 'duped' and 'sucker' were spinning around Deb's head. Somehow they didn't seem big enough for what was happening to her.

Summer carried on. 'Yes, I know there are a few laws we will have to pay lip service to and we, the company, will honour all those we have to. But you are in for a big surprise ... a big, bad surprise.' Summer was gloating now. 'It has taken two decades to get it all in place, from the worthless contracts and promises to more recently making you look like an incompetent, bigoted, racist clown.'

There was a brief pause for breath. 'And how dare the likes of you presume to be classed as a friend of someone of *my* standing?' Summer looked down her nose at her victim like she was nothing more than a pile of something she wouldn't want to step in.

'What worthless contracts?' asked Deb, in a still smaller voice.

Summer came around the desk and sat on its front edge, so she was close to Deb but still towering over her. 'Boy, am I going to enjoy this,' she thought, preparing her assault. Her dress suit was tight and the position uncomplimentary. Her flesh was squeezed and was oozing alarmingly over her skirt top. Her large chest was heaving as the adrenaline pumped around her body. She could smell her own sweaty musk and flowery perfume mixing and wafting around her in a heady mixture. She was going to make damn sure that this little bitch left with her tail between her legs and knowing that she, Summer Ponsenbury, was superior in every way.

'I know you had your suspicions about the contracts at the buy-out but I allowed you to have a little chat with the company lawyers to put that trusting little pea-brain of yours at ease. Who do you think they work for? You really believed all that crap I had them sell you about security for you and your future.' A pause. 'What was it?' Summer made a mocking, dramatic gesture of taking an oath. 'Give me fifteen more years and I will guarantee the world for the rest of your life! Not going to happen, dear. I made sure all the promises I made were all kept well out of the Articles of Association, just like I was advised. I know we all sat there with our hands on our hearts and promised to the heavens they were legal and we would honour them – but we lied.' The last three words were said in a voice reserved for a toddler. 'They were just worthless bits of paper to keep you loyal and working your little heart out, you stupid, trusting bitch, you were never ever going to make the fifteen years to qualify.'

'But ... but ...'

'Stuck for words?' Summer leant forward intimidatingly, her size making the position uncomfortable, very uncomfortable.

The seams on her clothes were dangerously close to splitting but this was a moment she had been waiting years for.

'Over the last eighteen months or so I have ruined your reputation, your future and your health, and it just needed a few small lies to do it. Everyone knew you were the one who kept the company going so I stopped investing the company funds where you said they were needed, which means things are beginning to not work quite so well. They all knew it was your job in the past and are blaming you now it's stuttering. I've over-ruled or ignored your advice on the senior people the company has employed over the last year or so and they are all failing in their jobs. Most of the morons in this company know that recruitment is *your* job and you have failed in that too. Your perfect recruitment record is smashed and now they all think you have lost the plot. No-one knows it was really me behind the scenes sabotaging your efforts ... The famous Deborah in her prime would not have allowed these people to be taken on in the past but everyone can see you and your damn forms and charts are failing completely now and no-one has faith in what you have to say. And then there is what you did to poor Yvette!' Summer was smirking as she delivered the last statement.

'But I didn't do anything to Yvette!', said Deb in a very small voice. She was sobbing now.

'I know – but isn't it fantastic that everyone else thinks you did? I could not have asked for a better reaction to you "bullying that poor, innocent, skinny little black girl".' Summer's voice was full with sarcasm.

'I didn't do that.' The denial came between more sobs. 'I did not do any of that.'

Summer resumed her 'talking to a toddler' voice. 'I know, that's why it is so good people believe you did.' Then, with more venom, 'This is why I am superior to you. A few lies, a few half-truths. I mix in a few broken promises made on your behalf that you didn't even know about and then blame you for not keeping them and start a few rumours – and I have completely destroyed you.'

Summer paused to gloat and shift her position. 'I have turned you – in the eyes of these parasites you looked out for all those years – from a heroine almost god-like in your purity and honesty, to some anti-depressant pill-popping, red-neck bigot. I have turned them all against you in just a few months. Two decades of commitment, trust and success and in seconds they have forgotten all you have done for them.' She gave a wave in the general direction of the factory. 'They all hate you now.' Summer lurched off the desk and straightened her suit before returning to her seat.

'But why? I couldn't have done more for you. I couldn't have been more honest. What else could I have done?' sobbed Deb.

Summer spun on her heels and hurled herself at the distraught wreck that was now Deb. Startled, Deb tried to force herself as far back into the chair as she could to escape the garlic-and-red wine breath and the body odour of the crazy woman looming over her and invading her personal space. But Summer had her trapped, her flabby arms grasping the arms of the chair to stop Deb attempting any sort of escape. She started her rhetoric again but there was no baby voice this time, just hatred fuelled by years of jealousy.

'Did you ever truly think I would let some working-class whore take the company away from me? I had to let Frank fuck me just to stay here. I should be back home working with my father, by his side, helping him and learning the business. All I had to do was show him I could make this shit-hole work. Then you fucking show up. Suddenly everyone sees your ideas and your work getting this company back on its feet and working. They should have been my ideas. I would have had those ideas and got the credit if I'd had the time.' Summer's voice was getting louder with every sentence.

Deb wanted to scream: 'But you didn't. You didn't have the know-how, you didn't have the ethics and you didn't have the commitment to make it work', but her small voice was hiding where she couldn't find it.

'All I had to do was prove to my father that I was as good as any son,' Summer hissed. 'Then I could have left and gone home. You spoilt that, you spoilt it all.' She screamed at Deb. 'Every time he asked or talked to anyone here it was "Deb has done this" or "Deb has done that". All he ever fucking heard was "Deb, Deb, Deb".' There was a short pause for breath. 'There was never anything about me. What I had done. What I had achieved. You stole everything.'

The last sentence, like so many before, was simply not true. Deb had stolen nothing. All she had done was her job, the job she was paid to do. As for Summer's achievements, what could be said about things that didn't exist? Deb was frozen and the shock had been so great she couldn't find a voice to fight her corner. There were flecks of spittle on her face and neck from Summer's rant but at that point she didn't care or notice. Summer released her grip on the chair and took a half step back confident she had broken Deb.

'I have taken away your future, I have destroyed your job and I have destroyed you! I could have just broken you so no-one else would want you and then let you crawl away too ill to work.' She sneered, picking up the papers Deb had placed on the desk just moments before. 'I could have signed this so you got your money but I did not want to pay the increased premiums if you tried to claim. But that is not going to happen now anyway. I made you that ill you could claim then I cancelled the policy before you could.' Summer took the documents, ripped them up and threw them at Deb's feet.

Again she leant forward and grasped the chair's arms. 'No-one is taking my fucking money. I will not allow you to sit on your arse enjoying life while I am stuck here.'

Deb wanted to point out if the papers had been signed it would technically be the insurance company's money, not Summer's or her company's – just one small fight-back to show she was still in there somewhere – but the effort seemed pointless.

Summer stood upright again. Her close proximity kept Deb seated and she took a few seconds to compose herself for the next part of her speech. 'I have thought long and hard about what I will let you have. We have to pay your redundancy but that's only your basic salary without bonuses and incentives, just scraps. I think £500,000 will show me in a good light. Shall we call it half a million, as that sounds a much bigger amount? I will let those moronic plebs of yours know how generous I have been, even though you have let the company down so, so badly. You fight it and I will simply start sacking people – your friends first – and you can be responsible for them losing their jobs. What's a few £20,000 settlements to get rid of you?'

From the profiling and unofficial assessment Summer's counsellor friend had done, she knew Deb would never be able to take being responsible for losing an innocent person their career and job. Summer was banking on that fact.

Deb sat in silence. Her world was being shredded in front of her. 'Those scum won't know your shares are worth more than £2 million already and would have easily topped £5 million by the time you retired. If you try and fight this I will make sure it looks like you are an ungrateful, greedy, spoilt little bitch who's just trying to fleece the company. All those poor little working-class twats will be thinking "Wow! Half a million pounds! That's life-changing". They won't see how much I have ripped you off for, and they won't care.'

Summer paced in font of Deb as she reeled off what she thought would happen once Deb was gone. 'Let's see, nobody will remember or even consider you will have to pay Capital Gains tax on it. Then you will have to pay your solicitor and that will cost you – I'll make sure of that. I'll drag it out and drag it out and you will try and fight it because it "shouldn't be like this". It should be fair and honest and right, because if you don't win it will make all you have ever stood for worthless.' Toddler voice again then back to more pure venom. 'I know you will never be able to beat me. What are you going to have left? Enough, if you're lucky, to pay off your mortgage after twenty years loyal and dedicated service, working all hours and doing all jobs needed … All that for nothing, NOTHING.'

She gave a short, barking laugh. 'I will have destroyed you in everyone's eyes. I will have destroyed your perfect career, and destroyed your perfect little marriage too, because your husband will leave you. He told you all along what would happen to you and you did not believe him. You will never work again and everyone will hate you and mistrust you and people will see me as the glorious saviour of the company.' And there it all was, the reasons Summer was being so evil: jealousy and greed, nothing more.

Deb sat there. How could Summer be so jealous of the hours she, Deb, had worked, the achievements she had made for the company and what it had cost her? She had missed her family growing up, sacrificed for the good of the company. Early starts and late finishes meant the only time she had seen her son in his early years was when he had been asleep in bed. It had only been her husband's efforts that had kept them all together. The pay-off was that she was working to guarantee all their futures – and that had all just been ripped away from her.

The person who had benefited the most from Deb's efforts and had spent all her life enjoying and spending the profits now stood before her claiming she was the one hurt and suffering. The woman must be completely crazy to be jealous of the hours and hours Deb had put in, especially with the privileged upbringing and the burden of being able to have absolutely anything you wanted whenever you wanted it like Summer. To claim to be jealous of a straightforward, working-class marriage, struggling to make ends meet, find enough hours in the day for work and everything else that had to be done, then collapse into bed too exhausted to move, was beyond ridiculous.

'Are you listening to me?' Summer screamed. 'I have destroyed everything and taken everything. I win. I WIN!' Summer flicked her hair, looking like Miss Piggy off *The Muppets*, before dramatically beaching herself in her luxurious, fully reclining, executive leather chair.

It was time for Summer to make the call she had longed to make for years. She had planned and schemed to make this day possible. As she stroked the soft leather of the chair, the call connected. 'Harry, my office now. It is time to take out the white trash.' She had worked on that line and little jibe to get it just right. Harry would be in in seconds, ready to please. The day could not get any better. The snivelling, shell-shocked, simpering Deb would soon be history. A few lies, a few schemes and the company money had stayed all hers. With a bit of self-promotion and marketing she would soon be able to take all the credit for everything that bitch had done over the years. I *win*, I WIN she thought to herself … I win.

* * *

Harry almost flew into the room, not even bothering to knock he was so eager to please. The broken husk of Deb was slumped in the chair in front of Summer's desk. She had been all right as a person, he supposed. He would have given her one if he'd got the chance. He had managed to get her to do most of his work by simply doing nothing. So what if she was collateral damage? Having her gone was going to increase his share and when it came down to it he wasn't going to worry about anyone else but number one. It was a bit cold-blooded but he felt no regret about helping to set it all up. If you were naive enough to believe that you got what you deserved from doing your job better than anyone else and being whiter than white, then you deserved to be in the situation Deb was now in.

Summer was sitting behind her desk ignoring Deb snivelling in front of her. 'That was quick,' Summer exclaimed. 'Nice to see someone is actually keen to please.' She gestured at Deb.

'Take her out of my sight. Take her company keys. Clear her personal belongings and get her into a taxi and off site as quickly as possible. And make sure she speaks to no one or gets anywhere near to a computer.'

'Do you want the company to pay for the taxi?'

'Why? I'm sure she has some small change left.' The answer was accompanied by a small smirk at another witty dig at her victim.

Harry walked over to where Deb was sitting, lost in her own disintegrating little world. 'Oy!' he nudged her arm. 'Oy! Get up. I'm talking to you. Come on move, I haven't got all day. Some of us have still got jobs to do.' Deb didn't register yet another snide comment and not so subtle dig.

Harry grasped the top of Deb's arm and forcibly dragged her to her feet, his fingers grasping so tightly that there would be bruises the following day.

'Come on, move.'

Deb was paraded in a shattered and traumatised state through the corridors of the company she had served with complete loyalty and commitment for a quarter of a century. She was only distantly aware of where she was. It was like she was in a dream and trying to walk knee-deep in treacle ... She was aware of people coming out of their offices and passing her like she didn't exist or recoiling backwards and closing the door. Harry's grip was like a vice and he guided her without resistance in any direction he wanted. No-one tried to talk to her and Harry took every possible chance to imply to everyone that she was drunk and her condition was solely down to alcohol and she had no fight left to counter the claims.

The people she should have been able to trust the most were the ones who had turned out to be her worst enemies, abusing and twisting that trust. But as she walked, there was one little shred of dignity she tried to hold onto, one little voice telling her to keep walking and not collapse. It was taking a gigantic effort not to break down and let these people complete her humiliation but she would not give them the chance to pick her up off the floor and throw her out like garbage.

* * *

'Miss, Miss!' There was knocking from somewhere. Someone tapping on glass. Where was she? 'Hey, darling, that's £14. Come on, I've got another customer to get to.' Some of her senses returned. She was in the back of a taxi outside her home. Her coat and handbag had been thrown on to the taxi's floor and the bag had spilled, losing some of its contents. She couldn't remember getting into the taxi, the journey or arriving here.

'For Christ's sake, luv.' The taxi driver was getting irritated. A flustered Deb managed to retrieve her spilt belongings and fumble in her purse for a £20 note, lurching out into the fresh cool air without waiting for her change. She'd barely got both feet onto the pavement with what was left of her belongings before the taxi sped off.

She braced herself and tried to walk up the short drive to her front door. The world was spinning violently and she was afraid that after a few steps she would fly off at a tangent. She was only just managing to stop herself vomiting across the front lawn.

Fumbling with her key, her hands shaking, it took four or five attempts to locate, unlock and open the door. She stumbled into the hall and closed the door behind her. Taking a couple of steps forward, the effort became too much and she collapsed, breaking her fall a little by sliding down the wall. She had not realised she had stopped crying but now the tears returned in floods. She screwed herself up into the foetal position on the carpet and sobbed. That was where, hours later, Bob found her when he arrived back from work as the day merged with twilight.

11

End of the World

'My god! Deb, DEB! What's the matter? What's happened? Are you all right?' Bob fell to his knees next to his wife. 'Deb, have you been attacked? Speak to me.' There was panic in his voice as he feared the worst.

She gripped his hand like she'd never let go again. 'I am sorry, so sorry. So, so sorry,' was all he could get out of her? She kept repeating that she was sorry – but for what? She was clearly in no condition to tell him, so he sat on the floor, cradling her and trying to comfort and calm her. She just kept repeating that she was sorry.

He stroked her hair and gripped her as tightly as he dared. He could see no physical injury and his fears dropped a notch or two but Deb was clearly traumatised. After what seemed like hours but was only minutes she calmed down a little. Bob adjusted his position and rose. Picking her up gently, he carried her into the lounge and laid her down as carefully as he could on the sofa. The dog seemed worried, its usually bouncy, happy greeting missing, and it stayed quietly in its bed, watching.

'Deb, please, what is wrong? Do you need a drink, a doctor, what can I do to help? I can't help if I don't know what's wrong, Deb, please.' All she could do was cry into the sofa's cushion and grip his hand, her nails almost drawing blood, sobs and shudders wracking her body.

Finally she calmed and she loosened her grip. 'I'll make a cup of tea, then we can talk, OK?' Pathetic response he knew but he wasn't good at this sort of thing. She nodded her approval, but she did not want to talk. She did not want to tell him what had happened just in case Summer's black prophecies about her marriage would come true. But he had the right to know. While he made tea she wiped her eyes and tried to make herself look less pathetic and beaten. She could not do anything about her red, puffy eyes but she could wipe off the smeared make-up and try and tidy her hair a little.

When he returned she was sitting upright and managing to keep her tears in check. Now she had to tell her husband that all the fears and worries he had always had about the company and the people she had worked with had all come true – or worse. All their dreams and all the promised rewards were gone, taken away by some jealous, twisted excuse for a human being.

Once Deb started, the words just kept coming. What Summer had done, how she had swindled Deb, the hatred, the bile and the jealousy. Deb recounted the threats and what would be done to her closest friends if she tried to fight. She spewed forth all the evil things Summer had taken pleasure in doing to destroy her.

Bob sat there stunned, his tea undrunk in the cup. The few questions he asked, hoping to get some small chink of inspiration to fight what was happening to them, were met with how or what Summer had done or put in place to prevent Deb fighting back. Summer had planned and schemed meticulously with the psychiatrist friend helping to find all the right buttons to press to do the most damage and destroy all resistance.

As the night went on, long silences spread between the questions. Bob had always suspected, even known, that these so-called friends and work colleagues would let his wife down, but not even in his wildest nightmares did he imagine the depths they would sink to and the pleasure they would take in what they were doing. He noticed a change in Deb's demeanour. Over the last few minutes she had veered from being totally beaten and depressed to an unsettling and chilling new calm. 'What is it, Deb?'

'I know what I can do. I will go and crash the car and kill myself. Then at least the company will have to pay out on the shares. Our family will get something. All I have to do is die in service. It doesn't matter how. That's it, that's what I have to do.' There was a look in her eyes that chilled him to the bone.

Bob almost spilt his cold tea as he tried to get in front of his wife and stop her rising from the sofa. 'Are you crazy? You cannot be serious? We will fight it together. Whatever happens this isn't worth killing yourself over.' Inside, Bob was panicking. It would be a crazy solution at the best of times but Deb's logic and grip on reality had obviously snapped under the stress and torment.

'I can and I will. I will get something for my family. I will get something for you. You gave up everything to help me and I would not even listen when you were warning me.' Bob was physically holding her by the shoulders to stop her getting up. 'I cannot believe I trusted these people, that I stuck up for them when you tried to tell me what they were like and I wouldn't listen. I just could not believe I worked with people like that … that there were even people like that.'

'Please stop. You're scaring me.' He was still barring her way. 'We'll always work it out together. Suicide is not going to happen. Anyway …' He knelt before her and looked deep into her eyes. '… don't you remember you told me she had cancelled the cover? There is no policy any more. The sacrifice would be for nothing. Let's go to bed and sleep on it. We can start to work things out in the morning. You're exhausted. And no more talk of suicide. We will survive this.'

As he talked, he had seen what he thought was comprehension in her eyes as she realised the obvious flaws in her desperate plan and that it was not the answer. They were together as they always had been. OK, the lifestyle was not going to be what they had worked for or earned, but they would survive. They always had.

* * *

After all that had happened in what was only a few short hours, neither Bob nor his wife could have felt any lower. Their world had been ripped apart. He had tried to get his wife to go to bed and get some sleep, hoping a few hours of rest would help both of them to think clearly and assess what had happened and even maybe find a solution.

The reality was that Deb was traumatised and his belief that he had calmed her enough to see sense had been false hope. Suicide had become the only topic of conversation for the next few depressing and frightening hours, Deb feeling it was the only way she could get anything out of the situation for Bob and her family, her mind so traumatised it could not or would not allow her to comprehend that Summer had cold-bloodedly taken even that option away. Bob was left in agony trying to stop his wife throwing away her life for nothing in one final grand but futile gesture.

Relief only came when exhaustion took over, Deb finally giving in and falling asleep on the sofa with Bob sleeping as best he could propped up against her so that if she moved he would wake. He was convinced that if she managed to 'escape' whilst he slept, his greatest worry and fear might come true before she regained some semblance of sanity.

The following days, then weeks, didn't really improve. At times Bob had to go to work, spending any free moment praying to any god that would listen to keep his wife safe. Every day was an agony on the return home, not knowing what he would find as he turned the key and opened the door. He'd be strangely happy or just plain relieved to find his wife still sitting where he had left her hours before, a half-drunk cup of tea or coffee stone cold on the side table next to her. At least it was not the worst thing he could imagine coming home to, even if it was far from the best.

Days were spent taking legal advice, Deb barely coherent at

times, completely broken. Bob was allowed no voice and no input because it was not his contract, not his signatures and not his agreement. Again and again they found lawyers only too willing to review the case for a price but they all came to the same conclusion. Unethical, unfair and what most people would call dishonest ... but in the bleary eyes of the law, everything had been legal or at least impossible to prove in favour of Summer's victim. After living hard-working and honest lives, Deb and Bob found it impossible to comprehend how easy it had been to 'con' her and how little support or protection she was given as the victim. How could signing one contract and then being told by your CEO and the company lawyers that the secondary document would be supplied for the guarantees and promises only to be told these documents were not legally binding and were worthless and were just a ruse, be anything other than a calculated, cynical and a clever scam. Surely this must be fraud.

Deb's whole career had been built on honesty and integrity and that had been her undoing. She had expected the senior people around her to have and to share the same beliefs. She had honestly believed that they had all reached their positions, and would not be in those positions, without those underlying beliefs. She could not see she was unique.

The agony of returning home to imagined tragedy when he had to work became too over-powering for Bob, the situation coming to a head one evening when he returned to find an assortment of pills and tablets put ready for use in a nice tidy pile on the kitchen table. Deb had had the strength to walk away that time, but would never admit to the episode ever happening.

Soon after, there was an incident with one of Summer's lackeys coming to the house when Bob was away. Another unbelievable coincidence – or was it planned? One of the senior members of Summer's happy little band arrived and convinced Deb that the company had seen the error of their ways and were prepared to welcome Deb back into the fold. Deb had been so desperate to resurrect her former life and make things all good again in Bob's eyes that she had agreed to come back and talk to them. Her fragile mind hadn't seen through the lies and bullshit when her deceiver convinced her not to tell anyone until she'd had the meeting and things were finalised. It was going to be a meeting between friends without outside influence.

But the meeting had been a sham, set up so the company could claim she had taken part fully and willingly in disciplinary procedures. They had calculated that it would help their case against her if they showed that they had done everything by the book. The meeting was a show trial and a witch hunt with the result already agreed and recorded long before Deb ever got there.

She arrived alone as agreed, not wanting to give them reasons to cancel before they had started. She found the 'court' already in session and her accusers and their legal team arrayed before her. The sham had been set up to complete their own agenda and to find out how she was going to fight them in court and what evidence she would use so they would have time to find a way to counter any potential problem, and what condition she was in mentally and physically.

Bob had insisted that she record her meetings with her own lawyers so he could hear what had been said and make sure they both understood the implications. Luckily Deb had had enough about her to record the initial conversation and invitation from her former company, and then what actually went on at the so-called 'friendly' meeting.

Bob listened to the tapes but it was too late. Again, Summer had manipulated her victim exactly as she wanted. It was clear from the start that there had been an ulterior motive. Bob believed these tapes proved how unethical and deceitful the company was being. He was horrified to hear them setting about Deb like a pack of wolves. She had been too scared, too confused and too alone to do anything but stand there and be bullied and tormented. Anyone who listened could hear his wife had been deceived and that she was in no condition mentally or physically to meet these people alone.

He presented this new evidence to Deb's lawyer, only to find out that the law was stacked against them again. In legal terms the tapes proved nothing, he was told. Even when the recordings were being played back and Deb could be heard sobbing and pleading for them all to stop. It was clear that Deb had been prevented from giving any defence to the company accusations but the lawyer rejected it as proof because she had acted alone and it had been her choice to go, despite the deception. The lawyer was more concerned that Deb had taped these meetings without getting written permission from the people working to destroy her. She had gone to the meeting in hope of something better, but the stake had already been in place with the kindling stacked around the base and Deb had been bullied into lighting the fire herself.

She was in such a state by this time that a few days later her divorced cousin and family arrived and squeezed into Bob and Deb's home to look after her when Bob was unable to be there.

* * *

Since the day Deb had been shown the factory door, every day had had its challenges. They were both trying to come to terms with what had happened and how it had been done. Bob was trying to help but because the threats and blackmailing were targeted at people he barely knew, there was not the same emotional manipulation his wife was tormented with. He wanted her to take her knowledge and skill to a competitor and reveal what had been done to her, stirring up a hornets' nest, but she would never forgive herself for the job losses and her friends being hurt if she took that course of action. All Bob's suggestions and demands fell on deaf ears. Deb had completely withdrawn into her own little world. There were glimpses of the person she had once been but they were fleeting, like a scared deer in the morning mist.

Nights proved to be no place to escape or hide from the ordeal, either. They shared a bed but Bob could not share his wife's nightmares, although the bruises were testament to him knowing when the worst of them were happening. Deb would lash out into the dark to protect herself from the demons. All he could do was put his arms around her and try and calm her.

Since Deb's cousin had moved in things had improved a little. Having her damn kids around was a small price to pay to keep Deb safe and Bob and the cousin worked in relays to try and protect their charge. The cousin working twilight and between them there was no repeat of the small pile of pills or any more traitorous, so-called friends trying to make bogus truces. Still, there was no-one who could help with the nightmares.

* * *

Soon the day arrived when everything would be officially finished – the day when all the dreams, sacrifices and achievements would be tallied up and found to be worthless. They both tried and failed to eat a small amount of breakfast before they set off for the agreed location where the mediation would take place. Bob had no misconceptions about what was going to happen but Deb still clung to the hope there would be a last-minute reconciliation or some recognition of what she had done and a thank-you.

Bob let her hope. It kept the peace and he was sure in her fragile state of being she would not go if she felt there was absolutely no hope – and who knew what sort of penalties and new cons Summer could come up with if Deb was not there? He was on tenterhooks, his only hope for the day 'that it didn't do irreparable damage to his wife'. It had been lucky their lifestyle had been nowhere near as excessive as those worthless bits of paper had suggested it could be. Always fearing the worst, he had kept their spending in check, although it hadn't been that hard, because Deb was so dedicated to her work and job there hadn't been time to be too frivolous.

The drive to the conference rooms deep in the heart of Birmingham city centre had been in stony silence. The neutral ground chosen between opposing legal representatives was a faceless and featureless business high-rise block with a few conference rooms rented out as required. Three small rooms had been reserved, two to keep the opposing parties apart and one as common ground for the lawyers and the mediator to come together and do what they had to do.

The day went worse than expected. Mr Smythe, the mediator, was good and had worked with Deb before for the company. He had been horrified to hear about the situation and had jumped at the chance to help someone he had professional respect for, but even his enthusiasm, well-practised skills and commitment to get Deb justice and fair treatment came to nothing.

The day had started with a general discussion on the whys and wherefores, to give everyone some sort of base line and to bring Mr Smythe up to speed. Since arriving in the conference room Deb had sobbed almost continuously and had to be coaxed into giving her input. Bob had made sure he had brought everything that was connected to the last few months to try and help the mediator; all their notes and thoughts, the offending documents and the recordings.

They had naively thought (or maybe they had just been clutching at straws?) that the overwhelming achievements and good works Deb had done for the company, once clearly written down and correlated, would at least influence Summer to be fair in her settlement, even if they were not enough to inspire reconciliation. These efforts, presented by Mr Smythe had been dismissed out of hand, Summer claiming that if she had been given the time, or recruited who she'd wanted, or just recruited more staff, the success of the company would have been the same.

Mr Smythe had countered that it had been Deb's unique skill-set, training and experience brought to a failing company that had been the more likely cause of the company's success. He referred to the great leaps forward in technology and manufacturing, sales techniques, recruitment and training that she'd introduced, and the financial benefits of all that Deb had done and put in place – all of which were now working perfectly, and all because of Deb. Again, these were all dismissed by Summer as something she herself would have done over the course of time, even though she did not and never had possessed the skill, qualifications, experience and know-how to do any of it. Even when specifics had been held up, amounts quantified and the financial benefits and claims shown to be built in stone, Summer maintained the 'I could have done that if I'd wanted to' attitude.

Mr Smythe fought and fought on Deb's behalf. How she had arrived at the company, then changed, corrected and improved everything, even how her first success and its cost savings had been the springboard that had triggered the launch of an international company. This one contribution had led to faster, better and more consistent manufacturing and production throughout the company, competitors being left in the company's wake unable to compete with the quantity, quality and profitability of their rival thanks to Deb. They were now old arguments but he insisted the obvious needed to be clearly stated.

Summer merely rejected what the mediator said, claiming she could not see how a little tweaking and tinkering had done even a fraction of what Deb claimed she had done for the company, and so it went on and on through the hours. For every great leap forward brought to the company and achieved by Deb, for every great problem solved and put right and made profitable and presented as proof of Deb's loyalty, contribution and dedication to the company, Summer simply countered with the claim that she herself could have and would have done the same if Deb had not been there.

Summer then dragged up that it was a sales technique copied

from another company that had led to the company's success, glossing quickly over the obvious flaw in the argument: that all their main competitors were selling the same way within three months. Mr Smythe was amazed that Summer could stand there and make such ludicrous claims. He had worked with the company for years and had seen how competitors had copied its style. He also knew that many of these copycats had come and gone, not able to match the important 'behind the scenes' work Deb had done. Did Summer truly believe that the company was on top just because their vans were newer and prettier? Was that all she thought it took to keep the company on top?

The day dragged on and on. All valid claims and arguments were dismissed until even Mr Smythe became disillusioned. Eventually, when all sensible arguments had been exhausted, he had to accept defeat and the lawyers were called to finalise the paperwork.

Deb joined her lawyers as they went over the details. Meanwhile Bob and Mr Smythe – Gary, now he was off work – found a small, discreet refreshment area at the end of the hall to slink away to. It was well past 10pm and the day had started over twelve hours ago. Both were stunned by events, nursing half-filled plastic cups of liquid that bore no resemblance to what the machine claimed it had served out. The chairs were wooden frames covered with bright orange fabric – obviously an attempt to make this dreary little corner brighter.

'I don't get it. Deb has always delivered, always got it done. Year after year she found ways to make that damn company profitable and keep them in front of the pack. It wasn't just re-labelling old products and giving them a new name or tarting up the packaging. She improved everything for everyone connected to that place and not one of them is grateful for what she has done. Not one of them has stood up for her or even said thank you.' Bob was talking into his cup; Gary could listen if he liked.

'There should be a bloody great statue in the car park of the company that proclaims: "Here is the person that made us what we are today" and it wouldn't be a statue of Summer fucking Ponsenbury. You know …' He turned to look at Gary, who was also staring into the dregs of his cup … 'I've watched Deb do stupidly long hours and take on monumental tasks for that company for over twenty years and she has never, NEVER failed to complete anything. Not just do it but do it much better and much faster and always far exceeding any reasonable expectations anyone else in that bloody company could ever hope to achieve.' Bob took a breath.

'Two-and-a-half per cent of the shares was all that she was given – as if that wasn't insult enough. Sorry – I meant promised, and they won't even honour that now. Two-and-a-half per cent should be two million pounds, yet she has made ten times that and more for them every year for two decades. The company is so profitable they wouldn't even notice that amount if it was gone. Two million pounds is one slow month's profit at point-of-sale. The salesmen could have taken out all of their overheads, paid all their bills and taken their wages as well and *then* sent the profits still left in their money-grabbing hands for just that one month to Deb, and she would have got more than she was promised by that woman.' He indicated where Summer and her crew were holed-up down the corridor. 'One small thank-you for the millionaire lifestyle Deb has given them and their sixty per cent profit margins.' Bob's rant petered out.

There was a few minutes' silence.

'I've known Deb for years,' Gary said, eventually. 'It has been my privilege to work with her. She has always been professional and fair. In my job you only get called in when things have broken down, in the hope you can negotiate a magical compromise that will please everyone, to settle things and sort things out so both sides can walk away with something. Sometimes it can even be only an explanation of why things have happened. On the few occasions I've worked with your wife I've seen her control the situation and find ways to explain and resolve situations so everyone is satisfied. She has calmed the unreasonable and explained and reasoned with the stubborn and misguided. She has taken time to explain and gone over things again and again if necessary. She's always left me feeling that the negotiations have been fair and honest and that is all that can be asked and I have never seen her lose.' There was a small pause. 'Like I said, I'm called in when everything has broken down. Some of the reasons for these breakdowns are so stupid you cannot believe.' Gary swirled the dregs around his cup and thinks that he would be better off not to take the last mouthful and drops the cup in the rubbish bin.

Bob looked over quizzically. 'It's not always just about business. The "I own 51% and you own only 49%" fallouts are the easy ones. You can find a common ground, a solution, without too much trouble. But today I have put forward more reasonable arguments for the most honest and professional employee I have ever met and ever had to help. These arguments should have at least guaranteed something for your future if they had been put before any halfway decent employer.' Gary paused again.

'I have truly been disgusted by the unreasonable response today. I never talk about the cases I have dealt with. This is the first time and hopefully the last that I feel strongly enough about the injustice to make some kind of comment. I hope Deborah will forgive me for failing her. When we started this morning, you told me your version of what had gone on. I believed you were not being honest and had enhanced what had happened. The anger you felt had obviously built up inside and was clouding your view of what had happened, and by exaggerating the facts you felt you would be helping Deb. This is the usual starting point. I apologise to you here and now for not taking your words as fact. I know it will not seem like much but all I can say is in all my years of doing this job and helping people all over the country and even abroad I have never ever come across anyone who deserved to be treated less like this than Deborah. When you told me how they had set your wife up I believed that things had possibly been misheard or misunderstood.' Gary took a deep, cleansing breath.

'I now know and share your belief that Deborah has been cold-bloodedly swindled by an unscrupulous boss who will stoop to any lengths to make money and is completely jealous of your wife to the point of obsession. Ms Ponsenbury has purposefully misguided and misled Deborah. She has twisted and bent the law with the help of her disreputable lawyers who have played their part in all of this and profited greatly, I am sure, from their efforts and poor conduct.' This was said emotionally, giving away Gary's feelings that all he had stood for or believed in had suddenly been tarnished and soiled.

'I am aware after talking to the legal counsels of both parties that in the eyes of the law no actual law has been broken, even though in any honest person's eyes this statement could not possibly be believed to be true.' Gary leant forward and put a hand on Bob's arm. 'Robert, I am sorry. You have tried your best, we have all tried our best, but there is nothing else we can do. The only thing now is to walk away with what little money they are offering and for you and Deborah to try and help each other get over this. The world is not a fair place and I know neither of you deserve this. Try not to judge the rest of the company on what a few have done. There will be some who believe all the lies, however unsubstantiated, but I am sure the majority will toe the company line just to keep their jobs and they will always know the truth. They are just too scared to say anything out loud.'

Bob spoke up. 'Gary, I know you are trying to help and make me feel better. I know you tried as hard as you could. Deb has always said great things about you so I know you would not have sold us out and that you will have exhausted all reasonable efforts. But for fuck's sake, don't ever try to make excuses for the sick, spineless bastards at that company who let this happen.' Gary removed his hand and Bob turned to face him.

'I took a temporary job at some company as a supervisor-cum-coordinator when my own work was slow. I had about thirty people working for me and I got the job because nobody else wanted it. The crew all said it was a poisoned chalice. These people were classed as the lowest of the low because all they did was deliver the parts around the factory to be made into something else. Every time production stopped they were blamed for not having the parts in the right places or the stuff just not being there at all. It didn't take long for me to sort it out. My crew were actually quite good at their job but I followed them around and watched what was happening. These so-called skilled machinists and machine operators were moving these parts that had been delivered correctly to make seats and card tables for their breaks and not returning them to their proper places. Some of these people were just moving parts off their section so they could cry wolf and create a little unscheduled break, knowing the attitude of the management and that they would simply blame my crew and not investigate further. The company was big and probably lost millions each year to lost production because of people not caring because they were not the ones getting blamed.

'I put things right and made sure the right people knew what was happening and stood up for the people working for me. I know the world is not fair. I presented figures to prove how good these people were. We reduced the so-called mistakes to zero. I gave them a belief in themselves, pointing out that they were not trained monkeys but had to know all three of the company's computer systems to do their job and trained on many other types of equipment. It was simple, basic stuff. Don't get me wrong, theirs was a shit job but once I stopped people using the team as an excuse to stop work and actually got them credit for what they were doing, life was much better for them. I was still disposed of after three months, though. The company used the excuse I was not in my office waiting with radio in hand ready to fly to the next problem and fire-fight, even though I had all but eradicated the problems and bad practices. I'd much improved the production and profitability and everything about the production side of the place but I never got any credit for that either.' Bob paused.

'Now the point of this little story is this. People I knew for less than three months and who I had no real connection to or had shown no real loyalty to, walked out and stopped the plant dead when they heard how I had been treated. All the savings I had made for the company were written off. I had to go in and talk to "my crew" to get them to go back to work. I had to tell them it had only ever been temporary and not to worry about me. But they still had that sense of fair play – doing the right thing was important, so they stuck up for me.' Bob stopped to emphasise his point.

'All I did was stop them being shouted at and they were willing to risk their jobs for that. Deb has done everything for this company and for the people employed by it for twenty-odd years. Every job, every pay-packet and every perk is down to her in one way or another. There are hundreds if not thousands of people who are connected to this company who have her and only her to thank for what they have today. She has worked alongside them and helped these scum all her working life and not one of them raised a finger to help her or even took the time to say thank you. We walk down the street or go shopping and these cowards run and hide. We see them turn and go in the other direction. Deb has put her neck on the line again and again for these people. Every decision she ever took has made these ungrateful scum safer and more secure in their jobs. I had more loyalty from thirty complete strangers than Deb has seen from these people after working together for two decades.

'Gary, I know life isn't fair but all that these so-called friends needed to do was show a few minutes' loyalty and protest, and stand up for someone who was unable to protect herself. Was that too much to ask? I am not militant but sometimes there has to be a point reached when something is so obviously wrong that something should have been done.' There was silence, as Bob's soap-box speech – sadly heard by an audience of only one – drew to a close.

'You know not one person sent a card, or got in touch or sent a few cheap flowers. Even cleaners after twenty years get a big send-off. These bastards just turned their backs and shunned her and they all owe her everything. Life is not fair – we never believed it was – but Deb made sure the people who worked for her got treated more fairly than most. Gary, we've spoken to lots of lawyers over the last few weeks and they have been next to useless, all saying that this happens all the time. But how can that possibly be acceptable? Even the police say this isn't fraud but how can it not be fraud? Summer got Deb to stay and keep working by producing false documents she knew would never stand up in court. Surely you cannot just deceive someone into working all their life for you and then simply deny ever saying anything despite the proof and the law just stand aside and accept it?' There was another pause then …

'I even tried to get the papers interested,' Bob confessed, 'but there seem to be more laws to protect the guilty than there are to help the innocent and they wouldn't get involved.'

Gary leaned across and put his hand on Bob's shoulder. 'At this point in time, none of us can do any more. Maybe the papers or maybe a blog are the way to go. People need to know and be warned about things like this and you can use your experiences to help others. Deb is more intelligent than most out there and she believed there were laws in place to protect her and people like her. She believed the documents she had asked for and been given were legal and were all the proof she needed. If you can make people aware of what might be out there and waiting to happen it could be the only good thing to come out of this mess. I am not saying break the law but there has got to be a way to get the warning across if you ever feel up to it. Change the style of what you say and maybe months or years from now someone will listen. You will never be able to name Summer and her company out loud and in public because they have too much money to fight you with but you could help others not to suffer like you two have done.' Gary thought on. 'Search the net – there might be a website out there where you could discuss this stuff.'

'Yes I like that idea,' said Bob. 'People out there with a "come the revolution" hit list. Like-minded people planning together ... I do like the sound of that.'

'NO, no I didn't mean that.' There was panic in Gary's voice.

Bob grinned. 'I know you didn't. Don't worry, I was just rattling your chain!'

All Gary could do was nod his agreement and condolences. They fell into silence until they were summoned back to where the proceedings were coming to an end.

* * *

Bob and Mr Smythe returned to the allotted conference room. Deb was still sobbing, as she had been doing most of the day, only now there were no tears left, just dry croaks and whimpers. Bob felt the reason Deb the person had been so deeply destroyed by all that had happened and been done to her by Summer, was because she had achieved so much and had risen so high against all the odds, and without succumbing to the temptations that power had brought. To give your trust and loyalty for so long and so completely to people who did not care and only wanted to abuse the privilege would have broken most people.

All that was left was for Mr Smythe and the lawyers to witness the final signatures and it was all over, and everything was lost. Mr Smythe went around and did what he could to make things run smoothly and without drama. All Bob could do was comfort his wife and silently promise to himself that this was not over.

Formalities completed, it was time to leave. Bob never knew whether it was fate or whether the opposition had laid in wait to twist the knife one more time. Mr Smythe led the way opening the doors, with Bob behind, supporting his wife as she shuffled along like a hospital patient learning to cope with a traumatic injury.

Their little group had been given the room furthest from the lift and stairs down to the outside world. The room's door closing must have been the signal for Summer and her entourage to appear from the room nearest the exit and bar their way, leaving the three of them stuck in no-man's land. First came the team of lawyers, the least senior holding the door open so his superiors and their clients could emerge into the hallway and onto the landing. The party had grown to include all the company's shareholders and directors and they all appeared in mock procession. Most had not been there throughout the day, and none had been needed but they'd all been summoned – no doubt for this latest performance. Summer appeared last, to applause and mutual back-patting, as she made her way to the lifts past her subjects and received their accolades as she went.

Bob and Deb had to stop and were made to witness yet more scorn and humiliation as Summer's group waited for the lift to arrive. The only exception was the most senior of the lawyers, a small, harmless-looking man with thick-rimmed, prescription-style glasses, despite the fortune he made every year from plying his trade. His receding, white-grey, slicked-back hair gave him the appearance of someone's nice old granddad or ageing uncle.

As the laughing and the cheers continued at the far end of the hall, he strode towards Deb, Bob and Gary Smythe. The lawyer put out his hand in a gesture of mock friendship, or an acknowledgment of a competition well played. Bob wanted to cut the hand off at the wrist and delight in shoving it somewhere unsavoury but he was supporting Deb. Deb herself was in no condition to go through the sort of polite pleasantry this piece of scum felt the situation required. Mr Smythe gave the hand one shake, a professional courtesy to satisfy its owner.

'My dear,' said the lawyer to Deb, 'we allowed you to play our game and you lost, simply because we deemed you unworthy of knowing all the rules. Good evening.' He turned on his heels, his statement delivered. At that precise moment the lift bell chimed like the bell at the start of a boxing match, announcing it had arrived and the doors were going to open. Bob released Deb with the intention of picking up the poisonous little shit and throwing him over the banister so he could splat on the concourse floor several floors below.

Before Bob could act, Deb started to fall, Bob only just managing to catch her before she crumpled to the floor. Her mind was reeling. All she wanted was to curl up in a little ball and fade away. Bob started to rise immediately his precious cargo was out of danger of injury but Smythe blocked his way.

'Stop it. Do not bite. They are not worth it.' He was gripping Bob by the shoulders to prevent him from rising. 'If you do anything rash you will not be there for Deb and she needs you. Please let it go.'

'HEY!' Harry called across the open space as they all packed themselves into the lift. 'We would ask you out to celebrate and have a drink but I'm guessing you couldn't afford to pay your round.' The lift erupted into laughter. It was too much. Bob broke free and grabbed the nearest thing to throw in the lift's direction ... Gary's briefcase smashed harmlessly into the closing lift doors, denting the metallic finish but not spreading its contents across the floor, which was testament to the quality of its primary function as a briefcase but its failure as an effective weapon.

'BOB, PLEASE.' Gary grabbed at Bob's arm again. 'Bob, look after Deb. Bob now!' Gary retrieved the briefcase and took the second lift down. His aim was to catch up with Summer's group and have a few strong words but he returned flustered and frustrated in his quest. By the time he had made reception the group had dispersed and gone. Their transport must have been waiting and ready to go. He found Bob and Deb where he had left them, now sitting on the floor with their backs to the wall, Deb with her face hidden and her head resting on her knees. The day had been too much to take. Bob looked up. There was a silent question on his face…

They were gone.

Gently they got Deb to her feet and eventually to the car. It was well after 11 p.m. and dark. 'Thanks for your help' and 'Anytime' was all that could be said. A few days later they found out Summer had disclosed all the details of the compromise agreement and how she had forced Deb to agree to only ten percent of what she had been promised- to all the company, carrying out her threat to market herself as the generous employer and missing out what they had actually taken from Deb and all they had reneged upon. This new breach in Deb's trust and personnel rights, was no doubt done to show Summer's domination, gloat at her victory and send a warning to others: 'If I can do this to your precious Deborah, think what I can do to you.'

* * *

It had been a couple of months since it all had been officially ended. Bob had spent most of his time caring for his wife. Her way of coping with what had happened was to shut down and act like it had never been part of her life. He knew she had refused much more lucrative deals and offers from much bigger companies throughout her working life but she had always stayed loyal and true to the company and the promises she had made – for all the good it had done her. If he did not half drag her around the local woods to walk the dog or around the local supermarket when he went shopping he was sure she would have simply stayed where she sat at home and done nothing until it was time to go to bed again.

He had had a few small-paying jobs but had spent the majority of his 'spare time' writing and e-mailing newspapers and magazines to try and generate some interest. Not many bothered to reply. There had been a few automated computer-generated

'Thank you for your interest' type e-mails confirming they had received what he had sent. The rest had not even bothered with that courtesy. He had written to the police, trying to get some sort of legal definition of what they classed as swindle and fraud and when in their eyes that just merged into normal business practice. From the short, sharp conversation he'd had on the phone after he had sent several letters and requests for help to all his local police forces he could only deduce that if it was 'rich doing it to the poor' that equalled business. But if it was 'the poor doing it to the rich' it became fraud and the police might consider jumping into action if it was a quiet week and there was no football on the TV.

Out of the desolation and emptiness had come one small letter from a national newspaper asking 'if he would like to call in for a chat'. He now sat in an ultra-modern reception area waiting to be summoned. He had spoken to a nice assistant to the assistant editor who had replied on the paper's behalf and had been firmly told it was a simple review to see if the story had any potential for filling a few lines for them. He now waited to present his story to the editor.

* * *

'Why oh why are you wasting my time with this?' The young, perky, moronic girl in front of Douglas Green had just given him the heads up concerning his next meeting with the great unwashed. Didn't the damn paper employ people like her to save him from twaddle like this?

'It is a good story. Human interest, corporate greed, little guy against the world stuff,' said Lucy, in her defence.

'For the love of God, are you for real? We are selling papers. Who cares if it is only one victim who got shafted after twenty years of loyal and faithful service?'

'Boss, we need something to fill a few paragraphs sometimes. I just thought we should have a listen and file it until we're doing something on bullying or greed. Just tuck it away until we have space to fill and put it on page fifteen or something, so no-one really reads it.'

Green looked over his glasses at the girl as he sat behind his desk. Well, girl to him, anyway; he was old enough to be clinging to the hope that someday soon he could retire before he actually died. 'If you ever bring me shit like this again you will be sucking my dick every day for the next three months.'

Green was overweight and sweaty. He had greasy black hair that he dragged straight back and tucked behind his ears where it hung just above his shoulders. He usually tucked it behind his ears to keep out of the way but when he got passionate or emotional about something it escaped and entwined itself around his glasses and across his face. Nothing was ever going to make him wear it in a ponytail like some ageing football star. Age and continual scowling had left crater-like furrows all over his face and his sickly skin colour screamed poor diet, too much booze and a deep hatred of that bright shiny thing they called the sun.

He used one finger to pull the glasses to the end of his nose so he could scowl more effectively over them. 'OK. Wheel this sad git in and let's get it over with.'

Bob entered the office with Lucy leading the way. The building was modern, very modern in fact but somehow the man in front of him had managed to get his office to the tired, condemned look long before its time. Green's clothes looked as though they were well worn even when they were clean and this wasn't a particularly clean day. His shirt sleeves were rolled up, the grime obvious on the folds and around the collar. His tie was at half-mast with a knot that had been loosened and tightened many times to take it on and off. It was probably black but it wasn't worth wasting money on the bet. A woollen tank-top and sandy-coloured cords finished the thrown-together look. The desk was cluttered almost to the point of collapse and the rest of the office would have made a hoarder proud.

Formal introductions were made and chairs found from their

hiding places. Lucy took notes. Bob reeled out his story, trying to give it enough bite and bile to make it interesting to Green, who sat back in his chair and listened with his hands and fingers intertwined at the back of his head, exposing sweat-stained armpits.

Eventually Green leaned forward. 'Bob, I may call you Bob? Thanks. It is a very sad and moving story and I wish the paper could cover this. Trouble is, it is a very small story in a very big sea. Papers want, need, even crave sensationalism. A hard-working, honest poor person getting ripped off by rich people won't sell.' This guy Bob had just laid bare his soul and it had been an interesting story, powerful and moving in its own little way. All it had done was to confirm Green's own beliefs that there was no good in the world and that any honest sucker out there would never get an even break.

'Bob, for this to make the papers something big and sensational needs to happen. It has to compete in the world of ... how can I put it? The world of scheming politicians, for example. We have Tony Blair and his cohorts destroying our country for generations to come. Our kids or even their kids will be paying for his cock-ups and the unrealistic promises he made just to win votes. He resurrected a war Mrs T could have finished years before if he hadn't led a campaign against her and stopped it. Then he needed votes and hey presto, the old foe was still out there and it was now Tony's mission to put things right – and it became the opposition government before that should have done more and had let everyone down. He has done everything, even down to implying he would make drugs legal to win votes. Yet with a great marketing company he has survived crisis after crisis of his own making and the public love him. If the world was fair his head and his followers' heads would be spiked on a modern-day Traitor's Gate somewhere but it is these stories and the people like that which sells our papers.

'Bob, do you see where I am coming from? There are national and international disasters with dead and dying strewn about the place with their dirty little faces looking out of the pages pleadingly.' Green made a sad face, or attempted to. It looked more like someone with bad indigestion about to belch.

'There are sex scandals and paedophiles and pop stars with their bits out. Occasionally we even love a fluffy, three-legged dog story. The only thing consistently there somewhere, mixed in with all that, are the tits and arses.' Green again leans forward, his elbows on the desk and his fingers forming a steeple under his chin. 'Where do you think your story fits in this menagerie?' Before Bob had time to answer, Green answered for him. 'Yes, a few might see the human interest angle or the bullying but it is not going to generate much interest. It is not going to sell papers.'

The man across the desk from him looked totally demoralised and beaten. Green got up and walked around the desk and moved a few files so he could perch himself in front of Bob. 'Look, I know it means a lot to you, it happened in your world. You have lived it, loved it and been ripped apart by it and I do truly sympathise with you and applaud your efforts. But the only way I can make this work is if this was all somehow bigger.' Green emphasised this with a hand gesture that could be anything from someone dispersing gnats to illustrating an explosion. 'It needs someone hurt or dead. Factories burnt to the ground. Naked chests chained to the railings in protest.' There was a pause. 'Bob, you should be proud of what you two achieved and how you did it honestly and ethically. Even the sacrifices you made to protect others at the end. You actually did that for real. Yes, people should look up to your wife as an example and be inspired and outraged by her mistreatment, then get revved up to make a stand about it. But this country is apathetic and as long as it is only one person suffering or lots of single people suffering on their own and not getting together, no-one will care. Truth is, I stand more chance of getting the "Bitch Boss and how I ripped Miss Goody Two-Shoes apart and put her in her place" story into the paper.' Green extended his hand. 'Sorry – honesty and being nice never helped to sell papers.'

Bob took the hint and stood and shook Green's hand. 'At least you listened and gave me some of your time.' Bob turned and left, the last glimmer of hope now extinguished. He was at a new low.

Lucy returned to the office of her malevolent leader after showing Bob out. 'That was a bit harsh. Shouldn't we as the voice of the people show a little sympathy to the little guy and a good cause? Isn't that what the free press is all about?'

Green stared at her like her 36D cup chest had magically been revealed. 'Fuck you,' was her response to his snigger and she turned to leave.

'Lucy, Lucy, hopefully I have inspired our hero to go out and do something a little more newsworthy. It is a nice little story but it needs a spark – something to make it big and grip the imagination. Do some quick research on all concerned just in case and we will sit and wait and keep our fingers crossed.'

'You old bastard.'

'Please ... "You cunning old bastard" accompanied with a mock regal bow. Now let's get on with the best part of the week. Bring me the file with all the C- rated celebs who have forgotten to put on any underwear and have flashed an eyeful getting out of some taxi somewhere for a bit of free publicity. And if you are not going to suck my dick, fetch me a coffee.' He gave a stupid grin in her direction to say he was only joking about the blow job. He wouldn't want her to start complaining to the psycho bitches in human resources.

Lucy left to fetch the file and the coffee giving him a one-finger salute to show there were no hard feelings ...

The coffee on his desk was hot and he opened the file of photographs and started sorting through them. He smiled to himself. 'Life is good. Not great ... but good.'

12

Mr T and the Path to Enlightenment

The time crept from days to weeks and then started to become months. Bob had witnessed so-called friends and colleagues manipulate and scheme to drive someone who trusted them first into depression to try and get rid of her. When that wasn't enough, they had humiliated her more, pushing their victim to the point where suicide seemed the only way out just to satisfy their greed and to add to their bulging bank balances. Bob's reaction had been anger at first but after all they had been through, the feeling had become an all-encompassing numbness. Trusted people had let them down. No-one cared or was interested in the truth and they had been left with nothing from an honest, hardworking life that should have yielded much more.

Deb had become a victim of tactics that a slum landlord would be proud of, from lies and bullying to blackmail and threats against friends and their futures. The few people who knew everything and were not part of the web of deceit or connected to the company had also been amazed at the lack of support, loyalty and help from people close to Deb. They were also surprised at the lack of interest from institutes that were supposedly there to protect and support the innocent and honest, and to help by being their voice and strength.

The fight could and should have been about many things and fought on many levels but when it came down to it, it was the total injustice of it all, because the victim was just a poor, honest girl with a few ethics and the only one playing by the rules.

Bob had now had endless nights of sleep resting by his wife but disturbed by her nightmares. On the few occasions the chance of a full night's sleep had been on offer his own demons had taken over. What should he have done differently? What could he do? His conclusion on these nights as he re-lived being powerless to stop what was being done to his family was that he *would* get justice for Deb. His faith in the law and the ethics of others had been completely shattered. His world had become a place void of truth and honesty. Was it time to go 'Tarantino', do the only thing left and stand up for what was right?

Would you get out of your chair in front of your television if there was an alarm going off and it was not your own? Or would you be more likely to turn up the volume on the TV, so that you could no longer hear the alarm going off?

Had Bob been pushed too far and been let down too much? Was it time to do the honourable thing and to pick the sheriff's badge up from where it lay in the dust? Did the situation require frontier justice to protect the common citizens and the good guy to make a stand against overwhelming odds?

Bob lay there in the dark and reflected on his new outlook to the problem he was trying to rectify. The instigators and manipulators had to be stopped somehow and somewhere. They all had to shop, some might jog and there would be times when they were just going out to the local pub. At all of these places they could be alone and would be vulnerable for at least some of the time. Maybe just a few seconds as they were concentrating on opening the car door or with an armful of shopping and as they struggled … thwack! They wouldn't feel that piece of steel until it was firmly embedded in their back. As their life slipped away, they'd slide down the rain-splattered car in a dark, dank car park somewhere where they thought they were safe. If the gods did have a sense of theatre there would be the sound of AC/DC playing 'Night Prowler' coming from the local pub. As they listened their breathing would get shallow and slow – and the shadow that had just done this would walk away into the darkness where he had patiently been waiting for his chance. Death is only one more breath away for the person sat on the rain-soaked floor…

Bob considered that even where he lived there might be a few cameras dotted around the town centre but there had to be times and places where an assailant could do the dirty deed and then slip away unnoticed. The biggest risk, he supposed, was that instead of slipping away into the shadows or merging into the crowd as justice was dealt out, some bystander would try and stop the clean getaway. As the blood spilled across the pavement and realisation dawned on the guilty and soon-to-be-dead, the hero would be caught up in miles of red tape and crowds of misguided busybodies.

Deb stirred a little but Bob was well practised now at not letting the situation escalate and she was soon back deep in slumber. Sometimes, he thought, you just want to make a statement, something spectacular enough to attract everyone's attention and get the justice needed. Every day he saw more of the person he loved fade away and be lost for all time, her health deteriorating as she gave up. It seemed he could do nothing to stop it, but he had tried, he had tried.

Now with a little planning on his part he felt things could get very troublesome indeed for the guilty. There was a whole Internet out there these days, even for the mildly technophobic like himself, where there were nasty things you could buy or nasty people who could make some of your problems go away permanently! The thought lingered.

Before those bastards had ripped his wife's life apart he had been close enough to their lives to know their families, their hobbies, some of their routines, and of course where they worked and lived.

As he lay there, he suddenly realised that for someone his age, and a home-owner, there might be a solution where he would have no need to risk shady back streets or dodgy deals over the Internet. He had been a householder for years and a pillar of the community and he saw no reason not to use these facts to make his life easier and get exactly what he needed now. He could take this forced retirement to look after Deb and find a way to use it to his advantage. Suddenly a straightforward answer popped into his consciousness. He would join the local clay pigeon shoot.

He would become just some old codger out to have fun blowing things out of the sky. Deb might even be convinced to come and join. Soon his probation period would be over and all his new friends would be full of advice and help, the background checks would be done and the security locker fitted in his home to comply with police requirements. Then he could buy a couple of repeater twelve-gauge shotguns to fill the empty space in the locker, all legal and above board. You know the sort of gun, those pump action things you see on every violent TV programme on the box. He could splash the cash and get a 'his and hers' matching set and he would not even come close to breaking the law, not just yet! He could get a few lessons and have a few sessions down at the local range so he could actually hit the side of a barn. Surely he would not have to be that good? He just needed to put himself in a situation where he kept pumping the cartridges and pulling the trigger. The members at the club might think his choice of weapon over the top for a few clay pigeons but that would not be the real reason why he had them, would it?

* * *

Deb, of course, knew nothing of the 'other' motive behind this new hobby. Bob felt that the moment would soon come when he and Mr Justice would go calling on the Queen Bitch herself, and all her little parasites. Soon Bob would contact – and use – some of their old friends at the company to get where he needed to be at just at the right moment. These were people that should have stood up for Deb as she tried to get justice and were now eager to put things right and lessen their own guilt for not stepping up to the plate in the first place, people Deb could not ask directly for help at the time because of the bullying, the blackmail and the threats. These people were now ready to put right their mistakes, although none of them had been brave enough to step out of line and act at the time, even when they knew it was the right thing to do.

If Bob was to carry out his plan he was going to have to lie to friends and he was uncomfortable with that. The plan was not that complicated. He was going to tell the friends that he was bringing more legal documents to try and fight on for Deb. All he had to ask was when all the shareholders and directors would be together. He would claim he needed them together so he could present the bogus and non-existent documents to all concerned and it would be better if they were in one place. In the grand scheme of things, it would only be a small deception and a small lie. He would ask for the security codes to the outer doors and for a phone call as soon as everyone was assembled, and he would do the rest. He could move through the factory without involving anyone else or causing unnecessary trouble.

When the time came, everyone was prepared to help. He could have even found out which types of biscuits were going to be served with the coffee if it would have helped him. Within an hour of starting his quest Bob had the dates and scheduled times for all the meetings that would involve the people he had asked about. Some of the meetings were unsuitable because some or all of his main targets would not be attending but there was a choice of three that fitted his criteria over the next couple of weeks ... a shortlist for Bob to ponder over and select from and choose the most convenient time.

* * *

On the chosen day, Bob called the company first thing and spoke to one of his contacts to check there were no late amendments to the scheduled meeting. He prepared himself as he made breakfast as normal for Deb and himself. A little tinkering in the garage and a small amount of tidying up and he could claim he had a load of rubbish ready to be taken to the tip. There was also an old and now poorly-used set of golf clubs across the back seat of the car, just in case an excuse was needed and he was away longer than expected. Bob felt it was better to have Deb thinking he was giving golf one more try before he was too old to walk around the course than to suspect the truth. He hoped the day's weather would improve. He visited the tip in the rain quite often because it always lessened the queues and saved him time. He never liked playing golf in the rain however, even when he was interested in the game, and he was worried Deb might suspect something if he acted out of character.

As his tinkering kept him out of sight, he loaded both shotguns and put them in the boot of the car with a few broken-down cardboard boxes over them to conceal the guns from prying eyes.

Deb as usual was sitting where he'd left her, on the sofa in front of the TV. He informed her he was off to do his errands, not expecting any acknowledgement. He left home and drove to a country lane close to the factory, waiting for the call to confirm the meeting had started.

It had turned into a miserable day and he watched the rain splatter and pool on the car windscreen. The golf excuse was now redundant. He knew there were a hardy or stupid few who would play on but he was not one of them. The radio changes from Ian Gillan's 'White Face, City Boy' to Kid Rock's 'All Summer Long' and Bob hummed quietly to himself. There was his bad singing, the music from the radio and the rain splattering against the car but it was strangely peaceful as if the world outside no longer existed. The road was deserted and the rain had driven everyone indoors and out of harm's way.

There were no nerves, just an inner peace he hadn't had for a long time. The spell was soon broken by the mobile phone vibrating on the car dashboard, as a precursor to it ringing. Bob reached forward and switched off the radio before picking up the phone and checking the caller ID. He then switched the phone off completely, satisfied it was time to go and visit a few old acquaintances. He took one long, calming breath and then turned the key in the car's ignition. It was only a short distance to his destination, the factory.

Bob drove through the gates, as he had done so many times before. The security guy in the gatehouse took down the car's registration number but he would not come out of his warm cosy office unless Bob or anyone else stopped, and in this weather Bob was sure the guy was happy this driver knew where he was going. Bob kept looking forward as he drove on and let the faceless guard go back to watching whatever it was he was interested in on his portable TV.

The car and driver eased past the vehicles already parked until they were at the end of the building and there Bob turned and parked his car. He put the hazard warning lights on to signify he was only going to be a temporary obstruction, got out and went to the boot of the car. The rain was getting harder but that was somehow better because it meant less chance of people milling about outside and witnessing his actions. He knew that the few orange and white plastic bollards had been put there to stop anyone taking his place ... a simple and nice gesture from his contacts inside.

To a casual observer he looked like someone loading or unloading. The car park was empty of people and there are no onlookers. Even if someone ventured forth from the main reception he would see them but chances are they would have their head down running for their own car and wouldn't even notice little old Bob waiting in the shadows.

He had customised a strap that he attached to one of the shotguns so he could position it over his shoulder and under the long waterproof coat he purchased especially to cover the gun up. Any weapon on show when he went in would create an outbreak of hysteria. He was happy to let that happen later when he wanted it to happen along with chaos and confusion. Bob wanted to control his environment and did not want all hell to break loose by mistake because of a casual glance from someone as he walked by. He did not want the screaming to start too soon. The day was cold as well as wet, so no-one would question the long coat – another happy set of circumstances to help him along his chosen path. The second shotgun went into a box of flowers he had purchased on the way there (if it was good enough for Arnie and the Terminator it was good enough for him).

Box under arm and coat pulled close he tried the set of codes he had been given for the small side entrance next to his car. A gentle push and the door opened and he was inside. It had never even crossed his mind the door might fail to open.

A few 'hi Bob's and 'how's Deb?' accompanied him down the corridor as he passed open doors or met people as he headed to where the meeting was taking place. He looked straight ahead and ignored all, trying to keep a good strong pace without running. He was determined not to get distracted from his task. He was worried that if he was stopped he would lose his nerve.

There was only one security door left, then there was nothing that could stop him.

He was within three steps of the door when it started to open and someone he didn't know blocked his way. 'Delivery for Ms Ponsenbury. Reception has sent me down this way because I need a signature,' said Bob. The man nodded and stepped aside, even holding the door open to let Bob pass. Fate, it seemed, was on his side and he was now in the large, open-plan office area where the meeting was taking place. There were only twenty steps between Bob and the guilty little fish seated in the room behind the large glass panels at the end of the open area. It was like some enormous weird aquarium. Anyone and everyone who was there was revealed but none were looking in Bob's direction.

He could just about make out Thin Lizzy playing 'The Boys are Back in Town' as the music seeped through the walls from the production area on the other side.

Bob was only seconds away from his goal and he strode across the space in front of him. The music changed to 'Born to Bad' by George something-or-other. He could see the big ugly boardroom table that Summer insisted on, Much too big for the room and the number of people who are summoned to sit around it. What is her thing about big furniture, does she think it makes her look smaller or something? Another extravagance to make herself feel more important, just like wanting the biggest and most expensive car in the neighbourhood. Bob could remember joking about the size of the table at home with Deb after he had first seen it, when a comedy sketch came on the TV. It was about a wealthy couple who spent the whole sketch shouting back and forth in a kind of silly game of Chinese whispers 'PASS THE SALT, DEAR' followed by, 'SORRY, WAS IT PEAS AND BEER YOU WANTED?'

This giant room had only one way in or out and no-one would be able to rush him because of the table and where his quarry were all seated at the far end. All the supplicants were transfixed as their Queen spoke to them and they would not see Bob making his entrance until it was too late.

People in the surrounding open-plan offices were beginning to recognise Bob and were making moves to get up and come over to him. He could not hesitate or they might get involved and he didn't want that. He didn't want the innocent getting hurt. He reached into the long cardboard box and his hand found the cold stock of the gun. The box and its non-useful contents were discarded and dropped to the floor. Like an Olympic runner, he lengthened his stride as he approached the finish line. As people caught sight of the shotgun, fear or maybe even conscience stops them screaming out a warning as they begin to scatter and take cover. The people in the oversized goldfish bowl are unconcerned, the sound-proof double glazing not allowing the outside world to distract its occupants. With shotgun in hand Bob opened the office door and made his entrance. 'HONEY, I'M HOME!' He didn't know why he chose that way to get their attention but in a split second their focus was totally on him.

Suddenly there was a Tarantino lookalike there beside him directing the action. Bob was sure it couldn't be the real one. This version was wearing pink Doc Martens, a green tartan kilt, sequined pink tank top and large white rimmed sun glasses. The giveaway is the long ponytail the look-alike is sporting. The real Mister T would never do that, surely.

It now became like a very old movie called *The Boondock Saints* that starred Willem Dafoe as a gay FBI Agent. In the film the action would be taking place as agent Dafoe recounted to his colleagues what happened at the scene of every crime. As the crimes were committed he would be there mirroring what was happening. The guns would be shot and the slow-motion cameras would capture the gory details. Dafoe would be in the thick of it with his fingers raised like a kid playing cowboys and Indians working out and following the perpetrator's every move.

Bob, he and the Mr T lookalike moved in harmony and as one. BOOM! BOOM! The first two got it. Bob had the gun, Mr T was improvising. Bob wanted to work around the table, saving Summer for last. The faces of the first two victims were turned to mush and bits of gristle, the red slop splattered theatrically over the glass to the right and behind where they were sitting. The film crew in the corner were getting it all on tape. Mr T narrated and kept score as if the action was happening in slow-motion.

First to go was Kathy, who was promoted from part-time to team leader before Deb had left the building, thanks to some creative witness statements put forward as her own but supplied by the company and designed to help Summer's case. Deb had even helped turn around the life of Kathy's self-harming teenage daughter. Kathy, you obviously forgot Deb's unselfish and non-judgmental support when everyone else shunned you.

The second was the whingeing and whining production director Trevor loyal to Summer but only really good enough to caretake all that Deb had built and installed for the company over the years. When Deb had been thrown out, he had been the one who later called around to tempt her back so the company could humiliate her further, the deceptions carried out to show his boss how loyal he was and to secure his position in the company. All this done by a man who had also greatly benefited from Deb's help in his private life. When he and his wife had struggled to have a family of their own, Deb had found a clinic abroad who were willing to help. This man, who owed his family to Deb, had turned on her just like the rest to get his share of the spoils. How could Deb have known the rewards for helping to create a happy, healthy baby would be betrayal and lies?

Mr T stage-managed – Bob and he turned as one. Luckily, the company lawyer was there … BOOM! No more lies and dodgy dealings. Remember telling Deb all those worthless documents were legally binding just to keep her working away like a good little girl until Summer was ready to make her move? You were there just to make the swindle believable and to make the cheating run a little smoother. That was number three and you are now legally dead.

Seconds passed like lifetimes but fear, adrenaline and self-preservation stirred those who were left still alive in the room into action. The first two just sat there and got what was coming but the lawyer had started to rise. Quick on the uptake but not quick enough and he had been nearly cut in half by the blast of the shotgun. Now the other little fishes in this barrel were desperately trying to find somewhere to hide and be safe.

BOOM! Number four. Sapp was next. Bob spun to the left, pumping the next round as he went, Mr T still shadowing his every move. Sapp took the next cartridge packed with death full in the chest as he also tried to rise to his feet, flying three feet through the air. As his lifeless and tattered body crumpled to the floor, a red splatter was left across the window behind him. If anyone was still left outside the room watching the action it could now only be seen through the red haze covering the glass like a macabre puppet show from hell. A fitting description because Sapp had crumpled to the floor like a puppet whose strings had been cut.

The question Bob would have asked if he had had the time or the inclination was, why try to stand? Wouldn't you just dive for cover? In Sapp's case, was it just another example of poor decision-making? Or was his latest designer suit a little too tight around his fat little body for any sudden movements? Maybe Sapp had even glanced at the floor and thought to himself that it looked too dirty to go rolling around on?

It had been a nice suit. Sapp was the original chef/chemist but had always had a reputation for not having any backbone (literally now!) and would sell his wife and kid to keep his fancy suits and fancy cars. He had known about the Black Queen fiddling figures and continually screwing up, then using her friendship with Summer to get things covered up, and had for a split second tried to help Deb. Well, until Summer growled in his direction and his resistance folded. His fortune and his wardrobe saved by the quick U-turn.

Harry was being very butch and had taken the opportunity to grab the Black Queen, Yvette, and was trying to use her as a human shield. From all the rumours he had spread over the years about his previous life in the Forces before he became an insurance salesman, you would have thought there would have been a different reaction. Maybe he should have been the one diving across the table and wrestling Bob to the floor, saving the day and becoming part of legend. Guess all the top-secret missions on the Play Station or Xbox don't really count in real life. Only Harry believes the bullshit Harry spouts and from the smell, Bob concluded that Harry's bull was mixing with the Black Queen's around their ankles and over their highly-polished shoes at that very moment.

Harry ... a man with no real talent. Successful in his job only because he could take credit for the work Deb had done. All that tedious work essential to the company's success. What commitment and support shown from a man without morals and ethics. To think Deb made you a multi-millionaire and all you had to do was read off the crib sheets she wrote for you and you couldn't even do that unless you were supervised and checked up on regularly. A man who had no qualms about using his staff as collateral damage to take the fall for his own failings. Harry, the man who used his position to abuse the women of the company and who classed them as mere toys for his amusement to be used and played with behind his wife's back

The Black Queen was putting up a fight, squirming around and trying to break free of Harry's grasp even if human shield was the only useful job she had ever done. Yet another talentless wonder employed by Summer and able to spread poison and hurtful gossip in equal measure wherever she went. Always hiding in the wings waiting to take credit for other people's work. When things went wrong, she relied on the colour of her skin or sexual preferences to make herself a special case, untouchable, unaccountable and un-blameable for her mistakes. Always ready to set her big bullying friend Summer on to you, Grrr!

Mr T. "Fire!"

BOOM! BOOM! Five and six. That pink frilly shirt wasn't as good at stopping shot as you both thought. Still, they died in each other's arms … romantic?

What pretty patterns the carnage had caused across the three walls of glass. If a psychiatrist was to glance an eye over them they could find all the sheep and clouds they could ever want, if they looked hard enough. To the rest of the world it was just slime and goo and mashed body parts. Bob could not believe the stench that now filled the room. They don't tell you about that in the cinema.

The little bits of confetti that were now settling all around the room were nice, almost festive. Bob hoped they were some very important memos or reports or something. The only person missing – and Bob would have liked to have been here to share the fun – was Summer's psychiatrist friend. An oversight by Mr T, surely not? Maybe the missing character would be killed as Bob made his escape, ridden down in the car park with an armful of files, his head smashed across the bonnet of the speeding getaway car. One last glance at the driver to recognise who had dealt the final blow.

People would be grateful in the end. Several had been invited to a session or two with the guy, Summer happy to help them over their wobbles. The visits, in hindsight, were a chance to find weaknesses and information Summer could use against unsuspecting victims. It must have the same feeling as a premiership football manager receiving the 'full backing of the board'. You must know that your days are numbered.

Deb's psychiatric assessment must have highlighted her honesty, ethics and integrity, the immense pride she had in her achievements and the relationship she had with the workforce. All had become targets for Summer to attack as she weakened her victim before going in for the kill, knowing how and what to attack to do the most damage in the shortest possible time.

The room was large but Bob's ears were still ringing from the blasts of the twelve-gauge shotgun. He could hear a few muffled screams and shouts from outside the meeting room as the people left now thought of themselves and ran like hell.

Bob knew Summer was in the room when he entered. She must have dived for cover as he dealt with the others. He was close to the door and no-one had made any attempt to sneak off. He took a vacant chair and wedged it under the handle of the door. If anyone tried to leave it would take too much time to free the chair. Time they did not have.

The film crew was still rolling in the corner like a silent three-piece band. Mr T was no longer by his side but halfway along the table, with a small, hand-held camera pointed directly at Bob. He was pointing at the table, either indicating where Bob needed to be for the next scene or trying to give away Summer's hiding place. Bob delicately, even lovingly, put the first shotgun down on the table like a treasured and precious piece of artwork and took its fully-loaded twin from under his coat. If he had realised how much time he would have he would have brought cartridges and reloaded. He could have brought one gun and saved the price of the flowers. Every little helps, as they say.

He took a step forward, then stepped up onto a chair and then onto the monstrously large table. It was a good job there were illuminated panels in the ceiling or he would have had to crouch down a bit so he didn't bang his head on a light fitting and have a nasty industrial accident. Bob slowly walked across the tabletop to the point where he thought Summer was hiding below. The director was now filming crouched down at the side of the table, looking up at the 'hero'.

Bob crouched down, too, and used the barrel of the shotgun to tap three times on the table's highly polished surface. There was a sharp intake of breath from below and a muffled squeak.

TAP … TAP … TAP again. 'Oh Summer, dear, please get up – you are not going to die.' Bob knew she was there and that she could hear him but she was trying to be as quiet as a little church mouse, well not so little. He took comfort from picturing her crouched beneath him in soiled underwear, petrified, with flab bulging out of an over-stretched business suit. Maybe now she was even a little repentant?

TAP … TAP … TAP. 'Stand up, Summer, I am not going to kill you.' A short pause.

'STAND UP NOW,' he screamed, as she tested his patience.

A shaky hand crept above the table top for leverage and support, followed by a wiry mop of ginger hair, slick and dark with sweat. She stood before him, her body visibly shaking. She wouldn't look him in the eyes but complied with the request rather than die. Bob had laid the gun casually across his knees as he continued to crouch. The barrel of the gun he kept levelled at the top half of her over-generous body. Her eyes were transfixed by the sight and it seemed to have a hypnotic effect, just like a dancing cobra as it pauses for a split second just before the moment it strikes. Was she hoping to see Bob as he started to pull the trigger and be able to dive back below the table and to safety before it went off? Her reflexes were going to be that good my arse, he thinks to himself.

With the gun firmly pointed at her, Bob started to speak. 'Summer, look around. If I wanted you dead, you would be dead.'

It took a few seconds for the words to sink in but he allowed her the time to follow his instructions, look around the room and take in all that had happened. The piles of offal scattered about that were once her co-conspirators. As he continued to crouch there, his big leather winter coat bunched around his legs, a humid, sweaty smell from all the excitement and exertion started to escape from within and mingle with the even more unsavoury smells now filling the room.

'Summer, you caused this to happen and you will have to live with this on your conscience for the rest of your life.' Bob looked slowly from side to side, gesturing with his free hand towards the mess. 'You will have to make peace with whichever god you think will forgive you and take you in. All of this is down to your greed and your jealousy.' He pointed a finger at the centre of her chest to emphasise what he was saying.

Realisation started to dawn on her face. Her mind was fighting the numbing shock of what had just happened. She was now beginning to understand the words Bob had spoken to her. 'You mean I am going to live. I am going to keep my … money?'

There it was, just as he knew it would be. No concerns or worries about what was left of the people around her. Then a flicker started at the edges of her mouth and grew into a smirk. She barely stopped herself from clapping and whooping with joy. This time she looked him straight in the eye. 'I am going to keep *all* my money.'

BOOM! Bob had lied.

Bob stood, turned and walked to where he could step down from the table. As his feet touched the floor he reached back and retrieved the second shotgun from where he had left it. A few steps and he kicked the chair away from the door and made his exit. Director and camera crew started to cheer and he heard 'AND CUT' from behind him. In the deserted offices he could now hear Lynyrd Skynyrd's 'Sweet Home Alabama' coming from the other side of the wall and he started to smile. It was an old song but he has always liked it.

* * *

Bob woke up with a start. He must have fallen asleep. What a dream! Ten out of ten for gratifying, glorious and justified but he might have to work on the ending. Well, more the escape if he ever did it for real. As his mind tried to get into gear, caught up between the dream and his body suffering another restless night, he thought to himself, 'Dream ... that explains why the glass didn't shatter!'

Deb stirred a little but he stopped her waking. He lay there and thought, 'Could I do that? Is that the answer?' If he wanted any sort of justice it was clear he was going to have to take it himself. Had the dream shown him the way? Would he have the nerve? He slipped out of bed and went to the bathroom, swilling the sweat from his face and taking a drink of cold water from the tap, wishing it was something stronger. He had a lot to think about.

13

The Quest

It is still dark outside the farmhouse and Bob is sitting patiently waiting for revenge on the person who had heaped so much misery on his family. After his dream, Bob had come to realise that if he wanted justice, he was the one who would have to find some way to mete it out to the woman who had taken everything. Bob had given up on waiting for God (any god) to protect the innocent, and the chances of a plague, skin-eating disease or a terminal dose of cancer befalling the guilty any time soon seemed a bit of a long shot. He had contemplated over the months about the world and the sorry fact that any god of any race, creed or colour would never be around and helpful when they were needed. His conclusion had seemed simple and straightforward: get a man in! You know the type of guy – cash, no receipt – and let him deal with the problem. How much would it cost and where to start looking?

As a teenager in the seventies, Bob had known a few nasty bastards and despite what today's parents say to their kids, there were knife-wielding street gangs and bike gangs back then and even a little gun-toting from some of the more extreme groups. These gangs and groups supplied anything and everything, including the right people for any job, at a price. Boy, how things had changed since back in the day! Like everyone around him, Bob had read the papers and watched TV and believed the hype that you could walk into any dodgy bar or darkened alley and get exactly what you needed. Not a bloody chance. All the places and people he knew had changed and become respectable and old.

Even the rules had changed. In the good old days you could walk into a gang pub on business and be able to walk back out again. There was no honour to the trade any more. Now you had to be the right colour and creed for the area and needed the right references. It also seemed you needed to know several made-up languages just to state your case. And after all that the bastards were still likely to attempt to knife you. It had become more like a bloody job interview than a bit of horse-trading to get rid of an irritation in your life. If you failed your interview you got a beating or worse. Maybe Lord Sugar could liven up his show with something similar now we're all a little tired of the same old scenario each series. Wouldn't it be more inspiring if being fired actually meant what it said? Don't you think it would be really great motivation for the contestants and cut down on the whingeing and hissy fits?

Bob had risked beatings for the cause revisiting places that once guaranteed someone who knew someone. The places and people he had known had all changed and gone, changed beyond recognition or disappeared completely, overgrown by urban sprawl. Now trendy little three-storey places and quaint little bungalows with a Lexus, BMW, Merc or Porsche proudly displayed in their one designated parking space had replaced what had been the familiar and friendly in a past life. The pubs and clubs where he might have found what he was looking for had now turned in to Harvesters and the like with 'real' open gas fires and all that crap.

It had been sad to see that one of his favourite early locals, had succumbed in this way. It had been called The Trappers and had been hidden away in the heart of the Malvern Hills. It had boasted primed bear traps under every pool table and was a safe haven for all the local bikers for miles around, a sort of common sacred ground where all were free to hang out and individual gangs and groups had no preference over any other. There was very little trouble, the bikers appreciative of its unique position in their lives. Somewhere that was a nice ride away, and you were left alone when you got there.

It was not up-market in any way, with its sawdust-covered stone floor and old mismatched tables and chairs painted black. Apart from the bear traps, there were shelves of empty bottles as decoration and loads of sharp, pointy farm machinery – donated knowingly or unknowingly by the local farmers – hanging from the ceilings or resting between the empty bottles. With all the potential for harm, no-one had ever gotten seriously hurt inside the bars for as long as Bob could remember. It had been years ago now and maybe something had kicked off and destruction and mayhem had ensued and the place had been closed. The health and safety executives in their nice suits taking their chance.

When Bob pulled up early in his quest he saw a building standing there that looked nothing like the original. Gone were the bear traps, the bars and the purple haze, the snake bites and the petrol fumes. Instead of a piece of local history and folklore, a lifeless franchise pub had taken over the site. The only features that had stayed the same were the fantastic views and the nice drive up there. Bob had not even bothered to get out of his car. The thought of the local bar owner still being the same giant of a man covered in tats and road-rash but now reduced to wearing a formal bow tie and smart trousers had been too depressing to risk discovering.

Bob needed to do something. It had been time to think laterally and 'outside the box' or whatever the saying was that month. All these sayings used by people who can't have ideas of their own and have to just wait around and steal someone else's and then copy the ideas parrot-fashion to try and gain 'street cred'. The one Bob had always hated the most was 'Never assume, because it makes an ASS out of U and ME'. It had been a favourite of one of his more moronic bosses, used daily even though the job would never have been workable unless a large degree of assuming took place. Just think about the saying for a minute. In everyday life you spend most of your time assuming. You would never function otherwise. You always assume the brakes on the family car will work when you need them. You assume the lift isn't going to plunge out of control downwards as soon as you step inside and take you to your death. You assume the psycho flipping your burgers hasn't snapped and there isn't rat poison all over your lunch. Even with a simple cup of tea at home you assume the handle is going to do the job it is supposed to and is not going to fail and send scalding liquid into your crotch.

Time to move on. Hawkken has been mentioned before and had once been a friend of Bob's and Deb's. He was from Finland and had been able to boast the true Hollywood Viking look: tall with long blond hair and all that. Why as a middle-aged man he thought a ponytail was sexy, no-one knew. It had not been that successful even when he was young, and now he was in his fifties it was still wrong. There had been lots of speculation over the years that he could now unclip it when it was time for bed. Everyone was ready to give him a little ribbing about it but none were brave enough to walk up and give the offending hair-do a good yank to find out, so the mystery continued.

He had been married when he joined the company but had left his wife when their marriage had not produced any offspring and he had become richer and had fancied someone younger to play with. You could have given him the benefit of the doubt about wanting a family and settling down if he hadn't chosen Pattaya in Thailand and a procession of very young Thai ladies in his search for a prospective Mrs Hawkken Mark Two. As far as Bob knew he still had not found Miss Right even though every time he was in Thailand Hawkken's search took him out every night scouring the night clubs and bars only to move on as the Miss of the previous night faded away and the search for perfection continued.

Thanks to all Deb's help, Hawkken was rich enough to split his time equally between his work in Finland and his search for happiness in Thailand. It had been a shame and a bit of a shock when he wouldn't even consider helping Deb when everything was going up in smoke around her. He had known the truth for a long time and by the end had been a big enough part of the company to have a say in the final outcome but he had been another who had thought more about his own wealth than thanking and supporting a friend in need. Another one who had conveniently forgotten who had made him rich and protected his interests in the first place ...?

* * *

Pattaya! Not everyone's cup of tea. Full of neon, sexy girls, loud music and cheap booze. This former Vietnam War, R 'n' R party town by the sea for the American servicemen who had been out there was showing no real intention of growing up or changing even now. Loud, proud and outrageously sexy, it is too expensive to get out there to attract the 'Costa yob' set so there is no trouble and no violence. You are probably safer out there than walking down dark alleyways and lonely car parks at home. It is all about customer service, no pun intended; if there was any trouble at all, the customers and tourists would simply not come.

It is a place where you can have one hell of a lot of fun with a capital 'F'. Hawkken's argument about it being just another seaside holiday resort was blown out of the water when there was bar after bar full of the sexiest, scantily-clad ladies you are ever going to see. It did, however, help a little to explain why the poor guy could not find his Miss Right; the guy was just spoilt for choice. For all those readers now tutting, grow up – the world is full of places like this and it is only the British who seem to have a problem with it.

OK, when the neon lights go on and the sun goes down it is for the more liberally minded and sexually liberated single older male. The place really comes alive after dark when the free clubs and nightclubs take over. Drinking, dancing and playing pool until the early hours were – still are – the norm. The seedier side of the place doesn't encroach too much unless you are one of the young (well, young at heart), free and single males who frequent the place. Then you are at the mercy of every girl around who is looking for a husband.

Bob had flown in alone this time from the UK via Dubai. He had finally made it through passport control in Bangkok airport. He had reconsidered his mission at least a hundred times as he stood waiting patiently in line for the nice man in uniform to call him forward and stamp his passport after the tedium of the long-haul flight. He had felt mildly turned-over by the local airport taxi service, but that is the fate of any tourist anywhere, and to be fair it still wasn't the extortionate prices he would have had to pay back home. Compared to those prices, £30 for a journey of almost two hours to Pattaya seemed very reasonable, even if it would only be £20 coming back the other way.

The taxi ride had been uneventful. The car's air-con had worked and he'd tried to snooze a little, not really to catch up on lost sleep but more so he didn't have to watch the scary traffic hurtling by. In every country the world over, the local drivers have their own views on what is considered as safe driving. After reviewing the evidence, Bob was pretty sure there was no such thing as a Thai highway code, or for that matter any restrictions on what or who can be carried in or on the back of a pick-up truck. Once his cabby had exhausted his limited knowledge of English football clubs, Bob was able to nod off and let the world go by, oblivious to the passing billboards, the roadside poverty and the palm trees, only regaining consciousness as they hit the bustle and traffic of Pattaya city.

He had been here several times to visit Hawkken with Deb and his family. Sometimes they had stayed with Hawkken in his condo in the centre of the city, and sometimes it had been a nice quiet hotel away from the hustle and bustle. Hawkken's place was very nice but it was essentially one extra-large bachelor pad and the neighbours and residents of the condominium all seemed in the same place with their own lives as Hawkken was with his. He did behave when they had been guests but Deb and Bob strongly suspected he was toning down his act for their innocent British morals. The amount of young and attractive Thai ladies they had seen leaving different apartments first thing in the morning when they themselves had been up early and going to use the swimming pool before the day became too hot or the pool too crowded, had been quite staggering.

As they had walked around the local streets doing the more normal, touristy things, there had always been an abundance of nice hotels and places advertising rooms available, even in high season, with access to swimming pools and all boasted air-conditioning. This time, Bob had not bothered booking long distance via the Internet. After listening to endless chatter from Hawkken and his crew of drinking buddies, it had become apparent that the usual passport and credit card formalities were dispensed with if you paid upfront and in cash. Bob had not given himself long to accomplish what he hoped to do, so he could not see himself in need of a swimming pool, but a working air-con was essential.

He paid for the taxi and set off looking for a room. After the dream and a few days thinking it over, he had made a commitment to put things right. He had spent weeks risking life and possible incarceration trying to get his plan realised back in the UK and a few minor scuffles and threats had convinced him to extend his search elsewhere. There could be better places in the world to try but here at least he knew a few faces and with the lack of success so far it felt somehow more promising or less intimidating. He had got the cheapest flight he could, spending thirty hours on a trip that even with a stop-over to shop at Dubai normally took well under twenty. He had told Deb and her cousin he was working in Spain for a week, tarting up the holiday home of an old customer he had back in the UK. Now he was in Thailand in the sweltering heat and finding that poorly-made plans had unforeseen problems.

He had arrived a few days before the final of the worldwide Ladyboy beauty pageant that was held annually in Pattaya. It had started off a bit like the American baseball world series and all the contestants were from the host country, but unlike the baseball, the Ladyboy pageant could now boast competitors from all over the world. Pattaya is swamped with tourists for two weeks before the main event, all hoping to have a chance to see and meet the Ladyboys as they promoted the show.

After two hours, Bob finally found a hotel. He had had many offers for rooms that he could rent by the hour but he had quickly passed them over. He was now sat in a slightly unnerving room in an area not far from the gay quarter of Pattaya. There were many mirrors all over the walls, a king-sized bed and disco lights that could be set on multiple settings, 'off' being the last button he managed to find. The large sunken bath was a blessing, baths of any kind being rare in most hotels, which favoured large showers. The mirrored walls and disco lights also crept into the bathroom. Bob could see it could have possibilities but a fully mirrored bathroom lost some of the fun element when you were sitting on the loo and you could see yourself from every angle. Back in the main room there was a raised platform and pole for pole dancing, a leather net contraption hanging from the ceiling that if you took time to read the literature provided, claimed to be a 'love swing'. There was also a very large television and once you had scrolled past the twenty or so porn channels you could find the more normal sports and news programmes. It would not have been Bob's first choice but on the up-side he was sure no one would ever think to look here if they were trying to find him, and reception had been very helpful and given him a big discount on the room for cash, so he guessed he could class it as a result. The air-con worked and there was a kettle and coffee. There was even room service if you were brave enough to order something off a menu written in Thai with food not being the only thing that might be on the list? It would do.

When Bob had visited Hawkken before, he had always taken the guy's protests about the bad publicity the place got and Hawkken being here for the family beaches with a pinch of salt. True, Hawkken always signed every petition going that claimed it was trying to clean the place up and make it respectable. Somehow, though, when night came and the neon went on, the big Finn always managed to end up in Walking Street to witness first-hand all that was supposedly in need of being cleaned up and would enjoy himself in one of the world's sexiest party streets. The joy of being rich and single?

Bob had witnessed Hawkken immersing himself in the lifestyle he claimed he had no interest in. Hawkken's side-kick and wingman was Trevor, an English guy who helped run the Finnish Company for Hawkken, and his boss took it upon himself on a regular basis to torment the weedy little guy. When they had all been there together, Bob had witnessed some of Trevor's trials and tribulations.

Putting Hawkken's dubious double-standards to one side, one night they had all been in a bar deep in the heart of Walking Street, supposedly because it had cheap booze and a good pool table. Hawkken had taken great delight in paying for some of the working girls to flaunt their wares at his poor unfortunate wingman. Trevor was middle-class and painfully shy about all things sexual. He had visited one of the company conferences in the UK with Hawkken and the factory girls had set about him like a pack of rabid she-wolves. It could have had something to do with the money his boss was spending on drinks for the girls, and or the fact he was telling all the ladies Trevor was a thirty-five-year-old virgin. There was 'blood in the water' and Trevor spent most of the night in hiding.

Bob had seen Trevor chat up numerous girls, becoming their friend for life in seconds because he was a true listener – but as soon as the question of sex raised its ugly head he was always off and running in the opposite direction. Still, Hawkken took great delight in trying to procure girls for his employee and then sitting back and watching the ensuing debacle, their poor mutual acquaintance reacting like someone had thrown a burning witch into his lap. A humiliation, if the rumours were correct, Hawkken repeated when they were out and about across Europe at work or on a jolly. It had even gained 'tradition' status if you listened to some of the group's closest friends. The only comment Bob could make was that it was easy money for the girls, once they got past the shock of rejection.

Back to the action. The only reason Bob was here was that Hawkken had inadvertently introduced him to places and people where for financial reward anything can be found or done. When Hawkken was in the country one of his favourite watering holes was a bar just off Walking Street, with a couple of pool tables, lots of loud music and the obligatory gorgeous girls. Bob was once told prostitution was illegal in Thailand and the bar had a sign stating that fact, right next to the 'bar fine' sign. (That's the commission taken by the bar from customers wanting to take the girls off-site for the evening.)

Sadly, and to his shame, Bob had asked on his first visit why the bar would have a fixed penalty for rowdy customers likely to cause trouble or damage the place. Once everyone had stopped laughing and the sign had been explained and a wave of embarrassment had washed over him, Bob accepted it as the way of life. There weren't places like this in the sticks in the heart of the Midlands, or at least not that he knew of. Different country, different culture, different set of rules.

Trying to describe the place back home to someone would make the place sound seedy but it is just a different way of life. If you want to, you can sit in a bar as a couple or group and it's just a good quality pool bar with loud music and good-looking waitresses. Every bar or club has its girls but if you don't want to pay, you don't have to play. As part of a group, Bob had spent nights taking on the girls at pool, playing for vodka or tequila shots. They always graciously let the punters win, even when they know you are totally hammered on the cheap booze and it is just good clean fun.

The bar is run by 'The Tsar' and she or he, whichever way you look at it, is the most gorgeous ladyboy you will ever see. Think Jerry Hall on a 'Roxy Music' album cover and you are about halfway there. Hawkken had introduced The Tsar to Bob and Deb several years earlier and over the few holidays they had spent in Thailand they had become sort of friends. Not really Christmas card list buddies but if they were in town on holiday and didn't visit, there was hell to pay. The Tsar always thought it fantastic that Bob and Deb had been together and in love for so long. From high school sweethearts and now into their fifties and still at it without the need of the little blue pill ... When all you see night after night is a procession of one-night stands wandering in and out of the bar, or older men looking to replace old wives with much younger versions to boost their flagging libidos, Bob and Deb must make a nice change. One night when they had all been drinking and chatting, Bob had joked how their son complained bitterly all the way through his teens that he was the only kid in school who had only one set of parents and one set of Christmas presents, and sadly he wasn't far wrong.

Well, on occasion Hawkken had let it slip that The Tsar could get you absolutely anything you wanted with a little time and the right amount of cash, 'nudge, nudge, wink, wink', followed by the best Monty Python impersonation he could muster in his strong non-English accent. This reputation was what Bob was hoping she could live up to.

So here Bob was in Thailand. He had taken the chance to get a few hours' sleep, because who knew when he would get the chance again? He had not rushed to get out on the town once he had found a room because the person he wanted to see would not be up much before 6 p.m., and definitely would not be starting work until at least 8 p.m., and that was more likely to be closer to 10 p.m., well after dark and when the fun had just started to warm up.

Bob showered and spruced up a little at the hotel, choosing to walk to the bar through the crowds rather than to sit in one of the local taxis inching forward because of the congestion already building as tourists flocked to the central hub of nightlife in the area. The Street would be subdued this early in the evening but the excitement and energy would build as 10 p.m. passed, reaching a crescendo in the early hours. Bob's plan was to arrive unfashionably early so he would have the bar to himself and maybe a chance to catch The Tsar on her own, or with only a few girls working the early part of the shift before the evening really got started.

Bob entered the neon, the glamour and the glitz of the street, thinking what a great anthem T. Rex's 'Dandy in the Underworld' would be for the place. At this time of night, all the wannabe bands were playing in the bars. The better bands would kick into life much later in the evening when the crowds had swollen and the party was in full swing. The transformation of the place was already amazing. You walked in the same place in the day and almost everywhere was closed. There would be people cleaning up and you could see the spaghetti that masqueraded as electrical wiring, linking all the signs hanging above your head – you were just stunned that any of it ever worked. At night you could not see past the lights, everything hidden behind the glare, just like the place itself.

Bob approached the bar, knowing he would have to be subtle, not just walk up and ask directions to the local hit man. It wasn't a supermarket back home with millions of little helpers ready to take you to what you want because the powers that be have moved it for the tenth time this month playing supermarket hide and seek. He could not see himself going, 'Oh! By the way, do you know anyone who will come to England and kill someone for me, please?'

Hawkken, if Bob's information was correct, was taking time

off to actually do a little work back in Finland so there was no real chance of meeting anyone he didn't want to meet. He joined the crowd that would later become a throng of tourists and sexy locals until he reached the bar he was aiming for. One last deep breath and he stepped across the threshold. The place was comfortably and reassuringly the same. He took a seat at the bar and ordered a drink for himself from the new face now serving the drinks behind the counter. Soon there were girls milling about there he recognised from previous nights out with Deb, Hawkken and his entourage. (Note to anyone wanting a PA: Bob knew what these girls sometimes had to do for a living and how many people must come through the bar each year, but he was still amazed when they could remember his name, his favourite drink, ask how his wife was and the multitude of other trivia they could recall specifically about people. He always found it incredibly impressive and much better than many of the PAs he had encountered back in the UK.)

A few other customers had entered and most of the girls had departed to do their jobs and it wasn't long until The Tsar glided in. She was always glamorous and stunning and Bob could never understand why she hadn't snagged her Mr Right and left for what most people would consider a better life. Maybe that was the curse of the Ladyboy … they only ever appear at their best in their natural environment? She was the perfect hostess and took time to meet and greet everyone in the bar and have a few friendly words with each girl. Bob was at the far end, and she worked her way over. They greeted as friends and she made small talk and asked how everyone was. She seemed genuinely to like them both as a couple and was disappointed Deb hadn't made the trip this time. Of course he knew it was more likely that she was coming over to see if he was alone tonight and looking to become a customer of one of the girls.

Bob confessed to being there only for a drink and a game of pool. The Tsar could leave if she wanted to but her long, sexy legs and the masses of long blonde hair stayed perched on the bar stool next to him and they chatted and drank. He knew the hair was dyed but the effect was sensational anyway. Eventually, Bob summoned up the courage to turn the conversation in the direction that he wanted. The drinks kept coming and he spilled the beans about what had happened to his wife and how badly she had been treated by the company. When you can get a Thai Ladyboy Madame to be genuinely disgusted about what the company had done to Deb it showed how low these parasites had gone and how far they had crossed over the line in everyone's eyes.

The night was creeping on and Bob had now had quite a lot of alcohol in a short space of time. He was, however, trying to act a little drunker than he actually was. Despite a few quick trips away to take care of her business, The Tsar had stayed chatting to him in their private little corner of the bar. He wasn't sure but the girls and the tourists seemed to be giving them space – or maybe it was just the alcohol gently warping the world to how he wanted it. Bob decided with all the background noise and loud music it was time to make a move.

He leaned forward and a little closer to his hostess. He took her beautifully manicured hand and started to slur a little tearfully as he looked deep into her incredibly sexy eyes. 'If I could find someone to kill the fucking bitch doing this to my wife, I would pay them to come to England and do the job.' The expletives were for effect. In all the time he had known The Tsar he had never felt the need to swear in front of her or any of her girls.

He hoped he had pricked her business instincts and it would bear fruit, but with his drunken act he had left himself a bit of plausible deniability so he could claim it was the drink talking if he needed to. With a grand gesture and a slight sway as he got off the bar stool he announced that he was off to play a few games of pool with the girls and sober up a little. He kissed the Tsar's hand. 'Thanks for listening. I know you didn't really have to.' All he got was a serene smile as he started off towards the pool tables. He knew she was an expert pool player but it was a busy night so she would not join him even if he asked, her prowess reserved for the few quiet nights when there were only friends in the bar. It would also give her time to think about what he had said and whether or not she could help with a solution.

Two hours later and he still hadn't lost a game to any of the girls. He had sobered up a lot and was now at the stage where he was trying to leave his opponent's pool balls over pockets, so they couldn't make out they were missing by accident. No one noticed the bizarre game they were playing. It wasn't as if they didn't end up all drinking shots at the end any way. He smiled to himself as he listened to the music and recognised a CD he made for the bar a few visits ago. It had a lot of tongue-in-cheek titles that he hoped someone might see the funny side of if they were actually listening to the music. The likes of Deep Purple with 'Strange Kind of Woman', Whitesnake's 'Rock 'n' Roll Women' and Ted Nugent blasting out 'Cat Scratch Fever' were all taking their turn blasting away in the background. Outside there would be many other bars with Thai bands playing live homage to rock superstars to entertain the masses.

Bob decided it was time to settle up his bar tab and wandered over to where The Tsar was now sitting on the other side of the bar. He apologised for dumping all his troubles on her earlier in the evening and asked her to come to dinner so he could make it up to her. It was still early by Walking Street standards and she would be there for hours yet, so at some stage she would have to slip away to get something to eat.

He knew that when she had been invited to join one of Hawkken's group get-togethers, the standard of the food and service had gone through the roof and at every restaurant the best tables were suddenly free and available. The Tsar had even joined Bob and Deb when Hawkken called off one time after he and the latest applicant for the vacant Mrs H's job went down with something nasty or they had found something more interesting to do.

They had had a great time, international businesswoman and international bordello owner, chatting away about business. Bob had just sat back, enjoyed the view and listened to all the stories and comparisons. He had been surprised by how much both businesses had in common. Obviously he now knew there was a lot more slime and dishonesty in the international business sector, but at the time the evening had been very entertaining.

As a couple, it had been one big holiday every two or three years for Bob and Deb. They could have done the usual places twice a year but it was each to their own and their preference was the more unusual and out of the way. Of course with Deb's work commitments they knew holidays would always take second place. On their travels they had made friends wherever they had travelled to and could boast friends who lived in jungles and struggled to make a living, where they would sit all night telling stories and eating local grilled bugs. To friends at the other end of the spectrum like a business manager for one of the posh hotels in the 'Bund' in Shanghai, where they had ended a holiday one year before flying back home. They all finished up on the balcony of the 'in' place overlooking the river and drinking drinks that were way too expensive and were nearly at a price where you would need to re-mortgage your house to buy a round. But you only get to visit those sorts of places once in your lifetime, unless you are very lucky. Bob's outlook and advice after his experiences of the last few years would be if you get the chance, do it and live for the moment, because you never know when or if you will get the chance again.

The logic of Bob's dinner argument to the super-sexy bar owner had been sound and he and The Tsar set off in search of an evening meal. Of course, she got them both into a fantastic restaurant with great food and great service. Bob had a few colourful stories and at fifty-five he had seen enough interesting places and done enough interesting things to keep a conversation moving on if need be. The Tsar on the other hand had stories that would make your hair turn white. They took it in turns with their monologues and a pleasant evening was had by both of them.

Bob had never been one to find amusement in giving a puppy a toffee for entertainment's sake and letting the poor dumb animal writhe about once it got the toffee stuck to the roof of its mouth. Also when he was abroad he respected the cultures, laws and beliefs of the local people, even if he did not entirely agree. It was their country and their lives and it was up to them and the differences across the globe were what made travelling fun. Only the likes of Tony Blair would want a one-tone monochrome world, just like he wanted for Europe. But on your travels there are the Yanks – and suddenly everyone wishes they had a toffee they could pass on.

Bob had made friends with people of many colours, creeds and of varying wealth but he could never bring himself to totally embrace the Americans. He and The Tsar had come to the end of their meal and were just enjoying the peace and calm before she had to go back to work. Just relaxing and not really in any rush to move on. Then the invasion started and a large party of Americans arrived as their 'see the real world by bus' tour had stopped for the night in Pattaya. Unfortunately the only tables that were free were close to where Bob and his guest were sitting. Soon they were almost surrounded by ageing, sixty-plus Americans. It had taken a while to get the organising and fretting about who sits next to who over with, but finally they had all sat down.

In that perfect twenty-twenty hindsight people have after the fact, Bob knew they should have got up as soon as the bus pulled up and started to unload. The trouble had been that he had not paid the bill and they both had only just started extra-large expensive brandies and it had seemed a waste to rush them.

Their conversation had been put on hold and they both now sat transfixed. As one, the seated Yanks produced antiseptic wet wipes and antiseptic hand creams from various pockets and bags and proceeded, as one, to wipe and polish everything that they might come into contact with. Bob and The Tsar sat there in silence clutching their very strong drinks and watching in amazement at the ongoing performance. After all had been cleansed, on and around the tables the waiters arrived and brought the menus which were all inspected and also cleaned before viewing, and ordering took place. Next the waiters brought the appropriate cutlery and glasses to match the orders. Even as these things were placed on the tables, sterilised hands snatched them up and proceeded to disinfect all that was laid before them. Cutlery wipe, wipe. Glasses wipe, wipe. Side plates wipe, wipe. It was synchronised health and safety eating-out to Olympic standard. The group's actions would have been bizarre in most places but they were sitting in what would have been a five-star establishment back in England. The staff were impeccable and Bob was pretty sure the cutlery was fresh from the steam cleaner.

Though their conversation had been entertaining, this phenomenon had taken over. It was like having the television on when you have a few friends around and it sits there in the corner and starts to become the focal point and the talking stops. When their eyes could be drawn away from the Americans for a second or two it was clear most of the other people dining there were having the same sort of reaction to the late arrivals. Meals and conversations had all been put on hold.

Bob knew his guest didn't really like the Americans that much. Out of all the nationalities that visited this part of the world the Yanks on the whole did not treat the girls that well. They were always trying to get out of paying. Somehow the men seemed to think they were still owed something for Vietnam. Silly boys, let it drop – it was a different century and it is the wrong fucking country anyway.

Bob and The Tsar both sat mesmerised and, like any occasion when you should absolutely not giggle, they lasted until they glanced at each other. Then it was too late. Luckily only the closest couple cottoned on that the two of them were finding the group's actions ... shall we say intriguing? The lady of the couple leant over towards them and Bob would have to admit that he had been expecting an ear bending and rightly so, after acting like a drunken schoolboy. What he got (in the condescending way only the Yanks seem to have mastered and can get away with) was a 'Well you have to be careful in these Third World countries. They still have the plague, you know, and there is no boiling water to sterilise anything.'

At this point Bob's eyes were watering with the effort of trying to keep a straight face. He called on the years of training way back from when he was at school, relying on the old tricks and refusing to turn and look at his beautiful co-conspirator. All around was the evidence to confirm they were all in a five star restaurant. There were plush fittings, fancy décor, electric lights and even running water. He had just eaten a fantastic meal accompanied by expensive wine and followed by brandies that would cost a local farmer a month's wages. He was aware that even though he had offered to pay for these luxuries earlier, being a friend of The Tsar would mean that when he attempted to pay later, more likely than not he would be told 'That's all right, sir, it has been taken care of.' Maybe it was the reward for treating The Tsar like a person and not attempting to judge what he had no knowledge of. Still, this part of the Third World seemed very comfortable.

Well, he could not stand the absurdity of the whole situation any longer and just like being back at school, it only took a glance in the wrong direction and his will-power dissipated into fits of laughter. The Tsar burst out laughing, too. She was gorgeous, glamorous and more graceful than most women but she was still a Ladyboy and the laugh was just a tad too deep for the glamorous, sexy female vision sat there. Bob saw the penny start to roll in the mind of the dear old American lady. It was rolling but hadn't dropped, so he quickly and graciously apologised for their childish, if harmless behaviour, trying to step in and railroad the conversation back towards safer ground.

'Well, what do you all do out in the jungle and places like that? I am sure your trip must have taken you to more wild and out-of-the-way places than central Pattaya city.' He was pinched in the soft midriff of his aging body by The Tsar. It is only the Yanks who don't get sarcasm. The rest of the party seemed deep in their own private conversations.

'We all have our regimes and stick to them.'

'OK, I understand that a few precautions are prudent and I will confess to checking the caps on bottled water so I can make sure it is not old bottles topped up with tap water,' says Bob. 'But when you are out in the cafes and bars what do you drink? Personally I would drink bottled beer in the out-of-the-way places and leave the water well alone.'

'Ah yes – but you are English (good, she didn't guess Australian) and you are all heavy drinkers, even in your own country. We would not drink alcohol in this climate, it's not good for the body. It affects your metabolism, you know.'

Bob was stunned; the English heavy drinkers? Where did she get that from? 'OK, you drink soft drinks or juices with lots and lots of ice in to keep you cool, that's very sensible.' The American agrees with the statement. The Tsar is looking at Bob with a 'Why are you having this conversation' type of look?

Bob continued. 'I think I will stick to my fermented, sterile and fully processed beer and alcohol if you don't mind. I am not being funny but these people all over the Third World are not going to be making ice for your drinks out of expensive bottled water, are they?' There is a blank stare. Bob leans forward. 'Where do you think they get the ice from?'

He thought the conversation was just between the two tables and the little bombshell was dropped as a sort of slow-burn question he could leave the Yanks to mull over and would gently spread around the group like a toffee they all could chew over. The thought that he was doing his little bit to get the Yanks to 'chew the toffee' and think that they were all at risk drinking contaminated, filth-filled drinks by the gallon would give him a mild sense of wellbeing for the rest of the night. But he had not been prepared for the synchronised gasping for air from all the eavesdropping fellow American travellers.

He felt a little apologetic later towards the trusting American tourists who he might now have turned into budding alcoholics, thanks to those one or two small sentences. But they were American and they were all bloody hypochondriacs anyway. They should get out and crunch on a few deep-fried bugs, like the rest of us tourists, and get to know a few locals. It had been fun though to see them all pick up their drinks (as one) and hold them up to the lights as they contemplated the ice statement.

He also felt he was doing the Third World a disservice. He knew you could see the ice being delivered daily by the bag load to most of the bars, clubs and restaurants and he was sure it was all manufactured in perfectly clean and sanitised factories somewhere. But if you can't mess with the Yanks, life just isn't worth living, is it?

With a quick smile from The Tsar, they took the opportunity and the break in conversation to get up to leave. Bob was satisfied he had fielded the ladyboy issue well and what the Yanks didn't know would not hurt them or cause grief for anyone else. Unfortunately, that particular penny had still been rolling and as they emerged from the American enclave it had finally chosen that moment to drop.

'Oh my God, they are perverts. That's ... that's a ladyboy.'

Well, a stunning ladyboy, or a ladyboy who is probably worth more than all of them put together would have been a more accurate statement. There were nervous and interested looks all around from the staff and the rest of the customers, and what conversations had restarted all hushed up to see what would happen next.

Nothing, not a missed step of the shapely legs on the extra high heels. Not one withering look. Just a quiet couple of words to the owner under her breath as they left. There was one rule of thumb Bob would say was valid anywhere in the world: you do not upset anyone who cooks or serves your food. In this case he would also have liked to add ‘or anyone who can influence the people who cook or serve the food’. People joke about ‘Chef’s special sauce’ but Bob thought that he would not have anything off the dessert menu that night if he had been one of the Yanks. He might have even skipped dinner altogether.

There must be a few grumpy and impolite people who get nasty rashes, upset stomachs and irritations and have no clue how they picked them up. That was one urban myth Bob didn’t want to put to the test, but it might be an episode of ‘Mythbusters’ worth watching.

If there had have been loud music playing as they made their entrance they would have entered the restaurant to Aerosmith and ‘Walk This Way’ but they would have left to Green Day’s ‘American Idiot’.

They walked back through the increasingly loud music and the vibrant heaving masses who had now found their way to this part of Pattaya. When Bob and The Tsar got back to the bar they found it packed and heaving. The staff were coping well and The Tsar was a gracious enough host to share a night-cap before Bob called it a night and headed back to the relative peace and quiet of his hotel room.

Just before he downed the last mouthful of his drink, he laughed a little, stared again into those deep sexy pools of eyes and became deadly serious. ‘I am not proud of how I feel but I really would pay to get those bastards killed.’

With that he downed what was left of the drink and departed, waving at the people he knew with a shout of ‘See you all again soon’. He headed out onto the street, dodging a couple of scantily-clad ladies half carrying their prey back to their lair for the night. He did not know whether he had spread enough bait or even if he was fishing in the right pool. He would have to wait and see what happened tomorrow … or later that day as it was well past midnight and technically he was already on his second day. If nothing happened he still had several days left to try 'fishing' somewhere else.

He walked back to the hotel alone and deep in thought but on his brief travels two slogan-covered T-shirts were amusing and distracting enough to make him smile. The first was simple and to the point and tightly stretched across the surgically-enhanced chest on yet another gorgeous little thing walking along minding her own business. It read: 'WHITE GIRLS CAN'T HUMP'. The second was stretched across a slightly less attractive, barrel-shaped gentleman with a very long, almost white, unkempt mass of hair with a full beard to match. Day-Glo grubby Bermuda shorts with knee-length white socks, one of which was at half-mast and open-toed sandals, completed the picture. Plastered across the expanse of his chest was: 'YES I AM THE REAL FATHER FUCKING XMAS'. Well, Bob had been on a long flight and it had been a long day going into a long night; and Santa must have to holiday somewhere – so why not Pattaya?

He fought with the control to the lights in his room and finally managed to win, plunging the room and its mirrors into darkness. Even the noise from muffled cries and squeaking beds that seeped through the walls from the surrounding rooms could not stop him falling into a deep sleep, the couple of hours he had managed earlier not making up for the hours lost travelling cattle class on the plane to get here.

* * *

Bob was awakened later that day with a call from hotel reception to say that he had just had a message delivered. After his 'night before' he was a little bleary-eyed and could have probably used another couple of hours in bed asleep. Reception had offered to send the message up but he made the decision to get up and go downstairs and collect it himself as a gentle way of getting his day started.

He was handed a plain white envelope with his name on it.

He took the paper knife as it was offered by the receptionist, to open the envelope. Anywhere else in the world she would have been classed as attractive, even close to stunning, but around here she almost became average. He slit open the envelope and inside was a short note telling him that he was invited to a pool party come BBQ that night and that he would be picked up around seven. He had never seen The Tsar's handwriting and the note wasn't signed, but who else could the invitation be from? He spent or more accurately wasted the day channel surfing the sports channels on the TV until he was politely chucked out by room service so they could spruce the room up a bit. He departed the hotel for a little while and started to mooch around the market stalls that are jammed in and around any place a tourist might have to pass on their travels from hotel to beach or to bar or any combination of the three. 'Who needs pavements anyway?' seemed the locals' viewpoint.

He elected to have a beer and do a little people-watching from one of the many open-air bars that filled the spaces or competed for the spaces between market stalls. The beer was cold and the fans were on, creating a cool breeze every time they made a sweep in his direction. The bar had a short menu and he selected noodle and chicken thick soup with a large spoonful of dried chillies. Full English is obviously the king of breakfasts but noodle soup isn't that far behind, eaten in the right surroundings. His first night had been a pleasant evening socialising that hadn't ended until the early hours. Time was precious and he hoped that tonight's little gathering was going to somehow get the ball rolling. It would have been helpful if the note had been a bit more informative or he could have spoken to the person who had delivered it just to see if anything could have been gleaned from them. He was not completely sure what had been arranged on his behalf but his time was limited, so it would be on with the concrete Wellingtons and jump right in.

* * *

There are some countries where punctuality and being on time is important. Thailand isn't one of them and by the time his ride arrived about an hour and twenty minutes late he was hot, his deodorant was only barely working and he had been propositioned by several ladies and pretty boys misjudging his slightly nervous behaviour and his pacing in front of the hotel. He retired from the outside heat for enough time to grab a cool drink with lots of ice from the hotel bar living on the edge of health and safety and to hell with the Americans! But his ride was late, even by Thai standards. It was an observation that Bob could make from past visits that the Thai people are kind, courteous and helpful but have no sense of time at all. He is English, so this sort of thing niggled him a bit – god knows what it did to the Germans or Japanese, the Russians and the Scandinavians just moan and bitch all the time so you never know if their complaints are justified anyway.

He was on his second stint outside the hotel when a large 4x4 taxi pulled up. He was glad to see that in the back was one of The Tsar's girls and not a complete stranger – they had played pool together in the past. He was a little disappointed The Tsar hadn't come herself but he had taken up too much of her time already. At least he would know one person at this little get-together. His guide gave him no clue as to where they were going and said with a little shrug, 'It's just a party'.

After twenty or so terror-filled minutes trying to make up time, the driver started to slow to a more sensible pace. Bob's assumption about making up time was based on the zigging and zagging through the heavy traffic, followed by flying down back streets and even across what appeared to be wasteland at breakneck speed until they started to leave the city and head out into the countryside. The pretty little passenger at his side on the back seat was taking no notice and was texting away merrily oblivious to the passing dangers. Fields and palm trees took over from hotels and bars in the headlights of the taxi. Even the cars, scooters and overloaded pick-ups became fewer in number. Half an hour later they were on one of those British, expat type housing estates found all over the world. At least this one was a little up-market and none of the home owners had felt the need to put a tacky glass conservatory on the back or side of the house for when it dropped below thirty degrees. Yes, Bob had seen it and got the pictures to prove it, thanks to his travels. It wasn't hard to see why the Brits find it hard to get on with their foreign neighbours; they are all scared of us and think the Brits are bloody nuts.

These expats are a few British lads, a couple of Swedes, a guy from Finland who isn't any relation to Hawkken (the country isn't that small) and a German. There were a couple of Thai guys around, and not the pretty boy kind, plus several Thai ladies making up the numbers. Bob's escort for the night was called Na and he was introduced as her friend. They met the host and Bob was told a few names of the people there as they mingled. Na and Bob got on well enough and there was a lot of dancing in and around the pool as the party went on and the music blasted out. Attire of the day for the gentlemen was Bermuda shorts and flip flops with a T-shirt as an optional extra. Bob was a little overdressed in polo shirt and chinos, but he could live with that. Showing up in black bow tie and tuxedo would have been much worse – or going for the reverse and slouching in if everyone else had been dressed up to the nines. All the ladies were looking fabulous in clingy short dresses or hot pants and tight T-shirts. The food and drink were plentiful, it was a warm and pleasant night and everyone was friendly and chatty. It was a lot better than a distant party he was made to suffer through and can remember from way back in the mists of time.

As the night and party went on, Bob began to think he had misunderstood the invitation and became a little disappointed. Maybe The Tsar was just trying to cheer him up a little after his sad little performance the night before. Surely if things were more in line with the way he had been hoping the night would go, he would have been taken to a back room and 'shaken down' by now, just like in all the old Bond movies. Here there seemed to be no real villains going, 'I understand you want to do business, Mr Bob?' The only sign that these guys might be what he was looking for was that they all seem to be ex-military. They had that air about them ... not just a gang of lads who got 'Call of Duty 23' for Xmas.

The party was good and everyone was talkative. When they weren't dancing Na, who knew everyone, kept them mingling. As the evening went on, Bob confirmed his earlier suspicions that the lads were retired ex-military and now had various jobs such as tourist police which they were using to bulk out their pensions and retirement plans. Somehow the conversations revealed how much they actually got from their respective governments to spend on the good life and Bob was amazed. He had never made that much when he was working full time and he hadn't ever earned enough to be able to afford to put a pension away. All his and Deb's hopes had been tied up in the company and all the false promises and guarantees Summer had made. For all the good it would do them now.

Bob thought that some of the lads just needed their uniform fix now and again with the whole tourist police thing until one of them let slip that as tourist police they got a firearms' licence and could now legally carry and keep firearms as essential equipment and part of their working environment.

Despite their military backgrounds most had enough interesting stories not to have to visit the 'what I did in the war' type stories, unlike the squaddies who visited Bob's local back home. A couple of the lads here had left the Forces and gone into business and ended stitched up like Deb. A few had made investments back home that the botch-up brothers, Blair and Brown, had made absolutely worthless as they took it upon themselves to screw up the British economy for generations to come. The Scandinavians, the two Swedes and the guy from Finland were trying to find themselves or re-invent themselves and were creepily open about the amount of prescription drugs they were on to help them get over whatever it was they were trying to get over. Bob wasn't clear why they were in need of the drugs, especially because none of them had seen actual combat from all the teasing the other guys gave them.

Bob was glad he was English, and as such did not have to share such things with the rest of the class. Even if you are on happy pills, pills to help digestion, pills for blood pressure, pills to help your body detox and pills to get your dick hard you don't have to confess all and be happy about it. After meeting a few of our Viking friends thanks to Hawkken, Bob knew that a bottle of vodka a day before they actually started the serious drinking in the evening could also be added to the mix. It was no wonder they had to round the evening off with Viagra to get a stiffy – and they all put it down to stress?

Bob's advice to the three of them – had he been asked – would have been get rid of all the pills and cut down the booze and if they still needed pills to get it up with the good-looking girlfriends they had in Thailand it was time for the long walk off a short pier. The German was just a smug bastard who was trying to bonk himself to death, or that was his claim. The very thing he was trying to kill himself with was probably providing him with the exercise that was prolonging his stay on the planet and keeping him alive longer.

Later in the evening they all got a bit reflective on life. Bob gave the edited highlights of what had been done to his wife by so-called trusted friends when it was his turn to speak. All seemed able to joke about nearly being millionaires on paper at some time during their lives and having other people, or other people's decisions, spoil everything and the conversation dipped in to what would happen come the revolution. Bob had a pretty good idea where his ice pick would be heading.

He tried to introduce a little bit of 'bait' into the conversation and joked about incentives and bonuses he would be prepared to pay if he could find the right person to remove his little problem. No-one seemed to take him seriously, so he let them think it was just the drink talking again. Again it was all fairly light-hearted stuff anyway, and it soon degenerated into the group making up the stupidest ways to get rid of people they didn't like and deciding who would be on their Christmas 'hit' list. For Bob it was amusing but sadly the fun wasn't getting him any nearer his goal and a solution to his problem.

They seemed a good bunch of lads and it had been a nice time but it was creeping into the early hours again and he was ready to call it a night. He was obviously going to have to pursue a different way of finding the type of people he was hoping to talk to. The drinking and joking had slowed and the music had changed to something sexy and aimed to get the guests smooching on the dance floor, or wherever they were dancing. He had a good idea where the party was heading. The smooching was getting more intense and a couple of the guests were already skinny-dipping. Bob was ready to leave; he wasn't here for that sort of thing. He wasn't a prude and he had always had a great sex life with his wife but it was a private thing, whether it was at home, in the jungle, on the beach or anywhere else you could find a little time and privacy to yourselves. The thought of a bunch of old wrinklies getting their white bits out did not appeal, no matter how good looking their partners were.

All he could say was he had an E-type Jag at home with all the curves and though the new Jags were sleek and had lots of fancy bits. But if they were parked side by side and you had your choice most would take the E-type home.

As he contemplated the best way to bring up the subject of escape without offending anyone, he reflected on what he considered quite a good top five places where he and Deb had done the dirty deed. It was amazing what you could do and where you could go on a budget when you were young. Five, would be horse riding in the Pyrenees Mountains, the mountains and forests all to yourself and stopping when the mood took you. Great views, great wine and great sex rolling around naked in the wild flowers.

Four would be a snowmobile trip in Lapland. They had headed out into the wilderness alone and made love under the Northern Lights. It was hot and passionate until they had finished but at minus thirty or so, there was no hanging around for a cuddle or being romantic and loving.

Number three would be out in the wilds again. They had been near the Italian and Yugoslav border before Yugoslavia was bombed out and broken up. Bob couldn't remember the name of the river or the names of the landmarks near it. They had been hiking in the forest and had found a surreal turquoise river and had made their way down to its banks. The river obviously ran a lot deeper in the winter and much stronger. The water's edge was a mass of very large smooth and flattened white boulders large enough for the two of them to lie next to each other on. There had been no skinny dipping. The colour of the water had been amazing but completely unnatural looking. They had enjoyed the primeval view and the hot sun on their bodies and forgot about the water probably having the ability to melt your skin off.

Two … this one had cost money but had definitely been worth the trip. It had been their twentieth wedding anniversary and they had visited the Ice Hotel. Every year the hotel is reborn and rebuilt from ice which then melts away in the summer. The rooms are all themed and decorated with ice sculptures and you sleep on piles of reindeer skins. They had paid for the main room. It is the only one which has a lock and if you are going to the place to be romantic you don't need strangers walking in on you. It was a fantastic place and a sensational experience keeping warm under the covers. Sadly, some of the other guests seemed to miss the point.

Of course it had been way below freezing and a loo trip in the middle of the night meant getting fully dressed and walking through the ice corridors and passageways back to the main and more conventional part of the hotel and the toilet block. They had made the trip wrapped up in fur coats and bobble hats and very little else, not expecting to meet anyone and trying not to giggle all the way there. They found they needn't have been quite so quiet. Most of the guests seemed to have forsaken the ice to huddle together across the flat surfaces in reception and in the changing rooms. Those awake and unable to sleep were moaning to each other about the unbelievable cold. Who said romance is dead? Well, most of this lot for a start. Bob and Deb returned to their room and did the only thing they could think of to get warm, again ...

Finally, number one. They had taken a couple of weeks to backpack around Cambodia. Most of their budget had been the flight tickets to get there. They had wanted to visit the real world and not just the Disney version for those who can't travel without their burger, fries and a large fizzy drink, and had finished that holiday at Ankor Wat.

Bob didn't know whether it was the sheer magnitude of the place and its overpowering sense of history, whether it was how insignificant the place made you feel and how little you were compared to the universe, or if it was the beauty of it and standing there trying to take it all in. It had been an honour to visit the place before the inevitable march of capitalism and tourism took its toll.

The temples and grounds had been almost deserted no matter what time you visited. One of the mornings they had risen before dawn and had started to watch the sunrise over the pools of purple lilies in front of the main temple. They had chosen their vantage point for privacy and as the lilies opened they had taken the opportunity to experience something special and perfect ...

Bob had planned and wished for a second visit when they were older and this time he had promised himself that they would stay at the Raffles Hotel in Siem Reap.

The memories and reflections made Bob morbid – it was definitely time to leave. He didn't know how long he had not been paying attention, or if anyone had asked him anything during that time. His little friend was talking to one of the other ladies, so he guessed that he hadn't been missed. It had not been the money stolen or the non-existent promised lifestyle that truly mattered, it had been the person he had lost because of Summer's greed and jealousy. Summer had taken away Deb's lust and passion for life and sent him back an empty husk who was unrecognisable from the person he had spent his life in love with. Deb had given up and was fading away and he knew he would never see the real her again. That was what hurt the most and that was why they were all going to pay.

He was back in the party. The music was still soft and sensual but it felt like it should have been Alice Cooper blasting out 'Oh my liberated parents' as the golden oldies surrounding him gyrated. He speculated on whether any of them would really be capable of dancing themselves to death ...

He had tracked down the host in the hope of being able to get a taxi back to the hotel. Bob eventually relented and let his host give them a lift back. They were chatty as they returned a little more sedately than they had arrived. Bob even joked about his unfortunate experiences and how easy it had been for the company to get rid of Deb. The host and now driver twisted his story and joked of making everyone at his father's company into shareholders. How he could reduce their wages, now he knew that all the promises about pensions and health care and how they would all be rewarded in the end could be ignored if he got the right paperwork in place and a shifty enough lawyer.

'Don't forget you can put it all in writing – just don't write any of it in the Articles of Association, put a time limit on how long they need to work and then make sure you drive them out before they qualify for any of it.' Bob joked.

'Yeah, it could save my dad a fortune and I guess they will find out way too late to do anything about it.'

Bob shrugged. 'That's what happened to us. Make it sound convincing and promise those poor unfortunates everything. Pay as little as you can get away with. Find a way to make them that ill they can't work then fob them off before they have a chance to receive any of the benefits.' The host smiled and Bob knew that the guy was just kidding and trying to help make light of something no-one should have to suffer.

As they pulled up at the hotel he invited Bob out on a boy's day out in the jungle with the lads. Bob tried to make his excuses but the host was insistent. It had been a good night out and the host had been most generous to Bob – and it was only one day, after all.

Bob got out of the car. Na had fallen asleep and was curled up on the back seat. He went to wake her and was waved away. The host knew where she lived and he was going to drop her off on his way back. Bob gently closed the door so as not to disturb the sleeping beauty. He turned to go and the electric window slid down. 'Bob, bring strong walking boots, earplugs and the strongest mozzy spray you can get your hands on. We will pick you up at 6 a.m., you can sleep in the truck,' he said with a grin, and sped off. Bob looked at his watch. Fuck, it was 1.30 a.m. now. Bob climbed the hotel stairs to his room and said a silent prayer to any god that might be listening to give him strength, and then tried to get a few hours' sleep.

14

AKs and Housemaids

Well, as Bob feared, the over-drinking, over-eating and over-partying boys' club all had constitutions like rhinoceros-sized goats. His plan had been simple. Get up and show willing at the allotted time and when no one had shown up thirty minutes later he would return to his bed, take the phone off the hook and hang the 'Do not disturb' sign on his door, taking the advice of Bruno Mars and spending the day in bed. As he sleepily exited the hotel main entrance without having eaten breakfast, two very large and shiny off-roaders pulled up like an episode of The A-Team. His host from the night before was already waving to him to come and join the passengers of the first vehicle.

All the British lads were there, alive and kicking. In an attempt to appear conscious, Bob joked: 'Come on, lads, have some pride. All ex-British military and all that, shouldn't we be in Land Rovers?' He was soon put right as they exchanged pleasantries. One of these cheap and cheerful beasties cost about a third of the price of a basic Land Rover and they claimed to have absolutely everything fitted as standard. Which from what he could see, they did. 'If they break down after a few trips you can just dump them,' Bob's host joked.

Bob felt a bit under-dressed for the occasion as he settled into the very comfortable leather seat in his corner of the air-conditioned 4x4. There was an abundance of jungle camouflage around him, which didn't work in the confined space and plush interior of the off-roader but was certainly appropriate to where they were going. He had managed green cargo pants and a plain grey, rip-off Armani polo shirt. That was the best he could come up with in the circumstances. Good boots and mozzy spray had been no problem. The A- Team comparisons continued and he now felt like ... what was the guy's name? 'Face', that was it. He was the sharply-dressed one who never really fitted in but always came good in the end.

The little convoy proceeded for the next four hours in the general direction of Cambodia, he was told. Their driver, as with all Thai drivers, was oblivious to the basic road lane system. The faster you went, the closer to the front of the traffic you were and the more lanes you had to choose from. Undertaking was expected and overloading was compulsory – what are passengers for if not to sit on whatever you are carrying and stop it all falling off? The billboards flew by, as did shanty-type homes that littered the roadside once they were out of the major cities. There were occasional garages or factories, old cars and trucks that looked like they should be abandoned and scraped parked up in front of the buildings, not giving any real clue to whether the place was actually open and still in use.

Leaving the ever-deteriorating roads, they entered the thick green jungle and followed an almost non-existent dirt track, going truly off road for an hour or so.

The rest of the party seemed intent on restocking the alcohol level in their bloodstream and spent the trip continually raiding the large ice-box lodged between the two front seats. Bob nursed a couple of bottles of Bud and tried not to fall asleep. He took a wild guess that if he did succumb, waking up with a marker pen moustache would be the least of the pranks aimed at him. Also, Bob suspected that the day out, bearing in mind the camouflage and the ex-military background, would contain fire arms and the use of live ammunition. Bob felt it might be prudent to stay sober enough so when these pissheads started shooting, he could dive for cover. The local drivers ploughed on regardless and Bob started to fully appreciate the comfort of these large off-roaders even if he thought they wouldn't last long enough to get them back to civilisation again.

The driver had tuned the radio into a local station and it was blasting away. None of the others seemed bothered by it. Bob loved the culture, the country and the people but he could not get his head around the Thai pop charts. Like some old codger, if asked he would clearly state, 'It all sounds the same to me'. With the off-roading and the merry band of companions the only song he thought would do the picture justice would be the old punk version of 'Nelly the Elephant'. Oh god, I must be really, really tired, he thought.

As they got deeper into the jungle, Bob's host explained that they were heading for a shack owned by the father-in-law of one of the other lads and they were following the road up to the shack where they could all let off a little steam. The host had turned and talked to Bob as though they were parked up in a service station. Bob now felt queasy from watching the head in front of him bounce and thrash across his eyeline as it spoke at him. If the positions had been reversed and he had been the one travelling backwards and being bounced around like a thong in a tumble dryer he was sure he would have puked.

All this new information had all been passed on with a slightly insane looking grin plastered across the host's face. Up until then Bob had been feeling comfortable with this little band. Now after the grin he was starting to think more *Deliverance* and Burt Reynolds.

OK, shack in the woods was the description. So, with what you can buy out here for your cash Bob jumped to the conclusion that it was going to be some kind of luxury pad and they were doing the off-road bit just for his benefit and taking the back way in. Wrong! Shack this time meant shack. All dirt, rust and rotting timber in the middle of the jungle. One assumption too many and the Deliverance nightmares were getting stronger.

There were a few Thai men of varying ages resting about the

rickety building but as the white boys all bailed out of the 4×4s everyone got animated and greetings were exchanged. The 4×4s were quickly unloaded. Bob noticed a few boxes being squirrelled away into the shack; the rest were spread amongst the locals to carry and they 'broke camp' almost immediately and headed off into the jungle. With all that was going on and could be about to happen, Bob was happy the mozzy spray seems to be working. One more blast for good measure. He was keeping to the background but with an eye on his host, hoping to catch any sort of prompts that might get sent his way.

As yet there had been no sign of anything lethal, just bottles of booze and lots of food ready to be cooked and the slightly swaying little band appearing to know where they were going. To be fair they only travelled about a thousand yards down a track even Bob could follow. Then they emerged into what would be lovingly described by these guys as a natural firing range supplied by Mother Nature herself. There was an area about one hundred and fifty yards long by thirty yards wide of clear space, with a forty-foot high rock wall running all the way along the left side and across the bottom of the clearing. The cliff tapered inwards from about fifteen feet high to the floor. Anything fired at targets set up there would ricochet harmlessly down into the leafy soil. To the right there was a sheer drop-off disappearing about a hundred feet down into the top of the jungle below. Bob had felt they were climbing but he hadn't expected to be this high up. Someone had rigged up a pulley system that ran the long length of the space where the targets could be set, retrieved and replaced without too much effort. Cross-ways there were what seemed to be railway sleepers planted upright in the ground near the rock wall, and pointing out across the jungle below were a couple of clay pigeon traps. As you came into the space there was a large shed half hidden in the tree line and two halved steel drums that had been turned into improvised BBQs.

The German patted Bob on the back as he passed, said

'Welcome to paradise' and went to join his friends. As everyone milled about doing what they were doing, Bob ventured out to the edge of the drop-off.

'You don't get views like that in north Brum, do you?' asked one of the English lads, emphasising his observations with a firm and enthusiastic slap across Bob's back that nearly sent him over the edge. Once he had regained his balance Bob nodded in agreement and stood there just taking in the spectacular view. From their vantage point there was a panorama of what looked like pristine forest stretching out in every direction in front of them.

His inner peace was broken as someone opened the shed door and its rusting hinges squealed. He was alone on the edge of the drop. He couldn't recall the English guy going but he turned and saw that everyone was now congregating around the shed, so he followed suit and wandered across to join the group.

With a grin that reminded Bob of Mr Travolta just before he started killing everything in sight as he played the bad guy in another blockbuster, the host theatrically pulled back a large tarpaulin to reveal a selection of small arms: several pistols and revolvers and the like. Another tarpaulin and a bigger gun rack this time. Here there were a couple of over-under shotguns, an AK47 and two smaller machine guns Bob with his limited knowledge could not put a name to. Bob guessed he should have paid more attention at 'Rambo' class.

With the continuous over-drinking he had got to the point where he was beginning to re-evaluate the guys and knock them back to pissheads who had not really seen any sort of combat. But the efficiency and skill they now showed as they inspected, cleaned and loaded the weapons on show meant that his first assessment could still stand good and they had been the real McCoy sometime in their lives. While Bob was watching, one of the Swedes came over and explained the ritual was because the Thais don't keep things that clean and the weapons were mostly ex-Vietnam and Cambodian military stock, all in good condition and good working order but a little old and in need of tender loving care to keep things working. Just like him and his friends, he joked. A Swede with a sense of humour? That's unusual, thought Bob.

Once the guns had been cleaned and loaded and lots of spare ammo had been distributed, the Thai whisky did the rounds and the guys set about blasting away at the targets the locals had set up for them. Bob went to the clay traps with three of the lads. He'd shot clays before and had even fired a few rounds from similar handguns to those on offer, at an open day back in the UK at a local army training centre. He knew the mechanics of the job but that did not mean that he could hit anything he was aiming at.

A couple of Thai lads took control of the traps and started firing clays out into space for the boys to blast away at. First up were two of the UK contingent, not even missing when they each started showboating a little and firing one-handed as they nursed a bottle of whisky with the other hand. Apart from the German, all the Caucasian lads were thirty to fifty kilos heavier than their ideal weight and that was being polite. Also they were a lot older than Bob, or at least looked a great deal older. They had partied into the early hours and only had a small amount of sleep at best, if they had any at all. They started drinking again as soon as it was light so should be at the least merry, if not pissed out of their tree, but every target and every clay Bob could see being shot at was being hit, and in its own way that was impressive. He watched engrossed as the friendly competition gained momentum. Eventually it was his turn up with the shotguns. He hit more clays than he missed and that was a personal success. It didn't stop the ribbing about how he would be the one at the front with the flame-thrower if it were a real war. More and more drink was flowing and Bob was also a little concerned at his failure in that department. He was only managing about a five-to-one ratio to the older guys and to clarify he was the one wimping out. He wasn't afraid of guns but a little respect wasn't a bad thing.

When it was his turn again he blasted away enthusiastically with the assault rifles and the handguns without much success and to the amusement of the others, and the complete loss of any street cred he might still have had left. At this point in a real war he would have been relegated to the one with the pointy stick trying to find landmines.

The BBQ had been started and was well underway. The lumps of meat were cooking up nicely. The games were coming to an end for that session and there was a lot of whispering that Bob was not privy to going on which seemed aimed in his general direction. It was soon announced that because of his poor performance so far Bob could not have anything to eat until he had hit a target specified by the committee. He took the insults in good humour and joked back that they should start without him because they could be here long after nightfall if they waited.

Bob's stomach was beginning to growl and he was a little worried that his new-found friends had found him a task that would mean breakfast might not be the only meal he would miss today. Still, honour had been insulted. When they had arrived at the range there had been a couple of small axes next to the pile of chopped wood ready for the fire. Bob walked over and picked them up. He then circled around and picked up two large, heavy, solid-looking knives from the cook's table. The rest of the happy band were following his little trek around the site with growing interest. There was even a little amusement when the chef growled at Bob when he took the knives. The audience stayed respectfully quiet as he took up position about fifteen feet from one of the railway sleepers. This could all go horribly wrong, he thought, and he could spend the rest of the day starving.

He took his time and adjusted his stance a little, then slowly and deliberately he threw first the knives and then the axes. All ended up firmly embedded in the wood and pinning the paper target in place. He turned and took a bow to the applause and cheers of the crowd.

Dinner was served. He had hoped to get two or maybe three

out of the four to hit and stay. Four out of four was a bonus but he wasn't going to confess that to anyone. There was no hidden ninja biker assassin past or mercenary training in some godforsaken training camp that he had to confess to, he had just worked as a production line butcher in a factory for five years. The tedium had meant he and his counterparts had ended up playing stupid games to break the monotony. Something else he wouldn't confess to. Why spoil the illusion?

After the meal, the host called Bob away from the group and they headed off alone back up the track to the 4x4s and the shack. In the distance the rest of the gang started blasting away again.

The host collected a very expensive bottle of brandy from the boot of the first 4×4 and hands it to Bob. 'There is a man I want you to meet. He might be able to help you with your problem. After you have talked, even if he cannot help, give him this' – he points at the brandy – 'as a thank you for listening.' There was that mad grin again.

Bob had questions but the host marched off towards the shack before he could ask any of them. He was not sure what was happening, so all he could do was follow the lead and go and talk to this man. The shack was rickety and what little light there was came from two small oil lamps. Bob was sure it was just for effect because he could see the bottom corner of a television set hidden away in the back of the room under a blanket, so he guessed there was power somewhere. The room was hot and stuffy. Not that outside was much cooler but outside would be brighter.

The old guy he was going to talk to looked well into his hundreds, as only Asians and Orientals can do, and was puffing away on roll-ups. Bob was no smoker, so wouldn't hazard a guess at exactly what the old guy was smoking. They sat in the gloom and had a general chat about Bob's situation but it soon became clear the guy was selling guns, and was not a gun for hire. For Bob, what was important was the safety of being somewhere else with an air-tight alibi. Bob wanted justice dealt out but not to be caught smuggling firearms before things had got started.

The outcome of the meeting in the jungle was that Bob now knew that to buy a shotgun in Thailand you need about £2,000 in cash. To buy an old AK47 was only about £50 and the pistols about the same. Seemed there was still a bit of a stockpile if you knew where to look thanks to some rowdy neighbours a few decades ago. Bob said he would consider the offer but the problem of getting his purchases back home would most likely be preventative. They shook hands, the brandy was passed on and they parted company still friends.

Once they were out of the shack the host told Bob the easiest way to get a couple of pistols home was to purchase a large piece of furniture and hide them in it. He counselled that unless you were very unlucky it was the easiest way, simply because customs only sweep for drugs using dogs. Tourists send that much tat home nobody has the time to spare or the inclination to strip down and search everything being sent out of Thailand. As an afterthought he also added, 'Don't touch anything you may send back. That way there are no fingerprints or evidence that can be traced back to you and you can deny all knowledge of what is going on if you are unlucky. Then you can claim all you did was buy a dining room table or a damn big wardrobe … If all does go well, in six to eight weeks, what you purchased here could be arriving on your drive via one of the many container ships heading to and from a port near you.'

Bob considered the sales pitch for about thirty seconds. He had plenty of time to get the bastards who robbed Deb. He could take as long as he liked and it would take as long as it takes because they didn't know he was coming for them … yet. Maybe it would be poetic justice to wait until they think all was forgotten and then he could spoil their retirement plans, too. Spending time in a Thai prison for gun-running wasn't in the plan, though, and it did seem way too simple to actually work.

He settled on considering a few more options first, which would involve a little more looking before a final decision. As his host said: 'We are always here and you know where to find us if you need us.'

Small explosions started to sound above the general chatter of weapons fire. His host gave him that Travolta grin again and they headed back to the range. They arrived back to see the lads making Molotov cocktails, setting them alight and sending them out into space over the edge of the cliff, ready to be blasted to kingdom come. It was spectacular and worth the cheer every time one went up. Bob got another informed explanation: 'It is just a way to get rid of the empties'. Good job the jungle was a humid, damp place, despite the almost unbearable heat. There were a few minor fires in the tree tops at the bottom of the cliff but they soon burned out.

The day's activities drew to a close and they headed back to civilisation, snoring replacing the earlier heavy drinking. It was nice to see they were human after all, thought Bob, as he prepared to follow suit. He was sure the boys would be up and at it again as soon as they got back. Great lads – but he wouldn't like their bar bill.

Back at the hotel Bob had a note to ring The Tsar or call into the bar when he got back. He was much too tired, so sent a quick text, ending with 'See you tomorrow xxx'. He hoped it wasn't an urgent request and he would be forgiven. He didn't even bother to switch on the TV and catch up with the news, or set his alarm clock. He just gave in to old age and alcohol and collapsed on the bed to sleep. Even the lights showed a little sympathy and didn't put up a fight and turned off straightaway.

* * *

Bob's time in Thailand was slipping away at an alarming rate but he now realised there was no hurry, as revenge was a dish best served cold and all that. Just keep looking, he said to himself, and get it right first time. The day after the trip out with the A-Team, another of The Tsar's girls showed up at the hotel. Bob was sure he was getting a good (or bad) reputation amongst the hotel guests and staff, depending on their point of view.

This little angel obviously couldn't wait for the evening and the bar to open. Missing breakfast for the second day, he pulled on the concrete wellies again and took another leap of faith and another ride into the unknown. His head was as fuzzy as his teeth, the electric toothbrush and minty fresh toothpaste left untouched in his bathroom because of the urgent request to come to reception.

The transport this time was not so upmarket just an old, mid-range Toyota saloon driven by the little angel herself. Everything in the car was a bit tatty and had seen better days, although there was the customary blessing and prayer to Buddha inked on the headlining. His chauffeur was slightly built – tomboyish would be the English description. Over in Thailand it is 'same, same' and a gesture to indicate flat-chested. She did have a mass of raven hair and a few good-quality tattoos just creeping into view at the edges of her crop top, though. She could barely see over the steering wheel but she got the ugly yellow Toyota to zip through the traffic with a fair amount of professionalism and they were soon flying along another country road in the middle of nowhere.

The main road became a one-lane track after about an hour's drive. Not the off-roading of the day before but if a car or occasional pedestrian pushing a fully-laden cart or bicycle came the other way it took a little manoeuvring to pass each other. They were in an area of farmland, a few trees here and there marking boundaries to fields, and a few more trees marking the edge of the road. In the fields there were neat rows of different types of green vegetables or rice, which seemed to be the biggest crop in the area. The green vegetables could be mostly the same plant but at different stages of growth, for all Bob knew. There didn't seem to be that much difference in the seasons here, so he guessed the growing cycles were extended or not as pronounced as at home. Here in Thailand you got few options: it seemed you got hot, even hotter, and hot and wet, whereas in England whole days could be lost talking about the different types of weather in any given week.

He didn't know if it would be better to shut the windows now the car had slowed. The speed was no longer sufficient to generate a cool breeze and it was slow enough for the bugs to fly in. At least with the window open the hot and humid air was circulated a little inside the car. They had passed a few small villages and now they pulled up and parked because they had found the one they were aiming for, he presumed. There were chickens running free and the dogs were too hot to bother about chasing them, preferring to sleep or scratch. An old blue pick-up was parked not too far away and one solitary buffalo was tied and corralled near the houses. Loads of near-naked kids came over to see the car, the driver or, as Bob suspects, himself, being the only white guy in the village. The adults gave them a cursory glance then continued with their chores.

They had parked at the far end of the village just before the rice fields started again and next to the home of the person they were here to meet. All the homes were similar, built of wood on wooden stilts that lifted the main part of the house eight feet off the ground. All the upper floors of the houses had large shuttered windows which were open to try and get a little air circulating. Underneath, some had washing hung between the stilts, others were used for storage and one or two had made the space more private by hanging plastic sheeting between the uprights.

This time things appeared a little more promising. His driver hadn't been over- chatty but from the brief information she had shared, he could be on the right trail. Again, he had been taken out into the middle of nowhere to meet a stranger. Was there some rule he didn't know about which said he could never meet anyone in an air-conditioned room or bar to talk business?

The house turned out to be owned by the big brother of Kaew

(pronounced Gail) who was the little angel driving him around. It seemed big brother had fallen on hard times. He had been a talented Thai kick-boxer earlier in his life and local champion on a regular basis, which gave him status in the community. He had lots of potential and was expected to have a national career and a very lucrative future to look forward to – until a drunken foreign tourist drove into his car. The tourist had been legless drunk and the one totally in the wrong.

If the accident had happened in England there would have been enough legal help to get the brother compensation for his injuries and damage to his car. In Thailand it went a little differently. Both cars were write-offs and the tourist escaped without a scratch but the brother had his knee smashed and his career ended. Somehow big bro' had got out of the car and staggered around to the other driver who was being a total arsehole about everything and had then proceeded to kick seven bells out of the guy and put him in intensive care for a very long time; no mean feat considering his injuries.

The Thai people value their tourist trade, so anything that upsets that trade is dealt with quickly. Big brother ended up doing eight years in prison for aggravated assault with no getting off for good behaviour or mitigating circumstances. Career, income and status were all gone because some pisshead was so drunk he couldn't see what he was doing. The tourist had walked away (when he was able) scot-free.

Big bro' had now been out of prison for a couple of years and the only jobs he could pick up had been playing the heavy for anyone willing to pay for his services. From the look of the guy, Bob could imagine he was very good at his job. He might not have been the champion-in-waiting any more but he was still solid muscle and the all-over tattoos added that little bit of menace.

They were introduced to each other by Kaew. Her brother stood there growling, his pumped-up body dressed in cut-off black jeans. Bob had seen variations of his sort making their way to Boy Town and the gay bars on the less attractive side of Pattaya. This guy however was more rip your face off than sit on your face.

The shacks here were not only for big bro' and Kaew but their whole extended family. There was no social services to claim off so everyone looked after each other and contributed in any way they could, several generations of the same family often living together. The responsibilities were something most Western men ran from as soon as they found out they were not just marrying a beautiful, sexy young woman but gaining a whole family to support as they were now the main breadwinner!

Being a white guy in the village meant they wouldn't get the chance to talk business straightaway. From nowhere, the whole extended family was suddenly present and being introduced, with Kaew trying to keep order and translating the random questions. Minutes became hours disappearing without much business being done. Bob had always been prepared to sit and chat and join in with the locals wherever his holidays had taken him and it seemed they were now staying for dinner and business was put on the back burner. From out of nowhere a meal was being served. It was a poor rural area, so the food was mostly rice, chillies and peppers with insects being the main source of protein.

Kaew seemed to be getting some pleasure from Bob's discomfort and his floundering as he tried to keep everyone happy and be polite. Two hours disappeared and they were all still chatting but not about business. Bob was sure if he wanted to marry Kaew the family would have her washed, packed and ready to go in no time. To try and get a private word with her he used the excuse that he needed the bathroom. Kaew showed him the way and when they were out of earshot of the family he thanked her for the day out but explained he needed to gee up the business chat and talk to her brother in private. She got the hint and when he returned it was only a few minutes until her brother called them outside to talk without interruption.

His price, no questions asked, was £10,000, the airfare and a hotel for a week so he could act like a tourist. Bob had no problem with that. Bob could get him close to where he was needed once he was in England and bro' would take care of the rest. Could this be problem solved?

No. There was a but. There was always a but…

It seems bro' wanted to include Kaew in the deal. He wanted her to come to England first and work for Bob as cook, cleaner, housekeeper whatever, for six months, so he had an excuse to come over to see her and it looked like he was just visiting his little sister. Bob didn't think he could sell that to his family and anyway, the trail would lead straight back to him.

Bob started running through what would have to be done to make it all work. It was so close it was almost tangible but it was getting messy. There would have to be a visa and a passport for Kaew. She couldn't be expected to come for nothing, so she would have to be paid some kind of wages, and Bob didn't think a little Thai house angel prancing around the family home would go down that well, even if it was for a worthy cause.

They were all talking and negotiating amicably when bro' threw another curve ball. Because of his criminal record he would have to get a false I.D. and false passport for himself, and he would also need money up front for the visa.

Bob could see so many problems on the horizon and the cost, even without any actual figures to work with, was going up and up. If he could pay cash for a non-refundable air ticket and leave bro' a little travelling cash, then sort him out when he got to England, there was no problem. Now it was becoming a major logistical nightmare with a much bigger budget than first thought.

Bro was saying he would need a lot of cash for wheeling and dealing to get the passports and visas etc. Even if Bob could convince Deb's family that he and Deb needed a housekeeper to help at home, some sexy, tattooed tomboy wouldn't be what they had in mind or found acceptable. Then there was the fact that suddenly all his anonymity would be lost. Too many people would know about his plans. Kaew and her bro' would know where he lived and there would be a paper trail a mile long leading straight to him if it all went tits up. He imagined he would be the main suspect anyway if Summer had an unfortunate accident, without making it totally impossible for him to get away with it. Also big bro' was hinting at the perks of having a super sexy Thai housekeeper and having your family pimp for you was just wrong, thought Bob.

Bob was suddenly aware of how unbelievably hot and muggy it was outside by the cars where they were talking. Having not made any attempt to cover himself from the scorching sun, he felt he was on slow roast, self-basting at an alarming rate. The air was completely still and he was a little light-headed. His mozzy spray was wearing off and millions of the damn things were arriving, not bothering the locals, of course, but his lily-white tenderness was now on the top of the 'Specials' board. He needed to get things wound up and get back in the car, on the road and heading for his hotel in Pattaya.

Big brother had gotten to the stage where he was just repeating himself and what had been said a hundred times before. The heat and bugs had become a major distraction and Big bro' had lost Bob's attention. The small amount of breeze from the moving car on the way back would be heaven and the hope was the old Toyota could out-run the insects.

Bob leant on the car wing and the pain was instant. Hands and backside had touched a furnace and he was now jumping around and seeing stars. Kaew was trying not to laugh and failing completely. Enough!

Yesterday gun-running, today human trafficking, and he hadn't even made it to the end of the week yet.

They were going over the same old ground without any new inspiration or improvements on the original plan. It was time to concede they were, for the moment, at an impasse. With the pain subsiding in his hands and Kaew in control of her giggling they left the negotiations open, saying Bob would price up what he could and see if there was anything he could work out. That seemed to keep everyone friendly.

They finished the meeting and all Bob craved was to get away. Normally meeting real people was one of the things he loved about travelling but the last few days were taking their toll. Bob would have killed at this precise moment for a cold room, a long massage and a very, very long iced drink. He reminded himself that a little discomfort might ultimately be worth it in the end, just to keep his morale up.

While the adults cleared away the remnants of the meal and he and big bro' had had their private meeting, the kids had caught a snake. As Bob, Kaew and big bro' move from their conspirators corner to go and say goodbye to everyone, Bob was amazed and shocked by the scene in front of them. The grown-ups were getting on with their lives as if nothing was out of the ordinary but the vision of young kids tormenting a lethal cobra as if it were harmless was chilling and sickening at the same time.

The game for these young miscreants seemed to be to keep out of striking range of the snake but at the same time torment it or frighten it enough with long sticks to make it lunge in their direction. Bob could not for one second imagine that Play Station or Xbox could ever come up with a game that gave the same kind of adrenaline rush. The kids were all laughing and shouting and didn't seem at all frightened.

Maybe a killer snake and what he saw as a game close to Russian roulette was just his Western viewpoint and over-protected lifestyle kicking in. For people living in places like this a deadly-poisonous and bad-tempered snake was probably a daily occurrence, and games like this could one day save a kid's life. Bob was sure that if one of these kids was cornered they would be able to act and cope with the situation and not freeze with blind panic like any soft, white Westerners would. Still, it gave him an excuse to ease back towards the car.

Just as his hand reached for the car's door handle, a little farewell drink appeared, accompanied by a whole bunch of Kaew's relatives. A couple of quick alcoholic shots and a lot of polite goodbyes, and he and the angel were finally heading back towards Pattaya.

So far the week had been a real eye opener, although he conceded that he could have found 'options' a lot closer to home, in countries with the same big gap between rich and poor. There would be people wanting to earn a little extra cash and without any damn visa problems if he had searched within the EU. To misuse a song from *The Rocky Horror Picture Show*: 'From respectable homeowner, in just seveeen daaaaays, I can build you a crime syndicate'.

He was beginning to suspect that if you wanted a job doing it was better to do it yourself. By the end of the car ride he had decided to spend the next few days wandering around picking up a few things that might come in handy when he got back home, and going to say a few thank you's and goodbyes to the people that had tried to help. He could not imagine he could get in any trouble sitting by the pool and chewing over what to do with his problem. He had an evening meal in the hotel, a couple of nightcaps and then a long, hot bath before settling in to get a full and uninterrupted night's sleep.

15

A Happy Accident

After a much-needed rest Bob got up refreshed. Over breakfast, he made a shopping list and then awarded himself a long and relaxing swim in the hotel's large pool before he set out to do his errands. The pool hadn't been a priority and it had been hidden away on the roof so he hadn't realised it was there straightaway, but once found it had been gratefully appreciated. He dropped off his keys in reception. There were a few fellow tourists milling about and all seemed to have gone for loud and trendy, multi-coloured attire in contrast to his white cotton short-sleeved shirt and tan trousers. Who would have thought he would be the one standing out from the crowd with what he had chosen to wear? He had his list tucked away in his shirt pocket, safe and sound, so he headed out to get the shopping started. He had a few days left to relax and work on a new plan.

He wandered around the tourist markets and the large shopping centres. These cathedral-style centres were great to hide from the early afternoon sun with their air-conditioning and tinted windows. He hadn't got up that early so breakfast had in truth been closer to early lunch. Bob ended up in one of the newest centres. The place was massive, with five or six floors already open for business and ready to sell you all you could possibly want or desire; the shoppers' choice was almost endless. There were hundreds of shops to search around and buy from and he was sure he would lose interest long before he got high enough to see what was hiding away on the top floors.

He had worked his way up a few floors and was now carrying a couple of store bags containing things purchased off his list, wandering along minding his own business and heading in the direction of the nearest escalator up to the next floor. He had soon left the ground floor. It had been packed with people ogling the gorgeous Ladyboys promoting the big contest being held later that night. Men who would run a mile if a gay man spoke to them were now in ecstasy with Ladyboys draped all over them trying to get photographs.

The banks of escalators were designed to give a spectacular and panoramic view of the shopping centre in all its glory. Bob suddenly heard shouting from the ground floor – it sounded like someone shouting 'Bob'. He glanced quickly over the rail in the general direction of the noise as he came off the escalator. Below was Hawkken. Even in the crowds and with the distance between them he had recognised Bob.

Bob turned, ignoring the shouting. Whatever Hawkken wanted, it was going to cause Bob grief. Bob ascended another floor. Hawkken had been trying to push his way up the lower escalator when he had been spotted, so Bob assumed Hawkken aimed to confront him. This was the situation he had been hoping to avoid. His Intel obviously wrong.

There were another four floors upwards and if Bob made out that he hadn't seen or heard Hawkken and kept quickly moving it should be easy to lose him in the crowds. The shouting had at least stopped, uncouth bloody foreigners. He made a quick plan in his head to go up and up, then along and down the far side of the massive building. The escalators were banked at either end and in the middle. Hawkken was following him up on the escalators at the beach end of the building. If Bob could put distance between himself and his pursuer he could escape and head back to the safety of his hotel by going out at the far end of the building onto the main road and mingling with all the traffic and the crowds. Bob took seconds to purchase a touristy, brightly-coloured T-shirt and a large-brimmed hat with 'I love Thailand' on it from a small market store, throwing a few notes down to cover the purchase. He intended to put on both, once he was comfortable that he had put enough space between him and Hawkken. He focused on moving at as much speed as possible, but without breaking into a run and drawing unwanted attention to himself.

He reminded himself that when all the lies and bullshit were being hurled at Deb, they had asked Hawkken, as a friend, to try and mediate and plead Deb's case, or just find out what was going on and why. He had refused point-blank, making it quite clear he wasn't going to help in any way and risk his money and lifestyle by getting involved, even if both had been totally down to Deb's efforts on his behalf. Bob had desperately resorted to an open letter across the company, pointing out what his wife was going through and underlining the lies and inconsistencies of the company's version of events. He had hoped that with all Deb had done for the workforce and the company for two decades that some, if not all, would be galvanised into some kind of protest knowing she was not the person the few people at the top were trying to say she was, and that she was totally innocent of all their slander. Like Hawkken, the workforce had disowned her to protect themselves and it had been more convenient for them to look the other way and make out nothing was happening, presumably with their fingers stuck in their ears and their eyes tight shut.

Three weeks later Bob had been arrested. The company and Summer had somehow convinced the local constabulary that these pleas for help were actually death threats and that they were all terrified for their lives. Bob spent an hour in the cells until the police could be bothered to actually review the evidence, then he was released without charge and given a sincere apology for the force's over-zealousness. It had amazed Bob how having seven or eight zeros after your bank balance could get you exactly what you wanted. Maybe Summer knew the Chief Superintendent's wife or something. Her influence had been great enough to get Bob arrested at 9.30 p.m. on his fiftieth birthday and at his party, more than three weeks after the email had been sent. If they had honestly thought that their lives were in danger, wouldn't they have done their 'he is trying to kill us' act sooner? The police did try and claim the date and time had been mere coincidence and not to read anything into it but did anyone or could anyone really believe that was the truth? The message from Summer and her buddies seemed clear: we can get you whenever we want to.

Hawkken obviously felt he had needed to show his loyalty to his masters and spent the next three days after the sham arrest and the 'death threat' incident calling Deb's phone, screaming and crying hysterically when Deb answered and claiming Summer had read the email and had committed suicide and it was all Deb's fault. He also claimed one of the other directors had followed suit because of the humiliating lies Bob had told. Now the company was in ruins, everyone was going to lose their jobs and they held her responsible. Hawkken had Bob's phone number and email address and if he or any of them had wanted to speak to Bob direct they could have. Again, they knew they could do more damage by attacking the soft target.

Once Bob had found out about the phone calls and calmed his wife down enough to make her listen to common sense, he was able to reassure her that the calls were untrue. Bob pointed out the obvious about Hawkken having his number and email address and the logic to why they were attacking her, because they knew they had already made her deeply ill. Once she was calm, even she could recognise the now familiar tactics; nothing written down and nothing that could be used as evidence. No emails or letters, just more of their tried-and-trusted scumbag tactics.

Bob didn't know if Hawkken had planned all this himself or acted out something concocted by Summer, but he had been at the point of giving up because of the stress of looking after Deb, keeping his own work going and doing the million and one things that had once been straightforward but were now making life as hard as it possibly could be. All the company had achieved with the attempt to warn him off was to reignite his resolve and make it stronger. Bob had made one quick phone call to confirm none of what Hawkken had been acting out was true. Unfortunately, all had been OK, as he had suspected it would be. Bob had managed to get a few of the latter rants on tape but they were nowhere near as vile as those in the first couple of days. Hawkken had obviously got bored with his little task, thinking he had done all he needed to.

Bob sent an email to the company wishing them all well and sending his best regards and hoped the supposedly dead would all be well and resurrected soon and well on the way to a full recovery. That small touch of sarcasm silenced the calls. Bob thought it was sick what they had done attacking Deb but he should not have been surprised as Deb had had to suffer that sort of treatment for almost two years before they broke her. The recordings were played to the police and all they said was, 'What did Bob expect them to do?' and that they were obviously not real death threats even though Hawkken had threatened to kill Bob several times. The suspicion about who knew who only grew.

* * *

As Bob made his way higher and reflected on what Hawkken had said and helped do against Deb, the bile rose. That a good friendship which had benefitted Hawkken had counted for nothing and meant nothing also meant Bob's temper now grew. Hawkken had been on Bob's personal 'come the revolution' list. Not at the very top, but not too far away. He wanted to dish out some justice but he wasn't going to end up in a Thai prison before he had a chance to visit Summer. His mantra had to be, 'that bitch first, that bitch first'. Then he could work through as many as he could on his 'to do' list.

He continued his hasty ascent to the unpopulated top floor. Nothing was blocked off but if there was nothing up there of value it was a good bet there would be no security either. If there was no security when he got there he would put on the new shirt and hat to change his appearance and run as fast as he could to the escalators at the far end of the complex and escape. Security was never that great in Thailand because it wasn't that necessary. Even in the street markets the stall owners simply covered their wares when they were done for the night. All their stock stayed where it was and was still there the following day. Could anyone boast the same in a market in England?

Bob had not looked back since the shouting had stopped and was quietly confident that he had given his pursuer the slip. As he came off the last escalator and onto the top floor he took the chance to take a look behind him and there was no sign of Hawkken. Bob's hope was that he had given up as a face-to-face meeting might not end well. It would be easier to keep his temper at a distance. He left the escalator and his vantage point and headed off towards the far end of the building.

What had looked like empty shops and an unused floor turned out to be a floor full of restaurants that seemed to cater for the evening and late trade and were not open in the day. He kept to the brisk walk rather than run because he caught glimpses of cleaners or staff preparing for later that evening. The floor had been a surprise. There was a massive food hall on basement level that served anything you could possibly desire, and cheaply. He had eaten there several times himself. It was all stainless steel, chrome and coloured plastic but the food was good.

He was suddenly confronted with a problem. There were no other escalators down and this last floor was only half the size of the ones below. The shape or construction of the roof meant the floor stopped to accommodate it and you could look down on the shoppers below. There was a double door with a sign for stairs on it to his right. He was in two minds … should he go back and take the escalator down to the floor below and risk Hawkken was still following, or go through the doors and take the stairs which would take a little longer but would hopefully mean he would be able to carry on with his plan by using this short detour for just one floor?

He decided to take the stairs but as he started towards them, the doors swung open alarmingly quickly and Hawkken stepped forward. Bob had barely moved from the rail, stopping dead in his tracks. Hawkken was now in front of him, barring his escape route down. The man was out of breath, doubled over and gulping in air like a stranded carp. He was crimson, not just red, and sweating like he had just run a marathon. It was his turf and Bob should have guessed that Hawkken might realise his plan and used a little local knowledge.

Between gasps, he stuttered: 'Stay … there … you … bastard.'

'Why should I, Hawkken, you piece of shit?' yelled Bob. 'What are you going to do, get your breath back and apologise? Bit late for that, don't you think? Or are you going to be all big and butch and threaten me some more?'

Hawkken was still too winded to talk. 'You and Summer had almost won, you know. Then came your antics with the police and the threats and it just made me remember why I was fighting you cunts in the first place!' By the end of Bob's little speech the man in front of him was still breathing heavily but standing more or less upright and not having to grip his knees for support and to stop himself puking.

Hawkken found his voice. 'We will all protect our own money by whatever means necessary, you arsehole.' He was still in front of Bob and blocking the route down, twelve, or maybe fifteen, feet between them. Bob considered his options.

'You're scum. You know what my wife did for everyone at that company and not one of you could be bothered to make one little protest on her behalf or help her just a little … or thank her for doing all she did. Do you get a bigger cut now?'

Hawkken spread his arms and shrugged, a stupid grin on his face. 'The company is built now and no one is going to risk losing out on all those profits. Summer wanted her gone and that was that.'

'FUCK YOU!' was all Bob could articulate, as blinding rage began to overtake him.

Hawkken was a bear of a man despite the blond ponytail, and he took a step forward. Bob took a step back, feeling the metal and glass banister behind him to stop him falling the seven floors down. It was Hawkken's turn to speak. 'You two have sunk without trace and we have shared the spoils around already.' The venom was evident with every word he spat out. 'You two are forgotten and what your wife did is being credited to anyone and everyone except her. No one will even remember her in a few years' time. History is already rewritten.' He had recovered enough to gloat.

Hawkken was much bigger, taller and a lot heavier than Bob, but Bob thinks he is fitter. He hasn't had the years of heavy drinking and drugs and he wondered if he'd be able to throw this arsehole over the banister and get away with it. 'You make any more trouble,' Hawkken said, a clenched fist waving at Bob to emphasise the point, 'and we will fuck you over big style.'

'What the fuck do you think you have already done? You pieces of shit have swindled a friend out of a life's work and the rewards she has fairly earned. You have driven her to the point of suicide and she is that ill now that she has to take pills every day just to be able to walk down the fucking street. WHAT THE FUCK ELSE IS THERE FOR YOU TO TAKE?'

Hawkken clenched both fists, pushed his jaw out and took another step forward. Now he was going bright red with rage again, red blotches covering his throat and face. The veins in his neck bulged.

The banister pushed into Bob's lower back and prevented another step back. In a fair fight his chances were slim against this man-mountain on the point of explosion. It crossed his mind that Hawkken's intentions could now be mirroring his own earlier ones. Bob was not going to let this creep win and let himself be the one thrown over the rail.

The mountain spoke. 'I will make it clear one last time. You cause any more trouble for us and I will use my contacts here and in Cambodia and get you sent a crate of "kiddy porn" and we will see how much more we can screw up your life.' All the threat needed was a stupid, theatrical laugh after it.

Bob was stunned. They might have beaten him this time. All it needed in England was for someone to point a finger in your direction and shout paedophile and it wouldn't matter that you were completely innocent. There was no need for evidence or proof, just mass hysteria and a lynch mob mentality. Hawkken was obviously convinced that this last threat was enough. He unclenched his fists and started to turn away, ready to leave. To him the matter was now closed, smug bastard. All Bob could do was stand there with icy fingers gripping his heart and bowels.

Bob gambled, making a snap decision to bluff his way out of trouble. 'Oy, you piece of shit. You're not the only one with friends here. What do you think I'm here for? How do you think I knew where you would be today? Why do you think I let you "trap" me here, where we can be alone?' Hawkken stopped walking away. He was listening but he hadn't yet heard anything to make him turn and face Bob.

Bob paused, trying to compose his thoughts, and that was enough to prick Hawkken's interest. He turned to look Bob straight in the eye. The big Finn was waiting for Bob to give an explanation and his face was like thunder.

This might be the stupidest decision I've ever made, or the most inspired, thought Bob. I could walk away beaten or stand my ground.

'I have already been here several days,' said Bob. The words were slow and deliberate, as if he was talking to a child. 'I have already found someone to take me to Cambodia without anyone, including the authorities, knowing.' A pause. 'I guessed you would try something to keep me quiet and, shall we say, get me "under control". Your paedophile thing might have worked if I had not already thought of it. I can come down to your level to play if I have to.'

Hawkken's rage returned. He was now visibly shaking, bright red and ready to pounce. He stood flexing and tensing his muscles, waiting to hear all that Bob had to say before smashing him to a pulp.

'I have placed an order, using your name, with some pretty nasty people, and on your passport I am guessing there will be a nice date stamp to confirm you were at least here at the time the shit was shipped. I even managed a signature a bit like yours. I know it wouldn't fool anyone professional, but no-one is going to be looking that hard.' Hawkken somehow managed to look fit to burst and confused at the same time. 'Just like your threat aimed at me, dickhead, a crate of that filth would destroy anybody. The shipping order is for a piece of furniture sent by you to a Ms Summer Ponsenbury. In six to eight weeks, she will receive a nice, big present from her favourite playboy of the month. And I will make sure there will be someone there to help her open it.' Bluff ... bluff ... bluff. 'An anonymous tip-off with all the shipping codes should be enough for someone to be waiting when the crate is delivered. NOW... how do you think your reputation will survive when you're caught importing kiddy porn, you arsehole?'

Bob didn't know how it had all escalated so quickly and become so twisted. He had wanted to make Hawkken squirm a little and buy himself some time. The subject has no grey areas. Hawkken with his lifestyle is the most likely to be able to carry out his threat, and there are millions and millions at stake for him and his new best buddies back at the company. 'At any cost' had been implied by Hawkken's little speech. Suddenly, rage overtook Bob. 'You will lose fucking everything. You all will. Maybe you can hide around here sucking off strangers to get cash for your next bottle of cheap vodka, you cunt.'

Like a raging bull, Hawkken flew at Bob, intent on ripping the smaller guy apart. Bob must have really hit a nerve with his improvised speech. There were only a few paces between them but it was enough for Hawkken to get his massive bulk up to full speed, his fury focused on Bob.

Despite his age, Bob was still quite nimble. He had played rugby and even a bit of American football in the UK when he was younger. Those years playing sport had taught him how to avoid or make contact. Reflexes and training took over and in the few split seconds he had, Bob dropped and rolled towards Hawkken, aiming for his lower legs. It was not a method he had been a fan of when he was playing because the contact was too easily avoided. Everyone would jump as a natural reaction to avoid the impact and that was what Bob was banking on.

Hawkken was no exception, and he jumped to avoid the feeble attempt to take him down. Bob sensed more than felt the other man's bulk fly over him and knew Hawkken was looking down and feeling smug at avoiding the challenge. Well, for a split second, until his bulk, his height and his momentum were joined by gravity. His jump was just enough to get him airborne and flying through the air. The jump had been impressive for a man of Hawkken's age and weight and he was high enough to hit the safety barrier at around knee height. Gravity took over as he desperately clawed the empty air in front of him. But it was too late.

Bob had rolled onto all fours but wasn't quick enough to see the fat bastard and his absurd ponytail disappear from view. All he could see was empty space through the immaculately clean glass and metal rail supporting it all. Hawkken had time to scream and his scream was soon joined by shoppers on the lower floors witnessing him swan-diving to the concrete and marble floor below. The scream, then the squishy thud followed by more screams and the sound of pandemonium breaking out from below confirmed there were no doubts about Hawkken's poor choice of where to land. Not even top billing from Cirque du

Soleil would walk away from that. Bob was still on hands and knees and staring into space, then the survival instinct kicked in.

He saw the two bags of shopping still at the base of the rail. He couldn't remember when he dropped them but he was thankful their contents were not spread everywhere. All the stuff in them would have his fingerprints and DNA on and that could be used to incriminate him. He couldn't leave the bags behind and run, so he stayed on all fours and scuttled forward to retrieve them, resisting the temptation to look down on the mess below. More importantly, he didn't want to give himself away to those looking up to see where the 'splat stain' took off from. Everyone would have dived for cover to get away from the mess but the more morbid would be returning to the scene already with cameras and tablets out, recording everything.

Bob retraced his way back from the edge, one hand clasping the handles of the bags as he dragged them after himself until he thought he was far enough away from the edge to rise and not be seen. He then headed for the door to the stairs, staying crouched down as he moved until he was in the stairwell and away from prying eyes. It was hard not to start blindly running in whatever direction seemed easiest. He leant on the wall with his forehead resting on the cold stone and within seconds his thoughts clarified.

Amongst the stuff he had bought today were the few items of traditional holiday tat that everyone one takes home plus what he had snatched up to camouflage himself from Hawkken. He replaced his white shirt with the red tourist T-shirt with Thai kick boxers fighting across his chest. He changed his plain, dull trousers for the brightly-coloured, knee-length swimming shorts which he'd bought for his son before remembering he was supposed to be in Spain, which wouldn't fit with the 'I love Thailand' logo on the backside. He had meant to bin them as soon as he got back to the hotel but now he was glad of his lapse in concentration.

He had always been brought up to tuck in any shirt he was

wearing and to look tidy, so now he left the T-shirt untucked. He had two hats to choose from: the 'I love Thailand' straw thing, or a fold-up waterproof golf trilby (another joke purchase for his son, who was making an attempt to learn to play golf). He chose the trilby – he didn't want to overdo the dickhead tourist thing. He now looked like a scummy tourist complete with sandals, the only original part of his attire that was on show. He should blend in well.

Bob ran down a couple of flights of stairs and then out onto the main shopping floor. He emerged to see the shoppers crowding up to the barrier to get a better view of the carnage below. There was still lots of noise but most of the screaming had stopped. Customers and employees alike had come out to see what the commotion was about and were jostling for position around the safety rails to get the best view. Inevitably there were camera phones and real cameras flashing away, as he suspected there would be. Bob was sure that there were already pictures on their way to every social networking site in creation. He worked his way close to a similarly attired tourist who was craning his neck for a better view. 'What's going on?' he asked him.

'It's great, mate. Some fat white guy just jumped off the top floor and went splat in front of all those sissy Ladyboys. Bet his girlfriend just told him she was up the duff and he didn't want his wife to find out.' Don't you just love the Aussie outlook on life? Still it confirmed that at the moment no-one believed there was a second party involved.

Bob nodded in agreement and started to walk away. The local store security guys seemed to be getting some sort of order down on the lower floors so Bob headed towards the exit he originally came in. Between some of the shops there were service hallways leading to customer toilets and the like, a hidden network to keep the facilities handy but out of sight. There was an entrance close to Bob which he made for, relieved to find it was the same design he had seen many times in places like this and he could now slip away completely unnoticed using the warren of connecting hallways to enter in one place and exit somewhere else entirely on that floor.

He came out as far away as possible to where he went in, close to the lifts and escalators and a way down and out. He joined a few of the squeamish and uninterested who didn't want to get involved and they all stood waiting for the lift to arrive. No-one really wanted to talk about what had just happened but there were still a few outbursts and mutterings of 'It's terrible, it's just terrible' and the like. They all travelled down and when the lift opened they headed for the nearest exits all trying to get away from the scene as quickly as possible.

Bob was amazed that most people in the shopping centre had headed towards the 'jumper' to get a better look. He had expected to be fighting to get out of the place and using the crowds as cover to help him to escape unseen. He contemplated staying and going to the police. Technically he had done nothing except avoid some lunatic attacking him. Whether that argument would be enough to convince anyone of his innocence he didn't know and decided not to put it to the test unless he had to.

Outside now and moving away, he guessed the police would soon arrive and lock the place down to try and get witness statements. He could already hear the sirens in the distance.

He headed for one of the hundreds of Baht buses that prowl around the main streets of Pattaya city, circling like predators around the one-way system to pick up passengers. It was a much more pedestrian-friendly system than the taxis back in the UK, and a lot cheaper. Here you stuck your hand out and climbed into the back of whichever converted pick-up with a roof and bench seats stopped first. You did the circuit until you were close to where you wanted to be and it cost less than twenty baht – that's less than fifty pence in real money. Bob found a bus and joined four passengers already on it. There were two Thai ladies dressed in matching uniforms as though they were off to work at a hair salon or massage parlour. There was one old guy sitting scrunched up in the corner and a slightly younger bloke listening to his iPhone with small ear phones plugged in. Bob thinks he can hear Ted Nugent playing 'Dog Eat Dog', but he could be mistaken.

As he sat there he wanted to shout, punch the air and proclaim, 'Who's the daddy now?' but it would scare his fellow passengers. His jubilation soon turned to concern as he rode the bus towards his hotel. He was soaked in sweat and he was sure someone would guess his guilty secret. As he looked around he calmed down a little when he realised every tourist was sweaty and stained. Maybe they were all guilty of something, especially knowing where they have come on holiday? Bob tried to keep under control and when he got as close as he was going to get to his hotel he got the bus to stop, paid his fare and walked the rest of the way.

The receptionist saw Bob enter the building and handed over the key as soon as he reached her. There was only a slight glimmer of amusement as she looked at his new attire. Once through the door of his room, with the deadbolts locked, the world suddenly started to spin and Bob sank to the floor, head in hands, adrenaline rush subsiding and nervous exhaustion taking over, and sat there.

He didn't know how long he was there – it could have been hours or just minutes – but the cold from the floor hit his bladder and the urge to pee got him moving again. When he returned from the loo and a quick shower to cleanse his body of drying sweat, he raided the mini bar and downed a couple of miniatures to get focused.

A couple of hours had disappeared and a couple more dragged by as Bob paced the room with more trips to the mini bar, trying to figure out his next move. There was no sudden, violent, forced entry by the local police and from his window life outside looked to be carrying on as normal. He had packed his suitcase and although he wasn't panicking, self-preservation was high on his 'things to do' list. He had the local TV news on in the background as he packed and paced hoping it would give him a sign of what to do or an early warning, but there had only been a few brief lines saying there had been an incident at the local shopping complex.

His dilemma was, did he run or should he stay? He hadn't said his farewells and thank-you's and there were still a few days to kill, yet he didn't want to draw attention to himself by trying to change his flight home. Also he didn't want to stay trapped in his hotel room and close to the scene, either. He could make out he was ill – he wouldn't be the first tourist to get laid up in bed with a dodgy stomach, even if he had never suffered before. The trouble with that was that the staff might try and help and he couldn't risk having them call a doctor – his actions might look suspicious and draw unwanted attention to himself. He could just take it in his stride and be cool, spending time working on his tan by the pool before he returned to the cold and rain of England. He could be self-sufficient here in the hotel and not venture off the grounds. With the restaurant and room service it was highly unlikely that he would starve, even if the prices in the hotel bar were a little higher than out in the real world.

The six o'clock news started on the TV. This time Hawkken was the lead story. It was still short on detail and Bob guessed that it would become more polished and in-depth as time went by. There seemed to be two schools of thought as to the apparent suicide. In the main everyone was assuming that a local businessman buckled under the stress and jumped off the top floor of the local shopping centre. The other version seemed to be focused on the ladyboy pageant, with some of the local god followers proclaiming Hawkken did it as the ultimate protest of the filth and debauchery dragging Pattaya down. Well, if that's what they want to think, who was Bob to put them straight? The piece wrapped up with the local police confirming that there were no suspicious circumstances and that they were not looking for anyone else in connection with the incident.

Bob sat down on the end of the bed in stunned amazement.

Could it really be that easy? He switched the TV off and sat there reflecting on what had happened. Could he be held responsible if anyone found out? He did antagonise Hawkken but he didn't actually throw him over the rail. And did it really matter? He could now tick this one off the list and move on.

Bob decided that to be on the safe side he would slip away from Pattaya but take his original flight home. His bag was packed just in case, so it shouldn't be too hard to find somewhere using the hotel's Internet. He could leave first thing in the morning. He was just about to rise from the bed when there was a firm knock on the door. PANIC!

What had gone wrong? Was it a cunning plan by the police to lull him into a false sense of security? Should he run? The answer to the last question was easy: he was nine storeys up and couldn't fly even if he could break the sealed window in his room. Was life going to kick him in the gonads yet again just as things were working out? No, if he is going down he decided to do it with dignity and a stiff upper lip and all that. He stood and walked to the door, opening it ready to embrace his fate.

The hallway was empty. He leant out and looked both ways. Were the Thai equivalent of a SWAT team waiting to pounce? Not unless they'd left him Champagne on ice as a welcoming gift, and an invitation to join them down the local nick, very polite. He bent over and picked up the ice bucket. He was tempted. It had been an eventful day, after all, and it could be seen as cause for celebration. He looked on the card to see which room it should have been sent to. Yes, that was his room, so he would have to ring reception and report the minor mistake. He turned to swing the door shut. A sexy foot in spike heels stopped it closing and the foot was followed by an even sexier leg. Then the door was pushed fully open to giggles and a loud 'Surprise'.

There, looking as beautiful as ever, was The Tsar. 'I didn't think you were up and about this early in the evening,' Bob asked, a little confused.

'Sometimes,' she said, the reply accompanied by a sexy pout.

'I want to give you as much time as possible to get ready. We are going out tonight and you have about thirty minutes until the car arrives.'

'Going out? Sorry, when did we arrange this?' He put his hands up. 'Again, sorry – but it really has been a bit of a long day.' He was not unhappy to see his guest but a night out on the town wasn't what he had planned and in hindsight the episodes he had managed to get himself into so far had bordered on chaos and catastrophe. Going out with the 'architect in charge' of organising it all could be pushing his luck too far.

The Tsar had made her decision and waltzed in, kissing him on both cheeks, throwing a tuxedo that was hanging over her shoulder onto the bed. 'Don't keep a girl waiting,' she said, opening the champagne before he even thought to offer.

The tux for him and the sparkly mini dress and all the jewellery The Tsar was wearing could only mean one thing, thought Bob. There was only one show to be seen at tonight, so Bob guessed they were going to the ladyboy pageant. He had gone with the flow so far and it had all worked out in the end. He resisted the temptation to attempt to striptease using the pole in the corner. Sexy girls could mesmerise but a fifty-something carrying two or three stones of excess baggage was probably not so good. He retired to the bathroom to change and returned transformed. The tux fitted him perfectly. He could not have done better if he had gone to the hire shop for a fitting himself. A quick rummage in his case and he had the requisite black patent shoes to finish off the outfit.

'My hero. Hope you are ready for a night playing my sugar daddy.' Another sexy grin.

'Yeah, about that. How much has the suit cost me? Do I need to visit a loan shark for the funds for the rest of the evening? You have been generous and fantastic so far but this is the biggest show of the year and I am a small fish in a big pond and I really don't want to spoil it for you.'

All he got was a derisory laugh. 'Poor thing, like I ever pay for anything … and neither do my guests.' She gave the love swing a playful push with the tip of her finger to get the momentum going and looked innocently at him with a raised eyebrow.

'I can explain … It was the only place I could get,' he spluttered in his defence. The Tsar just laughed and when the champagne had been taken care of they set off for the ball. The rest of the night was a fantastic, glamorous fantasy world. The Tsar was true to her word as far as the expenses went. They were VIPs for the night. They started with cocktails and mingled with the important guests before the show, sat behind the judges through the show and ended the night at the after-show party. Why he had even considered that she wouldn't know absolutely everyone on a night like this was just plain stupid. They danced all night to anything and everything that was played, mingled with the stars and ended up leaving the party to breakfast at the Pattaya Hilton, The Tsar leading, with an entourage of fifteen or so following close behind.

Exhaustion finally took its toll and Bob was taken back to his hotel. Somehow they had acquired a limo and they sat in luxury and enjoyed the moment. Bob tried to speak but The Tsar stopped him with a couple of fingers held up to his lips. There was a lot he wanted to say and 'Thank you for all the help' was the minimum but she was the only one allowed to speak.

'I hope you get the justice you want but we don't always get what we think we deserve,' she said. 'I saw your bags ready to go and I don't need to know if you had anything to do with the trouble at the shopping centre.' Of course, she would have recognised Hawkken's picture on the news. 'Come back and see me if you need any help in the future.' He took out his wallet. He wanted to leave something as a thank you and he felt guilty because in the chaos he hadn't managed to give the girls anything for their help either. 'Bob, there is no need. Just come back – we don't want to lose a friend.' With that the chauffeur opened the door. There was a small, awkward moment but she leant forward, kissed him on the cheek and said 'Be lucky'. He stepped out of the car and waited until it had pulled away and turned the corner before he returned to his room.

* * *

After the breakfast rush it didn't take long to find alternative accommodation away from Pattaya. He kept an eye on the news but there had been no new developments while he was out enjoying himself. When he told reception of his change of plans he was politely informed that he would be charged for the following night, but Bob didn't care and was soon in a taxi heading away from Pattaya. His destination was a small, quiet, out-of-the way island he visited many years ago with Deb.

First he would get to Rayong, a coastal town where he could get the ferry to the island of Koh Samed, a place he would recommend to any traveller wanting to relax. There were miles of beaches, a great nightlife and plenty of good sea-food.

As with most things, there is a tourist way and a local way. The first time he had visited, he and Deb had arrived by tourist ferry sailing close to a wide, clean beautiful beach. There had been a few tourists taking in the sun and a few small hotels peeping out of the jungle. He and Deb had been transferred onto a smaller boat for the last fifty or so yards to shore, the whole episode selling the deserted island thing. Then as they hit the beach a nice man in a uniform came and took money off them – some kind of eco tax. Fair enough, tourists were destroying all the places like this in the world.

They had then made a three-quarters-of-an-hour drive in a local taxi to their hotel. The taxi had been a no-name pick-up truck with an unpadded wooden bench seats and no roof. No luxury off-road 4x4s were anywhere to be seen. The trip, if it had been a normal road, would have taken about ten to fifteen minutes but on the local roads it felt like days. It was torturous – they had been bounced around, their spines being pulverised and driven through their skulls, until they got to the hotel. Whoever did the marketing had forgotten to mention the downside to secluded and out-of-the way. It wasn't just a killer on the backside, the dust came at them in clouds and so did the insects. Plus every ten minutes someone coming the other way would shower the tourist passengers in the back of the pick-up in shale and even more dust.

It could have been worse, they were told. In the rainy season the travellers arrive at their hotel soaked and covered in mud. A word of advice, if you do go to the island (and yes, it is worth it): catch the local ferry to Samet pier near Keaw beach. Most of the hotels are close and there are real roads at that end of the island. OK, it's not so romantic as option number one but your back will be grateful for the rest of your life. And don't do the late night squid fishing. It is sold as an all you can eat and drink during six hours of romantic fun fishing for your supper in paradise. When Bob did it the first time the ride out to the fishing grounds had been great. You are out on the sea watching the flickering lights along the shore and the stars and moon if it is a clear night (and it normally is) and all is well with the world. Then you stop to fish!

Bob had classed himself as a reasonable sailor. He had been on ships in high seas with the waves breaking over the pointy bit at the front and the captain worried somebody would get washed overboard. He had even sailed on boats with masts and the occasional yacht and worked on the sails and ropes with the world swaying from side to side – but nothing had prepared him for squid fishing at night.

The lights for fishing are rigged up and switched on and your whole world becomes the pool of light around the boat and the little bit of churning sea that is revealed. The boat had two tiers and you go down from the observation deck to sea level deck to fish. There is no skyline, however faint, and there is now no moon or stars you can use as a point of reference to steady yourself because the fishing lights are blazing away to attract the squid. The boat is just wallowing where it has stopped to fish. Bob lasted fifteen maybe twenty minutes. He had had no alcohol, only water, and no food – and he was still dying.

Soon they were on the way back to the harbour and not just for Bob. Most of the happy tourist fishermen had not made it off the observation deck and were a lot worse than he was. Once the boat had cut engines and come to its wallowing stop all the tourists had lost their sea legs pretty rapidly. The whole trip out and back to port had only taken three of the allotted six hours.

Everyone soon recovered once they were back on dry land and dispersed into the night to continue their recovery in a beach bar with a long and very strong cocktail or two. Bob and Deb had headed for the closest bar and something a lot stronger than water. It was only a few minutes until the boat's captain came in and he had come over and checked that they were both all right on his way to the bar. A few drinks later and he was confessing to the harmless local scam. The crew takes very little food or drink on the trips, it's not worth it. Everyone gets ill and the record is only about four hours from start to finish and that was only because the trip was made up of hardy Chinese tourists. No-one could remember the last time the trip lasted the full six hours, 'Ha bloody ha!'

So if you want squid, let the locals catch it and cook it for you. Bob had a couple of days this time, which he spent walking on the beaches and swimming in the sea during the day and eating fantastic sea food and watching the nightly fire shows down on the beach all evening. It could only have been bettered if he had not been there alone.

He left Thailand in the early hours to come home on the latest up-to-date plane, the one that looks way too big to ever fly. He now had a new clarity of purpose and a new understanding of what he had to do. As he sat there, thousands of feet up in the air, he reflected how he had first tried to make the job simple and it just got more and more complicated and out of control. He had tried to reduce the risk to himself and find people to carry out what needed to be done and at the same time keep himself out of trouble. All that had happened was that he had now realised what it would mean and that he would have to put his trust and his fate in someone else's hands if he continued down that road. He had considered many options and the only conclusion he could see was that he needed to solve the problem himself, alone, in control and totally focused. He now had the rest of an eighteen-hour flight and transfer time to start planning properly. The beach and the sea had been too good to waste.

16

Be Prepared

So, here Bob is, parked in a country lane with a big bag of 'essentials' ready to bring justice (if only a little bit) back into the world. He has spent time, whether he wanted to or not, continually reviewing and revising until he feels the plan could work. To get to this point, his journey had started on those first nights spent watching over his wife as the nightmares tormented her and he was left trying to comfort someone who had lost everything that gave their life meaning. He is probably on plan 13c, give or take a million or so. He knows the evil he is hunting down is unsuspecting and not even considering he might come calling. It thinks it is untouchable, it thinks it is all powerful and it thinks it is safe…

Over the last year he had looked at the simple, the spectacular, the elaborate, the expensive, the professional and all resolutions in between. They all led to that one final conclusion: that if the job needed to be done, it needed to be done by him. He didn't want to give this truly evil woman a chance to wheedle, whine and manipulate her way out of justice with someone who could be bought, or be conned by her into not completing the job. He is the only one who cares, and that is his resolve. The greed-driven harpy he is waiting for will not be able to talk or bribe her way out of anything with him.

There will also be no opportunity for a third party to blackmail him after the deed is done. He will not fight one tyranny to have it replaced by another. There will be no loss of nerve and there will be no attack of conscience at the last second to allow that woman to escape justice. The horizon is finally beginning to lighten and it makes him feel like things are beginning to ready themselves to move forward. The reality is that Bob might lose the cover of darkness and consequently risk his actions being witnessed, however slim that risk might be out here in the middle of nowhere. From his vantage point everything is still quiet in the house. He runs over the plan again in his mind. He rechecks his bag of goodies and nothing has been magically taken away.

The gun he now has is loaded, tested and ready to go. It had taken a while to get hold of it. He had returned from Thailand and lost his nerve and given the original plan of getting someone else in one last chance. He had again walked and stalked the city and its dark, unloved areas, trying to find someone willing to help. But he had not been able to repeat the 'successes' or find the opportunities presented during his little trip abroad. Here people were not interested in his problems and none were able to offer solutions. Here it didn't feel anywhere near as safe and he felt he was actually risking his own life, so he had decided not to push too deeply to find the people he needed. He could not even find a gun to help him with his task. If you were to believe the Sunday papers, this problem should have been easily solved in 'broken' Britain with just a quick trip to the back of the local supermarket and a chat with the local hoodie.

An opportunity had presented itself out of the blue, when he was almost at the point of taking a carving knife and waiting in the shadows of that woman's gym, or supermarket or pub car park, and to hell with any real plan. Bob had been at a family 'do' for his son and his wife, a family BBQ with all the husbands, wives, brothers and sisters, and this had been where the gods had finally given him a break …

Bob had met them all before at the wedding, of course, and knew some of the lads had reputations as wide boys. He had been told that if there was ever anything he needed which of the lads he needed to see. He was sure it was meant along the lines of TVs, DVDs or dodgy MOTs but needs must and all that. It was just how to bring it up in the conversation with all the family listening in? He decided to arrange a friendly pool night and drinks out with a few of the more noteworthy of the lads and to try his luck using the sob story tactics he had tried in Thailand. It wasn't hard to set up with a little schmoozing about how he had heard about their prowess around the pool table and how they should get together more often now they were all family. Soon a venue and date was set. The temptation of easy pickings was too much for the lads to overlook, Bob's reputation preceding him. He feared that these lads were not going to be anywhere near as sporting as the ladies back in the pool bars of Pattaya!

It was a men-only get-together and Bob and his son showed up on the appointed night, a few days later. His son was completely in the dark as to the real reason for the pool night out. A few drinks later, following a hammering on the pool table, and Bob managed to get one of the brothers away to a quiet corner of the bar and out of earshot of the rest of the group. Bob had touched on what had happened to Deb when they had been talking at the BBQ and again briefly as they played pool, and he had singled out the most likely candidate to chat to.

'Well, I hear you're still the black sheep of the family,' Bob joked with Damien, who was known as Daz to his mates.

'Yeah, you got to make your dole up somehow,' he replied, with a wink and grin.

'Well, we've all been there at one time or another. You heard about Deb and her forced retirement?'

'Yeah! It was a shame. Real bastards from the little I've heard. Can't believe they could get away with it. They are bigger criminals than the scum around here.'

'You're not the only one to say that. It's not like they can use the excuse they needed the money. But they did do it … and I think a little retribution is in order.'

'Yeah? Anytime or anything you think I can help with, just let me know. You are part of the family now.' (He must think it is an episode of the Sopranos or Ray Donavan).

Bob hesitated a little, like he was thinking before he spoke. 'Well, if you're sure you want to get involved, I do need an item you might be able to find for me, or the name of someone I might be able to talk to about finding something for me. If it is a bit out of your league, a name or a contact will be a great help. I don't want to drag too many people into this and you never know, you might even be able to get me a family discount.'

'No problem. I can get you anything. Just say the word.'

'Seriously, Daz, it is nasty, grown-up stuff and I don't want the whole family knowing my business. If you're sure you can keep out of the shit and get me what I want, that's great.' There was a short pause. 'That's if you really want to get involved with my problems.' He nodded his agreement and Bob leant forward conspiratorially and explained the type of item he was looking for. He had expected a shocked reaction from Daz and a 'no fucking way' but all Bob got was an 'I'll see what I can do'.

Bob didn't want any trails leading straight back to him but it seemed there were going to be a few small concessions. Between the two of them they arranged that if Daz could find the goods he would make contact by leaving a message with his sister about a decorating job he wanted Bob to quote for. Bob didn't want to be contacted direct, just in case. As if anyone would be checking anyway. If Daz said how much the 'quote' was for when he rang, Bob would bring the cash when and where they arranged to meet and only the two of them needed know anything about what was really going on.

The conversation ended and they returned to the beer, the pool table and the more normal small talk on a lads' night out.

* * *

Six days later, Bob had had a call from his daughter-in-law saying Daz was at her house and could Bob pop in because he had a job he wanted a quote on and it should be worth about a grand and a half. On his way, Bob visited the bank and took out the cash. He didn't know whether the price was good, bad or indifferent as he only had prices from a very different part of the world to compare with. Bob was actually a little annoyed – he had expected Daz to give him an address or location where they could meet, not just show up at his sister's to do the deal and risk dragging the family into the mess. He was expecting a little more discretion, but maybe he was being paranoid. It had confirmed the more people involved the higher the stress levels though.

Bob arrived at the house, where a bunch of kids were playing some music-based Xbox game with Daz joining in. Bob sat down with a cup of coffee and had to listen while the kids and Daz took it in turns to screech into a plastic microphone, trying to accumulate points. Bob finally got him to come outside and talk shop when the daughter-in-law arrived back from shopping and volunteered to supervise the screeching.

'What the fuck did you bring it here for? What if someone followed you? I'm trying to keep this low-key and low-profile so nothing can be traced back to me, or back to any of us,' Bob hissed under his breath when they were outside.

'It's no problem. It's been in the car for three days already,' said Daz. 'If anyone was interested I would have been stopped by now.' Bob didn't know whether Daz was trying to be careful in his own special way or having a little fun at Bob's expense. Or was he just a moron? Daz opened his car's boot and there was a box containing four tins of white gloss paint. He opened one of the tins and inside there was a small pistol and three magazines of ammunition, as requested. He pointed to the rest of the box. 'The other three are actually paint, so have fun.'

Bob knew he should be strictly professional and check everything out to make sure it was all working (something he could now do quite comfortably, thanks to his day out in the jungle). Instead he got Daz to quickly replace the lid and take the box of paint and firearms over to Bob's own car. The envelope of cash changed hands and there was a mumbled 'Thanks, see you later'.

All Bob could think of was getting out of there as quickly as possible and getting his cargo somewhere safe. He needed to check it out but he was desperately trying not to touch any of it until he could put on a pair of stretchy surgical gloves. Bob had thought he would be choosing the place to meet – somewhere well out of the way, so he could have given the damn gun a once-over. He regretted not saying his goodbyes before he came outside so he could have gone immediately but went back in to be polite and then he made a hasty retreat.

Bob did not go straight home but instead drove out into the deserted countryside. Over the last few months, he had used his new dog-walking hobby as an excuse to roam and reconnoitre just the right spot to be alone and unseen. The trip out into the country also gave him the opportunity to check if anyone was following the car after observing his little transaction with Daz. The idyllic and scenic empty country roads were great for this because there was nowhere or traffic for anyone to hide behind. He tried to convince himself the tightness in his chest was just a strong case of paranoia and he was only being healthily cautious. The main reason for the little excursion, though, was to check out the gun and make sure it was not just a toy. He only hoped he hadn't wasted his money.

The days of running factories were long gone and Bob now kept most of his decorating paraphernalia in his estate car. He had been very good at his job but when he and Deb had decided on a path for their future it had been her career that had been the most promising with all the wonderful guarantees and assurances. Bob had become a house-husband because they had a child, a house and a large garden which all needed care and attention and he had been the more qualified and capable of maintaining all three. Well, house and garden anyway; with the kid he just winged it. The decorating business filled the gaps in his diary if ever there were any spaces and it brought in extra income to help pay the bills. But it now meant that most of the time his car was full of junk.

Amongst the junk there was always a box of stretchy, disposable, surgical gloves to help keep the chemicals and paint from covering his hands as he worked. Once he had driven to the secluded spot and parked he found the box of rubber gloves and put a few pairs in his pocket, and then put a pair on, opened the box and examined the gun. Everything was in order. He had asked for a 9mm automatic pistol that would be small enough for a woman to carry and use, and that was exactly what he had received. He didn't claim he could tell anyone the make and model. There were a few numbers and letters that would mean something to someone but all he could say was it looked similar to what our man Bond carried in the early 007 films. It could be twenty years old or brand new, for all he could tell. There was no rust and it was clean and that was good enough as long as it fired.

Thanks to the day out in the Thai jungle with the A-Team, he knew enough to check the magazines and cock and fire the pistol, aiming into the ditch behind the car so that the evidence was instantly lost for ever. All was in order. Once he had fired the gun he replaced the stretchy gloves so as not to contaminate everything he touched with whatever residue they always find to break the case in NCIS and similar programmes. He put the pistol in a clean freezer bag and then put it in his pocket alongside the handful of spare gloves he had picked up earlier.

He left the parked car and walked down the grass verge of the lane until he could use the stile and head across the fields towards the woods in the distance. That was where he had chosen, thanks to the dog walks, for his little practice session. He was miles from anywhere. Once in the woods and out of view he went to the spot he had found, which had a muddy pool about twenty feet across. In the centre of the pool there was a rotting tree stump about three-and-a-half to four feet high. He took the pistol out of the bag, cocked it, aimed and fired. There was a small crack as the gun discharged, a small amount of recoil, and the bullet firmly lodged in the tree stump.

He took two more practice shots and hit his target both times (maybe his unspectacular efforts in Thailand had been down to the alcohol intake after all?). The stump hadn't exploded and shattered into sawdust like in a Dirty Harry movie. It was a small calibre weapon and not a magnum like in the movies but he was sure it would do the job. Without a close inspection the rotten wood just appeared as if it had been chewed or pecked a little by the local wildlife. He assumed as the stump rotted away the evidence would sink and disappear into the mire with it.

As satisfied as he could be, he headed back to the car, repeating the precautions of earlier. He resealed the pistol in the freezer bag and then when he was back at the car he returned it to the empty paint can along with the spare ammunition that was still there. He had a plastic supermarket grocery bag ready to take the used gloves. Hopefully he had kept the forensic evidence to a minimum and there seemed no reason to waste any more bullets. He expected his target to be close, very close, when he actually used it for real.

He was feeling happy with the world and dragged out his iPod from the glove box in the car dashboard. Time for a little 'Bad Boy Boogie', yet another AC/DC track. It must be his age …

* * *

He pulled up on his drive after the ride home. There was no barking from the dog so it was safe to assume one of Deb's friends had shown up and taken them both out. 'Another lucky break today,' he thought to himself. On with another pair of gloves and out with the freezer bags, then he squeezed through the back hedge into next door's garden. Bob came out immediately behind their old oil storage tank. Both his and the neighbour's houses were similar and they both had these oil storage tanks that were as old as the properties they supplied. Both tanks were overgrown and had become part of the hedge, with only the front of the tanks being kept clear for access for oil deliveries. The laurel hedge was now so thick you could almost walk along the centre unnoticed. He hid the freezer bags and their contents under the years of mulch and dead leaves collected under next door's tank. The gun should be safe and dry there until it was needed.

Going back to the car, he collected the small bag of used gloves and added the latest pair to the pile. He could put them in the trash because they would be long gone by the time anyone might be searching for any kind of evidence. But it was autumn, almost winter, and he had left a coal fire burning in the front room, so he committed his little bag to the fire. There was a bit of hissing as the gloves and bag melted before they burst into brightly coloured flames and then all the evidence had disappeared.

* * *

There is still no movement at the bitch queen's country pile, so we might as well run back through Bob's last twenty-four hours or so to keep you interested and get you up to speed.

Right, back to yesterday before the world starts to wake up. Now Bob had already bought a few things and arranged a few things so it had been a case of getting the ball well and truly rolling. First he had set off from home telling Deb that he had a few things to do and would see her later. There had been no acknowledgement – there very rarely was these days. He only managed to break into her world occasionally but if she needed to escape into the television to cope with what had happened to her, so be it. He would be there waiting if she ever returned.

He took his car and parked within walking distance of the local train station. He had paid for his parking like a good little shopper, not wanting to get a ticket and ruin the day. He had headed for the station and got a single into the city, paying cash of course. The ticket was for a couple of stops past where he actually wanted to get off. Paranoia again, but better safe than sorry.

The majority of people have a mate who would lend or rent a beaten-up, non-descript white van for a few quid, cash in hand. Bob's had been a short train ride away, in the heart of industrial Brum. He really didn't want to hire one when all that paperwork could be traced back to himself. He couldn't use his own car and be placed at the scene of the crime later by some random passer-by remembering make and model and a few letters or numbers from the registration. He had considered stealing a van but the risk would be that there might already be people looking for him and the car before he had even started. The aim was to keep off the radar as long as possible, if not completely. The best option had been the mate, a little cash and a small sob story about his car being in the garage and needing to finish a job for a grumpy customer who wouldn't wait the extra day – and Bob had his inconspicuous set of wheels at a reasonable price.

After the short train ride he had taken possession of the van, thanked his friend for the help and driven out of the yard feeling that things were beginning to move forward. Soon justice, soon! With him Bob had a small kitbag of bits and pieces. When he had picked up the van he had covered the driver's seat with a plastic disposable seat cover. (He had kept the one from when his car had been serviced but he could have picked some up from any company selling car valeting stuff.) If the van had been really dirty he would have joked it was to keep his trousers clean. As it was, he just made a joke about how messy decorating was and how he didn't want any sort of claim for cleaning when he returned it. The mate had looked a little worried about what state he was going to get his van back in but had finally been convinced it would be OK when Bob prised his friend's fingers off the set of keys so he could get going. If you can't wind up one of your mates when there are no Americans about, who can you wind up?

He also had a few sterilising wet wipes and a few pairs of the stretchy gloves. If you're skint try the local supermarket, the one with the ninja assistants ready to pounce as you touch their Granny Smiths with bare hands, as the rest of the bloody world goes by with their kids wheezing and coughing and carrying the plague behind you. But they are OK because they have gloves on. Full respirator equipment should be standard in every supermarket fruit and veg section by now or is that too Rhod Gilbert? Bob drove a short way from the yard before pulling over and wiping down all he had touched. He then put his stretchy gloves on, just in case.

The gloves stayed on until the van was safely parked where Bob had chosen to leave it until later, a few streets away from his home. Another good reason he'd found not to hire had been the tracker issue and the big brother scenario. If things went horribly wrong later Bob didn't want anyone being able to tell the police where he was and what route he had taken. He had parked within walking distance of the train station and his home, legally and with due care for other road users. He didn't want the van reported and the damn thing towed away.

Bob got out of the van and locked it, then took off the gloves. He had a new carrier bag for wet wipes and used gloves in the kitbag that he had taken to carrying around. More evidence to burn later. He could just have thrown them in a random bin on the way to reclaim his own car but burning seemed more permanent – and the blue flames were pretty. He got his own car from where it had been parked and drove home and relaxed. All in all, a round trip of about an hour-and-a-half and his transport needs were sorted.

He had already done a little prep work for the van ready for later. He would need to replace or disguise the number plates. He wasn't planning on meeting anyone when he went visiting Ms Ponsenbury but he would be parked on her drive for a short time and he didn't want a stray passer-by remembering a few digits. It had been a fuss, to say the least, when he had tried to get a set of plates for his trailer. Are you the owner? Do you have the log book for the car you will be towing with? Another bloody jobsworth. He had ended up like most people and written the number on a piece of card and stuck it there with tape. Again, stealing a set of number plates seemed too much trouble and another risk of being caught before the main event.

The answer had been inspired by the card and tape botch job. He had done the whole Blue Peter thing. Two sheets of white paper, one clear, see-through plastic folder and one yellow, see-through plastic folder, a black marker pen and some black duct tape – all available from any stationery store. He had cut the plastic folders to size to cover the van's number plates. Clear for front and yellow for back. He had written out some made-up numbers on the paper roughly the right size. He hadn't been cocky; there were no personalised numbers and he had kept the year's prefix close to the original on the van. He didn't want plates from this year on something ten years old. The paper was inserted into the folders and they were ready to be duct taped over the originals when needed. It had been a lot easier than making Tracy Island but he was fifty years older now. OK, they were not permanent but if you wanted something you can use quickly and will burn away to nothing when they have outlived their usefulness, they would do the job. Let's face it, as long as there is some kind of number plate no one is going to look twice. On the other hand, a van without plates would be spotted straight away.

The day was moving on but he had reached a point where he couldn't really get on with anything else until his wife was out of the way. Nothing permanent, you understand. Again, he had thought about his options. He could have suggested she go and see friends or relatives but there was no valid reason and he didn't want her interested or suspicious in what he might be doing. After careful consideration he had settled on a plan that would make her part of his alibi without her even knowing, and make getting rid of the evidence easier later too. Go, team Baldrick!

Most people these days have a BBQ or fire pit that is dragged out on an irregular basis and used to spoil perfectly good food. Bob and Deb were no exception. Their weapon of choice had been the fire pit-cum-cauldron. Bob was proud of the fact that he had never wasted food trying to cook on it. Bob, his wife and their friends had spent many nights over the years and the seasons around the pit with the flames leaping high into the night sky, drinking large amounts and solving the world's problems long into the night, or 'staring into the gates of hell', as one of their melancholy Irish friends had put it. He had been on his fourteenth Guinness and a few shorts by then but the image had stuck. The night was still and dry, so Bob would soon make an argument for the fire pit to be out and alight and the plan could move on.

It would only be Bob and Deb tonight. He made sure she was wrapped up warm and they sat by the fire drinking. Soon they were even chatting a little. It must be the 'primitive' thing; once there is a fire, conversations start easily. It was only mundane, run-of-the-mill stuff but even that was better than what had become the norm over the past few months. There was a small spark, a little flash of what used to be there. Bob wanted to sit and savour the moment a little but he knew his chance might be lost if he hesitated too long. It was one of Deb's more lucid times and it hurt him to be underhand and dishonest, even in this small way. She deserved better.

Bob kept the red wine flowing – that is, red wine for Deb and blackcurrant squash for himself. Who could tell the difference in the evening light? Only the taste would give him away if he got them mixed up by mistake. As the night wore on, he started to add crushed sleeping pills to the wine. He did not want to kill her, just give her a good, long night in deep and blissful sleep. The pills were one of the purchases brought back from Thailand once he had the outline of the plan and were much stronger than the UK equivalent, so not so many were needed. The imports strong enough to actually do what they were created for and the staff not going into fits because you have tried to buy three packs of paracetamol at the same time.

He kept them both downing their drinks at a brisk pace and not too far into the night he took his now very tired and tipsy wife to bed, and tucked her in. As her head hit the pillow she fell almost instantly asleep. He hoped the deep sleep would last long enough for him to complete his mission.

He left her in peace and went to the spare bedroom where he had been hiding his little bag of goodies. He had the false plates for the van, the duct tape and a few other items ready for later. He also had the gun that he retrieved earlier from its hiding place under the oil tank. He laid out the gun and ammunition on a sheet of newspaper and with clean, stretchy gloves on he removed the bullets from the magazines. He wiped and cleaned everything as best he could with a degreaser from the garage. He then reloaded the magazines and reloaded the gun, making sure he had replaced the half-empty magazine with a full one. The gun was then replaced in the freezer bag, with the spare ammunition in a separate bag and both were then added to the rest of his inventory in his kitbag. He took the newspaper and the rest of the rubbish down to the fire pit and watched it all burn away. He took the opportunity to stack the fire high so it should still be 'in' tomorrow when he returned, if all went well. He went back inside, set his alarm on his phone so he could get a few hours' sleep and headed for the spare bed. He'd estimated it would take an hour to get ready and to drive to his chosen spot, ready to watch until it was time to act.

* * *

The alarm went off at 4.30 a.m. Not too loudly, no harsh ringing, just a few gentle chimes to start the day off peacefully. A quick brush of the teeth (standards please) and he got dressed. Just underpants, an old T-shirt and socks and an all-in-one waterproof jump suit he had from when he was into motor biking. No press studs or zips, only Velcro to keep the weather out. It should burn down to nothing. To be honest, he was a bit chilly but Bob was sure things would warm up later. A pair of cheap £10 trainers a couple of sizes too big which he had padded out a little, purchased from a discount sports shop and again highly flammable, and his ensemble was almost complete.

From under the bed he produced his disguise. He'd purchased a long ginger wig in Thailand. He could have purchased anything from shocking pink to neon blue but given that the family colouring of the firm's original founders was ginger and freckles, a realistic ginger had seemed most fitting. A quick trip to a local costume hire shop in England had found him a matching long ginger beard and eyebrows. He sat in front of the small mirror and followed the directions he got for applying the glue for both from the helpful hire shop assistant. With the beard and eyebrows in place Bob donned the long wig. It finished off the disguise nicely. He let the hair fall seductively across his face to make sure it hid as much of his real features as possible. OK, he now looked like a Scottish Liverpudlian paedophile but that was probably a good thing in its way, for today only.

He took a bundle of normal clothes downstairs, not forgetting to pick up the kitbag with all its goodies. Bob risked a quick listen at the bedroom door where Deb was fast asleep to make sure he hadn't disturbed her. He didn't try to open the door because it creaked but more importantly he didn't want to scare her to death if she did wake up and saw him in his new disguise as 'Paedo Paul'. That would not help the plan at all.

Downstairs, he had a 'travel wee', as old people say, then he departed. He had two sets of keys – his own and the van's – his mobile and the goody bag. He slipped out of the side door trying hard not to trip or fall over anything, including the dog. At this time of the morning it gave him a 'do you really think that would fool me?' look and went back to sleep. He had left his car unlocked when he parked it so there would be no thunk and beep-beep from the central locking as he opened it and got inside. Modern cars, what a pain in the backside with all the beeping as everyone comes and goes. At night it is like trying to sleep with a giant space invader machine playing under your bedroom window.

Luckily he lived on a slight hill, so with keys in the ignition to release the steering lock, and the hand brake off, he coasted down the drive and started up the car a little way along the road, then drove to the van.

He slipped on the stretchy gloves and transferred all his stuff to the van. He had now added a large, empty cardboard box and a clipboard that he had in the back of his car to his stash. Beep-beep clunk! Sorry, but it's not his van so he couldn't leave it unlocked. He turned the key in the ignition and 'Houston, we have lift off'.

Bob headed out into the countryside, stopping at a spot picked to be away from any prying eyes so he could doctor the van's number plates. The home-made plates were taped into position in seconds. He hadn't considered rain and was lucky it was a dry night, so the tape had stuck just fine. All done and back on the road in less than a minute with the van's new identity in place. Bob was now just another deliveryman in a white van with an early drop-off to do. On with the high-viz vest left helpfully by a previous driver, and he was on his way.

17

Just Before Dawn

For the next part of the plan there was another 'prepared earlier' moment when Bob had cobbled together an identity badge. He pins that proudly to his chest, just to look official, for a little later on. Another 'If it wasn't there someone would notice' detail but when the badge is there no one would bother to give it more than a glance. Who cares what the name tag says? Who wants to know who is delivering you a parcel or serving your meal? Certainly not Ms Ponsenbury. Bob had kept a visitor badge from when he was out working. Now it had an official-looking crest taken from a local council round-robin letter (see, there is a use for them), plus a blurry picture from a magazine that in the right light might look a little like Bob's new ultra ego 'Paedo Paul'. As soon as some life shows at the Bitch Queen's house he will pull onto the drive and make a delivery.

Once he is parked there on the drive he will get out of the van, put the goody bag over his shoulder, pick up the fake delivery (the empty box has lots of black and yellow chevron tape around its edges to help sell it as real and very important) and then he will take the clipboard and walk up to the front door. He is considering limping a little – we have all seen the film *The Usual Suspects* and it might be worth a try for the sympathy vote and to come over as harmless. It could be 7 to 7.30 a.m. before there is evidence of anyone awake in the house and the more harmless he can look when he is struggling to carry the large parcel to the door, the more chance there might be of Summer having the door open wide for him when he gets there with his load.

Thinking about it, she is more likely to enjoy the show and let him hobble along and struggle to pull the bell chain. She will then obviously expect him to wait respectfully until she is completely ready, after a suitable amount of time has elapsed, just to show how important she is and give him time to see how big the house is. Eventually she will want to see what the menial has brought her. It looks certain he is going to have to ring the bell and wait, never mind, 'patience is a virtue' and all that!

Thanks to all those early morning deliveries these days everyone accepts some unshaven, dishevelled cretin loitering on their doorstep at first light looking about two years older than the local hoodies that are terrorising the neighbourhood. The cretin will be there asking for a signature for another piece of 'must-have' crap that you have bought over the Internet and which probably cost less than the price of delivering it straight to your door for your immediate enjoyment.

Just to clarify the need for the box ... This bogus parcel is there so Bob's dear victim has to open the door so that it can be delivered, and it is big enough so that in the event that dear Summer has a safety chain on, she will have to take it off because the box is too big to pass through the gap. The aim is to get into the house as quickly and quietly as possible – and what easier way than a large, unopened, box of treats important enough to require a signature? While she is thinking 'What's in the box, what's in the box?' like some demented Jack Russell, Bob should be able to take the opportunity to make his entrance ... He could kick the door open as she unlocks it. Let's face it, door chains seem more of a gimmick to make the home owner feel safe than any real deterrent. That ten centimetres of five-millimetre chain link held in place with a couple of quarter-inch grub screws would surely keep an invading army at bay, wouldn't it? Anyway, who wants all the noise from a big entrance? If he can help it, Bob wants something more subdued so as not to awaken anyone else in the house before he has completed the first part of the plan and he is inside and everything is under his control.

* * *

Has he over-estimated his quarry? He has parked up, opened the van, retrieved the parcel and started heading for the front door, now opened wide. He is being instructed to come in and to place the precious parcel on the hall table, without him having to say a word. There she is, the picture of loveliness. Seventeen stones of tousled, still sleepy and sweaty ginger bitch in a flowery, one-man tent disguised as a nightdress to try and hide the bulges.

'Morning. Ms Ponsenbury?' Bob inquires, keeping in character and putting as little enthusiasm as possible into the question. 'Recorded delivery. I need a signature.'

'Yes, yes that's me.' She rushes past him without a second glance, she is so eager to get to the parcel he has placed on the hall table.

He hasn't been officially dismissed but he is sure she is trying to get rid of 'Paedo Paul' so she can get to her 'precious' and open the box. She has pushed past him to look at the label and is paying him no attention at all now, assuming no doubt that he will touch his forelock on his way out. She is probably expecting him to rake the gravel flat as he leaves as well.

Instead, Bob puts his hand into the goody bag, grasps the gun and steps forward. 'Ms Ponsenbury – a signature, please.' As she turns to face him again he quickly shoves the gun under her double chin.

'Not a fucking word and you will live, bitch,' he hisses menacingly. Her hands fly up to cover her mouth and stop herself screaming. Her face is screwed up with the exertion of not saying a single word. Now he has her attention, he has stepped back but is still pointing the gun at her face. She is trying hard not to look directly at the pistol as if it will disappear as soon as she cannot see it, but failing miserably.

He reaches behind himself with the empty hand and pushes the door to, until he hears the latch click shut. The gun is still raised and he signals for her to step back. He follows her until she has her back against the wall. The stone must be cold because her nipples have suddenly gone hard under the flowery material and are pointing in his general direction. The parcel is no longer her main source of interest. It has been seconds and he is in the house and out of sight of the rest of the world and their prying eyes with the door shut tight behind him to keep unwanted guests at bay.

'Keep still and not a sound, understand?' A small nod of her head. She still has her hands over her mouth. 'I am only here for cash and jewellery. It is a robbery, so do not make it anything more, clear?' Another nod.

'Co-operate and I am gone in five minutes and you have an insurance claim and a good story. If you want to be clever I will blow your fucking brains all over the wall.' He is still speaking in hushed tones, so as not to wake anyone else who might be upstairs still asleep. A more vigorous nod this time from Ms P. 'You all alone in this big house?' She gives a negative shake of the head this time. 'Your husband upstairs asleep?' An affirmative nod. 'Anyone else? You lie and I will kill the fucking lot of you.' Again Bob is hissing as much venom as he can at the woman. She nods to confirm it is just the two of them.

Bob takes out the duct tape and rips a piece off. 'Mouth,' he says as he hands her the piece of tape at arm's length with his free hand, and raises the gun to point directly at her face again. She is not that stupid after all and she covers her own mouth with the tape straight away, no further instructions required. Next he takes out an already-threaded small cable tie from the bag. 'Hands out and thumbs together.' More hissing and more venom to scare her (this is the easy bit). Compliance, arms outstretched, hands together with the thumbs in the air. The cable tie goes over the thumbs. One short sharp yank and the bitch is secure. There is a muffled yelp as the cable tie bites around the flesh and he can see her eyes watering … He is not here to make friends after all, he is here to make amends.

A minute-and-a-half or maybe two minutes after he closed the front door and she is leading him up the stairs to where her husband, Little Anthony, is fast asleep. The obnoxious Scouse twat must be hung like a donkey – or she is trying to upset her daddy and has taken in a bit of rough just to piss him off. Every staff do Bob can remember going to when Little Anthony was there had ended in trouble. The moron got pissed and started picking on random members of the company, trying to provoke a fight. Everyone knew who he was so they had to take it or else the Bitch Queen would sack them on the spot for attacking her poor little baby – scrawny, poisonous and protected little shit that he is.

Once Bob had witnessed Anthony smash a glass door into one of his victims. God knows how the victim had walked away with only a few bad bruises. Bob would not have liked to guess how far Little Anthony would have gone if he had not stepped in on the victim's side. Bob would have bet money that in his drunken state Anthony would have handed out a good sound kicking to the poor lad who had somehow been chosen to become his victim for the night. But once he had been seen by Bob, the twat had swaggered off shouting back at his victim, 'Let that be a lesson to ya.'

Anthony's victim hadn't wanted trouble so even after Bob had offered to be a witness if the police were called, the lad had taken the blame. He had apologised to the hotel staff saying he had tripped and hit the door and it had shattered on contact. One good thing from the incident was that Little Anthony never came to another company get-together, only the open air shows the company tried to sell their products at. The call of all that free booze on offer to try and get people to come in was too much of a temptation to keep him away. Not even the call of Jeremy Kyle or whatever crap he watched all day long could put up any resistance to the endless supply of free lager on those few days.

They get to the top of the stairs without trouble. No mad run for safety, no fainting from the excitement, no attempt to get away or even to swivel and karate-kick Bob back down the stairs. In real life there is no retake if it all goes horribly wrong. There is just the possibility of death. The gun stuck in the base of her spine is more than enough of a threat to keep her well behaved. They stand at the start of a short landing. He puts his hand on her shoulder. She nearly jumps through the ceiling. The sweat stains are spreading over the nightdress. He stops her outside the first door. He opens it carefully and quietly. Just because she has said there is no-one else in the rooms leading to the master bedroom, it does not necessarily mean she is telling the truth. Fibbing a little seems to be one of her more irritating traits but this time it is an empty spare room. The next is a bathroom and then another spare bedroom all empty.

She walks forward to the last door at the end of the landing. It must be the master bedroom. Again, he carefully opens the door, this time to find Little Anthony snoring away happily on a large double bed. Naked, blue white, hairy, loads of badly done tattoos and pimply. It is some small mercy Anthony is face down and his white pimply arse is just about covered by the scrunched-up bed clothes but Bob is still glad that he hasn't eaten breakfast. There is a slight dribble stain on the pillow Anthony is cradling under his head.

Bob silently signals for Summer to stand still at the far end of the bed and keep quiet. He takes another cable tie out of his bag ready and then puts the short muzzle of the gun right behind Anthony's ear and prods. Like some skinny white maggot trying to rouse itself from slumber, reality slowly dawns and Little Anthony breaks wind. 'Hands behind your fucking back and keep your trap shut.'

'Fuck you!' Well, what had he expected? Even naked and with a gun stuck in his ear this smart arse was never going to be quiet. Anthony goes to move across the bed. Bob pushes down hard with the gun (a vision of all the blackheads popping shoots across his imagination, gross! Again he is glad breakfast is still so far off).

'You want to die, big boy?' Bob doesn't know whether it is the pain from the pressure of the gun or the muffled squeal from Summer, but maggot boy calms down and lowers himself the two inches he had managed to rise off the bed. He puts his hands behind his back without being asked. Bob secures Anthony with the cable tie, this time around the wrists, and he does his little speech again about it just being a robbery and the benefits of co-operation.

'Right, where is the money, the jewellery and your porno DVD collection?' No-one laughs at Bob's attempt to lighten the mood. He tries to push the gun further into Anthony's ear as some sort of incentive and only gets mumbled obscenities. He looks across at Summer and he can see fear there.

'Now, children, I have played nice so far. Your insurance details say you have a safe, so money and jewellery ... NOW!' Bob didn't know if there was a safe or even if professional criminals could get access to that sort of information but these people were multi-millionaires and it's a big house, so he is guessing that they would want at least some of their stash close at hand to stroke and cuddle when the need takes them. From the reaction on Summer's face it seems he has struck lucky and this is immediately confirmed by the maggot. 'How the fuck you know that?' Bob must get around to taping the guy's mouth shut to keep him quiet.

'I am a professional. Now which one of you is going to show me where the safe is?' Summer is sobbing and fidgeting at the end of the bed. She seems to be attempting to will Anthony into not opening his mouth and revealing her secret stash.

She is shaking her head and raising her hands to remove the tape. Unfortunately Anthony can't see her from where he is lying face down on the bed. 'Say nothing,' is the subliminal command for Anthony to obey, but nothing is getting through.

Bob points at her with his free hand and at the same time jams the gun hard into Anthony's thick skull, making him squeal like a pig. She puts her hands out, palms open as if surrendering and showing she won't resist any more.

'For fuck sake, I'll take you, I'll take you.' Finally Anthony was being useful. 'There is no problem, I will take you.' Anthony is even sobbing a little now. 'The safe is downstairs. Down in the cellar. Show him, Summer, please. Take it all, take it all.'

From his position face-down on the bed, Anthony cannot see the glare Summer is giving him. He may have lost a friend for life, if her laser-eyed stare doesn't melt his brain to stop him talking first. A million pound payday as minimum every year and she looks like she is going to rip his tongue and heart out and try and make him eat them before he dies over a few grand in a safe ... It could be a very large safe, Bob muses over to himself?

Anthony has now confirmed there is a safe, told Bob where it is and implied there is something of interest in it as well. BANG! Anthony has now made himself surplus to requirements. One shot to the back of the head, quick and clean. Summer drops to the floor, her legs giving way. She is too scared to scream and just a whimper escapes from her throat. Bob steps sharply back to stop getting splattered with blood, the small pistol only making a small hole. There is a pause and then the blood pumps out in decreasing spasms as the heart stops pumping. Bob takes a small Stanley knife from the kitbag and removes the cable tie from Anthony's wrists and moves the dead man's arms into a more natural position for sleeping. It now looks like he was shot when he was still fast asleep. The used cable tie goes back into the kitbag with the rubbish.

There is no fear that anyone outside the room heard the shot. The neighbours are over a mile away as the crow flies and the house is double-glazed with the windows shut tight to the chill morning air. Someone standing on the lawn below the bedroom window would not have heard the shot. Besides, even if the window had been open, they are in the country and anyone would assume it was a farmer shooting something small and fluffy at this time in the morning ... well, any time of the day really. The shot wouldn't even have disturbed the early birds on the bird table.

There is no turning back now for Bob. Summer is on the floor at the bottom of the bed sobbing, so at least she hasn't fainted. He goes over and grabs her by the shoulders where she is half lying against the bed and gets her into a better sitting position, ripping the duct tape off her mouth. That too goes in the kitbag. Then her cable tie is removed. He shakes her to get her attention.

'Stop snivelling, bitch, I have just done you a big favour from what I can see with your choice of men.' He leans in closer and calmly whispers in her ear what he wants her to do.

'Listen, if you want to live, follow orders.' Summer is in mild shock but she has enough about her to realise that she must follow the instructions to the letter. Bob opens the wardrobe and takes out a suit and shirt and drops them in her lap. He then roots around in a drawer until he finds a bra and adds that to the pile. She already has knickers on, he can see them through her night clothes. Romance must be dead if you can sleep almost fully clothed every night – and it's so unhygienic. 'Put that lot on.'

The request had been reasonable but at first she makes no attempt to comply. 'GET DRESSED NOW.' He bends forward, shouting directly into her face. She stands and turns, her back now towards dear Little Anthony so she does not have to look his way. She has gone into under-drive but with some basic snarling under his breath she is encouraged to complete the task, although not as quickly as he would have liked or wanted. He wasn't going to help her dress, holding her sleeve arms open like she was some sulky toddler he was trying to get ready to go out when all she wanted to do was play with dolly.

Once fully dressed Bob commands her to hold her hands out and cable ties her thumbs again so she is free to open the safe but is restricted if she tries to escape. It wouldn't be completely impossible to get away, he wouldn't want her to give up all hope … not just yet. He sees no need to replace the tape as she isn't overly chatty. The bitch could start screaming anytime she wants to, but who is going to hear? He grabs a handful of the ginger mop she calls hair and propels her out onto the landing. She has become a mixture of zombie and the local supermarket's Saturday-only staff, but at least she is moving and that's better than the Saturday staff.

He is sure she hasn't recognised him, thanks to the disguise. He worried about his voice but fear must have fuddled her brain and so far she hasn't recognised or placed it as his. He has been to the house before, when Summer had wanted to show off her wealth to all her friends and colleagues, so he knows where he is going. He is leading and dragging her in his wake and he doesn't care if she realises he knows the layout of the place. Down the stairs, through the hall, across the lounge, into the kitchen and they are finally standing in front of the cellar door. The unhealthy cow is heavy breathing like she has just run a hundred metre dash. He glances at the kitchen clock – if it is correct he has been here just under fifteen minutes. He doesn't know if that's good or bad. What he does know is that it has felt like hours, but maybe that is the effect of his adrenaline-charged system.

Through the cellar door and down another flight of stairs, hitting the light switch as he passes to illuminate in front of them and the cellar beyond. He cannot see a safe. There are two walls that are bare brick and two which have been plastered over. The plastered walls have an array of naff paintings on them and there are two free-standing Welsh dressers strategically placed dead centre up against each of these walls with the pictures fanned out around them.

'Where is the safe?' Blank look from Summer. Was the little shit upstairs lying and playing for time, hoping Bob would take Summer to explore and he could make his escape? Were his last words a lie? There is too much assorted household crap piled up against the brick walls, so the assumption is it is behind one of the pictures ... or maybe one of the dressers? Enlightenment! There is nothing on one of the dressers while the other is overburdened with assorted books, empty jars and bric-a-brac.

He drags the unhelpful Queen Bitch by the hair over to the empty piece of furniture. It doesn't take much detective work to find out that the top is hinged down one side and not the other. He runs a hand down the unhinged side of the dresser and finds a loose section of moulding. One gentle push and hey presto! A spring lock releases and the top swings open to reveal a sweet little safe.

'Open it.' No response. 'OPEN IT.' This time the request is enhanced with a tug of the hair and a prod in the ribs with the gun to get her attention and she takes the hint. She twiddles the knob on the safe back and forth a few times then there is a click and the safe's door opens a fraction. She steps aside and sinks down the wall until she is sitting on the floor with her hands and arms covering her head as she rests it on her knees.

'There. Take the lot,' she mumbles. Jackpot! There are a few official-looking documents and a couple of jewellery boxes on the top of the pile. The rest of the space, about one-and-half-foot square, is packed with bundles of cash, all new £20 notes that Bob is sure the tax man knows nothing about. There must be thousands. It had been a shot in the dark but he should have known that the bitch would have a secret stash hidden away somewhere.

Greed seems the overpowering motivation in Summer's life, an all-consuming force. The risks she takes to add even more money to an already meaninglessly high bank account would seem stupid to most people. Maybe it is an attempt to show she could make money without Deb's help, even if she wouldn't have had the money to play with in the first place if it wasn't for Deb. If it wasn't for Deb's professionalism or if it hadn't been for Deb's diligence, what disasters might have happened? Bob supposed that when you are getting a fortune out of a factory and company someone else built for you, you must become blasé about your funds knowing that it will all reappear like magic every year. Bob and Deb had seen the world on a small budget. They had made friends all over and seen things most tourists never see because of those friendships. He just didn't get it. There was more to life than having to hide your cash from the taxman, surely?

Bob empties out a large cardboard box of old clothes and starts to fill it with the contents of the safe, all except the documents. He is amazed at how much cash is there. Once past the twenties, the stacks became bundles of fifty pound notes. Summer seems to have given up completely, so he leaves her to take the first box-load up the stairs and empties it across the kitchen breakfast bar. He makes a second trip and backtracks downstairs to empty the safe completely and get Summer back up on her feet and up into the kitchen.

His approach is more understanding and encouraging now. 'There, that was easy, wasn't it? It will all be over soon and I will leave you in peace and be gone forever.'

The kitchen is a rural but modern affair with a big breakfast bar and he sits Summer down in front of it away from the doors with the pile of money in front of her. He removes temptations like a knife rack, large kitchen utensils and anything that could be thrown at him and puts them out of harm's way. He opens the jewellery boxes and empties the contents onto the pile of cash for her to stare at.

As he had been here in a former life he knows where all the hard liquor is kept. Summer is a two bottles of wine a night kind of girl; her husband preferred the spirits. Soon Bob has a bottle of vodka and bottle of gin out on the counter, and one glass. He then takes out the medical box. Everyone has one at home just in case, and the box is full of half-taken prescriptions, half-used cough mixtures and a few tatty old bandages and plasters that are so old they are either frayed and or curling up at the edges.

He has brought with him a selection of tranquillisers and

sleeping pills that he bought over-the-counter abroad. It does cross his mind that they might have unique and specific ingredients that could be traced back to the country of origin and he is aiming for zero leads, so as he searches the medical box he is happy to find an abundance of sleeping pills and anti-depressants. Perhaps the snivelling bitch in front of him had a conscience after all and felt guilty about what she had done to Deb.

Nah! Don't think so, all these packs are untouched. It was more likely to be props for a little more play-acting. Summer could have got them from any doctor and then made sure they were found on the top of the stuff in her handbag or somewhere like that so someone would see and she could claim that she was suffering too ... Pathetic, the suckers back at the factory must have lapped that up. All of them falling over themselves to ask if Summer was all right and "Please, Ms Ponsenbury, can I be one of your new sympathetic best friends."'

Bob pours Summer a cold drink and starts popping the pills out of their packaging in front of her. He could have made a hot drink but he didn't fancy a face full of scalding coffee if she suddenly sprang into life. The glass is risk enough but with her thumbs tied, any attempt at throwing it in his direction should not be that accurate. There is a little pile of mixed yellow and white pills. He is playing nice now and apologises for the mess upstairs and again claims it is for the better. He thanks her for her cooperation. There has been no screaming, shouting or pleading, no real attempt at bargaining, and it has made his job much easier.

Maybe she knows everyone hates her and no longer trusts a word she says now that her true colours have been revealed, and she was subconsciously waiting for something like this to happen as a kind of penance. Now she has just accepted it as bad karma and what goes around comes around. Ultimately she knows that she will get daddy's casino business and money. That's the good thing about being an only child, you don't have to share. As if she would give a flying fuck about a load of whingeing Brits and what they think of her anyway. Maybe she is quiet because she is scared witless? It does make Bob wonder why she attacked Deb like she did, knowing what she was going to inherit. But he knows the answer to the unasked question: greed. It's more, more, more all the way. The only other answer would be 'Because I could' and that would not surprise him either!

Time to focus again. He stands next to the sitting Summer and he explains what he wants her to do. 'I'm going to let you live because you have been a very good girl. There is just one more thing you need to do. You need to take these sleeping pills so you can go to sleep and I can be long gone before you get the police involved. There aren't that many. It will just knock you out for a few hours.' Like Bob would know. She has zoned out again.

'Look at me. Oy! Look at me.' He snaps his fingers in front of her face to get her attention and she focuses again. He steps back, the gun ready in the other hand in case she tries to bolt. 'Now, don't get stupid, I'm going to leave soon. Eat the pills. Just a little more co-operation and it is all over and you can go back to your life.' With his free hand he passes her some of the pills. She takes them in her hand and puts them in her mouth. 'Swallow!' she takes a drink and the pills go down. They repeat this little game until all the pills are gone.

He then pours her a glass of vodka. 'Drink!' She complies and he keeps topping up her glass. She starts off like she is a teetotaller but after a little encouragement with the gun she is soon knocking the alcohol back with gusto. Atta- girl! She gags a few times at the start because the vodka is neat but it goes down more easily with every mouthful.

'Don't worry,' Bob encourages, 'you will be out for the count for twenty-four hours and you will wake up with the hangover from hell, but I will be gone.'

Inside he wants to scream at her and ask her why she did it. Why betray someone like Deb who thought she was a good friend? Why destroy someone who had worked tirelessly for decades making you millions of pounds and building a company that now spreads across the globe? A company that rewards you with dividends each and every year worth more than most people make in a lifetime, all down to Deb's unappreciated efforts.

But most of all he wants to know after all the lies and manipulations, the unfounded abuse and bullying, when Deb was broken beyond repair and so ill all she wanted to do was commit suicide to make the hurt go away. Did Summer actually feel anything about what she had done? What justification was there for her actions, for making another human so ill she would never work again and would spend the rest of her life on medication. And why had Summer cancelled the policy? The insurance would have allowed Deb something and cost the company nothing, was it spite? Summer was going to benefit from Deb's achievements until she retired, hadn't Deb earned that small mercy.

Bob can feel the rage rising. He could quite easily beat this woman to a pulp but he is not going to. Instead now the drugs and alcohol are beginning to kick in he will get on with his plan.

Summer looks up at him, trying to focus with bleary eyes from a world that is beginning to spin of its own free will. 'You won't touch me ... now you have drugged me?' she slurs.

'What?'

'Please don't rape me. I am a good girl.'

He stands there perplexed. God, what a horrible thought. He doesn't know whether to take her seriously. If only half the stories he has heard about her over the years were true he would be worried about catching something nasty and itchy. Anyway, Bob is not that desperate or stupid enough to leave all that DNA evidence around.

'No, luv, the money is all I want. Now finish your drink.' That seems enough to settle her troubled mind. He turns the radio on to try and lighten the mood. There is some nondescript boy band shredding what was once a pretty good song. He is sure most of the band's followers wouldn't know that this is not an original. Someone else taking all the credit and getting rich off someone a lot more talented than themselves. Unfortunately it seems the way of the world these days.

He takes an M&S plastic carrier bag off the side and puts all the £20 notes in it from the pile on the kitchen counter. There is still about two thirds of the stack left, made up of the fifties. Why waste the whole lot? He leaves the jewellery where it lies. He doesn't know where to get rid of it and it looks good quality, but he doesn't want anything that could be recognised as Summer's. The empty pill packets and the almost empty bottle of vodka he leaves in front of her, plus the still full bottle of gin. She carries on slurping away and trying hard not to fall off her chair. He arranges her handbag next to the money along with her mobile phone and car keys. It all looks like she is getting ready to leave in a hurry.

The cocktail is obviously working and he just manages to catch her and stops her falling off the chair and onto the floor. 'Beesh gentul wiv me. Plish don't bee wruff.' And she downs the dregs out of her glass.

She is well and truly out of her tree now. He removes the cable tie and puts it with the rubbish in his goody bag. He wipes the gun and puts it into her hand. She can't even sit upright now. If she had had more conventional bar stool type furniture with no arms or back there would be no way to keep her seated. As it is, it's become like keeping a sack full of puppies sat on the stool. He puts his hand over hers and raises both and the gun up until the little pistol is aiming at her temple ... Bang.

As with Anthony, a little hole appears and he steps back, letting go and letting her fall. He has time to step aside before the blood starts pumping out. This small calibre weapon seems ideal for the job. Hollywood must have been the ones that created the market and the need for massive handguns that blow half your head off and splatter blood and brains everywhere. Far too messy for real life.

She had teetered and then fallen forward onto the breakfast bar and as she collapsed, some of the money, the jewellery and the bottles had fallen with her as she slithered off the chair. The gin bottle had smashed on the tiled floor and its contents were spreading and soaking into the business suit he had made her dress in as she lay there crumpled on the floor, the bank notes spread about her. The gun had stayed in her hand for a short time but with the grip no longer tight as she hit the floor it had worked loose and fallen a little way from her hand.

The perfect little scene was left for the casual observer of a deeply disturbed woman unable to cope with what she had done to her best and most loyal friend. In her despair and guilt she had killed her unfaithful husband and had been set to start a new life. She had emptied the safe of her secret stash of cash and jewellery ready to run. But before she fled she had had an attack of remorse, the most likely conclusion being that she realised that she had blown everything with her jealousy and greed. Her temper has clouded her judgment and it is futile to run. She has lost everything; her husband, her job, her fortune and there is nothing left for her. Now she just wants to destroy it all. End it all.

He throws a pair of her shoes under the breakfast counter as a final touch. She would not have been getting ready to run barefooted, after all. This had been his plan from the start. Why would anyone look further than this little domestic? He heads back down to the cellar and takes out some firelighters and some matches from his bag. He puts several of the film-wrapped squares amongst the junk and lights them. He doesn't wait to see if the fire is catching. There are enough dry paper and rags about not to have to worry too much about it not bursting into flames. He heads back up the stairs and into the kitchen avoiding the spreading blood and mess.

He would have liked to have heard 'Fire' by Arthur Brown or 'Fire Starter' from the guy with the hair, but the radio is aiming for the younger market and there is some totally inappropriate and happy tune playing.

He steps carefully over the debris in the kitchen, going over to the gas cooker where he switches everything on to full. He doesn't light any of the escaping gas but leaves it hissing into the air.

Across to the cupboards, where he puts another lighted firelighter amongst the cleaning clothes, polishing stuff and aerosols. He closes the door. The aerosols should make a nice bang as they go up. He picks up the carrier bag full of money and goes into the lounge. The smell is getting a bit ripe in the kitchen, our newly departed deceased's bowels having opened.

In the lounge there is a gas fire and he switches that on full too, again leaving it unlit with the gas escaping. A couple more firelighters under the corner of the sofa and amongst the DVDs and magazines. Things are hotting up. He can hear the crackling and popping from down in the cellar.

Out into the hall. He originally wanted to go upstairs and make sure a fire was set in the master bedroom but he doesn't want to get trapped and chooses not to. Time and the urge to get out of there are beginning to become his main motivations. The clock on the hall wall tells him he has been here forty minutes already. There is a nice wooden staircase with a storage space underneath. He opens the door and it is full of even more junk and paper. The last two firelighters go into there and he closes the doors. Once the fire gets going, the nice wooded staircase will spread the blaze for him. A quick glance around. Has he forgotten anything? He can smell the place burning. He grabs the empty box and the clipboard, opens the front door and steps into the early light of the morning.

The door is on a latch and closes with a clunk. It will take a lot to force it open now it is locked again. He keeps to a brisk walk back to the van rather than run, just in case someone is passing. Running would look suspicious, Paedo Paul creepy he can live with for a while. A quick check back and there is nothing that he can see that would give him away, not even any blood on his costume.

He opens the van and throws his collection of bags and boxes on to the passenger seat. He gets in, starts up and drives calmly and unhurriedly away. One final look back across the fields from a safe distance and he can see the faint flicker of fire in a couple of windows. Soon the place will be a pile of rubble and ash.

And the local papers will have the headline: 'Vodka and pills binge tragedy'.

18

Greed-driven Harpy

SHIT ... SHIT ... SHIT!

The bitch is coming out of her front door. It had all been a daydream. Boredom had crept up and finally got the better of him. There had been no lights switched on or off anywhere as far as he was aware. It was still dark, he knew he would have seen them. His soul would have felt them. Her closing the front door must have woken him. Only on the horizon is there any sign of the new day ahead and the sky brightening. Shit ... she is jogging up the drive!

All the planning and preparation are now completely blown. Bob's mind is in turmoil. Does he run? Does he wait until she comes back? She has a 'Green Goddess'-style jogging outfit on with fluorescent stripes down the arms of the tracksuit. How long will she be gone? She will see the van, see him if he stays, and when she gets back and he is still here will she be suspicious. Shit ... Shit ... what can he do?

Panic subsides and he gains control of his emotions. Think ... think. This could work in his favour. His alter-ego is a white van man and he has on his disguise; she will never recognise him. She is getting closer and closer. She has jogged the length of her drive, so maybe she will stop at the open gate and then jog back once she has reached the road?

He watches. No, she turns onto the road and heads towards where he is parked. Red shaggy hair, with the green tracksuit and the fluorescent stripes trying to hide the four or five stones of extra weight she is carrying. No wonder she jogs in the early hours when no-one should be around to see the spectacle. Inspiration! As she closes in on his position, he takes up the mobile phone and puts it to his ear so that it looks like he is talking to someone. He has the clipboard perched up against the steering wheel. Hopefully she will assume that he is checking an address or something with the imaginary person at the other end of the fictitious phone call. The clipboard even hides most of his face but if she looks she will only see Paedo Paul.

She is going to stomp past him in seconds and he is trying not to look her way but all that swaying and swinging and heavy breathing and the reflective strips flashing makes it impossible. It is morbidly hypnotic. Will God strike her down with a heart attack as she passes, and save Bob from his sins? All the adrenaline is making him hot, sweaty and uncomfortable but probably not as hot, sweaty and uncomfortable as she is.

He had worried for nothing. There was not a glance or a look in his direction. He was just a white van man, one of the array of menials and underlings who magically transforms her life and gets everything done in the shadows. To her, people like him did not exist. He was one of the unclean that one would not talk to and never ever socialise with, one of the unappreciated going about his shitty little life, not even worthy of an acknowledgment of his existence. He has been to enough company functions to know her views on the workers making her millions. If robots could do it she would be ecstatic. Bob didn't even work for her company and he knew more names than she did of the people who worked for her and their likes, dislikes, skills and aspirations.

Over two decades Bob had seen his wife grow into the role of guardian angel and mother hen to the whole workforce and guide them so that the right people were where they should be and where they could achieve the most for themselves and for the company. Perhaps some of these people would reflect one day on how they'd enjoyed working for someone who actually cared and still had more than enough skill to make the company the success it had become. All Summer wanted was the workforce to touch their forelock when she passed or before they had to speak to her ... and of course agree with her every word.

Under Deb's influence, the company had grown in size, status and profitability. It had also become a trusted name in its market. Looking back he could see that once the company had made it the good people who had got it there had been subtly replaced with Summer's lackeys and 'yes' men. Lackeys and yes men had been the cause of all the company's problems before Deb arrived. Maybe he could hope history would repeat itself, but that was a long shot. The indestructible superstructure Deb had built the company on would guarantee that wouldn't happen. All-out nuclear war would be the only thing that could do any real damage to the company and its profitability now and it had all been thanks to Deb's achievements.

This needs to end now! Think ... think, he has done too much to let this evil woman just jog off into the sunrise. He considers going in and killing Anthony and ringing the police hoping she was the one blamed but she could end up getting the sympathy vote as the grieving widow.

He just cannot walk away ... No, this bitch destroyed Deb, destroyed their life, their future and their dreams. Summer cheated, lied about and abused Deb to the point of no return. Bob is sure there would be people who would applaud and praise the way Summer manipulated and schemed so convincingly to steal someone else's achievements and rewards for herself, and managed to destroy that person in the process so much that the victim couldn't fight back. The world would be a better place if he could find a way to put an end to this woman. To be that greedy for money and accolades that you can destroy a friend just to claim their life's work as yours is beyond any normal person.

Summer is disappearing into the gloom. If it wasn't for the

fluorescent strips she would be hard to see. Bob checks his bag. The gun is ready. Decision made. He starts the van. He knows the road, he has travelled it several times to scout the area. There is only one road in the direction she is going for a couple of miles and then it comes to a deserted crossroads. There are no people, no cars and no houses. He pulls away after her. He can see her in the distance, thanks to the headlights. The radio goes from chat to Queen playing 'Fat Bottomed Girls'. He wants to laugh but keeps himself under control. He has never been into stick insects and curves will always win outright but there is a point where the scale starts to tilt the other way. Anyway, nervous tension might soon turn to hysteria if he doesn't focus and keep a grip on things.

He soon catches up, the headlights doing nothing for the now fully illuminated enormous wobbling backside of hers. He considers flooring the accelerator and driving over the bitch but there would be too much evidence left around the crash site for the police to work with. He could stay and say he was dazzled by her go-faster stripes or he thought it was two people and he tried to drive between them before he realised, but that probably would not get him off. And how could he explain the fucking great dent in the front of his mate's van when he returned it?

If he was in Canada he could put it down to a stray caribou but unfortunately he is on a country lane in Staffordshire and that particular animal doesn't roam this far south. The van could even come off worst and be undrivable; then how would he escape?

He indicates out of habit and pulls around Summer. Just another white van on an early morning mission. He doesn't go too close or too fast as he passes. She appears, plodding along in the rear-view mirror until she is swallowed up in the darkness again. He guesses she uses the crossroads as a target point and will turn back once she has reached it, so that is where he will wait for her. If she doesn't show in ten or fifteen minutes he can always return to plan A.

Within a couple of minutes he reaches the crossroads and has a short time to prepare. She could stop and turn around but she maybe fitter or more determined than he has given her credit for and aiming to carry on, choosing one of the other directions. He is sure this time of the year she won't be off-roading, school cross-country style.

Bob pulls up and parks near to a sign showing all the possible local destinations and leaving the engine running. He has parked on the road to ensure he doesn't leave tyre prints on the grass verge. He did the same near the house, choosing a concrete slab a farmer had conveniently laid as access to his land with the gate set a little way back, it gave Bob the view he wanted.

It is getting noticeably lighter now. Bob has sat and waited, watching patiently in the van's mirrors as Summer crests a small dip in the road, still heading in his direction. He gets out of the van with the bag over his shoulder and the clipboard in his hand. He then makes a show of looking at the road sign. He is taking time to see if fate is going to be kind and give him a little alone time with Summer. He can see no other headlights in any direction.

He can hear the heavy footfalls and deep breathing that announces the woman's approach. His right hand is inside the bag gripping the pistol, keeping it out of sight but ready. It feels cold and lifeless even through the plastic gloves and all he can ask is that it is reliable and works when needed. He has the clipboard in his left hand and he hopes he looks suitably confused so that she will stop and offer guidance. Plod, plod, closer and closer.

She is level with him and then she goes past without stopping. Bob calls out after her, 'Miss, Miss, excuse me, sorry to trouble you'. She obviously is no Good Samaritan and considers ignoring him and takes a few extra strides, then stops and turns. He has to go to her. She is standing there like a big green annoyed primary school teacher with her hands on her hips. She has a look on her face of 'How dare someone like you interrupt someone like me!'

'Yes?' She sounds irritated.

'I am sorry to trouble you but you are the only one around. My dispatch seems to have given me a non-existent address. Do you live around here? You might recognise the name.' He keeps talking as he gets closer, raising the clipboard as if to offer it to her for her perusal. He had hoped she would stop by where he was stood waiting and see if he needed help. They would have both been shielded from view thanks to the size of the van. Now she has run past they are in full view of anyone watching, and they are on the opposite side of the road to the vehicle.

She reaches for the board. 'Buy a sat nav. It may help.'

What she means is, buy a sat nav and don't bother me. She is at almost at full arm's reach away and as she makes to take the board, he does not let go. The resistance surprises her and she looks at him. It means he now has a clear shot at her chest and in the split second it takes to question his actions he has raised the gun. He has an overwhelming urge to start quoting Judge Dredd: 'I AM THE LAW ... PREPARE TO BE JUDGED', but he resists.

A fraction of a second feels like hours. The gun is chest-high and he fires ... Bang! He has chosen the small-calibre weapon to help convince the police it was hers in the original plan. There is no massive flash as it discharges. There is no lifting her off her feet and throwing her six feet backwards as her chest explodes and her backbone is shattered into a million pieces.

He thinks he has failed. There is a small, slightly smoking hole just off-centre in the middle of her chest and then a dark stain starts to creep out and spread across her clothing. She is not dropping dead at his feet – she just looks surprised, as if she has been stung by a bee or wasp. He raises the gun higher and fires point blank into her face. This time she drops. Dead meat.

What little momentum there was from the second impact sends the body backward in a slow graceful arc, the only time this bitch has been graceful in years, he thinks. The body falls into a drainage ditch, twisting as it goes, to land in the mud and water almost completely hidden from view by the weed – without any assistance from Bob. Yep! There is a God.

Ms Summer fucking Ponsenbury is now face down in slime, duck weed and fox shit where she belongs. He wants to check and make sure she is dead, cut the head off, drive a stake through the heart and all that sort of thing but he is still with it enough to realise not to push his luck and the desire to leave no evidence prevails. No footprints in the mud, just a big green arse poking out above the pond plants that grow in the ditch. With the green tracksuit nearly the same colour as the surrounding vegetation and the fact she is now well below eye level, it should mean she will be almost invisible to anyone driving past. A fitting end.

Bob puts the gun back in the bag. He doesn't know whether he is savouring the moment or too shocked to move, so he just stands there. He takes the stretchy gloves off to give his sweaty palms a chance to breathe in the cool morning air. Hawkken had been a happy accident, and technically Bob had simply got out of the way of some aggressive maniac attacking him. This had been different. After a short time he replaces the gloves with a new pair and takes a few deep breaths to keep his heart rate in check. The gloves are so cheap, who cares how many he uses as long as they work. This frugal thought is strange at a time like this.

Focus is back and his mind is again on track. He is not worried about the shot being heard – it's a different scenario to his daydream but the same result; something fluffy has just become lunch. Now he moves quickly. In the original plan he was going to drive away from the house and then replace the false number plates so if he was spotted the numbers would be useless and untraceable. He looks around and the place is deserted except for him and the green arse in the ditch. He quickly goes to the front and back of the van and peels the makeshift plates off and they also end up in the bag. Why find anywhere else to stop and change them? In seconds he is in the van and pulling away, heading for home.

The drive is surreal; no panic but no joy either. Perhaps he has mentally envisioned killing that women so many times as he watched his wife suffer nightmare after nightmare that he has become numb, or it may still feel that it is unreal and it has not registered that the job is finished. Maybe the elation will come later when he is safe and at home again?

His escape route has been pre-planned and he has made sure that it is totally different to the way he came. The way home is a mixture of country lanes and poorly used 'A' roads, just a quiet ride in the country where there are no cameras on every junction and no potential witnesses watching on every street corner, like there would be in the city. The invisible white van is slipping through the lonely early hours on the roads he now knows well. He had followed Summer enough times over the past few weeks as he checked her route home looking for a spot to ambush the bitch. He had borrowed cars and motorbikes so she didn't suspect anything and notice the same car following her as she carried on oblivious to her impending brush with fate. He had toyed with playing the broken-down motorist or motorcyclist on one of the narrow lanes where she would have had to stop and if not help, she would still have had to wait. Then a simple request to use her mobile to summon assistance from a struggling stranger and as she searched her bag, he could have reached in and blasted her in the back of the head.

He had even considered dropping a brick off a bridge she passed under regularly. Her bright red BMW and private plates were easy to pick out from the crowd. He'd have aimed the brick so it smashed through her windscreen as she zoomed up the dual-carriageway, oblivious again to the danger. Only concern for the safety of other drivers stopping him using this most simple of plans.

From deserted crossroads to home in around twenty minutes. On the way he sees a couple of cars travelling in the opposite direction and a few more on the outskirts of town. Probably early commuters heading for the business estates somewhere or even into Birmingham. He pulls up and parks a short distance from his home. He picks up everything that he has brought and put into the van to be used on his little quest – the bag, the box and the clipboard – and takes it with him. The day is much lighter now and the estate is coming to life. The disguise can still be useful if anyone is taking any notice. He heads for his home.

He tries to be as quiet as he can when he enters, still trying not to fall over anything or drop anything and make a noise that might give him away because he still has a few things to do before he wakes Deb. The dog is now full of energy, unlike earlier, but is well trained enough not to start barking and jumping around dementedly. The disguise didn't fool it the first time so it won't be a problem now. A quick fuss once he has put everything down safely and he lets it out into the back garden to look after itself. Now it is just a case of getting rid of the evidence.

He goes into the garage and spreads paper across the worktop, then puts all his stuff on it. First he takes the gun and ammunition out of the bag and with a sterile wipe gives everything the once-over and then seals them into waterproof, re-sealable plastic food bags, one for the gun and one for the magazines and ammunition. The bags are airtight and he places them to one side. This is a problem he didn't think he would have to solve. In the original plan the gun was going to be left at the scene as evidence of Summer's guilt.

He takes the unused pills and returns them to their usual resting place at the back of one of the kitchen cupboards. Back in the garage, everything else that is left should burn down to nothing. He opens the top of the bogus parcel and inside he puts the kitbag with all the used gloves, the cable ties, the tape, the homemade car number plates and finally the clipboard. He is just about to take it all outside to burn and he remembers his ginger wig and disguise. The wig comes off easily but the eyebrows and the big beard take a little more effort than just a sweep of the hand. But he is soon outside in his nice secluded garden standing near the fire pit.

The dog had come over for a second or two but has now disappeared and found something more interesting to do. Sometimes the fire pit will stay hot for a couple of days so it takes nothing but a quick rake and a little fresh wood to bring it back to full life, the hot embers bursting into flame when they are disturbed as the oxygen mixes in with them. The box and its contents are first and instantly the flames take hold, the cardboard peeling as it burns. A few more bits of wood to keep it all going and the fire stacked up, then he strips. The trainers, the waterproof jumpsuit and high-viz vest, then the T-shirt and his underwear. All are committed to the flames as he stands there stark bollock naked watching it all burn, close enough not to feel the chill air around him. He piles on what is left of the wood he had left ready and leaves it to burn away.

There had been a bit too much smoke to start with but as soon as the heat had built up the smoke had disappeared. It is only 'cold' fires that give off smoke. He leaves the fire and takes out some detergent he has for cleaning the car. It is a strong de-greaser and he hopes if there is any evidence he has missed it will be washed off or contaminated so it is now useless. He can't risk having a shower inside and waking his wife with things still to be done so he uses the garden hose. For several seconds all his mind can scream is 'Fuck! That is cold' – and he could really do without the damn dog trying to help. A cold wet nose where you don't want it is not the most pleasant thing in the world and does take you by surprise. What is it with big dogs and water?

He dries off using dirty towels from the washing basket. He had been organised enough last night to leave fresh clothes ready and he quickly dresses, but towels had not crossed his mind. He has to risk creeping around the kitchen again so he can get dog food. The damn thing is getting bored and becoming a pain in the arse and is bouncing around and being playful. The result of a full night's sleep and then playing in cold water, no doubt. Bob feeds it in the garage to keep it quiet. It will definitely be cats next time. Small, quiet and happy to crap in someone else's garden without your help or encouragement.

Bob takes a second or two and runs through what he is doing. He has returned the Stanley knife to the junk drawer and the pills to the medical box and he then makes another check on the fire, fetching a little more wood and adding it to the pile that has burnt down now. Back to the garage and on with more stretchy gloves. He thinks he has a plan and a hiding place for the gun now he has had time to think. He didn't want to use the original hiding place as a long-term solution because anyone could have found the evidence if he was unlucky. Now that he has kept the gun it might come in handy at some later date.

He roots about the garage until he finds some fishing line. The dog is back in the garden chewing something and no longer has any interest in what he is doing. Bob puts the bags with the gun and the ammunition in his jacket pocket and removes the ladder from the wall bracket it is hanging from and goes outside. There is an unused chimneystack at the rear of the house. It had been connected to a big wood-burning stove when they had moved in but when they had opened up the kitchen the stove had gone and the base of the chimney had been filled in.

He raises the ladder up against the back wall and up the chimneystack so he can gain access to the roof. He is trying to keep as quiet as possible, which is no mean feat with a set of thirty-foot ladders. He is glad he has no fear of heights because the solution, if it works, should make things easy. Once he is on the roof he ties the fishing line to the first bag. He uses the one with the ammo in because he doesn't want to risk the gun straight away. He then lowers the bag down inside the unused chimney and ties off the line around the chimney pot so he can retrieve it whenever he needs to.

It works perfectly. The clear line is almost invisible even when he is this close to it. He quickly repeats the process with the bag containing the gun and goes back down the ladder. Soon everything is back in its place in the garage. From outside you can look up and there is no trace of what he has done. The fishing line is invisible and it shouldn't weather too badly out in the rain. It is eight to eight thirtyish and it's a work day, so if there was a little noise from his exploits no-one should care. Over the years the neighbours had seen him working on his house at all times of the day so this wouldn't be out of the ordinary enough for anyone to notice.

Back inside he listens at the bottom of the stairs for movement from the bedroom Deb is in, but cannot hear anything, not a sound. The master bedroom is at the front of the house and he has been at the rear so at the moment it is so far, so good. He had been a little worried about the ladder idea but it was too big a risk not to hide the gun and get it done straight away.

Right, only the van to return now. He picks up the keys, gives the dog a chew to keep it happy and is on his way down the drive. All is going well.

* * *

'Hi there! What's up with the roof?' Jack, one of Bob's neighbours, catches him off-guard as he goes down the drive, heading for the van and trying to complete his escape. It's one of those 'minute before or a minute after' scenarios where either way their paths would not have crossed. Now Bob is trapped into being polite and he really has more important things to do.

'Oh! Hi there. Nothing really, just some stupid bloody pigeon that had managed to get itself down the chimney and I wanted to get it out before work so it didn't suffer.'

'Sooner you than me, mate. Three rungs up a stepladder is far enough for me. See you around, got to fly.' With a cheery wave he fucks off.

'Yeah, see you.' Too damn cheerful for his own good, that guy. Nothing you can put your finger on but you are always left wishing you had something pointy or heavy and blunt to hand when he starts. At least this time he was quick. The pigeon story had seemed lame but Bob did genuinely get two or three of the damn things each year down the main chimney on the other side of the house that led down into the front room. The stupid birds tried to roost on the chimney pot in the escaping warmth and they'd fall off, the unfortunate one or two dropping the wrong way and ending up covered in soot, toasty and a little crispy.

Jack is off, walking the other way. Bob walks around the corner to the van, putting on another new pair of gloves (he didn't want to be sloppy now). Three-quarters of an hour later and he has fought his way through the tail-end of rush hour traffic and is parking the van back in the yard he borrowed it from. He is careful to park away from the yard office so no-one can see when he takes the seat covers off, closes the van and removes the last pair of gloves. The rubbish is conveniently burned in a small fire one of the lads has going in an old oil drum in a sheltered corner in the yard.

As Bob crosses the yard to return the keys, his friend comes out. 'All done, any problems?'

'No, smooth as smooth. Thanks again, that got me out of trouble. You know how it is, the garage tells you the parts will be in to fix your car in plenty of time and then guess what?'

'Yep! Sounds familiar, we have the same problems all the time. Just try it with a fleet of the fucking things.' They chat for a short time and Bob drops him £40. Well, he isn't supposed to let people borrow the vans, 'nudge, nudge, wink, wink, say no more'. More Monty Python impersonations, Bob would bet it is the most quoted bit from the show. He leaves and walks ten minutes to the local train station. He gets a ticket for home and within thirty minutes is collecting his own car from where he parked it earlier.

Commuting, who wants it? There had been another potential 'Rhod' moment waiting for the train. On his side a train with six carriages and six passengers. On the opposite track it is armpit to sweaty armpit and the ones at the front are worried about being pushed on to the track to certain death. Again six carriages arrive but with people already standing for lack of space. Best of luck.

Bob was feeling quite happy on the ride back. He has already rid the world of a greed-driven harpy before breakfast and that does seem to lighten the day. He would thoroughly recommend the experience to anyone. Put it on your 'things to do' list, right at the top of page one: 'Destroy true evil incarnate before a full English'.

He starts his car, as reliable as ever despite the 140,000-plus on the mileage counter. There is a quick drive to the local shops to buy some bacon and eggs and even a lottery ticket (no, he didn't feel that lucky but the date and time stamp helps his alibi). The ticket and the till receipt are added to the rubbish in the pocket on the car door. Where does all the rubbish come from? He doesn't smoke or even eat sweets and still the car is full of wrappers and cigarette packets. Does he have a local tramp camping in his Volvo overnight? He must keep an eye on the lottery this week though, just in case – or is that being greedy?

He pulls onto his drive and he is not being quiet this time. He makes sure the door bangs shut. He also bangs the front door as he takes his shopping through to the kitchen. There is a little time taken to wind up the dog and get it barking, then he bounds 'Tigger'-style up the stairs and makes a dramatic entrance into the master bedroom.

He is greeted with a sleepy and grumpy, 'What the fuck?'

'Do you want breakfast? It has just gone 10.30, dear.' Then another Tigger impression. 'You shouldn't drink if it makes you grumpy in the morning.' Chaos instigated, and hangover ignited. He had considered letting the dog come bouncing along too but no one deserves that first thing in the morning. Bob gets off the bed and goes to the door. Deb seems to be signalling from under the covers that she wants two eggs, so he departs to cook breakfast and lets her come round and join the land of the living. While the bacon is cooking he checks the fire pit. Everything has burnt away nicely. He rakes the pit and leaves the red-hot embers to burn away completely, then glances up quickly to check that the fishing line securing the gun wasn't visible. Then back to the cooking.

A really hot shower, two very strong cups of coffee and a full English and all is well with the world. He checks the fire again and is sure no evidence could have survived. Deb is back in the land of the living, or as close as she gets these days, and has put the 'lie-in' down to the alcohol and lots of restless nights finally catching up. If he is honest, she seems a lot better in herself for a solid twelve hours' deep sleep, even if it was drug-induced. It is easy for him to claim that he has only been up an hour before she was and he reels off the made-up story about the pigeon and being purposefully vague about the details and which chimney it was, just in case they meet up with Jack at some point – the guy is bound to bring it up. It is then a simple case of mentioning that he went out for supplies and spent ten minutes in front of the TV catching up with Sky News, just in case he is asked. It's a good job it is repeated over and over again.

* * *

All the trouble building up his feeble but believable alibi reaps its rewards much later in the day. Actually, he had wanted the police to show up a lot earlier, when the car engine was still hot and they could have dramatically arrested him on the spot without any real proof, and later let him go because they had no evidence from the crime scene or off him or the car. The car would be clean of any incriminating evidence and given a little time the security camera in the car park in front of the local shops would confirm his alibi. The lottery ticket and receipt would be the icing on the cake.

As it was, the police did not arrive until early evening. Then instead of a full SWAT team, dogs and helicopters, an older, grey-haired, plain clothes detective arrived, along with a rookie cop who looked like an overly tall and lanky twelve-year- old who was going to a fancy dress party with his granddad dressed as a policeman. After confirming who he was, and that it was his wife's house and yes he did live here etc, etc, Bob let them in. He made out he was a little panicky and asked if his son or any of the family were hurt. That started to panic Deb a little but the detective soon calmed them down and confirmed everything was all right with the family and he was here on a different matter entirely.

They all ended up in the front room. 'Well, we've told you who we are and you have told us that none of our family is injured, in trouble or dead – so what's the visit all about and how can we help?'

'Well, sir, we have been informed that you have a dislike for a Ms Summer Ponsenbury, your wife's former employer. There was an incident earlier today which we are now investigating.'

'What's that bitch trying to pull now? Hasn't she done enough damage to my wife and me already? She has destroyed our life and my wife's health. That whore should be locked in a cage to stop her doing any more harm. Whatever she is trying to claim, trust me – she is lying. Whenever she opens her mouth the lies just spew out. She gets off on counting her money and screwing innocent people over.' Bob doesn't have to fake the emotions and anger he is presenting to the police.

The detective was sitting at the end of the sofa while Bob and the young constable both stood, the constable by the door, presumably to stop any kind of escape attempt. Bob prowls in front of the fire. Deb is quietly sitting in a chair to the side. 'Well, er … yes. If you could confirm where you were early this morning please, sir, we will try and get this over with as quickly as possible.'

'Here, of course. I got up half nine-ish and my wife maybe an hour or hour-and- a-half later.' He looks at Deb and she confirms what she believes to be true. 'We sat around the fire pit last night and got drunk. We got up late this morning. Slept in a bit, it's not like we have a lot to do these days.' Again Deb confirms what is being said to the officer.

'Can anyone independently confirm any of this?'

'No, it was just the two of us. But the fire pit might still be warm and the empty wine bottles are in the recycling bin outside if that proves anything. The blue bin if you want to look.' The officer says he will check and can Bob show him. Bob doesn't know why but both policemen seem to be finding Deb's German Shepherd a little unnerving. The dog had barked when they had arrived and now she was watching them intently, giving them the evil eye. Bob is sure they have seen the local force's dogs growling and snarling around the station with their handlers trying to keep them under control. Maybe not putting her on a lead and not stopping her glaring at them as they try and complete their interview is putting them off their game a bit. They all trudge out to the pit and then to the bin for what any of that can confirm or prove in the grand scheme of things to the policemen.

The detective opens the bin and takes one of the empty bottles out and starts to inspect it. Bob has a moment of panic. The detective turns to look at Bob like he has some secret spider sense and can somehow make out the residue left from the sleeping pills inside the bottle. Bob is getting worried.

'I quite like this one myself. It's from M&S, isn't it?' Bob confirms the observation and the empty bottle goes back into the bin and that seems to be all. Then Deb suddenly pipes up with the pigeon story. She doesn't know it isn't true but once Bob has confirmed the story and that the neighbour from down the road had witnessed the episode, all again becomes calm. It is the first thing she has said in months that has not been prompted and pushed or cajoled out of her. Bob takes the opportunity to 'remember' the trip to the shop and makes a show of finding the ticket and receipt. It couldn't have gone better even if he had rehearsed it.

Bob really wants to say a few things about the darling Ms Ponsenbury and be helpful and give the police a few leads to chase but as yet they have not given away any clue as to why they are there and what sort of incident they are investigating. It would be hard for Bob to convince them of his innocence if he starts talking like he knows Summer is no more.

'Officer, we have co-operated as best we can. Please can't you tell us what that bitch is trying to pull or accuse me of this time?' Bob asks. 'Last time she made out I was making death threats because I had written a small blog about what had happened to Deb and asking if anyone could offer any sort of advice or help. Summer managed to sucker some of your comrades-at-arms to get me arrested before they actually bothered to take the time and looked at the evidence or lack of it. I did get a nice apology but I would hope it is on record what Summer is like and capable of and that she isn't manipulating you again?'

Well, God bless the sweet young copper. 'She was mur-!' A glare from his superior shuts him up instantly but it is just a little too late. The plain-clothes guy has cut him dead but Bob has caught enough to open up and to look innocent whilst he is doing it, all at the same time.

Bob isn't quite jumping up and down with joy but for appearances' sake he is trying to look happy. Why try and deny how the confirmation makes him feel? 'Someone has killed that bitch? RESULT! Well, that has made my day. No, that's made my year! Well, maybe even my lifetime,' he enthuses. 'If ever there was someone who deserved to die [he almost says *horribly*, which might have given him away but he manages to stop himself] it was her.' More reflectively to no-one in particular, he adds: 'Well, who would have believed it? There must be a God after all.'

'Sir, that's not the reaction most people have been giving us.' Yes, but not everyone knows her like we do, Bob thinks.

'You don't know the bitch or the scum she mixes with as well as I do. Sorry, I mean did.' Plain-clothes and junior are soon back in Bob's lounge and they sit back and listen as they are given the low-down and details of how Summer Ponsenbury had swindled Deb out of millions of pounds, destroyed her reputation, taken her pension and all Deb had worked for. Bob missed nothing, explaining how with the help of her lawyers Summer had fed Deb page after page of promises and guarantees to keep her working at the company for years, and that they had all been found to be worthless. He went through the lies and fabrication of evidence they used to destroy Deb's career and reputation. How Summer and her cohorts had conspired, and made Deb so ill they had been able to drive her out of the company with next to nothing and it was all done so Summer wouldn't have to pay market value for his wife's shares and to leave the way open for Summer to take the credit for what had really been done and achieved by Deb. It was an old story now, but it was a new audience and they both sat there horrified at what had been got away with in plain sight of the law.

'She appears to have been a very calculating woman. It would seem to me that you have a very clear and personal motive. Is there anything else you would like to say or even … confess to?'

Is he trying to imply it was Bob? How dare the guy think that, even if it was a little true? 'Don't go jumping to conclusions – but don't get me wrong, I wanted her dead and to die horribly if at all possible. Did she die horribly? Never mind, but my wife still has nightmares and still needs medication to cope with life, thanks to what that woman did.' Bob pauses slightly. 'I wouldn't risk doing something if it meant there would be no-one left here to look after Deb.'(Deb has been allowed to go to bed so there are only the two policemen, the dog and Bob left in the room.)

He continues. 'Almost every night the nightmares come and I have to stay awake and watch over her until she finally falls into a deep sleep out of sheer exhaustion. Some nights I have been so tired myself that I have dozed off and woken up to find my wife gone. Imagine what runs through your mind knowing what has gone before. Should it be right that I have to feel relieved when I find her curled up on the front room carpet crying and she can't even remember how or why she came to be there? Some nights she is still sleepwalking when I find her and I can guide her back to bed without her realising what she has done. I spent six months not being able to work or leave her alone because I didn't know what I would return to. Even now there are days when I worry.'

They take notes and listen. 'Yeah, I could and would have killed that bitch and all the rest of the bastards who helped stitch up my wife. All the people who sold her out for a promotion or a little more cash in their pay packet. Deb made all the shareholders multi-millionaires by salvaging a company about to go under and showing them all what to do and how to do it. She spent two decades of her life and worked sixty to eighty hours a week minimum while the others sat back and did as little as they possibly could and she didn't even get a thank you. Those parasites even went out of their way to celebrate in front of her when they had managed to screw her out of everything. All of them high-fiving each other and boasting how expensive the night out was going to be to celebrate their win.'

'You want to know who killed Summer fucking Ponsenbury? Try the people who will benefit the most from her death: the other two bastards whose shares will have at least doubled. How many millions do you think they are suddenly worth now? I know a few years back Summer was worth well over ten million and she was easily taking another million or so out of the company each year, plus the value of her shares. Someone is going to be in line to benefit from that now she won't be there. You don't have to believe my figures – anyone can contact Companies House and buy a copy of any company's accounts for a few quid if they are interested enough and don't believe the toned down and well edited version they are being fobbed off with. They will even include the dividend pay-outs the CEO has probably been hiding or not mentioning, because most people forget about them or just don't know about the extra yearly pay-out.'

He had not meant to make it a rant but he was on a roll. 'Then what about that poisonous little shit of a husband? If she has died in service, the company's insurance will pay him off, no questions asked. I know Summer cancelled Deb's policy but I would bet money no-one else's was tampered with. Perhaps Anthony has got a little greedy – there are over ten million pieces of motive there.' The climax was building and the police were getting it all. 'Then there is her family over in Hawaii and all their dodgy dealings in their casino business.' Bob leans forward like a conspirator about to spill a juicy secret. 'There has been some kind of family feud about who owns the business or part of it and there are rumours about some dodgy tax dealings. They tried to drag Deb into it to help sort it out but she wouldn't get involved. There seemed to be connections with some heavy-weight local crime bosses and money owed. It could have something to do with that?'

The two country coppers are stunned. They obviously didn't know what they have got into but at least it was more interesting than chasing down the odd missing tractor. 'My friends, if that bitch is dead, that's absolutely great and couldn't be better but it wasn't me. She was rotten to the core and would turn on a friend or member of her family in a blink of an eye if she could make money out of it. The people she has surrounded herself with are as corrupt as she was and that goes for both the company and for her family. So best of luck with the inquiries. I am positive I am not the only one who would be glad to see her dead but I am certainly the one with the least to gain.'

The performance is all but over. Bob gives the officers copies of emails and notes sent between himself and the company. He also promises to make available all the documents, recordings and photographic evidence connected to what Deb went through if they should need it. Plain-clothes leaves with junior in tow. Bob is thanked for his co-operation and the many possible new leads they now have. Bob says as they are going that if there is anything else he can help with, please don't hesitate to get in touch – and the officers go.

It seems Bob's show of righteous indignation has convinced

the policemen the killer is to be found elsewhere. Bob doesn't know whether the sidekick will be rollicked for letting everything slip and giving the game away, or praised for helping to find all the new leads they now have. Bob isn't off the hook yet but there is light at the end of the tunnel.

It had been a blessing that Deb hadn't been there for the rant and forced to relive bad memories. Once she had found out Summer had been killed, she had become ill and excused herself. The police had sympathised and to Bob's surprise let Deb go up to bed.

The following day two more policemen arrive to take samples of mud and debris off the car. They also take the receipt and the lottery ticket as evidence. Bob jots down the lottery numbers just in case. He is sure they won't notify him if he wins. It all seems routine and casual and they are gone in fifteen minutes.

Deb is a little shaky but seems happy that it wasn't Bob, and that a little justice for what happened to her might finally have come their way. Once she had left the company, all the things she had been trying to do or improve for years and that had been stopped by Summer had suddenly been done. New computer systems and higher staff levels in the key areas that Deb had been trying to get all happened straight away and without fuss. Even the car park was resurfaced. No doubt the gullible would have been taken in and deceived into believing their new masters were all great and it had all been because of them that things were now being done and improved.

19

Bad Penny

It had been nearly a week since the police had first visited them and after only the second visit they had been left alone. Bob had expected some fall-out and to have to spend lots of time trying to convince people of his innocence but the reality had been that so far the world had not stopped spinning and he could still get Sky Sports on the television, so that seemed to be a good sign. No-one from the company had rung or called in to spread the gossip … or try and get some. Bob suspected that in the canteen there would be a tote running and the employees would be betting on the outcome of the inquiry and investigation.

As he sat in his front room half watching the early morning news and half listening to the music on his iPad as it played ZZ Top and 'I Thank You', he mused to himself as to whether or not he would be the favourite for main suspect. He wondered if he should call around and place a little wager. Should he bet on himself? Would that send the wrong message? Should he bet on one of the other candidates in the hope of leading the police to some new ground? He gave a small smile and carried on with what he was doing.

After the initial shock, Deb had seemed a lot happier, calmer and more relaxed. Bob had resigned himself to the fact that they would never get their money back for the twenty-five years Deb had dedicated to the company and the people connected with it. Their future was now in the balance and uncertain; Deb couldn't work and he was in his mid-fifties and without qualifications anyone recognised these days. But Deb being almost happy was great and as far as she was concerned the police were looking for someone who had hated Summer even more than Bob had. For once it felt as though the gods were actually conspiring together to do a good thing.

A car pulls up outside. The door slams shut, but Bob is not that interested. If it is anyone coming to his house he will wait until they ring the doorbell and set the dog off barking. He hears the stomp of booted feet marching up his drive. Oh, joy, it is someone coming here, he thinks. Deb is upstairs cleaning. Last night they had made love for the first time in what felt like years. It hadn't been all-consuming passion as most of their love life had been but it had been the first, small, hesitant step to recover something else that Deb's ordeal had taken from them. A little normality beginning to creep back into their lives …

BANG, BANG, BANG. 'Come out, you bastard. I know you are in there, come on out.' BANG, BANG, BANG on the front door. 'Come on out here, I am going to kill you, you fuck!' That will be Summer's better half, Anthony. Bob would have recognised those dulcet tones anywhere and the poor boy sounded pissed off. Bob should have known the nice morning wouldn't last.

Even before the first bang on the door had stopped vibrating through the house, Bob was up out of his chair and moving quickly into the hall, ready to protect his family. The dog was going wild in the back garden, sounding ready to take on any intruder. Anthony was still ranting and banging on the door. Deb was halfway down the stairs and looking like a rabbit in headlights.

'Stay there,' Bob commands. She is clearly shaken and he wants her away from danger. He gives her his mobile even though he can clearly see the outline of hers in her jeans pocket. 'I will sort this out. Go back upstairs and call the police, then if you can, use the camera on my phone to record as much as you can of what happens.' Bob takes a few steps back down the stairs and goes to the back door and lets the dog in. It is still going mad but it stops barking when it is told to. Bob returns to the bottom of the stairs. 'Go upstairs, take the dog and ring the police,' he tells Deb again, because she has not moved. 'I will stall him until they get here. Just go!'

Deb turns and calls the dog after her. Bob can hear the beep of the phone numbers as they are being selected and dialled as his wife ascends the stairs. She was always good in a crisis and always under control when people were falling apart around her. She had once marched across a cricket pitch at a local charity match to give one of the players the kiss of life because he had keeled over with a heart attack and no-one closer was doing anything other than standing and pointing.

The banging and requests for Bob to come out and play had stopped when the dog had gone quiet. After a brief pause they started up again even more loudly. Bob was determined not to let this animal outside intimidate his family or himself. He knows he will protect his wife at all costs this time. Against unethical and unscrupulous lawyers and their red tape he had not stood a chance but this was more straightforward. Bob will not put Deb's safety in someone else's hands just to be let down again by people she should be able to trust. He is going out of the front door and as soon as he can get close enough he is going to kick seven bells out of this cretin. He is sure that by now there will be enough neighbours watching to prove self-defence easily enough.

'OK. I AM COMING OUT,' Bob shouts, trying to make himself heard. He is right by the door and he shouts again and this time Anthony hears him and shuts up. 'I am coming out. I don't know what your problem with me is but I am coming out to help. Is that OK?' It has gone quiet. Bob unlocks the door. Will Anthony barge straight in as he twists the handle or will Anthony let him get outside before he tries to strike? The first thing Bob wants to achieve is to get out and let the door close behind him. The catch will drop and at least that will give Deb a little protection if he can't overpower Anthony.

Bob starts to turn the handle and open the door. There is no great weight suddenly thrown against it. The door opens wider and he cannot see Anthony at all – he must have stepped to one side or the other to let Bob out. Bob thinks to himself that this guy is definitely after me and takes a cautious step out. He is expecting at any second a fist or a lump of wood or something to swing at his head. Anthony isn't known for fighting fairly.

SHIT! He has seriously misjudged the situation and the threat. He had been expecting some whining, whingeing bully who would take a few swings until Bob fought back and then would stand down or run away. Unfortunately, Bob now has a shotgun aimed at his head.

That had been careless. These people had been mega-rich and had lived way out in the country owning lots of land. Of course Anthony would have a few farming toys to play with. The back of Bob's neck is now getting a little hot and sweaty and the instinct to try and run is becoming overpowering. At this range and only having two shots is not going to be a problem: it wouldn't matter how good or bad a shot Anthony is, he should still find the target and that would be most unfortunate for Bob.

The danger to Deb is still there, and very clear. Bob takes one step forward and he raises his hands in surrender, hopefully looking submissive and not letting any of the contempt seep through. The door swings shut behind him and he hears the latch click as it drops and it seals the door tight. Bob has completed his first aim even if he doesn't get a chance to do anything else. Deb is now relatively safe and there is no way back for Bob. It is just him and Anthony. Can Anthony pull the trigger? Bob knows he can if he can turn the tables.

The tattooed ginger toss-pot is glaring daggers but hasn't said a word. It is hard for Bob to be really intimidated by someone who looks like a seventies porn star in too-tight flared jeans, too-tight T-shirt and with several large, garish rings on his fingers to go with the obligatory pair of shades – even if he is the one holding the bloody gun.

'I'm going to blow your fucking brains out, you bastard.' Good, at least they are now talking. 'You killed my little angel and I am going to make you bleed.' Bob resists the temptation to question the terms 'little' and 'angel'.

Bob takes a couple of slow steps away from the door and backs away from Anthony. Both men are staring intently at each other and the gun stays firmly aimed at its target. Bob lowers himself to his knees, keeping his arms outstretched and in a neutral position as he tries to appear less of a threat to the gun-wielding dickhead in front of him. Bob is quite proud of how fit he is in his fifties; there are kids in his street who would have had to use the wall as support to get down this low.

'Anthony, I don't know what you want. I had nothing to do with the killing. Ask me whatever you want and I will tell you the truth (well, as much as Summer would have). Anthony you are making a big mistake, I am totally innocent.'

'Shut the fuck up. They told me it was you. Everyone has told me it was you.' He is swaying almost on the point of pacing and the gun is waving around like he is about to start conducting with it.

'Anthony who are … they? Think, is it the same people who have gained the most from Summer's death? Could it be the same people who might be using you to cover their tracks? Anthony, if anyone thought it was me I would be banged up in prison by now. I haven't even had to go to the police station to make a formal statement because I had proof I wasn't anywhere near where it happened.' Bob is kneeling there in front of the mad man with the gun, arms outstretched and hands open, looking like some saintly martyr of Christendom, although his knees were beginning to ache a little now.

Anthony's face is screwed up as he tries to concentrate on all those conflicting thoughts bouncing around in his skull, and he has started pacing one or two steps from side to side like he is practising some weird barn dance step or imitating a chimpanzee that has been caged too long. This moron should be giving Bob a big friendly hug and a large bonus because he has just become a multi-millionaire and can now do whatever he wants. He can go and buy all his own toys, like a big boy. There will be attractive women throwing themselves at him. He could even marry one and start a family, because that is just what the world needs, more little Anthonys.

'Anthony, you are a very rich man now. The company will pay you at least ten million pounds, probably more, for the shares Summer had. Don't let them twist everything and make you lose it all just for the few lies they are prepared to tell you to get you off their trail. You have been married for years. She had your wedding photos on her desk. I know it won't bring her back [Bob hopes the decision not to cut off her head and stake her heart won't come back to bite him] but it is all your money now and it will help you move on. That bitch stole everything from us ...'

Damn! He'd almost had him. The pacing had stopped, the gun was being lowered – and then Bob had to let his feelings show. The gun is back, aimed straight at his chest, and Anthony has aggressively taken a couple of steps closer. Bob considers risking a lunge forward in the hope that his reflexes are quicker than Anthony's.

'My sweet angel wouldn't have done that. You take it back! Summer gave your wife everything. She gave her the chance to climb out of the gutter and off the council estate. My angel helped her out of sympathy and let her have a little title just to make her happy.' Anthony never was too bright.

Bob glares at the moron standing a few feet in front of him. His hackles are well and truly up now. He wants to stand and scream into the guy's face so that he might just understand that if it hadn't been for Deb the company would have failed years ago but he reins it in.

'You're right Anthony, we should all be grateful.' Bob doesn't add 'now that the bitch is dead,' he just thinks it. 'But I think something is being covered up here. All those years our wives were friends and then Summer turns on Deb for no reason? Perhaps someone was jealous of them and was trying to break them and their successful team up. Anthony, walk away and go and spend your money. Whoever is behind this is manipulating everything. Deb has already lost all she worked for. They even convinced Summer to cancel Deb's illness cover to grab a little more for themselves. I know you have lost Summer now but she died in service so you have become a very rich man and that is a lot better than the treatment Deb got.'

Anthony's eyes are watering up and it looks like he is about to burst into tears. Bob hadn't considered that he had made his case that well. He had been a little under pressure and it had all been off-the-cuff stuff. Bob rises slowly and pain shoots through his knees, legs and lower back. Maybe it is time to accept he is old, after all?

Tears start to run down Anthony's cheeks. 'But … but they say I don't get anything. We aren't married, so her dad gets everything.' He has taken off his sunglasses to wipe his eyes and he looks like a puppy that has been told off and given a smack for shitting on the carpet for the first time. 'After the funeral, I have a week to get out of the house (sob). They say it is not "our" house, (sob) it is Summer's house. They say she paid cash for it and it is only her name on the deeds (sob). I get nothing. No-one will look after me.'

Bob isn't sure what shocks him more – that Summer had turned over someone else close to her or that the gruesome twosome had stuck together for so long when they were not even married.

'Did you say you're not married? I've seen the wedding photos. You were married in Hawaii at her dad's casino.'

Anthony has forgotten all about the gun in his hand and it's now pointing straight down at the drive. 'The picture was a fake. It was a photo we had done for advertising for the casino. Free gifts or casino chips for newlyweds playing there or something like that. It saved her dad paying for actors.' What a lovely family. Bob doesn't know what to say. 'She said when the time was right that we could get married and have children. She kept a copy of the picture to stop people asking when, that was all!' (And it saved her money on inviting people to the wedding, Bob contemplated quietly).

'Anthony, something is very wrong here. Someone has driven a wedge between two friends and is taking over the company piece by piece.' Bob hopes he sounds sincere. Anthony has the blank look of a person who is having trouble figuring out the plot of an episode of *Eastenders.*

'Think about it. First, they manipulate Summer into getting rid of Deb [like she had ever needed encouraging]. I bet they thought I would snap and go after your wife and kill her for what she did to Deb. Maybe they made a mistake and went too far and made Deb so ill I had to stay and look after her? Maybe they are trying to get someone else to do their dirty work?'

Bob starts to go a little off-track. 'Anthony, the police claimed it had been a professional "hit" and that she had been killed with a shot to the heart and a shot to the head, is that true?' Bob risks a few facts he shouldn't really know to help embellish the story and make it more believable for Little Anthony. 'Deb and I have lost everything. How could I afford to pay for a professional hit man?' A little pause to let the rest of the class catch up. 'You have to believe me, OK? This is someone bigger and higher up the food chain than we are who is controlling everything. They are trying to get us working classes to kill each other off and tie up all the loose ends for them as they sit back and watch, laughing at us.' Bob tries to give him and Anthony a little false empathy.

Bob knows the conclusions he wants Anthony to jump to all by himself but it is like pulling teeth. Surely, the police should be on their way by now. Perhaps Deb mentioned the shotgun and health and safety won't let them come out to play until the big boys arrive with their big guns?

'Anthony, who will benefit the most from our wives not being in the company anymore?' Bob is smiling and trying to look all innocent and benevolent. Anthony just looks confused. 'Do you think it could be Sapp and Grant? They have always resented being told what to do by women. They must have taken over the company by now and they will have a fifty-fifty share each for doing absolutely nothing. Anthony, our wives have been played and we are being played now. Those two bastards that are left have taken it all and are trying to put the blame on us.' Anthony might be working it out now. 'When I didn't kill Summer they needed another fall guy. You are their second choice.' Bob lets him think it over for a second or two.

'If you had killed me today, everything would all be nicely tied up with a little red ribbon. The police would stop looking for the real criminals. I would be dead and unable to defend myself and you would be in jail and unable to get your money.' Bob doesn't remind him that Summer has already shafted him on that one.

Bob steps up to Anthony and puts a reassuring hand on the arm and hand holding the gun. The gun is still facing down and out of harm's way but from where he is now Bob should be able to put up a reasonable fight if he hasn't completely won Anthony over.

'Anthony, you need to finish this. You need to make things right. I want to kill these bastards as much as you do but if I am caught there is no one to take care of Deb. I can't leave her alone after all she has been put through at the hands of these bastards.' Mentally he had included Summer in that poisonous little group but he lets Anthony think what he wants, little angel my arse! 'Anthony, they have taken your wife, they have taken your money and they are now richer than God. You have lost everything and you are the only one who can now get close enough to get them.'

Bob can see hatred and determination in Anthony's eyes. He has raised the gun and is holding it across his chest waiting for the order to advance. He is convinced that those two spoilt rich bastards did it … did it all!

'Anthony, when you arrived you said that everyone is convinced it was me and that I did such an awful thing. They won't let me into the factory or into the offices but they trust you. You can go as the grieving husband and no one will stop you. No one will get in your way. Trust me, those two will be together gloating and joking and thinking up ways to spend the money that should be yours.' It is easy now Bob has found out what motivates Little Anthony deep down inside.

There is something close to religious fervour building in this new disciple's eyes. 'Anthony, you can just walk in and take revenge for both of us. I promise I will tell everything to the police so that they know the truth.'

As Anthony turns and starts to go they hear the first distant sirens of the advancing police. Bob looks skyward and silently proclaims, 'REALLY! Ten more minutes and this would all be over.' Anthony has become like a scared feral dog. Suddenly everyone is his enemy and the shotgun is pointed at Bob again.

'You bastard, you rang the police.'

'Anthony, I was here with you all the time. We are at the front of my house, out in the open and you are pointing a gun at me. One of my neighbours will have rung for help, don't you think?' The sirens are increasing in volume and between them they have seconds to decide what will happen here.

'Anthony, take the fucking gun out of my face. Stop wasting time. Decide, kill me here and let those bastards get away with it – or go now and finish it and kill the right people?'

'But you rang the police.' The moron, how does he even open doors on his own?

Bob stands right in front of him and spreads his arms religiously again. The police are getting closer. 'Anthony … the police will be here in seconds. Go and get in your fucking car and go and do some good. I will buy you as much time as I can. I will say you are heading for Grant's house and send them in the opposite direction to the factory.' Then a little less harshly. 'Please don't let those bastards win.'

No movement and the sirens are louder still.

'For Christ's sake make a decision … NOW!'

* * *

Well, things could have gone more smoothly and worked out better. There they were standing on Bob's drive with the sirens getting louder and louder and the police getting closer and closer. Bob had been convinced that for once Little Anthony was actually going to do something useful with the damn shotgun he had been holding onto so tightly for the last fifteen minutes. But as destiny continued to get closer and louder Anthony had transformed into a twitching, giant rabbit frozen in the headlights. The poor lad just stood there all confused and panicked.

Bob had hoped that he could have pointed Anthony's obvious anger and lust for vengeance at the people who deserved it the most. He should have guessed from what life had already thrown in his direction that things were not going to run as smoothly as he had wanted or expected. All that had been left was to look to the heavens again and ask, 'Can't I catch a break just this once?'

They were still motionless and waiting in front of the house when the police arrived. The sirens had stopped as they had turned into the road, like the calm before the storm, and then seconds later the police car had screeched to a halt across the end of the drive. There they were in all their glory, blue lights flashing but without the siren howling at full volume to let the crooks know they were coming and it was time to leave. You wouldn't want to draw attention to yourself, now, would you? Bob was facing the action with Anthony in front but with his back to the road, and the police.

The policemen had still been getting out of their car and adjusting their helmets as Anthony started to turn to face them.

Bob truthfully didn't know what Anthony had been going to do, or was thinking of doing, or even if the guy had actually made a decision to do anything at all. He could have been about to surrender or he could have been about to level the gun at the police and go down blasting. All Bob knew was at that moment in time he saw that the chance of getting the important job finished quickly and by someone else had disappeared into the ether right before his very eyes.

In the seconds it took for Anthony to turn to face the police, Bob saw an opportunity to swing this whole debacle in his favour and he took his chance. If Anthony wasn't going to be useful Bob was not going to let him get away with anything … Bob reached down and grabbed the cast-iron boot cleaner that stood near the door and leapt forward as well as any fifty-something-year-old could have done. He smashed the jagged weight as hard and as fiercely as he could across the back of Anthony's skull, smashing bone and flesh to pulp, with his forward momentum driving Anthony's still-standing body to the ground. The gun had gone off, blasting its deadly contents harmlessly up into the air.

The unarmed police had dived for cover behind whatever they could get between themselves and the lunatic with a gun. They were obviously convinced that they were the targets and the shots had been meant for them. Bob lay across the still-twitching body; thankfully the now-empty gun had been knocked from Anthony's lifeless hands as they had crashed to the floor. Bob started screaming at the police to get their act together as though Anthony was still a risk. The police were trying to sound big and butch from behind privet hedge and flowerpots. 'Throw down your weapons' and 'we are the law' type stuff. They finally joined the fray once they were certain the threat was well and truly over. The poor lads were obviously more use to the country crime scene and a bit of traffic control at the local fete than what their inner city counterparts encounter on a daily basis if you believe the *Guardian*.

It was soon apparent they were holding down a lifeless body and the handcuffs were not really necessary. 'Good job I managed to get to him before he could take aim,' was Bob's opening gambit once he got his breath back. 'That arsehole had a real attitude problem. He was going to spread you all over the pavement.' Bob managed a weak grin in the policeman's direction. 'Nice timing though – he was just about to do me as you arrived. Something about tying up loose ends. What he said didn't make any sense.'

If Anthony had still been alive he would have protested his innocence but Bob didn't think the boys in blue would have believed him. Being shot at had seemed to cloud their judgment a little and they hadn't been that careful restraining the suspect until they realised he wasn't going to fight back ... ever!

More police quickly arrived and Bob was sent back inside, for his own safety, of course, now the threat was gone. Deb had watched the whole thing play out from a bedroom window but without any sound until the gun had gone off. Once it had become clear everything was under control she had come downstairs and let Bob back into the house. He could only guess at the rollercoaster of emotions he had put her through as she had watched everything unfold in front of the upstairs window she must have been watching from. All Bob knew was he was welcomed back with the strongest bear hug he had ever known and one of the longest and most passionate kisses he could remember.

Bob had kept the explanation simple. Anthony had arrived agitated and he had gone out to calm the guy down. Anthony had then threatened to kill him but hadn't explained why and then he had saved the policemen's lives when Anthony had turned the gun on them. Everyone seemed happy with the statement. Over the next few days and weeks there were statements made and police interviews done. There was a court case and an inquiry but it all worked itself out. Bob became the gracious hero for a few weeks. Refusing to comment to the papers and press until they got bored and left. Just like the song by Suzi Quatro '15 Minutes of Fame', everyone left as soon as something else took their attention.

All the plans Bob had for exterminating the cockroaches left behind after Summer's untimely demise had to be put on hold now he was in the spotlight. He was stuck in some surreal middle ground where he could see his quarry but there was too much focus on his own little world to do anything without being noticed. He reconciled himself to waiting. The main greed-driven fraudster had been dealt with and one of her fellow conspirators. They were rotting in whichever hell they were now sharing and Bob would have to settle for the quiet life for the moment. He would sit there at the back of the bus – and wait …

20

The Greatest Loss

Time passed and he planned, he schemed and he prepared with all the free time he could spare. He was readying himself, but also keeping a low profile as he searched for better contacts and constructed better plans to use when the time eventually came and was right. He knew there was no reason to let the rest of the scum know that they were on borrowed time.

As the months crept on, his dedication wavered. The Deb he had known was gone, but they were enjoying the quiet time they were sharing. Bob and Deb revisited some of the places they had travelled to in a past life. They even found a few new places they hadn't seen before as they travelled around Europe in a second-hand camper van. Sadly for Bob, it wasn't enough. He could never reignite the flame, so Deb never regained her confidence, regained her faith in other people or in herself. She never found the drive to start again and Bob was left fearing that this once shining light was just petering out.

Bob had expected once the head of the snake had been cut off, so to speak, the empire would fall apart. He should have known that something Deb had built was much stronger than that. Summer had followed 'The Book of Deb' to keep things working and moving forward. Now it seemed Sapp and Grant were following the same text religiously. 'The Book of Deb' seemed to hold all the knowledge required to make any idiot capable of keeping the company going, and that did niggle at Bob.

Almost a year had passed since the shoot-out on the drive and they were taking a break from travelling so Bob could refresh their flagging funds a little. They had handed over their home to their son and his family, with the proviso they would keep a room going for when they were back in England and wanted a place to stay. The house was big enough for them all, as long as it was a short stay.

Deb had gone into town with her cousin. She was past not going out on her own but still preferred company she knew if she could get someone to accompany her. The two ladies of leisure trawled the shops and had been having a good time when they had crossed paths with Sapp, his wife and their unfortunately ugly son. They had all stopped because there hadn't been enough time to avoid each other. Sapp had spent time bragging, gloating or maybe praising – in a roundabout way – how well Deb had built the company and how successful it still was and what a shame Deb had made the decision to leave when she did. Like it had ever been her choice? They had parted company when Sapp had grown tired of the subtle taunting and Deb had talked her cousin into taking her home, the day spoilt.

The house had been deserted and Deb had been left alone claiming she was tired from the shopping expedition. All the horrors must have flooded back, all the nightmares re-animated. Bob had returned home too late to do anything to help. His once greatest fear, that he had honestly believed had been vanquished, had smashed its way back into his life. He found Deb in a cooling bath, her wrists opened and pill packets strewn across the floor.

Like a victim of a violent rape and assault, you can paper over the imperfections, brush yourself off, put on a brave face and make out you are coping. But only you know what you had to endure and what you went through and how much damage was done to you, how vulnerable it has made you and how scared you now feel about living. Only you know how deep the scars that no-one else can see have gone.

People who have never had to live through the traumatic experience that you have can say, 'Take a bath and it will be all washed away'. But you can still smell everything, see everything and feel everything that was done to you. In your quietest moments the horrors reappear and invade and you can no longer enjoy the present. What should be peaceful times are taken over and you find yourself drifting back and reliving the event and what was done to you. You relive the ordeal again and again.

Anything can trigger a relapse, with its cold dread down your spine or numbing sickness in the pit of your stomach. A face in the crowd that looks like your attacker. An innocent person standing there wearing similar clothes to those your attacker had worn. Aftershave he had been wearing wafts across your senses in the street or in a bar from a passing stranger. Even a person you knew and haven't seen for a long time somehow finding out and rushing to console you, their help and good intentions just triggering everything anew.

On the outside you are over it and it is long forgotten. But only you know it is eating you from the inside out and every day is a fight to keep everything under control as the real you is taken one small piece at a time. Deb hadn't been physically attacked, but the mental damage of losing everything she had spent her whole life working for was the same – and the attack had lasted years not hours, or even minutes. Bob and Deb had become sick of hearing 'What doesn't kill you makes you stronger' from well-intentioned morons who had no concept of Deb's ordeal and what it had cost her mentally and physically to protect people she saw as innocent. The saying was now redundant anyway, because it had killed her. Summer had come up with the perfect crime, the perfect murder. She had found a way to kill one of her minority shareholders and get away with it…

Bob and Deb had always joked and made a pledge that when the time came, the first one to go would be lowered into the flames to the sound of AC/DC playing 'You Shook Me All Night Long'. When it came to it, Bob had felt that what he and Deb thought appropriate and fitting between themselves, the near family would fail to see the humour in. He conceded to a more dignified but meaningless end and he kept all the wonderful memories to himself.

Bob spent a couple of months getting everything in order. His son had already taken over the house and the deeds had been transferred before Bob and Deb had gone on what had become their last grand tour. Bob had cleared as much of the junk as he could from the house and he had done lots of maintenance on the house and garden to help the kids a little, because he knew at some point he could be leaving for a long period of time.

His son and his family seemed happy he was still around, and for the help with the house and garden. It was a little reminiscent of Deb and the company – nobody really appreciates what you do if you are always there and always have everything under control. The finished article is all they ever see and that was also true in Bob's garden. No-one registers all the weeding, the cultivating, the prep-work, the bug control, the mowing and the tinkering. They all just arrive and sit in front of the fire pit or on one of the deckchairs with a glass of something in their hand and say how wonderful the garden is.

Bob revisited a few places on his own, the people around him seeing the lonely trekking as his own little homage to the past and the memories of Deb. There was no sign of anything sinister or strange to the outside world. Right from the start of Deb's ordeal, Bob had watched the person he knew fade away and there had been a sense of inevitability despite all his attempts to stave off what he feared was coming. He had become complacent, and Deb had been lost. He knew the blow had been coming and it had been bad but he had had time to prepare; it hadn't been like losing someone to an unsuspected heart attack or car accident. He had known he wouldn't be able to do anything about it in the end and would just have to accept it.

Since the spotlight had shone his way for his fifteen minutes of unwanted fame he had been banished to the naughty step and unable to touch the rest of the late Summer's little cartel. There had been too many deaths too close together, but now the domestic stuff was done he was ready to revisit old acquaintances. He hadn't really kept up with how Sapp and Harry were enjoying themselves now they owned the company. He didn't even know how the company was doing since their little falling out but Bob was sure it would still be there and 'The Book of Deb' would still be doing its magic.

For the funeral, Bob had taken Deb's body back to where she had been born and where most of her surviving relatives still lived. It had been a family request and he had no objections. He was not going soft, and dead is dead, and you can grieve as much as you like, but the startling truth is, you cannot bring them back. Being that far away from the company meant there was little risk of any of employees finding out Deb was gone. He wouldn't want the company forewarned and forearmed and knowing that he was on his way with something sharp and pointy to re-open a few old scars and hopefully make some new ones. All he had to do was figure out the when and how.

Bob had spent his months surfing the net, making new contacts and getting a little more professional as far as his plans were concerned. Even the contents of his goodie bag had improved. He had turned most of his belongings into cash and had squirreled it away in places near and far. He had gained what he hoped was a good fake passport and that it would pass as genuine when the time came to use it.

* * *

The time had gone quickly after Deb's funeral but it had been frustrating. All Bob wanted was revenge on the people who were left who had played their part in killing her. He had thought that his time on the naughty step was coming to an end but he had been trapped there waiting for an opportunity for longer than he had expected. All it had really done again was strengthen his resolve. Finally the frustration had won and he had decided to give the issue a little nudge.

His plan was to check in on the company by 'accidentally' meeting some of the salesmen at their local. The plan to keep Deb's funeral a secret had failed. Some eagle-eyed busybody had found out, so surprise had gone out the window. He had found out the company knew when a few cards had slunk their way into his post. No-one had rung or made direct contact, just a few polite condolences to ease their own consciences. Bob wasn't sure how the meeting would turn out but he could always find a plan B. As far as he could remember you couldn't be arrested for bumping into someone in a bar.

Bob was going to target a couple of salesmen Deb had known and helped years ago and he was making his way to their local hang-out, a designer pub claiming to be an authentic 'olde worlde' original, if you believed the marketing hype, but had been probably built less than twenty years ago.

When they had all been friends, Bob and Deb had occasionally joined the group. The lads were guaranteed to be propping up the bar through the week and spending some of their sixty per cent commissions. Their only deviations to this tradition were the Friday and Saturday 'pull' nights when both left their long-suffering but well-rewarded spouses to trawl the nightclubs and bars of the bigger local towns and cities looking for a bit of 'rough trade', as they liked to put it.

It was mid-week and Bob had seen their cars parked obediently in the car park, waiting to take their masters home later that evening because by then the lads would be too drunk to walk. They had joked about it being one of the perks of living in the middle of the countryside. Bob suspected that it was the only reason this pair of townies lived out here.

Bob wasn't sure what sort of reception he would get. The company was split on who or what had happened to Summer, even if most thought that she had deserved it. Whoever had been running the tote wasn't paying out on Anthony because the police hadn't tried to prosecute a dead man, so technically there was still no winner. Even so, there had been a small and loyal few, from the snippets of gossip Bob had managed to glean, who had actually suspected that he, Bob, had something to do with it and was responsible for Summer, like Elvis, leaving the building. He couldn't see the lads running with fear when he showed up on their turf but they might not want to chat.

Bob knew the lads would be in the public bar so he chose to go into the lounge, knowing from the layout of the place that when either of them came to collect their next round of drinks he would be visible through the open hatch and doorway the staff used to watch both bars at the same time. It would give them all a chance to check each other out and decide at a friendly, non-threatening distance what would happen next and how they would proceed. Bob ordered his pint and settled down to wait and listen to the music. It was always Slade, which wasn't bad, but it was the same every time because the bar owner's wife was a fan, and what she said was the law.

He needn't have had any concerns or worried unduly. Before he had even taken his first sip, two whirlwinds had burst through the adjoining door from the public bar. There were lots of commiserations and 'great to see you's' all enthusiastically mixed together in that way only well-meaning, thick-skinned people of slightly below average intelligence can do. It was like having two dense Labradors bouncing around. Bob should be grateful that at least they weren't wet or trying to shag his leg. Once it had all calmed down, Bob and the two lads, Chris and Jake, had been joined by another company salesman. This guy had joined more recently and had been recruited by Summer and her crew and he hadn't been there long enough to know or appreciate what Deb had done for the company and who he should really be thanking for his new luxury lifestyle.

Pleasantries and general chit-chat out of the way Bob was trying to bring the conversation around to things he actually wanted to know. The two lads were 'babysitting' – as they put it

– the new boy Gavin (another Gavin, the bloody sales team was full of them. Perhaps it was the only name Grunt could remember?). Gavin was about to get Best Newcomer Award for his first full year.

'Well, the company is shit without Deb – we might as well be bloody zombies. There is no team spirit left. No-one wants to help or tell you what you need to know. We're just like modern-day slaves. It is like being back at Borstal. Do this, do that, don't talk back,' was Chris's input on the latest regime.

'At least Deb told us why things had to happen this or that way and showed us how to do it bloody right,' Jake pitched in.

Gavin had tried to put his tenpennyworth in about how wonderful the bosses were but now sat perplexed and poleaxed after he had been put right by the lads without any prompting from Bob. All the people poor Gavin had rated were not the people the propaganda said they were and what he had been sold. Sales and marketing telling fibs, who would have thought it? Gavin had been going on about didn't Ms P do this or Harry do that and wasn't Sapp a nice man underneath, until he had been shot down by the lads and told the awful truth and given the real history of the 'world' …

Bob was keeping out of the conversation; he didn't want to become angry but the drivel this new twat had swallowed was so untrue. Bob just had to sit there and repeat under his breath that it wasn't Gavin's fault and he didn't know any better.

The lads were stupid enough not to see or realise that they were unintentionally winding Bob up. If they knew what Deb had done and what she had meant to the success of the company and the whole shebang, why had they acted like all the others? Why hadn't they tried to help Deb when they had had the chance? Bob had asked the two of them back at the start what everyone thought of how Deb was being treated and would they help. Their response had been one of the ones that had gone along the lines of 'what doesn't kill you makes you stronger'. Now that it had killed her and Summer had gone to hell for it, maybe they felt safe to say out loud what everyone knew. Now they were acting like Deb was a fallen hero and a comrade lost in battle, rather than shunning her like everyone else had done at the time she had needed help the most.

The lads had toasted Deb's memory several times with shorts between the pints of lager. Bob had gracefully declined because of driving home. Gavin had tried to keep up until he had passed out or fell asleep, having not been at the company long enough to get used to the rigours of after-work socialising.

'That arsehole Grunt is off to Italy soon. Him and that frightening wife of his are off spending their wad of cash in some bloody fancy hotel in Venice.' Bob's ears pricked up at the slurred announcement from Jake. 'I saw the brochures around his office and took a peek. It is some bloody big fancy dress party where I assume they all shag each other in the streets. They all wear masks, you know. Well, you would bloody have to with that pair, wouldn't you?' Jake and Chris cracked up laughing. Bob just smiled; it had been the sort of little titbit he had hoped for.

Bob wouldn't disillusion them about what they thought the Venice carnival was all about and what went on. They were right though about the masks, and that could present some possibilities. A couple of general questions and he knew he only had a couple of weeks before it all started. He could have looked on Wikipedia when he got home but was that any better than asking two drunks in a pub?

Bob knew a lot about the annual festival. He and Deb had done it on the cheap years earlier and had taken with them a couple of gay friends from the company. The two lads concerned were in love with each other like any regular couple but hid under their macho salesman exteriors. At company get-togethers they could be found with their contemporaries bragging about conquests and assessing their chances with the 'tarts' in marketing and going on about all the manly stuff they did. Deb's gaydar had picked up on all the little untruths. She had spoken to them late in the evening at one of these conferences about it and said not to worry, their secret was safe. They had chatted into the early hours of the next day and everyone had been happily drunk. Since then they had become close friends but had sworn Deb and Bob to secrecy about their love life and sexual inclinations. They were worried the company might find it unacceptable, saying out in the open that it did not matter but pushing them out on the quiet. Deb had pledged her support if they ever did want to 'come out' but they were content, if not happy, hiding in the shadows.

The Venice trip had been five years previously and they had all chipped in and rented a flat for the week and immersed themselves in the carnival experience, the gay guys taking great pride in the over-the-top costumes they had brought from England. They had been a little deflated once they had seen the efforts of the locals and the mega-rich who come to Venice for the week but they had soon perked up and camped up to compensate. It wasn't the shag-fest that Jake and Chris fantasised about, but it had been a fantastic experience. There had been lots of costumes and promenading for the tourists but if you weren't brave enough to be one of the ones promenading you could always buy a cheap, one-Euro mask, take pictures and still feel part of it all.

Venice isn't that big a place and the makings of an idea and a plan quickly shot into Bob's mind. Now he had a snippet of information that could be useful, he didn't have to tolerate the two-faced pissheads and their idiot sidekick he was sitting with any longer. They had been like everyone else and without any conscience at all had looked after themselves and shunned Deb, looking the other way after she'd spent years looking out for them. Their pathetic little act trying to curry favour with Bob and make out that it wasn't that they didn't want to help, it was just that they couldn't, had not won Bob over.

He stood up ready to leave. 'Well, I'm off, you pair of lying, two-faced, pieces of shit.' They seemed to sense the change that had come over Bob.

'What are you on about? We are all friends here,' Chris piped up, swaying slightly even though he was sitting down. 'We've sat and commiserated with you and called those arseholes … well, arseholes. What more can we do?'

'You shit-faced scumbags, Deb helped you the most. Neither of you would be here enjoying the high life you lead if it wasn't for her. When the company wanted to throw you out and stop you taking over the areas your fathers had franchised when they had earned enough to fuck off and retire, Deb stepped in. The company could have taken it all back – they were within their rights – but she fought for you. She argued that it would be better to keep faces the customers knew and people who knew the areas. You two dimwits wouldn't have your Mercs or Range Rovers or your big houses and endless cash. Deb could have let Summer and Grant take everything away from you because your dads hadn't bothered to train you properly, they just wanted their little boys working with them so they knew you pair of shits were keeping out of trouble. It was Deb who trained you and made you. She got nothing from the company when she was ripped off by Ponsenbury but when the company was trying to shit on you and take everything your dads had built and worked for and pay you nothing, she stood up for you and fought for you to be given a chance … she got you your chance. Now you have a millionaire lifestyle and she turned you into two of the best salesmen in the company. "What doesn't kill you makes you stronger" – was that all the help you could be arsed to give Deb after what she did for you? You wankers!'

There was a pause for breath and the two lads looked at each other as Gavin carried on sleeping to the side of them, dribbling down his shirt. Bob had no intention of taking it any further, these two were morons and not worth wasting any more time on. What had he expected, an apology?

'What did you think we could do? Nobody was going to risk upsetting Summer. Hell, why would any of us want to give all this up?' Chris was speaking the truth for once.

'You don't get it, do you? You wouldn't have any of "this" if it wasn't for Deb,' Bob replied.

'Yeah, but you don't get it – we wouldn't keep it if it wasn't for keeping Summer happy. Sorry and all that, mate.' It was Jake this time.

There weren't that many people in the pub, just a couple in the corner and an old guy at the bar, and the barmaid listening in when she didn't have to serve in the other room. The lounge wasn't that big, so Bob guessed everyone had heard everything. It was time to go. He wanted to smash the two lads' heads together but an assault charge would be an inconvenience.

There was a three-quarter full pitcher of cheap lager on the table that the boys had replaced several times already. Bob picked the pitcher up and emptied its contents over the two morons in front of him. The couple laughed, the old guy clapped and the barmaid cheered; all seemed to hold the lads in such low esteem that they wanted to share in the moment, too.

Bob placed the empty pitcher back on the table. The lads had not moved. They now looked at each other through dripping and foaming hair and started laughing themselves. 'Is that all you got?' Chris asked. Bob left, guessing that they didn't suspect him of killing anyone or they might have been a little more worried or respectful. Maybe they really were that stupid? However, he had got some info he could use and there were more important things to do than beat up a pair of drunks half his age. It didn't stop him hoping that they caught something nasty on their next illicit sexual encounter and their pricks shrivelled up and dropped off.

* * *

The Venice carnival was less than two weeks away, he had checked on the Internet. He had quickly found flights to Spain where he could access the Med and whip across the sea by ferry as a walk-on passenger to Italy, giving himself time to get to

Venice before anything happened. He knew he had no chance of getting a hotel or private room at such short notice. When he had been with Deb and the two friends, they had booked months in advance and then struggled and had to take somewhere further from the main square than they would have liked.

He guessed that with all the new-found wealth Grunt and his wife had, it would be a big hotel and a different costume every day and night, walking amongst the poor people of Venice so the two of them could be admired and photographed, their superiority could be acknowledged and their egos massaged.

Bob, on the other hand, would be sleeping rough and where he could this time, and his only disguise would be one of the white one-Euro masks and his camera. There were lots of small streets and poky alleyways and he hoped he would get the chance to deal with Grunt. The small pistol would stay at home. Maybe he could make it look like an accident or a violent Italian mugging gone wrong. But first he had to get there and find Harry Grant.

Bob had arrived the day after the official opening of the carnival and had instantly been swept along with the tide of costumes and opulence on show. The organisers claimed that this was how the Venice of old had been all the time. That was a nice thought, everyone happy and partying. No violence, racism or prejudices but now that world only lasted for a week or two each year.

* * *

Bob had now been there and searching for two full days and had not yet found Grunt. He was beginning to consider that the information he had gained might have been wrong and he should have taken the time to check. The two morons he had got the info from were unaware of its importance to him, so it should have been valid. He should have tried to confirm it but he hadn't wanted anyone knowing he was mooching around and spying on the company and trying to talk to its employees.

He was now sitting on a park bench about fifteen minutes from St Mark's square in the Italian sun, eating an Italian ham and cheese sandwich. It had crossed his mind he could have checked if Grunt was on holiday this week by simply posing as a prospective customer or franchisee wanting to join up. He could have claimed he was only in the Midlands for a couple of days this week and he had been given Mr Grunt's name as a contact. Reception would have been able to give him all the confirmation he needed as to whether this was going to be a wild goose chase or not.

As he sat, even this far from St Mark's, he filled his time watching the beautiful costumes go by and the occasional tarted-up pet. He would have liked to add 'beautiful people' to the sentence but that was not always the case. The gorgeous clothes were not always wrapped around appropriately gorgeous people or figures. Beefburgers and chips have a lot to answer for all over the world.

He considered that he could have simply set up Grunt with the same sort of phone call he had considered to find out if the guy was on holiday or not. Grunt was always on the lookout for fresh blood and new money to be taken on and taken in on the company's behalf. He'd heard that the turnover of disgruntled salesmen was much higher now Deb wasn't there to sort the wheat from the chaff or stop the company pocketing the franchise fee and fobbing off the next unlucky recruit once the probation period was coming to an end and moving on to the next one. He could have arranged anonymously to meet Grunt on some decrepit car park somewhere and done the deed. But Bob, after all, was hoping to make it look like another accident to give him time to get away and move on to the next one on the list. Still, he was enjoying the grandeur, the sun and with some of the time he had to himself he was enjoying revisiting and reliving the memories of Deb and better days.

He finished his sandwich and took a swig out of his bottled water. He could say without any question at all that this wasn't his diet of choice but he was trying to keep the costs down. Venice in carnival week was expensive, even on bread and water and sleeping rough. He hadn't been the only one sleeping rough, though. He had had to share the benches and the concrete steps with many revellers who were stranded, unaware that the public ferries stopped relatively early so they couldn't get back to the mainland and cheaper hotels unless they paid fantastic amounts of money for a water taxi. It bordered on legalised extortion at this time of year. Most had chosen to save their money and carry on partying as best they could, or resorted to the cold concrete to catch a few hours' sleep until the ferries re-started at first light the next day.

The local council or the Venetian equivalent had hidden away rows of chemical toilets for the masses of tourists who flocked to see the spectacle and were too tight to pay a little money to use a real toilet in one of the many bars, restaurants and hotels that were about. The queues were everlasting most of the time but in the early hours they were no problem and if you were lucky they might just have been cleaned for the following day as well.

Bob had set up a simple plan. He walked a circuit of what he considered the most likely places he might catch sight of the vacationing 'Grunts'. He started at St Mark's, walked around the tourist spots, then passed the better-known bars and restaurants, going back to St Mark's via the designer shops. Sometimes, to break the monotony, he walked it all in the opposite direction at a tourist shuffle. Whenever he found bottlenecks with a good vantage point so he could see the milling crowd, he would sit eagle-eyed and scowling, waiting for his luck to change. Venice wasn't that big ... where could they be hiding? The costumes might make it a little harder to be found but they were two of the tallest, most gangly people he knew and as a couple they should stand out from the crowd wherever they went.

A couple of times he had tried the tables and chairs outside bars and cafes to park his sorry arse but they had quickly been ruled out because once he sat down there was instantly a waiter waiting there at his shoulder. Too much eating and drinking also meant more wasted time in the queues for the loos, or resorting to peeing behind a refuse bin or down a back alley like many of our uncouth, uninhibited European cousins. When the trawling wasn't working, Bob had chosen a vantage point and just waited. Grunt might not even pass that way so after two hours he went back on patrol. Feeling then at least he was trying to do something.

* * *

Bob had lost track of the times he had done the circuit now but he started it again. It was late afternoon and there was a noticeable drop in pedestrian traffic as the tourists and promenaders retired for a little sustenance, a short nap or just went somewhere to repair, repaint and fluff up their costumes ready for the evening. He didn't know the names of the roads he was travelling around and around but by now he knew exactly where they all went and what led off any of them or was at the end of any of them if any lost soul wanted to know. He could quite easily become designated map-reader for any tourist if they could describe where or what they were trying to get to not using street names. Bob was confident that it would only take a distant sighting of his quarry and the hunt could start properly.

He had decided that it was time to take a short cat-nap of his own and join the ranks of the flagging tourists and the revellers who were up but had as yet not quite recovered from the night before. He found himself in a small square and had occupied a free corner on a set of steps leading to some large, locked doors that looked like they hadn't opened in years, maybe even centuries. The square had a couple of shops with tourist tat in them, a convenience store and a small café. Not the most promising fishing spot but at one corner there was a cut-through to another 'must see' big church for the tourists to visit if they could read a map, so there was some traffic he could watch and keep an eye on.

It was like counting sheep when he was watching tourists. He would wake up every now and again and try and hold on and watch a little more. Waking up for a few seconds when different bits of him went numb and the pins and needles started. Then getting comfortable again as the pain subsided. One tourist … two tourist … three … four … zzzzz!

He woke again and tried to revive the left hand that now felt detached from the rest of his body. The pain grew almost instantly as the circulation started again and then subsided. A quick look at his watch and he could see it was another fifteen minutes on from the last time he looked. In all he had managed to get about an hour-and-a-half of interrupted and patchy sleep but it would help to keep him going later on as he prowled about through the streets and alleyways crisscrossing the canals. There were a few like him littered about the place, stuck in corners or spread across public benches. All but a few, completely anonymous to everyone thanks to the various masks and disguises that they were wearing.

He had a swig of water and a good stretch to get his system up and running again. Now the big decision: did he do the course in reverse from here? The light was going, so soon everyone would be starting to come out to play and going against the flow would be hard work. Another stretch and he would decide. Then, as he watched the furthest bridge across the square, some half-dressed lanky guy lolloped across and headed for the convenience store and disappeared inside. Surely Bob's luck couldn't be that good?

Bob moved to a better and closer vantage point, now very awake and hoping it hadn't been some fleeting, half-conscious dream mirage that his mind was just seeing because it wanted to see it. Bob assumed the guy would go back the way he had come because he hadn't been fully attired for the evening. Bob stood in the new spot waiting, tension building. He touched his hand to the mask to check it was in place. It had become a second skin in the last few days and his senses had numbed to the fact that it should not really be there.

The guy had his back to Bob most of the time he was crossing the open space and pacing between the few people milling about. He had been tall and skinny enough for Grunt but Bob had to be sure. He had been wearing a French-style white wig, so the famous black flat-top, if it was still there, had been hidden. The guy had also had maroon and purple pantaloons, period socks, garters and shoes. But the thing that had made Bob think that this was his man was the fact that he had walked through one of the most beautiful cities in the world in a grubby white, English-style vest and had thought that was OK. That had been what had made Bob ninety-nine per cent certain he had found Grunt.

A couple of customers came out of the store. Neither was dressed up or looking like a tourist so Bob concluded that they were probably some of the few locals left on the island and had seen it all before enough times in their obviously long lives not to get carried away. A few seconds later, Grunt appeared in all his sweaty-vest glory. He even stopped and stared in Bob's direction as he opened the pack of cigarettes he had purchased, lighting one and inhaling deeply before moving away and back in the direction that he had come from a little earlier – and totally oblivious to the fact that Bob had been there and watching all the time. Bob felt the need to check that the mask was in place for a second time within minutes. He was amazed by how anonymous this cheap purchase had made him and how he had blended into the masses. He had only removed it to eat and to swill his face late at night or early in the morning from a convenient fountain to freshen up. He had even kept it on to sleep.

Grunt wasn't hard to follow. Fifty yards, one canal bridge and another fifty feet or so along the canal path and he disappeared into what was either a small hotel or a large B&B. All that grand build-up and the cheapskate was staying in what was little more than a guest house off a back alley. Worth millions and still doing something like this on the cheap. Bob was surprised he hadn't bought his ciggies from duty free on the way over, or maybe he had and had already smoked those.

Bob crossed over the bridge and walked the same route along the canal path past the 'hotel'. There were few tourists or locals walking this part of Venice but now the mask had been fully put to the test he didn't worry for one second about Grunt recognising him. Bob passed the building, which was a little bigger than the ones surrounding it. There were also, as he walked by, lots of key-code-entry number pads on very expensive wrought iron gates. Maybe his first impression had been wrong and there was a little more money here than the run-down little hotel suggested.

Like all of Venice, canals replaced most roads with many bridges scattered across them to allow foot traffic access to the other side so you were all not forced onto the main thoroughfares. Bob walked five hundred yards and came to the end of the street. At the T-junction it opened out in front of him into the Grand Canal. The traffic was still quite busy but it wasn't the chaos of the peak periods. A few yards back there had been another small bridge just back from the main entrance. He knew pretty well where he was, because across the water from where he stood he could see the empty stalls of the fish market, and he knew he could use the bridge and cut across to one of the main streets on the way to St Mark's. He wandered around trying to look like any other awestruck tourist and took a few pretend photographs with his camera as he surveyed the area and his options.

He walked back to the bridge and went and stood right at the apex. Again he did the pretend tourist thing and raised his camera, then he turned with his back to the Grand Canal and looked back in the direction of the hotel. From this vantage point no one could enter or leave either side of the canal without being in plain sight for most of their journey. The hotel entrance was in full view. Anyone looking his way would only see a tourist waiting with his camera for the perfect shot.

For once he wished he was a smoker so he could blend in more. In this part of the world there were always lots of couples or singles just chilling out, standing or sitting around and watching the world go by, and they were always accompanied by a cloud of smoke. As time passed, a few people came and went. Most must be local workers because they weren't dressed up. There had been two young ladies in very short miniskirts, stockings and long leather boots who had passed his way, arm-in-arm. They had both had flouncy, white, ruffled, almost see-through shirts and silver cat masks, their hair adorned with plaits of glitter and tinsel. Gorgeous and curvy, they were obviously heading in the direction of their favourite hunting ground. Not totally committed to the spirit of the carnival but curvy and good-looking enough to turn heads.

He had expected the Grunts to appear fairly quickly but the time had gone by and it was now dark. Late afternoon had been replaced by early evening and even that was pushing its way towards full night by the time his quarry appeared. They stood on the few steps of the hotel for a second or two to light cigarettes, and then they started walking towards Bob. He had expected them to go the other way and join the masses promenading with the crowds along the more popular routes. Their costumes were grand, if not spectacular, but they had obviously been in Venice long enough to know some of the short cuts.

Bob remembered when he had been here before that the gay lads had taken over the costume department, and all things related, for the group. They had insisted on doing this as a sort of thank-you because Bob had brought them to such a spectacular venue and introduced them to The Venice Carnival – something they had never heard of before. For Bob, it had been the stunningly sexy ladies with corseted and stocking bodies but he had a sneaking suspicion the lads were leaning more towards the men in tights.

On that visit the lads had made sure all their costumes were spectacular. Bob had been a little self-conscious but it was hard not to join in with the boys camping it up at every opportunity and dragging Bob and Deb around like their tolerant and understanding uncle and auntie. They had achieved in hours what Bob and Deb had not been able to, taking advantage of the gay underground, and soon the group was booked into several masked balls spread over the week. By the end Bob was getting a little fed up being abandoned by the other three as they trundled off, what felt like every thirty minutes, for a fag break.

In the end he had taken his revenge on the lads by setting them up with a couple of old Aussie ladies. He sort of implied both lads were single, could be considered players and were up for anything. He lit the blue touch paper and stood back as the old dears pounced as the guilty smokers returned. The boys had been eyed up all night by various females in the crowd. The Casanova-come-sportsman look going over well. He and Deb had left in the early hours. The boys staggered back after breakfast with more cash than they had started with and had taken a lot of ribbing about the two old dears making men of them. Accusations they denied vigorously.

Bob's reminiscing had allowed the Grunts to get quite close to him. He could hear they were in the midst of an argument, their voices hushed as they hissed at each other. Bob's mask had been of the 'Vendetta' film type just for a bit of irony.

'I am just saying, you own half the bloody company and we are in some fucking back-alley guest house. There better be a nice, big, NEW shiny car on the drive when we get back, or else!' Bob's plan was to follow them and hope to get Harry alone sometime during the night. Bob had purchased a long kitchen knife to do the deed. He had managed not to touch it by getting the sales assistant to take it down and wrap it for him in a paper bag. When the time came he would slip on a pair of stretchy gloves, take out the blade and spoil Harry's retirement plans. Not much of a plan admittedly, just simple, straightforward and to the point.

'Dear, you know how much that little hotel cost me. It is quaint and romantic.'

'It is fucking cheap and dirty, you cheapskate. I turn a blind eye to your fucking around but the rewards better be damn good now you are Mister Moneybags or I will divorce the arse off you.' The rest of the conversation was lost as they passed Bob without even noticing he was there. They were well out of range before Harry came up with a reply but it didn't stop Bob allowing himself a smug smile. Trouble in paradise, and all that money still couldn't help. Time to start following, he thought, he had given them enough of a head-start now.

* * *

Bob had followed the Grunts around for hours. It hadn't been hard, their height and coloured costumes making them easy to watch over even in a carnival crowd. Bob's new concern was that he had miscalculated how easy it would be to kill someone in a crowd. Hawkken had been a happy accident and technically even suicide; Summer's had been a planned execution, however badly done. But both had been done away from people. Harry's death was going to be a spur-of-the-moment sort of thing.

After gaining the info, Bob had soon been on a flight to Malaga where he had hired a car and had ended up in Granada at a friend's house. He had borrowed the friend's Triumph motor bike for a few days to be alone and headed for Venice. He had found a small hotel on the mainland where he could leave the bike and had then caught the ferry and sailed into Venice in full view and ready to hunt for Harry.

Once found, Bob had followed the Grunts around bars and tourist landmarks as they indulged themselves. Every time chances had presented themselves to end dear Harry, the crowds had ebbed and flowed and the chance had been lost. Bob had followed the still-bickering couple to a grand casino hotel that would stay open into the early hours of the following day. In all the films there was always that perfect moment as the crowd looks away, the assassin is close enough, the target is all alone and unprepared and the getaway is clear. The perfect moment had not appeared so far, lucky old Harry.

Bob had waited for an hour-and-a-half but he knew the casino would have a private water taxi waiting for the gamblers who had had enough or who had run out of money. The taxi was canal-side and he had walked to where he could get a view of the private dock but he could not cover both exits at the same time and there was no vantage point he could find that could solve the problem. Though frustrated, he now knew where to find Harry so it hadn't been a total loss. He had walked back to the little bridge by the hotel where he knew he could wait and watch until the Grunts came back.

It was almost 3.30 a.m. and he was yawning with almost every other breath, ready to quit for the night and find somewhere to doss down for a few hours before the crowds started to return. Just as he stood up in the shadows, a water taxi turned into his bit of canal, mooring by the hotel. Grunt and his wife staggered and tripped their way onto dry land and eventually swayed their way into the hotel and disappeared. He had hoped the bickering would escalate and they would have returned separately but no such luck. The water taxi was another inconvenience to overcome. Fuck it, he was tired; time to get some rest.

* * *

'Later that day' proved equally frustrating for Bob, and carnival week was quickly coming to an end. The venues had been different for the Grunts, only the casino as last port of call and Harry still breathing staying the same. Bob had left them to it as soon as they went inside the casino and went and found somewhere to grab another cat-nap and he had been back on his lonely vigil and waiting at the hotel by 2 a.m. He was beginning to recognise costumes and people as he slunk around. The kitten girls had become bright spots as he caught sight of them at different times pouncing and playing with their unsuspecting victims. He hoped people were not beginning to notice him because he was always wearing the same clothes and mask. Admittedly the girls were a lot more noticeable than he was and probably smelt a lot better too. He managed a quick rub-down in the small hours at one of the local fountains in stone-cold water but he could do little about his clothes. He had bought some cheap aftershave but he wasn't sure that was an improvement the way it made his eyes water when he first put it on.

Again, a water taxi had brought the happy couple safely back to the hotel, the drunken passengers disembarking and staggering the fifteen feet, or what the metric equivalent is into the hotel, and that was another day wasted.

Bob had two more days and then he would have missed this golden opportunity. He had the makings of a plan 'B' back in the UK but too many deaths close to the company might seem a little suspicious. He spent another restless night on an uncomfortable bench in a park until a drunken couple tried to brace themselves against the back of the same bench he was on and tried to copulate. He gave up on sleep then and left the couple semi-clothed in matching green satin outfits grunting and squealing noisily and oblivious to him being there. He returned to the area around the hotel and prowled around, seeking inspiration. There were a few people but whenever anyone came close he staggered a little bit and muttered a bit under his breath like a lost party-goer and he was left alone. He left as it got light to find breakfast, a loo and somewhere to get a little more sleep – but he had the start of a plan.

As soon as Harry and his wife appeared for their evening's entertainment, Bob followed, as he had before. There still might be a chance. He watched from outside as the Grunts entered bars that appeared to have only one entrance and exit, waiting until they re-emerged and went on to the next with him discreetly in tow. As the week had gone on, the crowds had got even bigger and the streets had become more packed. There had been a few fireworks but the big display was tomorrow, the final night.

Bob watched from a safe distance as the Grunts pushed themselves into yet another overcrowded bar. He thought about following but all those sweaty people in heavy, large costumes put him off. He couldn't imagine it was very pleasant in there. Maybe you don't notice so much when you are younger and here having fun. Both times he had been here before he had done exactly the same thing the Grunts were doing now, except for the gambling – his budget had not stretched to that – and he had found places to party long into the night with new-found friends. But this time, his days on the street were affecting his karma and his happy disposition, and he was also looking forward to a long hot bath.

He saw the kitten girls with two good-looking Nordic types, so he guessed their hunting was done for the night. Again, the night progressed the same as the others and the Grunts and their presumed gambling problem disappeared into the casino for a few hours when the bars began to close. This time he didn't hang around or take a leisurely walk but headed straight back to the hotel.

It was a quiet area and as soon as he thought it was safe, Bob started to get his plan up and running. Like most 'roads', the canals had to be repaired and maintained. Instead of bollards and chevroned barriers placed to stop and restrict access, in Venice there were floating pontoons doing the same job, secured across the canal entrance denying boats access. As he had mooched around the area Bob had found, only two canals away, one of these floating pontoons. He now unhooked the furthest securing chain and as that end of the pontoon sank he ran back across the bridge. He unhooked the chain from the side he was now on and dragged the lightweight barrier up onto the canal path, a concrete and stone quay that ran around most the edges of the canals in Venice to make loading and unloading easier and to help stop the city being washed away.

The float was easily folded in half and carried the couple of hundred feet back to the entrance he wanted to temporarily block. The whole Venice trip had been rushed and it was sadly turning into a farce. Now he had to position the float on his own, something you either needed a small boat to do or maybe even two men, one on each pathway and each holding a separate end of the chain. Even though this was a small spur canal and not much more than two boats' width across, it was something he hadn't planned for. He was quickly going off Venice and it had been one of his favourite places of all time.

He attached one end of the pontoon to his side of the canal and pushed it out onto the water as far as he could. Then he tried to lob the other end of the chain across to the other path. It wasn't a particularly heavy gauge chain, so it hadn't made that much noise when it had landed and there was still some background noise from distant revellers and passing traffic on the Grand Canal. The chain had landed, paused for a second and then like some weird serpent slipped into the water and sank, taking the far end of the float with it. He reeled it in and tried again, then again and again for fifteen minutes. With the main canal busy he had been forced to duck for cover a couple of times as commercial barges moved past close to where he was. He had resorted to trying to lasso one of the mooring points cowboy-style.

He had all but given up and with what he was sure would have been his last attempt if it had not worked, he finally managed to hook the chain onto some rotting timber nudge boards fixed to the canal walls at water level, which he speculated were there to stop the barges and boats damaging themselves or the ancient stonework. It had been what seemed like a lifetime of Mr Bean-type farce but the plan only stood a chance if he could block the entrance.

With the chain snagged, the float was still partially submerged below water because of the weight of the excess chain dragging it down. Again, fate was going to make him work for it. The water level was at least three feet below the top of the canal quayside. Once he was on the other side of the canal he lay on his stomach and tried to grab the chain. It was inches away from his outstretched arm and fingertips. He looked about for something he could use to hook or catch the chain but there was nothing. He was so damn close. He stood there trying to get his brain to solve the puzzle he was presented with, but he was tired, grubby and really pissed off with the whole thing and there was no inspiration that would propel his fatigued brain into action.

He tried to catch the chain with his foot, worried the slightest nudge on the rotten wood would send it all under the water again and this time he was sure he would just walk away. He took the weight on his arms and lowered his legs over the side. He balanced one foot on the rail, arms taking most of the weight, and trying to hook the chain with his free foot. He didn't trust the old timber enough to hold all his weight if he stood there and leant down to try and pick the chain up with his hand. All this accomplished in the end was Bob getting two wet feet as part of the wood gave way, confirming his suspicions, and he was only just quick enough to stop himself falling completely into the water, managing to brace his full weight on his arms until he could get a little purchase and scramble back on to the quayside. A few deep breaths and he looked over to see if the chain had gone. It was still there, tauntingly, like it was saying 'Come and get me, you wuss'.

Once he had seen that the chain was still snagged he went and hid in the shadows. Someone must have heard his splashing about that time? He got his breath back. No-one had come to see what was going on, so he decided on one last try. He took off his belt and looped it over the closest metal mooring point and again lay on his stomach and reached over the side, one hand holding onto the leather belt for grim death, the other reaching for the chain.

He inched forward and down, his legs spread across the pathway. He was hoping it would counterbalance his torso as he reached further. His endeavours paid off. He clasped the chain in triumph and tried to ease his way back. He had forgotten about his small shoulder bag that he had been living out of for the last few days. It had been permanently over his shoulder all the time except when he had been using it as a pillow, but at the very moment of his success, the bag decided to make a break for freedom, slipping across his back and off his shoulder. Somehow he managed to save himself and the bag and keep a hold of the chain. It had been a few seconds of thrashing limbs but all of him, apart from his feet, was still dry and he was now lying on the cobbles of the path and not falling through the air. He got up and secured the chain to the mooring before he had reclaimed his belt. The float was in place. The Grunts couldn't get to the hotel without walking now.

He sat back against the wall and waited. He even chuckled to himself at the stupidity of his attempts to solve a simple problem. He could have tied the chain across at the bridge or he could have used the mooring points and zigzagged back and forth across the bridge, making one end of the chain secure and then moving the other end to the next mooring point and moving slowly along until he had the pontoon where he wanted it. Stress and fatigue were taking their toll. Next time he would just shoot the fucker!

* * *

The chug of the water taxi woke him up as it pulled up at the canal entrance but stayed on the Grand Canal. There was a little bickering and a few protests from its two passengers as they were asked to disembark before they got to the hotel and they had the prospect of a short walk they didn't want or might not even be capable of. But what could the taxi man do when the canal was now closed?

Bob was up on his still cold and soggy feet, watching. He didn't know how long he had slept but if his feet were still wet it could not have been long. His hand went into the bag and he pulled out a pair of stretchy gloves and put them on. The Grunts were making a meal of getting off the taxi but being on the Grand Canal meant passing traffic rocking the boat a little and in their inebriated state it was making things that much harder. Bob reached back into the bag for the knife he had purchased … the knife. The bloody knife was missing. Everything else was there. When he had been all arms and legs and trying not to fall into the water the knife must have fallen out of the bag and he hadn't noticed and it was now in the mud at the bottom of the canal.

The taxi revved up and pulled away. Harry and his wife were trying to co-ordinate their efforts before they attempted the last five hundred yards to safety and they were giggling like schoolgirls.

Bob was angry. Grunt was going to escape again. He was that angry he couldn't think straight. The Grunts staggered forward. A few faltering steps. A sway, a stagger and a violent lurch to the side and they both nearly ended up in the canal, triggering more fits of laughter.

That was it, they had nearly done it themselves. Bob was sure one good push and the heavy costumes would do the rest. He hadn't planned on killing Grunt's wife but time was running out and she had just become collateral damage. The two of them going down together might even make it more convincing as an accident too.

Bob was on the opposite side of the canal to the drunken couple. He started towards them, keeping to the shadows as best he could. The couple staggered and swayed and made slow progress in the right direction.

As Bob started over the bridge to come up behind them and

push the two unsuspecting drunkards into the canal, Mrs Grunt started whining about desperately needing to pee.

'Come on, dear, we are nearly at the bloody hotel.'

'Piss off, it has just taken us ten minutes to do this far,' the lady observed. 'It's all right for you bloody men, you just get your knob out anywhere and that's fine. Up the wall, out the window, in the sink.' A charming scene best glossed over, Bob thought.

'Just hold on, honey, someone could be watching,' Harry said in his best sulky voice. She did have a point, though, it had taken a damn long time to travel a very short distance.

'You damn twat, I am not going to strip off in public. I will use this alleyway here and as if by magic ... PUFF.' There were a few hand signals implying that she had conjured the alleyway herself and for her immediate need, even though it had been there for hundreds of years.

'Hurry up, then, you mad bitch. A woman of your age can't hold it all night or even for three hundred yards, it seems.'

Bob couldn't hear the mumbled reply but the hand gesture was self-explanatory. She staggered a few steps closer to the hotel and then disappeared into the shadows of the alley to go and do what she had to do. Bob saw his chance and came across the bridge towards Harry. He imitated the staggering and the swaying the Grunts had been so good at and made out he was the worse for wear, just like the loving couple had been on their merry little walk.

Grunt had taken a few steps after his wife but then jumped as Bob magically appeared from nowhere.

'Hold on there, my good man.' Grunt put his arm up to Bob in an attempt to block the pathway. 'Sorry old boy, the wife's a little indisposed at the moment. She should be finished in about ten minutes.' He laughed at his own little joke.

Bob shrugged. 'No English,' he said trying to move forward.

It appeared Grunt didn't want his wife discovered and started to mime and use pigeon English to explain his problem to a fellow drunk. 'The wife.' He did a curvy shape hand gesture, which Bob assumed meant female. Harry staggered a bit, then regained his balance and squatted down. 'Is taking a pee.' Again more gushing hand gestures to accompany the squat and a silly PEEEE! sound-effect to accompany what he was trying to convey.

Bob was within touching distance. 'Si, si,' he said, hoping it sounded Italian and he had done a better job than Harry's attempt at an upper crust English accent. Grunt rose from the squatting position, still swaying.

Now Harry assumed the Italian gentleman before him had been made fully aware of the situation and would do the honourable thing and wait. 'Thank you, kind sir, for your discretion,' he said, following it with an unstable attempt at a gracious bow.

At that moment Bob stepped forward, interlocking with his prey, one leg behind Harry's, one hand holding Harry's arm away from his costumed body and one hand on Harry's chest. Bob then twisted and threw Harry almost judo-style with all the force he could muster to the ground. The aim was to get enough downward momentum to bounce Harry's head off the stone floor and then push the dazed body into the water.

It worked better than Bob could have hoped for. Harry's head hit one of the stumpy metal mooring posts as he went down and the thud was deadened by the big white wig he had been wearing all holiday. The rest went to plan: the body was rolled over the edge and quietly lowered into the water. The large heavy costume helped to conceal any kind of splash and then dragged poor, unfortunate Harry down under the water. One quick check by Bob and he saw the last of the purple felt disappearing and the white wig floating away. He didn't know if Harry was still alive or not. There had been an audible crack as his head had struck metal but that wasn't going to matter for that much longer.

Bob was on his feet and walking briskly back over the bridge and away from the scene, giving one quick glance back to check there had been no evidence left or that Harry had not miraculously surfaced in perfect health. From the alley he heard Mrs Grunt.

'Harry, Harry! You bastard! You better not have left me here alone … Harry … HARRY!'

By then it was too late and Bob had turned the corner and was heading for a water taxi. The price would be worth it for a long hot bath and a sleep in a proper bed before the long ride back to Spain. He had planned a few days with his friends there, relaxing in the sun eating tapas, but he would barely have time now to get back, pick up the hire car and get to the airport. Still, the car would prove he was in Granada all his holiday if someone in England got that interested. Deb's old company really was having a run of bad luck, although Sapp could now enjoy a few weeks as 'numero uno'.

21

Sad Sapp

Bob arrived back home without incident. He didn't know for sure if the Italian police had suspected anything other than a tragic accident but there had been no visits or questions from their British counterparts, so he would take that as a good sign. The travelling and time alone had given him opportunity to consider what he wanted to do next. Again, he had pruned the management tree and again, it had not been enough to cause any real harm to the company. The Book of Deb was still holding good. He hoped the company could take one more piece of pruning with no permanent damage being done. He had considered calling it a day, but then he had remembered that it had been Sapp's gloating, at that chance meeting in town that had been the final push that had taken Deb from him. Summer had been the jealous mastermind, unable to let Deb have the credit or rewards for what she had done. Hawkken and Harry had been the ruthless foot soldiers and storm-troopers enforcing their master's will without question or conscience. Sapp had come into that category as well, making one small little effort to help Deb right at the start but then he had folded and become the most zealous of her denouncers to show his absolute loyalty to Summer and hopefully stop himself being her next victim.

Bob had concluded there was only one thing to do and that was to finish what he had started, which meant Sapp would be next. The planning would be better this time. He had returned unscathed from Venice more by luck than judgement. He now had a new identity hidden away he could use when he wanted. The fake passport had worked on the few occasions he had had to use it on the Venice trip, but to be fair that was only for minor incidents and the people checking hadn't been that committed to their task. His extended family didn't really need him now, and his and Deb's home was now fully passed over to their son and his family.

Get rid of Sapp and then disappear and give the passport a real test was the goal now. He thought Hallowe'en or bonfire night would be the right sort of period to wander around in a disguise, and that gave him time to plan. Then he could go and find somewhere warm for winter. He toyed with trying to create another accident but if he had now made the decision to disappear and start a new life, why risk all the uncontrollables? He still had the little gun and he would work around that. He remembered sitting with wet feet in Venice and thinking, 'Just shoot the fucker next time' and that essentially was his plan.

Sapp had not moved, despite his now great wealth. His Indian wife's family had been rich, and when Sapp and she had had to get married, her parents had paid out a large sum towards a home so their daughter would not have to live in poverty. Bob guessed Sapp hadn't paid them back or even considered trying now that he had more than enough money to do so. The house was nice but you wouldn't guess the guy was worth millions and millions from looking at it.

Bob had become friendly with a new local salesman for the company in Sapp's area. The new guy had been quite open about answering a few questions once Bob had convinced him that he wasn't out to steal his area. It seemed once Deb had gone, along with her views about loyalty, commitment and obligation, the company had found a new scam to eke out even more millions from their unsuspecting salesmen.

The company had gone for the high staff turnover and tactics employed by franchise pubs and food chains everywhere, where only the top few people who own everything make real money selling unsuspecting people unachievable dreams. Once the victim's money is gone, the cycle pops up again and the bar soon reopens 'Under New Management' because the previous tenants have fallen foul of some unobtainable target or overpriced maintenance regime they have to commit to. The people at the top are only interested in the next franchise fee and how much they can get the next guy to spend doing the place up, before the new guy becomes the next guy replaced. The customer base stays the same, give or take. You lose a few because they are loyal to the guy before and you gain a few the new guy attracts in. But the people at the top keep getting their franchise fee every few years and all their equipment renewed and the property maintained for free by keeping on reselling the same dream over and over again.

Anyway, the new salesman had been quite willing to give Sapp's home address away when Bob had hinted he might be interested in joining the team and having plenty of disposable cash to spend. He didn't really need the address, he only wanted confirmation Sapp was still there without talking to someone who might still recognise him from when Deb was still working.

It seemed the company was now offering a 'bounty' for finding new recruits. Bob couldn't understand how these salesmen hadn't sussed what was happening. The books were kept full of new replacements in-waiting and the company kept the franchise fees rolling in as long as they were ready to jump in as soon as any minor excuse could be found to rid themselves of the old guy. Bob guessed the 'new' guys always thought it would never happen to them and that they were a special case, and that history wouldn't keep repeating itself.

As the time of year chosen came along, Bob turned what was left of his belongings he could into cash. His family were a little concerned about his latest planned trek, especially with winter coming, but Bob reassured them that like him, the old campervan still had one good long trip left in it and he would keep in touch from a hot sunny beach somewhere. When the time came, he gave his family a big hug and bade them a fond farewell in his best Sunday afternoon, B-movie style. Bob had then driven to a secluded bed and breakfast about sixty miles away from Sapp's to prepare. There were just a few things to arrange and few things to put in place and it would be time to reawaken the new and much improved justice system.

Bob had scoured the papers and car magazines for an old, dark blue, four-door Audi. He had found one quickly and in the right area, once he was settled in at the B&B. Bob bought it using cash and a false name and address. It had a lot of miles on the clock, but it would do. He paid for it to be tarted up and polished so it looked newish and could pass, at a glance, for something well maintained. It had been £20 well spent for the Polish car valeter to do his magic. Unless you are an Audi fan they all look similar and of undiscernible age. It was low season for the guest house, so they were accommodating when he asked if he could take up an extra car space for a few days. Bob made one small modification to the car while it was parked in the car park: he took about half an hour to install flashing blue lights hidden behind the car's front radiator grill.

The campervan had been sold to a local garage. It hadn't made him much money but it had been reliable and it seemed a shame to scrap it when someone else could find a use for it. Once he had finished with Sapp, a campervan would not be the ideal getaway vehicle.

It had been almost two weeks since he had left home. He had made a few calls using local public phones to his family to assure them all was going well. Bob still had the small pistol and a little ammunition that he had rescued from its hiding place before he had left his old home on the next leg of this journey.

The day before he was due to leave the B&B he made a round trip into the local city where he joined the crowds of shoppers and people preparing for the week of 'trick and treaters' and firework party-goers. He bought a false policeman's costume from a small hire shop hidden away on an estate in the back of beyond, ready for later. Over the week before he had spent a little time watching Sapp's house to get a feel for the family's after-work routine. As always it was Sapp's wife who seemed to do everything, while her lord and master did whatever with his time.

Bob had observed her taking the kid to various clubs a few nights of the week and on the others, when she was the one going out, Sapp never baby-sat. There had been a couple of nights when the wife had left wearing gym gear with the kid in tow. Obviously he would be dropped off somewhere until she finished, picking the lad up on her way back home. These nights ended about 10.30-ish and she was left to carry the tired kid into the house on her own. The simple conclusion was that on almost any night Bob would be able to show up and watch for the spouse to leave and he would then have a little time to go and reintroduce himself to Sad Sapp.

On the chosen day, he had packed ready for the real road trip. All the essentials were now in the boot of the car. His few clothes and personal stuff plus the two passports and about £20,000 in cash were in a large waterproof duffel bag. There was a second bag with the police uniform and a few other things in it – this was the new goody bag, ready and waiting. Bob had decided to revisit the old disguise and had purchased a short ginger wig and a matching false beard to replace the ones burnt. This time the wig and beard were well trimmed, because 'Paedo Paul' was now going to be a member of the establishment and he was going to be a little more well-kept in appearance than his previous reincarnation. Of course there was also the next generation of homemade number plates that had worked so well before.

After the drive to fetch the policeman's costume, he had visited a small storage company where he kept another of his recent purchases, a 600cc motor bike. Again, it had been bought for cash using a false identity. He gave it a run to charge everything up and filled it with fuel before returning it to the storage unit as part of his final preparations. After a quick chat with the owner of the storage yard to arrange late access for Hallowe'en night, he had gone back to the B&B.

The storage place was actually a farm and the owner/farmer had just bought a few cheap rusty containers and put them in a disused barn and was now subsidising his farm profits making reasonable money, or so he claimed, renting the containers as secure storage. Bob had used the excuse that he was moving into this part of the world but had not found anywhere permanent yet. He had put the bike there as a boy toy he had not got space for and then added a few empty boxes to pad out his story and the container. All the containers that were there and inside had large padlocks and a rudimentary light. Bob didn't know how many people were using this out-of-the way little site but other than the boss, he had seen only one other person and that was a farmhand, when he had called in to get instructions for the day from the farmer on one of Bob's earlier visits. Bob could be the only paying customer as far as he knew, or the place could become a beehive of activity on the days he wasn't actually there.

Bob had explained to the farmer he would be calling in late on Hallowe'en so if it was OK by him he would keep the keys so that he didn't disturb anyone else's night. He claimed he would be fetching the bike to go and see friends but had no idea when he would be able to leave work, and that had satisfied the farmer of Bob's good intentions. Bob would drop the key through the letterbox in the door of the Portakabin that served as the office, and everyone seemed happy with the arrangement.

Bob had checked the area out well around Sapp's home. He had already planned where he could pull over to change and then prep the car without being seen or disturbed. The house was in town but there was lots of countryside not too far away. As early evening began, Bob pulled up at his chosen spot, a little early and ahead of schedule. He put it down to being keen to get started. To his horror there was another car parked just a little further up the country lane.

He hesitated about staying and thought about finding some other place to do the necessary, or just pulling off and driving around and coming back later. As he made the decision to move and come back later and was about to leave, an old guy appeared from over a stile near to the other car, followed by a damned ugly collie dog. They both got into the car and it drove off. Bob had considered being discreet in case it turned out to be a dishevelled young couple re-arranging their attire as they returned to the other car and that would have been certainly more entertaining than 'one man and his dog'. But he was now alone and that was all that was important.

He had dressed earlier to help with his disguise. His mobile phone had been disposed of once he had written down the few numbers he wanted and needed. He could ring his family from anywhere on a public phone or use the net; he would just say that his mobile was lost or stolen. This time he was going to be careful but not over-cautious. He would be long gone before things really kicked off. He already had on black tidy trousers and a light blue shirt and these he would keep on until his night's work was done.

The interior car mirror was not as good as the mirror he had used at home for putting on the wig and false beard, way back before Summer's unfortunate little incident, but he would have to make do. Once the hairy part of the disguise was done he got out of the car and went to the rear and opened the boot. Out came the fluorescent padded police waistcoat with the blue and white patch across the back proclaiming 'POLICE' in large capitals. A black, clip-on tie and new, black, shiny boots were next to be added and then the imitation utility belt that looked as though it belonged to some mighty Gotham city hero. The belt even boasted plastic handcuffs but he didn't expect anyone to get close enough to see that they were fake and he was glad it would be dark because they wouldn't fool anyone giving them a close inspection. The gun in the holster was the real thing, even if it looked a little small compared to the dummy toy it had replaced. He took out the peaked cap that completed the outfit. Number plates were quickly covered and changed, then he closed the boot and went and sat back in the car, putting the cap on the passenger seat. He pulled on the stretchy gloves and waited. The radio was playing 'Ballroom Blitz' by Sweet. As the singer blasted out 'As the man in the back said everyone attack ...' Bob started the car.

It was mid-week, so it was a work night, but Bob was sure Sapp would have finished long ago and would already be back at home. The guy was never around even before he was the boss. The Audi pulled into the posh little dead-end road where Sapp's house was in the north of Birmingham. Bob made one circuit to check for cars – both Sapp's and his wife's were at the house – and he then went and parked just about in view so that he could sit and watch for the right moment. He was gambling that even if the routine wasn't going to be its usual self there would be something 'on', Hallowe'en being one of those times of the year when mums and kids feel the urge to come together – and that would take the rest of Sapp's family out for a while and leave the man of the house all alone. Other people's kids were not allowed in the house, unless there had been a major shift in power in the household over recent times. This Bob knew from when the people in Summer's little entourage were still playing nice and friendly and he guessed Sapp's attitude would not have changed. There hadn't even been a token pumpkin head in any of the windows.

The house was in one of the furthest corners of the fashionable dead-end. It was still a newish development and every house was uniformly the same, even down to the two cars in the drive – a big one for daddy and a 4x4 run-around tank for mummy to do the school run in. The lack of any sort of Hallowe'en decoration was the only thing that made Sapp's house stand out from the rest. Maybe he was making a stand against the 'trick or treat' custom those pain in the arse Yanks had managed to sell us Brits. Real All Hallows Eve seemed a much better set-up and a lot more sinister. Scare all the little kids shitless with the real thing and keep them off the streets so the adults could have all the fun for once. It is, after all, a religious and deeply meaningful night for some people.

After only about twenty minutes, the door of Sapp's house opened and his wife and son were briefly illuminated as they both headed for the 4x4. The kid had a costume on ready for a fancy dress party, although Bob could not make out what he was supposed to be. The wife was in leggings and leotard and Bob gave her the benefit of the doubt and assumed that she was going to some kind of keep-fit class and not her own adult version of trick or treat and some illicit and passionate affair. Her body still looked good from where he has parked and he was still amazed that Sapp and she ever got together as a couple. Would she still be there if she could see her hubby at the works get-togethers – following Harry's example – or see what happened after them, to be more accurate?

Maybe Bob would be doing her a favour? The 4x4 revved up and shot off down the road a little faster than he had seen her go when he had been watching before. She could be late or it could be that her and grumpy old Sapp have had a little tiff. Either way the speed had almost caught him napping. He had only just managed to duck down across the passenger seat as she sped past. Bob sat back upright. His minor worries that Sapp would actually be joining in with something to do with the family and he would have to wait until a different night were totally unfounded. One more track off the radio to give her time to be long gone and it would then be time to start Halloween off with a bang. The Beastie Boys started up. The sound was happy and loud and it fitted his mood just dandy.

He started up the car's engine and pulled off, doing the few hundred yards in seconds. He parked the old blue Audi on the drive in the space the 4x4 had left. Bob left the engine running and the headlights on full beam, switching on the added blue flashing lights. It all worked beautifully. The car was directly facing the front door and the blue lights were flashing off every reflective surface in the vicinity. It was almost festive.

He put on the peaked cap and did a quick check on the disguise in the mirror then he got out of the car and went to the door. Bang, bang on the door and a quick ring of the bell for good measure and then he waited, checking the gun was loose in the holster. The car had been parked with the lights on so anyone answering the door could only see Bob's silhouette and any curtain twitchers would see the fluorescent police jacket and cap but would hopefully not try and get involved. The house had almost all the lights on, so Sapp could be in any of the rooms. You would think with his hatred of kids and all that they do, he would be like the rest of us on Hallowe'en night and have the lights turned off and be sat upstairs in a back room making out that everyone in the house has gone out for the evening. Instead it looked like he wanted to proclaim he was in to the whole world.

It took several more knocks and blasts on the doorbell to get Sapp to reluctantly open the door. Maybe Sapp was upstairs with his tissues and lubricating gel and internet connection after all. Bob was just about to give up, but patience is a virtue and as the door was opened it looked like it was all going to work out happily. Sapp sounded really irritated and grumpy until he registered the blue flashing lights and the silhouette of the uniform. He has obviously had several visits from the local kids already and if he was trying to get a little 'me' time for himself he should have been better prepared.

'Mr Sapp?' Bob put on his best deep and menacing police voice. There was a nod from Sapp to acknowledge that Bob had the right person. 'Sorry to disturb you this late, sir, but may I come in and have a quick word?'

Sapp agreed to the chat but seemed to have no intention of asking Bob in, despite the retina-destroying light he was looking almost directly into and the request from a representative of the law.

Bob asked again: 'May we step inside for a few seconds, sir?' Sapp hesitated but he had an officer of the law standing on his drive, for fuck sake, and what would the neighbours think, so he grudgingly agreed. 'Suppose – if you must.' Helpful son of a bitch right to the end…

He stood to the side to let Bob pass. Bob's true identity was well hidden but he would still have been happier if Sapp had led the way and he had turned his back on him. Bob went in the direction that his gracious host was vaguely indicating. 'Straight through, the kitchen is down there.' Officer Bob walked down the hall. The lounge door was ajar and through the crack between door and frame he could see a part-eaten TV dinner on a stool in front of the sofa and porno frozen on the TV screen. From behind, Sapp suddenly moved quickly.

Bob was convinced he had been made. The 'Police' on his waistcoat misspelt like joke ones in Thailand? In his heightened state of awareness he instantly suspected that his cover had been blown and reached for the gun. The number plates had come from an equally stupid scenario he had seen on the TV. An American bomber had almost escape scot-free but had taken the number plates off his escape vehicle and was stopped for that. The devil being in the detail as they say.

Sapp disappeared into the lounge. He had gone for the TV remote to clear the screen of the incriminating evidence. Bob followed, gun raised, not realising Sapp's fairly innocent intentions and expecting an ambush or escape attempt. The remote fell to the floor and the batteries burst out and rolled in opposite directions across the shagpile.

'I was only … the TV,' Sapp spluttered and pointed, waving his arms about and yelling, 'Don't shoot, don't shoot'. He looked into Bob's eyes. What he saw Bob did not know but he had been clearly recognised from the look now on Sapp's face.

'YOU!' was all Sapp had time to say. One shot to the face and he dropped to his knees, then one shot to the heart. Bob was sure the slight change in the MO and technique was equally as deadly to Sapp as it had been to Summer. There was no pondweed to fall into but Sapp managed to wedge himself sideways between the sofa and one of the armchairs, knocking the still-hot dinner across the floor. Sapp's dead weight pushed the chair across the door. Another bloody cheapskate, all the money he had and his furniture felt like it was made from foam and balsa wood. Bob reached across and dragged it out of his way one- handed, so he could make his exit leaving the lights on. They were on when he arrived so he guessed that was the norm. Sapp had always been the same at work. You could track his progression through the company on any given day following lights and equipment left switched on and abandoned.

While he had waited in the car and when Bob had been in the house there had been background noise of occasional fireworks going off. Bob was sure no-one would have heard the shots through the double-glazing and recognised them for what they really were. Bob stepped out on to the drive. He gave a casual nod and a 'Good evening, sir' as a parting gesture to his imaginary friend, standing just out of sight, to keep the curtain twitchers happy if they were still watching and to sell that Sapp, at this moment, was still all right. Bob then pulled the front door to and got into the car. He switched the blue flashing lights off so he didn't cause any unsuspecting drivers stress and backed up off the drive and pulled away.

He headed for the farm. He had about an hour and twenty minutes' drive in front of him and with the cap back on the passenger seat he was just another faceless rep in a faceless Audi on the motorway and on the road to nowhere. He resisted the temptation to put on the blue flashing lights again and to put his foot down just to get to his destination a little quicker, common sense prevailing because if there was a real copper out there on the road it would end his night prematurely ... a bit like Sapp's.

He had not known the area around the farm that well, unlike his old stomping ground, but it had not taken long to find a suitable spot to dump and burn the Audi. He had found a service road that ran alongside the local railway track. At the end of the road there were a group of three bridges under the railway. The furthest away was to let a small river flow under. The second was dead space and the third looked like it was a small access way for the local farmer to get to his land and surrounding fields. Bob had seen people walking their dogs down the road on one of his drive-bys and he had returned and investigated.

Unlocked double gates had led to over a mile-and-a-half of deserted access road. No buildings of any sort were on view near or in the distance and the rail track was raised to block the view of anyone on the main road. It was perfect. If it hadn't been for the dog walkers' cars parked near the gates during the day, he would have missed it. Then it had been a simple matter of checking the local ordnance survey map of the area – and he had found a country walk that took him close to the farm with the storage containers. Once he was done setting things alight he no longer had a use for, he just needed to cut across a couple of large fields from the bridge end of the service road, pick up the hikers' track and follow it to roughly where he wanted to go … in the dark.

He arrived at the double gates and soon had the car on the inside with the gates shut behind him. He had switched off the car's lights as soon as he had arrived and once his eyes had accustomed themselves to the dark of the night he was able to follow the light-coloured concrete road easily, keeping the chance of being spotted to a minimum. All around him was darkness but without all the incidental lights from towns or cities and passing cars he could see well enough to get to the bridges.

He had considered leaving the motorbike under one of the bridges, hidden under one of the arches ready for the big getaway but common sense had again won out and he had convinced himself that it would be better not to risk someone finding it and then vandalising or stealing it. That could ruin his great escape before it even started.

He pulled into the middle one of the three bridges and parked the car right in the centre of the arch so that even in daylight it would have been completely hidden from view. He got out and quickly scouted the immediate area using a pencil light, checking the other two bridge sections to make sure no-one was dossing down and sleeping rough in them. Even if he had found someone, he was still dressed as his new alter ego, PC Paedo Paul, so he could have gently moved them on if he had needed to. All was clear.

He went to the boot of the car and opened it. The small, interior light came on and it seemed a massive intrusion into the dark. Off with the cap, police jacket, utility belt and finally the wig, eyebrows and beard. On with his own waterproof combat jacket and benny hat. He knew it was a beanie hat these days but in his youth it had been 'Benny' as a tribute to the old *Crossroads* star – and it made you look as big a twat as the character the guy had played. Bob still had the gloves on, so he salvaged the pistol from the utility belt, put it into a plastic bag and then into his waterproof bag, which he put to one side away from the car. He ripped the false plates off from the front and back of the Audi and they went into the open boot, too. He opened the windows and bonnet and liberally soaked everything, including the interior and the items in the boot, with the two gallons of petrol he had brought with him. He lit a couple of bits of newspaper and dropped one onto the driver's seat and one in the boot and the fire caught immediately. Hopefully that would make sure there was no DNA or fingerprints left to be found. He tossed the plastic gloves into the flames and headed off cross-country with the few possessions he had left.

He marched off but when he got to the top of the first field and looked back down the shallow incline he became very concerned. The car was engulfed in flame under the bridge and the flames were licking out from either side of the arch. The arch was four sets of rail tracks wide and the bridges went under the embankment the tracks were laid on. The surrounding farmland was undulating so there was very little chance of the flames being noticed unless he was really unlucky and a train went past in the next fifteen or so minutes. Even then from the train driver's view point he would only be able to see a red glow and probably just put it down to some down-and-out trying to keep warm and do nothing about it. Anyway, it can't take that long for a damn car to burn. The fire pit he had used to get rid of evidence before had worked well enough and this was the same idea, just on a bigger scale. Over the years he had seen a couple of burnt-out wrecks on the motorway and it looked like they had gone from pride and joy to melted lumps of scrap metal in minutes. Bob turned and headed away from the track, leaving the still-burning car. Hopefully he could find his way in the dark.

* * *

When he got to the farm, the main house had a couple of lights on but he didn't go over. The barn office was closed but as arranged, the access door to the barn had been left open for him; it was the middle of nowhere, after all. The motion sensors did their work and as he crossed the threshold, the barn's interior light came on. It didn't quite illuminate the furthest corners but it was plenty good enough to allow him to cross to his container without breaking his neck. There was also enough light to unlock the padlock without fumbling around for hours. He wheeled the bike out and started it up so it could warm up while he quickly finished packing and preparing for his ride.

He had considered breaking for the Chunnel and riding hell for leather and escaping into Europe that way. In the end he had thought the risk too big. Contestant number four (Sapp) would have been going cold for hours by then and could well have been found and there would be no guarantees that the police would not be there waiting and checking passports as Bob tried to get away. Maybe if he had been closer and the time taken shorter he might have risked it. Bob was sure he wouldn't have left any real evidence but he didn't want to become involved in any investigation and lose out to some unexpected unlucky break.

He put his helmet on after he had slung the rucksack, which contained what was left of his worldly possessions, back over his shoulder. He rode the short distance to the Portakabin, then dismounted and dropped the keys through the letterbox. He had squashed the empty boxes and binned them in the farm's skip the day before. He jumped back on the bike and rode out of the open barn door carefully and sedately and with due consideration for fellow road users, so as not to draw any unwanted attention to himself.

22

The Great Escape

The night was cold and dry and the roads were very quiet. He could see the occasional firework going off in the night sky, the result no doubt of some spotty youth failing to resist the temptation and wait for the appropriate evening. Soon he was cruising down the M5 south towards Cornwall, his trusty iPad on. Fittingly ZZ Top were playing 'I'm Bad, I'm Nationwide'. His family had originally come from Padstow (Steinville or Padstein as it is unofficially called these days). Generations after generations of family history bought out, like so many others, so some tourist could have himself a holiday cottage to use two weeks of the year. His grandparents' generation had capitulated to economic pressure and moved north to find work, giving in to the demand of the rich for quaint tourist homes by the sea. His family had settled in the Midlands in the hope of a more prosperous life but extended family and friends had spewed out all over the country over the years. Well, even if he had been old enough to have had a say in the matter, the outcome would probably have been the same. Why do shit jobs for shit pay and only be employed a few months a year if you can't even see the sea because all the rich tourists have all the best houses?

It had seemed strange over the years when he had returned as a tourist himself. Forty or fifty years ago as a young kid he had known everyone. The grown-ups looked out for the children, and not just their own, and it was safe to play in the streets.

Every door was left open and unlocked without fear of being robbed or having squatters move in. Now there just seemed to be a lot of dodgy 'put-on' Cornish accents by Londoners trying to sell imported Chinese crap to the tourists and convince everyone that it was made locally. Apologies to any real locals holding out.

The trip was uneventful. A few loo stops broke his journey and kept him awake, then he had arrived and was huddled up on a sheltered bench on one of the local beaches, trying to catch a few hours' sleep before the rest of the world woke up. It was cool but dry and the sunrise had been spectacular coming up over the fields at the back of the beach.

There had not been much risk of people being up and moving him on at this time of year. Even so, he was awoken by a local council workman opening up the beach toilet block and banging about to let anyone in range know how dedicated he was. Bob guessed that he was not the worst thing the guy had found on the beach this early in the morning. He would even go as far as saying an old guy sleeping on the beach next to a motorbike would probably not even get a second glance. Bob stretched and stomped about to get the circulation going again. His body was beginning to feel very old. Once the council workman had left, Bob walked over to use the now-spotless facilities. The bag and bike were left together; after all, who else was going to be around at 7 a.m. on the first day of November on a deserted Cornish beach?

Job done, so to speak, Bob started up the bike. The journey hadn't been hard but the second-hand machine was slowly bleeding to death, which was obvious from the warm, black stain underneath the engine on the sand. It finally died at a lay-by not too far away from Padstow. Bob had hoped to get around the coast to one of the larger harbours but he could work on that later. He ditched the bike and helmet there, dropping the keys near the bike to make it look like the rider had been careless, and in the hope that some passing yob would nick it thinking that Christmas had come early. The poor thing should be stripped and in bits in no time and should disappear without trace.

This was where he had spent his childhood, so he knew most of the local bus routes. He walked along the road and then waited at the stop for the bus to take him down into town. Thanks to the more professional circle of contacts and the new fake passport they helped to supply, Bob sat on the stone wall confident that the old Bob would soon be able to fall off the face of the earth.

By the time the bus came he was bloody cold and he was just about to give up and start walking the couple of miles or so to Padstow to get warm. So much for out-of-season timetables. Once in the bus and out of the now howling wind he started to get the feeling back in his extremities, thanks to the hot air being pumped around by the heating system. Soon he was down near the harbour, where he found himself an open café and went for a full English. He chatted to the staff – well, the one waitress and the chef. It was November, after all.

Padstow harbour isn't that big but it does get a few out-of-town nautical types calling in to get a bite at Rick Stein's place and then trundling on somewhere else. At the café he had found out that there were two, possibly three larger boats in at the moment, and they had all arrived over the last few days. The waitress had been happy to stand by the window in the warm and point them out. After a leisurely breakfast to give the boats' crews time to get up, Bob started his tour of the harbour.

He knew he might not be able to escape quickly but he wasn't in that much of a hurry and his plan now was to cadge a lift here and there, keep a low profile for a while and slowly slip away under the radar.

Over the next hour or so he found out as much as he could about the boats and their owners and more importantly their potential for helping with his escape. The first had been straightforward. A couple on deck were doing a few little jobs to their pride and joy and Bob had walked up and started chatting, friendly-like, about their boat and where they were heading to next. Sadly, they were now parked up until after Christmas and once they were all secured and tied down (their words, not Bob's) they would be off to their friends on dry land. The second looked as though it had already been abandoned for the winter, but he would keep an eye open in case the owners returned and he was mistaken.

The third boat and his last chance at the moment was a little posher than most in the harbour and as he made his way around the quay in its general direction he saw a fit-looking lady jump up on deck and then head off past the tourist shops in the direction of the local supermarket. He tried not to be too obvious but took off after her, following her through the town and then up the hill to where the fairly recent addition to the local facilities was perched. He found a good vantage point out of the cold breeze and waited for her to come back out.

The supermarket was a good size for the town but it was a bloody good walk up the hill to get there. He supposed that was better than having to buy the groceries, then start climbing, and the lady in question had set a brisk pace so she was certainly as fit as she looked from a distance. Must be a heavy smoker though, no-one else could have gone up at that speed. All his life Bob had been surrounded by heavy smokers and they had all been super fit … until they keeled over dead, just before they retired.

The lady concerned came out of the supermarket with three good-sized bags of goodies. He gave her a little head start and then followed at a brisk pace. His aim was to catch her up quickly and look as though he was in a hurry as he passed but then, being a true gentleman, stop and ask if he could help. As he overtook her he smiled and greeted her with a cheerful 'good morning'. He received a polite 'good morning' back, accompanied by a friendly smile. He had estimated the lady's age badly. He had judged from a distance and gone with the assumption from her general physique and appearance that she was a fit thirty-something or maybe younger. Up close she was probably nearer to Bob's own age. Most people (that includes men and women) let themselves go as soon as possible but this woman was definitely on the Honor Blackman 'eternally young' pill.

'I am sorry, I shouldn't let you struggle with all that shopping.'

'Wow! A real gentleman.'

'If I'm completely honest, I saw a good-looking tourist going the same way I am, but it is a start – and someday I hope to actually help someone in genuine need.'

'Local then?'

'Born here, sadly taken to the Midlands when I was young and sold to a factory boss. Torn from my heritage so people can eat cream scones and buy tatty souvenirs,' he said, with what he hoped was a cheeky and friendly smile.

She entered into the spirit of the banter. 'So what are you going to do? Mug me as I struggle back to the harbour burdened down with toilet rolls and tampons?'

'Don't need to. I have seen what they are charging for cream teas and that is punishment enough. Anyway that looks more like vodka and mixers from here,' he said, pointing at the bags.

She gestured for Bob to take a couple of the heavier bags and they walked down the hill with Padstow laid out before them. They chatted and harmlessly flirted a little but it was only a short walk back to the boat. He had mentioned a few places to see locally and things to do like any helpful local and she had commented on things already seen and done.

'Well, here is home and thanks for carrying my essentials.'

'Stocking up for a trip or just a good night in?' he asks.

'I'm catching the tide tomorrow, weather permitting, and carrying on around the coast. I would be heading for the Med but I've left it a little late in the year, so I will see how bad the weather gets and how far I can go. Hopefully I can get across the Channel and do a little shopping within a week or two and I will see how it goes from there.'

'Seems like a very interesting plan you have there. I hope you and your husband have a great time.' Bob had seen the wedding ring on her finger and guessed her old man was still sound asleep on board. She just smiled and waved goodbye as she stepped onto the boat with her shopping. Bob took a couple of steps, then turned back around. She looked up and he offered the name of a local public house he would be in that evening and pointed it out so if she and her husband fancied a drink on dry land with a 'bitter local' they could find him, then he walked off. He didn't want to push it and if he could talk to the husband later he might get his first 'lift' in return for a free couple of drinks. From the sound of it they were not planning on leaving until at least tomorrow so that gave him some time.

All he could now do was mooch around a bit to kill time. This could be his escape route but he didn't want to come on too strong and blow it. He hoped the invitation would get him an audience with the captain and if necessary he could always offer a little cash incentive against fuel for a few days as a passenger. He could even end up slipping into France unannounced, from what the captain's wife was saying.

* * *

Early evening came and went. He had retrieved his bag and all his worldly possessions from the café where they'd kindly looked after it for him through the day, after he contributed an extra tenner to the takings. He visited a few places and reminisced a little as he went around the town. This might be the last place he saw of England for a while. Now he was sitting alone nursing a pint, waiting and hoping.

From the pub he could see the boat and there were lights on but there didn't seem to be much happening and no sign of anyone coming over for a drink. The time was creeping quickly towards 10 p.m., so he guessed the invitation had been rejected. He had been gambling this was going to be his means of escape one way or another and it had seemed quite promising earlier. He made the decision to be blatant and ask before it was too late, and if they said no he would have to find another way and another escape route. He finished what was left of the pint – you wouldn't want to leave any at those prices. Bob picked up his things and headed for the boat. What was the worst that could happen? Being told to bugger off?

Bob would confess to not knowing the correct protocol for getting the attention of an uninterested boat owner so after a moment's hesitation he opted for leaning over the rail, reaching out and tapping on the window. The glamorous lady of earlier came up on deck looking relaxed and at peace with the world, wrapped in a big, furry jacket and with what looked like a good-sized measure from one of her earlier purchases in a large glass.

'Hi again.' He tried not to sound or look too creepy, even if he was a little embarrassed.

'Sorry about the drink. I just ran out of time and all that.' She was still being friendly but it did come across as a polite brush-off.

'No worries, you won't be the first or I imagine the last to crush my poor aching heart.' He didn't know if flirting was the right approach but she really did have a fantastic smile. 'I have come to confess all before it is too late.'

She arched an eyebrow and folded her arms across her chest as best she could with the large tumbler still in her hand. Then she leant back and perched herself on a convenient flat and supportive surface. 'Go on, then.'

'Well, to be honest when you said you were off to France I was hoping to cadge a lift. Don't worry, it's nothing sinister. I was just going to Paris for a Monet exhibition that's on for a couple of weeks and a boat trip sounded a great way to get the trip up and running. The beer invite was so I could ask you and your husband if I paid for some of the fuel would it be OK to travel with you as far as France.' Bob going with the slightly-eccentric-but-well-educated old traveller act, to set everyone's mind at rest. It's not like most serial killers are clean- shaven and well-educated and blend in now, is it? Did he qualify in that category now? he wondered. He hadn't thought about that before.

She made herself comfortable on her perch as she listened to his confession, arms still folded across her chest. The lights from the harbour were reflected on the water, shimmering gently. 'And the bag you have brought with you is all your luggage, I assume? Just a tad presumptuous, don't you think?'

He was embarrassed. 'Yes, I can see that it might be taken that way.' As he had been sitting in the pub he had concocted a cover story. 'To be honest, I was already packed and about to start hitching a ride towards the Chunnel.' He shrugged his shoulders. 'Poor artist and all that off on an adventure.'

'So you can't pay for fuel then?'

He realised she was winding him up when a malicious grin spread across her lips. 'Yes, I can pay and actually I can cook and clean as well,' he replied.

She gave a little pause, just for effect. Her shoulder-length blonde hair was being tussled by an intermittent breeze coming over the sea wall. 'Well, I don't usually take on passengers and just for the record I am the captain. I am not in any hurry, so we travel at my pace. If I decide I want you off my boat or you want to go that is fine, and I set you ashore at the next port of call, wherever that may be, OK? I hate cooking and cleaning so if that is OK by you, they are your responsibilities for the duration and if you do a good job I might not even charge you for the diesel.'

'I have no problem with that.'

'That is, "I have no problem with that, captain".' Again the malicious grin as she extended her arm and they shook hands. The deal was done and he was welcomed on board. 'By the way, I am Grace and I live alone, so don't get any ideas above your station, cabin boy.'

'Hi ... Captain, I'm Charlie.' That was the Christian name on Bob's fake passport and his new identity, so he guessed he'd better start getting used to it and getting into character. Strange how knowing the difference between Monet and Manet turns you from creepy, axe-wielding psychopathic killer into eccentric, harmless traveller in most people's eyes in one short sentence. (Manet paints lots of people and Monet lots of lilies, by the way). Still, Grace was safe. Bob only had one more little job to take care of before he could retire ...

He had expected to be sleeping on one of the bench sofas that ran around the main living area with Grace tucked up in the main and only bedroom but she had other ideas. Once he had been taken on-board and the hatches had been tightened down for the night he became (how could he put it tactfully?) a crew member with benefits. There had been a little drinking and mild flirting and then they had both been naked and almost as wild as teenagers. He now lay content and relaxed next to his stunning and sleeping captain. After all the downs of the last few years maybe a few days of meaningless sex (if there was such a thing?) was what he needed.

They left Padstow as planned as soon as the tide was right and the harbour gate was opened. Grace was doing her captain thing and Bob was below decks cooking breakfast and trying to tidy up a little and looking forward to making the place untidy again as soon as they were parked or moored for the night, or whatever sailors did. For the next few days they coast-hopped, with Captain Grace going ashore for supplies when they were needed. They had one bad day where the sea got a little choppier than forecast, so they had made for land early and as soon as the world stopped rocking because of the bad weather they decided to try and imitate the power of the sea and work through the booze cabinet in between.

Bob was having a very relaxing time escaping. He contemplated that the police were probably a little less relaxed. Grace's boat was well-equipped but there was no television by choice, so he wasn't worried about it carrying a shot of his ugly mug if the police were looking for him as a 'person of interest'.

Even if he had been lucky and had left no evidence to connect the dots to himself he was sure they would still like to interview him, just to cross his name off their list.

His plan of staying on board so that he couldn't be recognised, just in case, worked well until the Isle of Wight. Then Grace had insisted that he come and eat at a small restaurant she loved and always visited when she was there; her treat. He had tried the spoilt brat thing and asked if they really had to go out and had massaged her shoulders and poured out wine but the captain's word was final, even if they had found time to ruffle the bed before they went out. He spent a good three hours on tenterhooks in a romantic restaurant with a stunningly attractive, witty and intelligent woman. He made sure they sat in the darkest and most private corner with his back firmly to the rest of the customers and praying silently that his fears about the TV were unfounded and not going to happen.

He kept his order light because of the butterflies in his stomach and resigned himself to the feeling he was having, that if or when he turned around quickly he would catch everyone in the restaurant staring at him and trying to place where they had seen his face before. He was thankful that they made it back to the boat without the crime squad showing up and surrounding them. They barely made into the cabin before they were having sex. It was hard and passionate and they hadn't even had time to take all their clothes off. Bob put it down to the risk factor of their pleasant evening out. Grace put it down to an enthusiastic thank you from the cabin boy.

They soon reached the French coast, which had been the only objective at the start of the voyage. They had chatted and talked nearly all the way when they hadn't been undressed and in each other's arms. The boat was big enough for it to have outside and inside steering and they had spent most of the time outside wrapped in coats and waterproof jackets. He speculated that when Captain Grace was in the Med she would be sailing her boat topless or with only a flimsy loose white T-shirt blowing in the breeze and maybe a thong for decency's sake. Even in the cold grey Channel she could still make a windcheater look OK, if not sexy.

As they had crossed between England and France he had contemplated what to do. Should he enjoy the moment and walk away from that one last little task he had promised to complete? In the end the memory of Deb and the matter of honour finally being satisfied won out. He slipped downstairs and went to his bag. Coming back up he'd gone to the stern of the boat for a few seconds. He had made sure the gun was fully loaded but as the water churned behind the boat he had thrown the real passport and the empty magazines into the sea.

He was enjoying himself, so he allowed the captain to take him further around the French coast than was completely necessary. Just having Grace there was enough to entice him to stay a bit longer and his emotions were torn. Grace had lived up to her name and had been gracious when he had summoned the courage to ask her to put him ashore but she was obviously disappointed by his choice. The last night had been spent in each other's arms a little tearfully, drinking too much. He couldn't convince her it was just going to take a few days to settle a matter once and for all and then – if she would let him return – he would come back until she had had enough of him and she could kick him off her boat.

He left and went ashore in a small port north of Concarneau in Brittany. They had made a pact that they would meet at Motril on the coast south of the Spanish city of Granada two weeks later. She had friends there and he had promised that when he was back he would take her inland to see the Alhambra and eat tapas. The extra time spent together had put miles on his journey.

23

Loose Ends

Once back alone and on shore, he focused on the task in hand. He still had lots of cash and the pistol was tucked away in the deepest corner of his bag. He had a couple of places where he had stashed extra cash over the preceding year under his new name and he could call and collect it if it was required. It didn't take long to get another motorbike from the small ads. One map of the area, a bike magazine that showed bikes that were for sale and a local phone. His first two calls were to non-English speaking French bikers. The third attempt got him an old but well-maintained motorbike. Bob's non-existent French and the seller's limited English caused a few problems over the phone but when Bob had shown up with a newly purchased, full-faced helmet with blacked-out visor and a handful of Euros, things were soon sorted out.

A full tank of fuel, AC/DC playing 'Ride On' on the iPad and he was heading for Munich and the last known location of Yvette, the Black Queen. He had toyed with the idea of letting the poisonous little bitch go but she had been Summer's main tool of destruction with her made-up accusations of bullying and racism levelled at Deb. Nobody had really believed the lies but who would stand against a black, foreign lesbian with the full backing of the board in this day and age? What would all those human rights do-gooders have made of it, even if the black bitch was as guilty as sin? That would have been a real media circus.

There had been a quote from history class: 'The *only* thing necessary for the triumph of evil is for *good men to do nothing.*' On reflection it hadn't been much of a decision to go visiting.

After Summer had departed for the fires of hell, Bob had been forced to twiddle his thumbs for a time but he had kept an eye on the little lesbian playgirl. Without Summer's protection and manipulations, the Black Queen had become surplus to requirements and her contributions had been no longer required by the company. Her services or lack of them ended and she was asked to leave. Bob already had the address she had used when she had been working (for want of a better phrase) for the company in Germany. She had come up with a scheme agreed by Summer whereby she bought herself a flat and had got the company to pay the inflated mortgage payments for her. Bob guessed she would not have been asked to sell it straightaway and maybe she had even found a way to make the repayments herself – or found someone else stupid enough to do it for her.

The pull of the gay and lesbian scene in Munich had meant she had made her base of operations there, despite there being better, cheaper and more appropriate locations for the company elsewhere. All the neo-Nazi crew cuts and horse tranquillisers had won her dominatrix side over. Well, who had been surprised to learn that the little prima donna had enjoyed herself at the company's expense rather than giving work priority and doing what she was being paid to do? With Summer protecting the Black Queen, nobody had dared to see the blindingly obvious. It wasn't until Deb had gone out and taken on a German national to move things along that the market had actually started to take off. Of course, Summer had given all the credit for the success to the Black Queen, and again someone else had benefited from work completely done by Deb.

On one of their little tours of Europe before Deb died, Bob had made sure they had spent a couple of days in Munich. There Bob had made contact with a private detective he had found over the Internet and arranged for an eye to be kept on the Black

Queen and her whereabouts, so he knew where to find her when he needed to. Mr G Mann, the German detective (was he being humorous? Who knows ...) was good as his word and had checked in once a month with updates and to let Bob know the Black Queen was still in town. It seemed that once the free cash had been stopped from the company by the new regime of Harry and Sapp, Yvette had spiralled out of control. 'Drugs, more sex partners and then even more drugs' was the intelligence coming from the G Mann. She had kept her guilty little pleasures well hidden and secret for years but with no audience to deceive she was taking the opportunity to over-indulge. Most other people at worst confessing to a liking of Glam Rock as their guilty pleasure.

A few people had known about her little vices while she was at the company but Summer had laid the law down and not allowed anything to be said. Now Bob had real concerns that the vices had become addictions and he didn't want her overdosing and dying before he could get to her, so he had spoilt his short recreational because he knew it was time to mop up the last loose end.

Thanks to the new Europe and letting its members run free, he was soon riding through the German countryside following the sat nav and contemplating what he was going to do after he was finished. Was catching up with Captain Grace the right thing to do? Cruising around the Mediterranean or going inland and taking her to Granada for a few months of good food, good wine and a bit of culture, staying with friends where he knew he would be safe? Once they got a little stale with each other they could go their separate ways for a while, but keep in touch and then catch up to start over again, say in Rome or some other great city – or was that too Mills and Boon? He had cash hidden away in France and Spain, so he wasn't going to starve. He even had a large sum stashed away in Thailand, so should he try and find his way there and really put the fake passport to the test? He was in no real hurry to make a decision and, taking a page from his little boat trip, he could take the long way round and hope he made it in one piece. He could give it a year or so and see if he could find his way there. He could end up being the old guy sitting in the corner chatting with the gorgeous blonde ladyboy, one of her little angels sitting on his lap or serving him drinks.

* * *

He filled up the fuel tank of the motorbike on the outskirts of Munich, the logic being if he needed to escape he can do so quickly and put a lot of distance between this place and himself. He then started to fight his way through the city traffic to the Black Queen's flat. He is happy with his choice of transport. Like in most big cities, it is the only mode of transportation that you know you will be able to park close to where you want to be and that will be able to keep moving whatever the amount of traffic on the roads.

Bob arrives at his destination easily, thanks to the wonders of modern technology. He unslings the large bag and takes out a pair of stretchy gloves from a side pocket and puts them on. He then tries his luck again in the bag and finds the gun hiding deep in the corner. He takes it out. He is careful to make sure no-one is watching. He then removes the plastic bag around it and puts the gun in his jacket pocket. He had hoped to keep the biking gloves on but they were far too bulky to be able to shoot the gun easily.

The large bag goes back over his shoulder. He can't imagine it would still be there if he left it with the bike; it isn't a deserted Cornish beach in the winter, after all. He spies a pavement florist only a short walk away and goes over to make a purchase. He keeps his helmet on and his identity hidden. All the flowers are already bunched and priced up so it is easy to choose and pay in cash with the correct change. Soon he is in the stairwell of the apartment block and ready to search for the apartment he wants.

The gun is in his pocket and with the flowers he is now carrying, Bob hopes he can pass as a flower delivery boy. As soon as somebody comes and opens the security door to go out, Bob takes his chance and goes in, then ascends the stairs to the right flat. His next decision is whether to force his way in as the door opens or play it a little cooler and wait until the Black Queen accepts her gift and make his move then. Bob rings the bell.

Nothing! He waits and rings again, still nothing.

He has been careless and over-confident. His successes and the recent good times had led him to believe he was at the point where he could feel fate was on his side. He bangs the door a couple more times and tries the doorbell again out of frustration. Still nothing. He turns to go and find a place to regroup and re-plan but he is trapped at the top of the stairs.

'Are those for us?' he hears, followed by some babbled German. The two gentlemen blocking his way to the stairs seem to be British and from their dress code and mannerisms they are both gay. The Black Queen is nowhere to be seen. They are still babbling at him in German, clearly assuming the flowers are for them. They glide by. One takes out a key to the door, the other takes the flowers and starts to primp them. Bob is trapped on the landing and his only option is to back up and make some space, and let the one with the key open the door. They are talking between themselves in English, speculating on who could have sent them flowers. Then their attention is back on Bob and he assumes they are asking if he needs a signature in German, going by the accompanying gestures.

Bob gets his act together, unfreezes and opens the motorbike helmet's visor. 'Sorry, I am so sorry you caught me by surprise. I was ... again sorry, I am looking for Yvette. You have over-powered me a little.' Bob hopes the bumbling Brit abroad approach will endear him to these two gentlemen.

They have stopped doing what they were doing and in unison they exclaim: 'Oh! You are English.'

'Yes, again sorry – I was sure this was the address of an old friend. She is black, skinny and about so high.' Bob indicates a rough estimate of Yvette's height. He is a little confused and perplexed. The private detective had seemed to be doing a good job, reporting as requested and keeping him informed of changes. Bob had only contacted him a month ago to make sure nothing had changed and to end the contract because he had decided on what he was going to do and this was most definitely the right address.

'Of course we know Yvette. We bought the place off her about a couple of weeks ago and moved in. She was a special friend of ours too. We stayed here quite a lot and came here for a few parties over the years. If the walls could talk … or if someone had had a video recorder,' partner number one says, with a grin and a wink.

Partner number two finishes the story after gently slapping number one across the top of the arm and whispering, 'He may not be that close a friend?'

'Yes, when she suddenly said she was moving we snapped her hand off. The flat didn't even get to go on to the market. Quite a little coup on our part and a great result really.'

'Ah! I should have called,' says Bob. 'We are very close friends and I was hoping to surprise her. I know she was a lesbian but we meant a lot to each other. She even joked if ever she was going to give a man a blow job I would be the one.' They all laugh – the time for being subtle was long gone and he can guess the type of parties the Black Queen was into. Bob continues: 'She loved the lifestyle here and wanted me to come and stay, like her big brother if that isn't too Jeremy Kyle. To be honest I am a bit old for it; the lifestyle, I mean. Did she stay around here? Did she leave an address or phone number I could use to track her down?'

Partner number two goes on: 'She decided about three or four months ago that she fancied a change of scenery.' Bob wonders if Yvette had heard about Harry's little accident and put two and two together and had decided to run and hide. 'She found herself a lovely little place down near Rome. Lucky bitch, I say, and nice if you have the money to do that sort of thing. We are looking forward to the invite to the house warming once she gets settled in.'

Partner one adds: 'Hold on – she gave us a forwarding address for her mail, if that will help. We wouldn't want to keep brother and sister apart?' He ignores completely the fact that Bob and Yvette couldn't possibly be related. 'I could try her mobile if you like?'

'No, please, the address is great. We split after a few heated words last time and if I ring I am sure she will go all diva on me and hide if she knows I am coming. You must know how sulky she gets if she doesn't get her own way.' There are a couple of knowing nods. 'Better I man up and do this face-to-face and get it over with.'

Partner number two agrees wholeheartedly and disappears to find the address. Bob keeps the helmet on with the visor up. Having it on he is sure would make it impossible for these two boys to recognise him if they had to point him out at a later date. Even if it is hard on the cheekbones to talk wearing the damn thing. Partner number one and Bob exchange a few pleasantries until two comes back.

'Here you are.' He gives Bob a piece of old envelope with a scribbled-down address on it. He then slaps his partner playfully across the arm. 'What are we like? Please come in and have a drink, I am sorry Clay has forgotten his manners and hasn't invited you in. I am Craig, by the way.'

'That's no problem.' Bob looks at the address and confirms it is near to Rome, just like he had been told. He even comments that it is near where he and Yvette stayed in the past when they came on holiday together years ago. Partner two comments that maybe she is turning straight in her old age and they giggle to themselves.

'Thanks for your help, gents. Keep the flowers. A thousand miles tied to the back of a motorbike isn't going to do them any good at all. Call it a moving-in gift. It is only mid-morning and if I put this in the sat nav I can easily get five or six hours riding in.'

Partner two goes all 'Carry On' and exclaims: 'I should be so lucky?' This gets him another slap on the arm and a fit of giggling, so Bob takes his leave and swears the both of them to secrecy and promises to send them an invite if there is going to be a party.

He is soon on the road again. The Black Queen seems to be harder to get rid of than a case of herpes.

* * *

It would be wrong to say the trip was pleasant. He has travelled in Italy twice before. The last time was over ten years ago, discounting the recent Venice trip, and both times had been in glorious sunshine. This trip was rain nearly all the way. He had been lucky with the weather during his escape from England. The English Channel in a small boat and bad weather had not appealed, even with the promise of Captain Grace there to hold his hand, but the weather had behaved which was more than could be said for the captain. At least the food and wine were excellent in Italy, despite the weather on the few brief stops he made.

Bob arrives late in the evening the following day, just outside his target destination, and he makes the choice to stay overnight in one of the cheap and cheerful nearby hotels, caution put out to dry off in the wind just like his biking gear once he is in his hotel room. The cold and the rain have taken their toll and the call of hot food and a warm bed have overpowered all his objections and arguments to quietly go and get the job done without anyone knowing he has even been there.

He wakes to a sunny bright day in Ostia Antica, just a short trip from Rome. He picks up a tourist-style street map and with the sat nav in his pocket he tracks down the address he wants.

This time he retires to a safe distance to watch and wait for evidence of the Black Queen before he acts. He chooses his spot in one of the tourist cafés a little away from the small block of flats where Yvette now resides. Just off to the side of the café are some beautiful Roman ruins. He is sure the place must be a real money-spinner in the high season. Now at the start of winter there are just a few callers poking about.

There are many cafes in the area and the one he has chosen is one of the furthest away from the block of flats where the Black Queen is holed up. From where he is he can see all the exits. He has taken one of the outside tables but has stayed as far back in the shadows in the outside domain of the café as he can. Though it is a bright, slightly chilly day, he is hidden away in the gloom underneath a brightly-striped hoarding that protects the café's customers from sun and rain, depending on the time of year.

He expects to be there for most of the morning before any signs of life. Yvette hadn't been known for her early starts even when she was supposedly working. Bob has already made the decision that if the Black Queen hasn't shown herself by 3 p.m. then he will go and knock on her door regardless.

What a surprise! He has barely started his second cup of English tea (much to the disgust of his waiter who was obviously a coffee drinker) when the Black Queen promenades out of the front door and across the road to the café closest to the block of flats. From what Bob can see she has chosen to sit inside and has disappeared from view. Bob sits and waits. He assumes that at some stage she will re-emerge to go and take a little mid-morning nap. Bob orders another drink and pays his bill so he can move quickly if he needs to and won't have the waiter running after him.

His tea is cold and untouched when Yvette reappears forty-five minutes later. She comes out of the café, crosses the road to a newspaper stand and buys an armful of magazines, and then goes back up to her flat. Bob gets up and goes the other way back to his hotel, where he packs up all his gear and settles his hotel bill. One quick stop to fill up the bike again and he rides the short distance back, parking down the side street next to the flats.

Like most of these places abroad, the newspaper stand also has a few bouquets of flowers for sale, so sticking to what is becoming a tradition he purchases a couple of bunches and heads for the Black Queen's flat. It is on the second floor and a nice old lady coming out of the main entrance holds the door for him, so he easily circumvents what little security the place boasts. It has only cost him a nod of thanks and a smile, even if the old lady hasn't seen the smile thanks to the motorbike helmet still being on and the visor in place. It is the thought that counts, anyway, isn't it?

He climbs the concrete stairs, encouraged by the amount of noise coming from all around the block. He hadn't noticed the noise at the flat in Germany. Here there are TVs, radios, kids playing and grown-ups shouting, the music, the arguments and the general chatter all creating a wall of sound that surrounds him as he stands in front of the Black Queen's front door.

His visor is still down. He has taken the bike gloves off and put on the last pair of stretchy rubber ones he had brought from England. He holds the flowers in one hand in front of his chest in full view and with his free hand he reaches out and presses the door bell, immediately hearing the chimes from inside. He puts his hand back into his jacket pocket and grips the cold steel of the pistol in readiness. Just another flower delivery boy doing his job. The door is opened by Yvette.

He lowers the flowers and raises the gun, stepping forward so she has no time to slam the door in his face. Who said sales training wouldn't be useful after all this time? The Black Queen recoils and takes a few steps back. The hallway had been empty apart from himself and the noise. He enters with the gun raised, pointing directly between her eyes. He puts the flowers down on a side table and closes the flat's front door without taking his eyes off the woman directly in front of him. Bob gestures to

Yvette to be quiet by raising a finger up to the front of the helmet and then he steps forward and gets her to move backwards until she hits the armchair with the back of her knees and half falls, half sits down into it.

A quick glance around and it is plain to see that she isn't doing that well. The furniture is old and tatty. There is only one living space and the dirty washing-up is easily seen piled in the sink in the corner. There are magazines scattered across the floor and pizza boxes dotted about. She is obviously waiting for the cleaner to get back off holiday. A little tray on the top of the TV has what could be the remnants of her latest score on it, judging by the paraphernalia on it, and she is looking a little under the weather.

It is like a scene from any of the movies inspired by the film *Reservoir Dogs*. Bob has the gun pointed at her and he is standing slightly sideways on to the seated woman. He is just out of reach with his gun arm fully extended with the pistol locked on its target.

She is silent, trying to will herself to sink further into the chair and become an ever smaller target. Her bottom lip is beginning to quiver and shake. One tear is trying to find its way across her cheek. Her hands are gripping the arms of the dirty armchair and she is silently praying that this vision of death in front of her is not going to pull the trigger.

Bob hadn't planned any further than this. He considers struggling to take the helmet off or at least trying to take it off with one hand – but if he stops pointing the gun at her to take it off or loses sight of her as he pulls the helmet off his head she might be inspired to make one last final attempt at freedom. He settles for raising the blacked-out visor. He doesn't have a long speech prepared. All he wants is to let her know who he is before the end.

'YOU! You piece of shit. I knew it was you all along.' She spits out in his direction. She has misunderstood his hesitation. She thinks he is gloating and trying to form a suitable tirade of abuse to express his feelings. Maybe she is hoping he is a coward and he has frozen, unable to squeeze the trigger that last few millimetres. Maybe her imagination is racing ahead and she now thinks that he is waiting and he isn't going to shoot her straightaway at all, because he has decided that he is going to kill her slowly and peel her like a grape.

Bob reaches out and takes the TV remote. The TV is on but the sound is turned down. Did she turn it down to answer the door? He still has the gun pointing at her.

'WE stitched that bitch of yours up, no fucking problem. She was never going to get anything from the start. We ripped her fucking head off and shit down her neck and then we fucked the corpse.' The Black Queen has a wild look in her eyes. 'What is the point of being the best, being honest and having ethics if pieces of shit like us can tell a few lies and take everything away you have ever worked for and destroy everything you ever achieved?'

She leans forward a little. She is the one gloating. 'We took away all that mattered. We took away her reputation. We took away everybody's trust. We took away all the admiration for a fucking job well done.' There is a slight pause for breath and she sits back looking smug. 'Then we took all her fucking money, her health and her future with just a few made-up stories.' She crosses her legs and straightens her short skirt. 'I bet the bitch cried herself to sleep every fucking night after she had realised she had wasted over twenty years of her life just making us money while we arsed about and had a good time.'

While she has been ranting Bob, has flicked through the channels and has settled on a music one that is playing 'Nickelback'. Good, that should be loud enough and it had been one of Deb's favourites. He raises the volume. He has not said a word since he entered the flat. He wants to scream vengeance. He wants her to plead for her life. He wants fear to have turned her brain to mush and for her to be sitting frozen in terror in a pool of her own urine. The gun is still pointing at her.

'No-one cares. No one is bothered. No one gives a flying shit as long as it doesn't involve them losing out. Your stupid bitch wife will never get FUCKING JUSTICE.'

Wrong!

Bang … Mississippi.

Bang … Mississippi.

Bang … Mississippi.

Bob keeps firing until he has emptied the pistol's magazine into the Black Queen's torso. He takes a deep breath and turns the volume down. He doesn't want anyone calling around to complain about the noise. Yvette is slouched in the chair but still upright, her tatty hair hanging down over her face. She is like some kids' over-sized rag doll. He throws the gun onto her bloody lap and the top half of her body slowly falls forward.

* * *

There had been a few more involved that could have done with a visit from Bob but you have to draw the line somewhere and move on. As the chorus of 'How you remind me' comes around again the lead singer asks 'are we having fun yet?' Bob can honestly say yes, he really was … yeh oh oh o! oh o!

He checks his watch. He had almost a full tank of fuel and if he starts now he might just have time to make it to Motril to meet back up with the captain before she gives up waiting. For now, job done.